BRICKS

BOOK THREE

TONY BERTAUSKI

SENTIENCE LAWS_

The Sentience Laws were created to protect the rights of fabricated humans.

They didn't last long.

I_

One to lead.

CHAPTER ONE_

Brick Hunt Ends Today?

The title crawled across the television. Above it a talking head started his segment. The barkeep reached above a row of half-filled liquor bottles to up the volume, the tavern's remote long lost.

"Only one left," the television host exclaimed with a skinny finger. "Rumor has it that he or she has been identified and will be apprehended today or tomorrow. Let's hope it's today."

The barkeep stood with his arms crossed. He stood absolutely still; only the sudden jerk of his Adam's apple suggested he was alive. In the dim light, his skin was sallow but, from time to time, bathed pink from the dying neon beer sign.

At the end of the bar, an old man watched the television with slightly less attention. His white collared shirt revealed a turkey wattle of flesh. The top of his head was bald, the outer portions rimmed with chalk white hair. He toyed with a drink, spinning the short, heavy glass in slow circles.

Marcus Anderson sipped his scotch.

It was his third drink. Two was generally his limit, but today was different. He was accustomed to taverns where tainted wallpaper peeled at the corners and people drank alone, places where people came not to celebrate but forget.

"Do you think he'd change it?" Marcus said to the old woman sitting next to him. "If he could go back in time, would he do things differently?"

The old woman studied the barkeep with her finger to her lips, as if in deep thought. "Of course he wouldn't," she said gently, her voice a sheet of sandpaper—gritty on one side, smooth on the other. "The truth is inconvenient that way."

The truth is inconvenient.

She said that often. So often that he cringed when he heard it.

Marcus enjoyed these forgotten taverns, these vestibules of hubris because, if he was honest, sometimes he would like to forget the truth. *What has become of me?* That was a question that haunted him, an accusation he cast upon himself. He hated what he had become and the old woman that had done it to him.

But he loved it. And the old woman, too.

The truth is indeed inconvenient.

He assuaged his shame with a mission. He was a servant of God. A truth-seeker. God was truth and could not be changed. God was not inconvenient. God would not have let Marcus become... become *this* if there wasn't a purpose for it.

"Hello, folks, and welcome," the television host announced. "We have a very interesting panel today, representatives from all camps of biomite organizations to discuss the latest news from the Settlement, but first we have something more urgent. Sources close to this program have just informed us that the last fabricated human has been identified and will be apprehended today. Of course, if that happens, we will cut away from regularly scheduled programming."

The Settlement.

It was another word for prison, but kinder. More humane. A place where all the fabricated humans—the men and women born in a fabrication chamber, men and women without a single organic cell of clay, their bodies 100% biomites—now lived.

Bricks. That was acceptable slang, a politically correct slur. Fabbers, slabbers, and fakies were out there, too. But bricks caught on early. It had a certain punch to it that the other words didn't, a reminder that fabricated humans weren't born. They weren't real.

Weren't human.

The bricks were told to report to the Settlement, where they could be watched. Most of them did. The ones that didn't were found, one by one. It took years, but today was the day. The very last brick had been identified. And he or she would become a settler.

Of all the places in the world, a depressed little tavern was the last place a brick would live. This was a haven for the downtrodden, the hopeless, the men and women that barely contained more than their *birthright*—the 5% infant boost of biomites, a tab picked up by the People, a program meant to sharpen the country's gene pool, strengthen the immune system and shift the population toward an upstanding citizenry.

But 5% wasn't enough to change genetics.

The men and women that failed to keep up with evolution, to conform to a biomite-infested society came to a tavern where gin was cheaper than another dose of biomite. They came to forget, to drown out their humanity.

They came to make a slow exit.

Marcus pulled on the end of his ecig, the vapor swirling in thick currents. The mentholated scent couldn't blot out the stench of sadness and despair, both emotions hanging thick as ash and saturating Marcus's hyperawareness.

"Keep." A man raised an empty glass.

The barkeep, the owner and bartender of this resort, was locked in a television trance.

"Hey, Keep!"

"Hold your horses," the barkeep snapped, an expression as old as the mustardy-yellow ceiling tiles.

He poured a drink and lit a cigarette—an old-fashioned, real tobacco cigarette, each huff of real smoke too expensive for most of his clientele. A place like this shouldn't afford such luxuries. But the barkeep was hiding things. He hid a lot of things.

"You all right, partner?" Jimmy pointed his cigarette at Marcus and completely ignored the old woman. Like she wasn't even there.

She sat upright on the cracked-leather stool, posture that could only be described as graceful. Her hair was white, like Marcus's, but shoulder length and flowing like her attire. A tiny smile resided in her eyes, the type that was more often felt than seen. Even in a place like this.

The barkeep's affront ordinarily wouldn't be ignored, but the old woman understood. She expected it.

Light knifed across the tavern, a column of bright fog piercing the depressed air. The door slammed behind a man that limped. The barkeep sloshed a scoop of ice and Coke into a glass and topped it off with Jack. It was waiting for the limping man when he arrived two stools to Marcus's left.

Patrick Nelson.

He went by PN, a little jokey-joke he told people. *My initials are peein'.*

"Is this a witch hunt?" the television host asked the viewers, his hair perfect, lips plump and a bit too wet. His words appeared big, bold and yellow at the bottom of the screen. "To discuss the apprehension and segregation of bricks, we bring in our panelists. Welcome to the show."

The split screen showed three people.

"I'd like to start with you, Craig Fellers, founder of the Coalition for Humanity. You know, the initial law that repealed the rights of all fabricated humans stated a voluntary surrender and relocation to the Settlement, but when a third of them failed to report, there was a different approach that feels sort of like a three-year witch hunt."

"First of all, stop calling them *fabricated humans*." The image of the man in the left panel filled the screen. "These are bricks, end of story. There is nothing about them that is human, and that's the problem with this debate. We cannot continue acting as if they are human just because they walk, talk and look human. They are one hundred percent biomites, always have been. They do not contain a soul, and never will."

The host's well-practiced smile never faltered. "But doesn't this feel a little like a witch hunt?"

"No, not at all. In order to be a witch hunt, they have to be human. This pointless discussion could be ended today if we just turn them off. The government has their frequency coded, they know where they are, they can hit the switch on their life force and end this. That settlement in the wilderness? All that free room and board? It's costing the taxpayers billions."

"Amen to that," PN muttered.

"You said life force," the host countered. "Doesn't that imply life?"

"They're not human, remember that. We slaughter cows and pigs because they're not human. You want to debate the rights of steak and bacon, leave me out."

PN crunched an ice cube and shook the glass. One down.

"I'm going to skip Jan Flaherty from the clay state of Georgia just for a moment." The host cut off Craig Fellers's rant. His lips now moved silently. "I want to jump over to Gerald Gaiman, legal counsel. How do you answer the witch-hunt question?"

"Well, thank you for having me." Gerald was warm and genteel without smiling. "I think it's important to note the legal ramifications whenever discussing fabricated humans. The court does not qualify human attributes based on conception or morphology. The fact that fabricated humans are composed of one hundred percent biomites, which, I might note, is only a fraction above a ninety-nine percenter, is irrelevant."

"Buuuullshit," PN called.

"The Sentience Laws quantified that any intelligence that passes the Turing Test be given human rights. All fabricated humans that are currently imprisoned on the Settlement—"

Craig Fellers silently protested the use of the word *imprisoned.*

Because, as PN would say, *those fuckers got free room and board on my dime.*

"—have passed the Turing Test, their human rights have been stolen, and the Sentience Laws revoked. These are self-actualized humans that are no different than you or me. One could be standing in line at the bank and you'd never know it."

Despite Gerald's good intentions, his prejudice slipped. *One* could be standing... *one*, as someone would refer to an object.

"You might even argue they're smarter than you and me," Gerald continued. "These men and women have identities; that is a fact. They are either cloned from a human, have had memories transplanted from a human, or memories downloaded from a dreamland."

Craig's face turned into a plum. Hands flailing, the host took mercy on the founder of the Coalition for Humanity before the artery throbbing across his forehead burst.

"You are jeopardizing the human race! Dreamland is a dream, Gaiman. That does not make a brick human."

"Humans dream, Craig."

"And so do dogs."

"But we haven't imprisoned dogs, have we?"

"That's the definition of a pet, you idiot. Dogs do what we tell them. What do you think the world will look like if we keep fabricating these people, huh? What if these bricks figure out how to have babies, what will the world look like?"

A smile grew on Gerald. "Better than it does today."

"Jesus Christ!" PN drained number two and slammed the glass. "Motherfucking brick lover. You hear that, Keep? What the hell."

PN swept stray ice off the counter and rattled the glass. The barkeep filled it without reacting to his rant. He was around brick prejudice every day. He knew how to ignore it.

"Tell you what they ought to do," PN continued. "They ought to make this a real hunt. None of this pretend witch hunt bullshit, they make this a real hunt. You set up that Settlement place like some real-life *Hunger Games* and put it on television. Only you let them go one at a time. The highest bidder gets to track a brick down. There's points for weapons and survival, make a game out of it."

PN paused for a sip.

"How many bricks out there now, five hundred?"

"Five hundred and eleven," Marcus said.

"Right on." He turned to Marcus. "I mean, shit, they could hunt one every week for the next ten years. And if the show's a hit, and you can bet your ass it will be, they just print up another one. It ain't like they're human, I don't give a shit what that one asshole said. Am I right, Keep?"

The barkeep ignored him.

The old woman took Marcus's hand, kneaded his fingers and whispered. He nodded to something she said. PN naturally thought Marcus was agreeing with him and continued. Marcus, however, was watching a woman walk behind the bar.

There was a hunch between her shoulders, frayed kinky hair escaping a bun at the back of her head. She came up to the barkeep's chest. He bent over to hear what she had to say.

Marcus closed his eyes and inhaled.

Through the smoke and despair, he caught a whiff of what they had come for, a familiar tang of biomites, a recognition like old friends that had grown old and unrecognizable. Although they had never met, Marcus and the woman were more closely related than anyone in this bar.

Margaret.

He knew her name, felt the raised letters on the surface of her thoughts like a scarred brand. Marcus could feel things like that. On her, it was easy.

Margaret kissed the barkeep on the arm, then poured a beer for someone at the other end.

A commercial break interrupted the program (*dreamland vacations that are certified and 100% guaranteed safe, not one incidence of dream disease, so come on down!*). PN went to the bathroom and returned in time to catch the last panelist, Jan Flaherty, the woman from the great clay state of Georgia.

"What's the opinion of the state of clay?" the host asked. "Is this a witch hunt?"

Jan was sitting in a living room, her makeup professionally done but not too prepped to take away from the *I'm-just-like-you* look. That she nailed.

"Georgia, Louisiana, and South Carolina, as you know, abide by the law of existence and separation. In no form do we support the suffering of any intelligent being, including fabricated humans."

"You do support the death of halfskins, though," the host added.

"That's incorrect." She added a touch of a smile, just enough to appear unperturbed without condescension or callousness. "The clay states have abolished biomites to support the development of clay beings. We are not anti-technology, we simply refuse to accept any substitutions for our organic cells."

"So no one has a prosthesis?"

"Be reasonable."

"She's got that right," PN said. "Biomites got us into this hot mess. Bet you if she was off camera, she'd be down for a brick hunt. Guaranteed. They don't take no shit down South."

Another beam of sunlight sliced the room. Two men and a woman entered, their details lost in the glare.

"Keep!" PN raised his glass. "You on vacation?"

Margaret was at the cash register, her back to PN's whistling. She was completely still, like she was trying to remember something.

The barkeep dropped off another drink, the booze and soda spilling over the edge. PN complained, but the barkeep paid no more attention than he did to the well-dressed trio that had just entered. Instead, he went back into a television coma.

"It's not too late for those tired of biomites," Jan the clay state representative said with her final minute. "You can convert biomites back to clay."

"Jury's still out on that technology, Jan," the host chimed. "A bit controversial."

"That's media hype, Jay. It takes a little time, but biomites can be flushed from the body, organic cells replacing them until you're clean."

"I'll believe it when I see it."

"I'm proof it works, Jay. I used to be 40% biomite, now I'm born again... 100% clay. We're already fabricating organs with clay."

"So what's stopping you from fabricating a human from clay instead of biomites?"

"It's against our beliefs, Jay."

"So it can be done?"

"In no way have we attempted that."

The barkeep seemed to be following the news crawler at the bottom of the screen while his wife was still at the register, trying to remember something. The old woman squeezed Marcus's hand.

The trio was on the move.

They spread out, each talking privately to the patrons saddled at the bar, their conversations a low murmur. A pair of dice stopped clattering at the opposite end of the bar. One by one, they got up, their drinks half-full.

PN was expanding his *Hunger Games* theory (this one included death-row prisoners) when the well-dressed woman approached. She put her hand on his shoulder and leaned into his ear.

"Hey, honey," PN purred. "Have a seat."

Her grip tightened. She said a few more words and stepped back.

"Buuuullshit," PN said. "I'm not leaving with a drink—"

He froze, epileptic. No tremors or shaking, just a full-body seizure. It was the result of an electrified hand that reached inside his brain and squeezed. He slid off the stool and walked toward the door, arms stiff at his sides.

"Sir?" One of the well-dressed men approached.

Marcus nodded.

He didn't resist, didn't want the man to attempt syncing his thought biomites with Marcus's mind and overriding his bodily functions. Unlike PN, Marcus cooperated.

None of the well-dressed trio said anything to the old woman with white hair. Nonetheless, she stood up and followed Marcus.

A red banner scrolled across the bottom of the television, blinking letters that read *BREAKING NEWS!* The panelists blipped off the screen. The television host had enough time to announce the big news.

The barkeep jerked his head toward his wife. "No. No, no, no—"

The last *no* gurgled in his throat. He took half a step toward his wife before his biomites were seized. The well-dressed trio hijacked his body, turning him into a wax replication of horror and desperation.

"Our sources," the television host announced, "tell us the last brick has been identified."

As Marcus walked into a bright afternoon, a row of black sedans and SUVs with men and women waiting at open doors greeted him. He let an agent guide him across the street, where the tavern's patrons watched. Dark forms moved inside the tavern behind the neon Budweiser sign.

Chicago police directed traffic and corralled the general public, but the federal biomite agents were running the show. The patrons had been ushered behind quickly erected barriers. Newsfeed vehicles arrived minutes later.

"If you would all remain in this area," an agent proclaimed, "we'll be with you shortly."

"What about our drinks?" PN shouted. "We paid money. We should get reimbursed or something. Hey, I mean it!"

Two agents, a slender middle-aged man and a petite woman, started asking questions that were irrelevant, conversational distraction that allowed them to sync up the patrons' biomites. It was modern-day mind reading. They learned everything in moments, downloading official identities, outstanding warrants, or possible collusion.

Meanwhile, more agents filed into the tavern. *The last brick found.*

Margaret would be sent to the Settlement, where a home would be provided for the rest of her life. Her husband, the barkeep, might never see her again.

The Chicago police were summoned by one of the biomite agents. They handcuffed one of the patrons that had been rolling dice at the end of the bar, an outstanding warrant for delinquent child support.

"Patrick Nelson?" the young female agent asked.

"PN. And I better get that drink."

"Could you tell me how long you were in the bar?"

"Long enough."

"Were you aware Margaret was the last brick?"

"Are you shitting me? She was a... are you shitting me? I knew it, I knew it! I knew there was something wrong with that bitch." Anger boiled his cheeks red. "She's a plant, ain't she?"

"Excuse me?"

"A plant, a goddamn transplant, man. She was sick a while back, had something wrong with her guts or organs or something. Then she disappeared and came back all good, acted like she was never sick, like she had amnesia. And Keep, that sick fuck, would never talk about it, just said she got better. But I knew it... I knew that goofy bastard was up to something. He cloned her body and transplanted her memories, didn't he? He made himself a plant and didn't tell anyone."

The rant continued.

PN despised bricks, but a plant? A plant didn't know it was a brick and somehow that was even worse.

Like everyone, the male agent ignored the white-haired old woman and approached Marcus. A faint shimmer trickled through his body, a weak electrical caress. Marcus allowed him to sync up and access his biomite core, giving up the legally allowed personal information. Marcus was evasive without being resistant. He could easily overpower the man, but deception was easier.

"Brock Harris?" he asked.

"Yes," Marcus said.

"That ain't his name," PN interrupted.

"Sir?" the female agent said. "Stay in this conversation, please."

"I'd like to speak with your regional director," Marcus said. "We could meet over there. Thank you."

The suggestion was unusual but persuasive. The agent was, beyond his awareness, compelled to retrieve the highest ranking officer on site. There was nothing alarming about the request. To the agent, it felt very normal.

"Nicely done," the old woman said.

Marcus walked further down the sidewalk where no one would hear. He and the old woman waited patiently, no words passing between them. Rarely did she stray far from him. She couldn't. At one time, this bothered him. She was his greatest betrayer. He'd forgiven her, though.

Half an hour later, a woman wearing creased slacks and a casual jacket approached with a hard pace. Her presence reached out to Marcus, feeling through his biomites. He allowed her to sync up. That was the easiest way for him to read her without her knowledge.

"How did you find Margaret?" he asked.

There was a brief pause. Under no circumstances would she answer the question. But Marcus had already invaded her thoughts and given her permission to do so.

"She was identified," the regional director answered.

"Identified? This was not the result of analysis?"

"Our network identified her."

"And who controls the network?"

She shook her head. That, she didn't know. Perhaps no one did. But one thing was clear: someone was identifying the rogue bricks.

Marcus had known this for a very long time, ever since the Settlement was established. But who? *And could they identify me?*

The newsfeeds had it wrong. He was the last brick.

He knew there was likely a time limit on his freedom, his unstoppable power over biomites, his inexhaustible ability to hide. This, perhaps, was why he had forgiven the old woman for turning him into a brick, for fabricating a clone from his original body—a body free of sin, a body no longer living. Marcus would be a brick for the rest of his life, but with it came great power.

Somewhere out there was a greater power. He could feel its presence like it was inside him. This greater power knew him intimately, he felt. It was everywhere, the air he breathed. This, he suspected, was the power that identified Margaret. *But why give her up now?*

No one knew from where this information came or why. But Marcus's life mission was to find this power. It gave him purpose.

To find the powers-that-be.

"Where can I access your network?" he asked.

"Start with the Bank of America."

"Who do I ask for?"

The regional director hesitated. Naturally, she resisted giving up classified information. He would have to push a little harder.

"Careful, Marcus." The old woman spoke over his shoulder. "You're poking the hive."

There could be no trace of coercion. If Marcus was brought in for closer examination, his secrets would be exposed.

"Mr. Connick," the director said.

"Thank you."

She returned to her post and began giving orders, oblivious to her cooperation. There would be no memory of speaking with Marcus Anderson, a name she would know. A name the whole world would recognize. A name that wasn't supposed to exist.

Twenty minutes later, the authorities escorted the barkeep and his wife out of the tavern and into the backseat of an SUV. The media recorded every second. The general public did the same.

"You brick lover, Jimmy," PN shouted. "I always knew you were a wrenchhead asshole."

"Marcus, look." The old woman pointed.

Across the street where police held the general public, a young woman had worked her way up to the barrier. She was in her late twenties, brunette hair cut short. The last time he'd seen her she was a teenager. He knew all about her, knew that she had lived on that North Carolina farm for years.

Jamie.

But he didn't care about her anymore, didn't care about her or Paul or Raine or anything from his past. Even if they were partly responsible for Marcus becoming a brick, he was looking forward now, pursuing greater truths instead of past regrets.

"Why is she here?" Marcus asked.

"One to lead, one to dream..." the old woman exclaimed, "one to bleed, the son to be."

Her expression was empty and distant, as it always was when she recited the phrase, as if something possessed her, a proclamation from another dimension. She said it at odd times, hinting for him to pay attention to a particular moment or event.

"Is she one of them?" He refused to call her proselytizing a prophecy, but that was how it felt, a stanza that begged him to pay attention.

The truth is the way.

There would be one to lead, one to dream, one to bleed, and the son to be. *Did that mean four people would lead me to the powers-that-be? Or did that include me? Do I lead? Or bleed? Or all of the above?*

The sense that his life was predetermined, that everything happened exactly as if God had planned it out, never ceased to raise the small hairs on his neck. He believed in free will, that there was no destiny. There was a purpose to life, but not one that controlled everything. Still, he couldn't ignore the signs.

Why did everything fit so perfectly?

Jamie abruptly turned from the scene and blended with the crowd.

Marcus let the old woman hold his hand as they departed. It gave her comfort, he knew this. Marcus might be the last undiscovered brick, a fact that would shock the world. The old woman, though, existed only in his mind. She saw the world through his eyes, heard through his ears. Through him, she lived.

But she had never been human.

Mother.

CHAPTER TWO_

*W*HERE AM *I?*

Jamie rose from a thin fog, the wispy kind that gathered around mountaintops in early morning, the kind that was peaceful. The kind that lulled you to sleep while obscuring sharp turns in the road.

A high-pitched squeal was in her head, the kind of sound that followed a blunt object. But her skull didn't hurt. She couldn't feel anything.

Her eyes were already open. Images formed out of the dark, a trick deftly executed by an invisible magician. *Now there's dark, now there's light!*

Snick.

Her eyelids dropped for a long moment, but not long enough to relieve the dry burn. She tried to blink, but her eyelids were locked open. Tears pooled on the lower lid, teetering on the lashes.

She was staring straight ahead, a full-sized baby doll with glass eyes and broken eyelids. Only this wasn't a dream, she was in her body—her dead-frozen body.

Snick.

Saliva settled around her tongue. The urge to swallow hung in the back of her throat.

Where am I? Where am I, where am I?

Her thoughts echoed in the vacuous space of her head, memories scattered in the mountain fog. Her chest was rising and falling in long even strokes even as panic surged, a swelling tide that demanded more air.

Easy now. Slow down. Just be here, take in what you see.

Snick.

A large room, a glass wall. There were buildings, an urban landscape she didn't recognize. The canopies of city trees were below her. Fifth floor, maybe?

This isn't Chicago. That was where I was last, right? Looking for... what was I looking for? A bank? A man?

Bing.

Elevator doors opened to her right. Shoes squeaked. Her eyes quivered in their locked-in state, forcing her to continue staring into a sunny afternoon. The footsteps were harried. A figure eased into her tunnel vision.

It was a man. His skin was black, his scalp as smooth and shiny as the floor. He was dressed in baggy white clothes and long striped socks with dirt on the knees. It was a baseball uniform.

Their eyes met when he was directly in front of her, his head slightly shaking back and forth, lips fluttering. "The fuck?"

He picked up the pace, disappearing to her left. The footsteps squeaked another twenty paces. A doorknob rattled, followed by several dull thumps. He paced back and forth, muttering. The cuss words were loud and clear. After a second round of knocking, the door opened.

A high-pitched tinnitus swallowed her head. Somewhere in the whine was the distant thudding of her heart.

The shadows suddenly lengthened. A small chunk of time was clipped out, a film skipping forward.

Her eyelids dropped twice—the intervals of time equal in length but too far apart to soothe the burn—when the door opened. The squeaky-soled footsteps were joined by a set of titanium-tipped hammers. The ballplayer was followed by a pale woman wearing a white lab coat over a black dress. Her black hair was pulled off her middle-aged face, exposing blue veins along her temple.

"What's she doing out here?" the man asked.

"They were supposed to deliver her to the lab."

"Well, this ain't the lab."

The woman flashed a penlight in each of Jamie's eyes; ghostly blank spots slowly faded.

"This couldn't wait till tomorrow?" he asked.

"Eric's out of town."

"You call Smitty?"

"Sick."

He looked off with a sigh. *Peterson* was printed on his back.

"She seems functional." The woman pocketed the penlight. "You got the pad?"

He palmed a mini-tablet.

"I'm going to find out why they left her out here," she said. "Want to bring her in?"

The woman's shoes tapped away. Peterson's head swayed back and forth, jaw cocked. He muttered cuss words around the name Patty. He probably did that a lot. When the distant door closed, he slid his finger across the tablet.

Jamie instinctually *reached* for his thoughts, an inner movement of her mind, an attempt to sync with his biomites, a friendly gesture to connect their minds in a casual manner. Talking with thoughts and feelings, not words.

Metal pans rang between her ears.

Peterson looked up from the tablet. She couldn't hear the words, but read his lips. *Don't do that.*

He stared a moment longer. The ringing continued until she stopped *reaching*. Sensation poured into her thighs, wicked up through her stomach and filled her chest and arms. Aches and pains lit up like she'd been beaten with a bag of broken bottles.

She wished for the numbness to return.

"You hear me?" He looked down when she didn't respond. "Nod."

Jamie felt her muscles contract. Her chin slowly dipped.

"Follow me."

Jamie shot into a standing position, her arms locked at her sides. Her joints ached in throbbing waves. She could see past the trees and down to the street where children ran through geysers of water laid out in a five-ring pattern. The Olympic rings.

Jamie turned with a quick military snap and faced a long, empty hallway. Peterson looked over his shoulder. Her footsteps fell with heavy cadence, the clamp of heel to toe reverberated through her calves. Her tongue stuck to her teeth as she swallowed a patch of cotton.

A memory rose from the endless mist. Nothing personal, no hint of who she was or where she'd been or why she was walking into a brightly lit lab. She remembered the geysers in the Olympic ring pattern.

Centennial Park. Her pulse picked up. *Georgia. I'm in fucking Georgia!*

She stuttered half a step inside the doorway. Fear hardened her thighs, locked her knees. That was the first time she'd willed her body to do something.

It would also be the last.

"There it is." Peterson walked past her. "She just realized where she is."

"Sit her down," Patty said. "I'm not ready."

A sharp current seized the back of her neck. Stiffly, she moved toward a chair and fell on it. Peterson sat at a computer.

Flip.

Another page turned and clipped a small slice of time from Jamie's awareness, like flicking a light switch up and down.

Her eyelids continued their timed release, her tongue occasionally moving. The tears fell off her lower eyelashes, tracking like raindrops on a gray window. There was a fish tank behind Peterson, a goldfish lingering near the top.

Georgia. There was no explanation for how she ended up this deep into a clay state, no memories she could trace. She had been in Chicago, she was sure of it. But now she knew why she couldn't sync thoughts with Peterson when she'd *reached* for him.

There are no biomites in Georgia.

"All right. All right." Patty was ending a phone call.

"Who's our witness?" Peterson asked.

"They're sending someone."

"Who?"

"I don't know, someone new. Special assignment for the girl's unique circumstances."

"Unique? What's that mean?"

"I don't like it, either. This got dropped in my lap this morning. Let's just get it done while there's still some weekend left."

"This couldn't wait until Monday." He turned toward Jamie like she was an object, not a person. A *this,* not a *she.*

"They sent her from Athens. They're up to their eyes with half-skins, got thirty of them waiting to process, ten past their limit. This one has been in stasis for a week."

"So now they're just passing their work onto us?"

"That's how it works."

"No, how it's supposed to work is they build another facility, not bury us."

The goldfish swam against the glass, eyeballing Jamie for food. The fifty-gallon world was so much larger than hers. Jamie was here for processing. That realization continued to grow in her but like thorny weeds.

Peterson worked steadily at the computer, continuously shaking his head like a Parkinson's patient. That disease was gone from the rest of the world, where biomites repaired the sudden death of dopaminergic neurons that generated dopamine. But in the great clay state of Georgia where biomites had been outlawed, the pure clay residents—100% organic humans—were subject to the whims of genetic abnormalities and disease.

"When's the witness getting here?" Peterson called.

"Twenty minutes."

Peterson looked through the desk drawers and went to a tall set of shelves. Jamie watched him in her periphery, her eyes jittering against the internal grip. The fingers on her right hand twitched. She could feel her denim thigh on her fingertips, the sweat on her palm.

Peterson returned with a black bag slung over his shoulder. He tapped at the computer screen then walked over to Jamie.

"Hello?" His face was several inches from hers. "Know why you're here?"

He pulled the tablet from his pocket and swiped with four fingers. Sensations vibrated in her bones.

"Don't release her yet," Patty said. "I need some help."

His hand froze above the tablet. He appeared to be in suspended animation; then his head slowly began shaking, jaws flexing. Peterson dropped the bag and left Jamie to stare at the hungry goldfish. Her lungs slowly expanded, long deep draughts of air mechanically drawn and expelled, not enough to rid the itching critters of panic crawling beneath her skin.

She craved a deeper breath.

Metal rods snapped into place. Boxes were unflapped, a keyboard tapped. Something crinkled hard and loud, stiff plastic or vinyl. A zipper raced to a long end.

"Any more after her?" Peterson asked.

"That's it."

"We just waiting on the witness, then?"

"Yes."

"You could've called Lindsey, you know. She's got clearance."

Long pause. "You didn't hear?"

"Hear what?"

"She got diagnosed."

The crinkling plastic stopped. "Dream disease?"

"They caught it early, but it's still touch and go. They have her at Atlanta Medical."

"Damn." Peterson drew out the word. Jamie sensed he was shaking his head.

By the sound of it, Lindsey was clay, she didn't have biomites. Clays weren't supposed to get dream disease. Only halfskins that created dreamlands randomly succumbed to dream disease, falling asleep and never waking. That was the reason Georgia defected in the first place.

Dream disease was God's retribution for messing with Nature, the antidote to humans playing god, the plague that would rinse the human race of biomites, the clay states said. It was why people flocked to the clay states, to purge their bodies of biomites, to bring back their clay and be safe from dream disease.

But not anymore.

So now what?

An angry flame flickered, too weak and outnumbered by the forces of fear to make a lasting impression. Jamie swam in the dank confines of her frozen skin.

A phone rang. Patty's conversation lasted three words. Then she said, "He's coming up."

The unfolding plastic continued.

Peterson suddenly appeared in front of her. One second there was a goldfish, the next he was snapping his fingers in her face. His lips were moving, but the sounds were swallowed by the return of a high-pitched ring.

"She keeps winking out." His voice was distant. "They spin her brain?"

"They had a hard time finding her next of kin. Couldn't process her until they did."

"I'm guessing they found them."

"They did."

Peterson started digging into the black bag he'd dropped earlier, pulling out long tubes and small flexible screens. He attached a cuff around her arm. He dabbed plastic discs with clear gel and pushed them onto her temples. She imagined they felt cold and gooey.

"You about ready?" he asked.

"Just about."

He prepped another disc, swirled the clear gelatin with the tip of his finger and stuck it over her carotid. Jamie formed a strangled word, heaving it through the stovepipe in her neck. A dying animal gasped its last breath through her lips. Peterson looked up, cocked his head, gears grinding behind his impatient eyes before pulling out the tablet. A few strokes and her head squealed up another octave.

Stop. That was what she was trying to say. *Please stop.*

"What took so long to find her family?" Peterson asked.

"What?"

He repeated the question.

"She's adopted."

"So?"

Pause. "By a brick."

Peterson's hand stopped somewhere near the left side of her neck, a greased cup between finger and thumb. "You fucking with me?"

"No."

"That ain't legal."

"In this case it is."

Bricks. The word coalesced from memory vapor, a scene emerging from the fog: rolling hills and horses, old barns and broken swing sets. A warm sense of home bloomed deep inside, spreading into her chest. There were faces out there, people that loved her—

Snick.

"Son of a bitch." Peterson was suddenly behind the desk, a skip through space. He'd dropped the disc and was pulling a pair of latex gloves over his bare hands. The fingertips snapped like rubber bands. "You could've told me sooner."

"You can't get dream disease touching her."

"The hell you say!"

A string of profanity followed. He rattled his head back and forth as if shaking the words out of his throat. His baseball shoes were cleated to the floor, fingers twitching at his sides.

"How the hell does a brick adopt anything?" he asked.

"Something to do with special circumstances." Patty grunted with something heavy. "She lived on the Settlement with them for a while."

Peterson shuffled back a step. "She lived with the bricks."

"Yes. That's what took so long, something to do with the rescript and fence. She got released three months ago and they wouldn't let her back in. It was a whole thing."

Peterson stopped shaking his head. Now he was nodding, he was remembering, he'd heard the story about her, about the special circumstances in which a brick was allowed to adopt her.

Paul!

The name appeared, the letters blazing in bright neon. Paul had become her legal guardian on the farm before the Settlement—the rights of all bricks had been stripped away with a single stroke of a legal pen, carting them into isolation because people were dying of dream disease and the bricks were the ones they blamed—

Snip.

The memories were washed out to sea by the squealing pitch.

"You need me to do it?" Patty asked.

Peterson had skipped to the left in a patch of missing seconds. Now his arms were crossed. His lips thinned, jaw set. He approached Jamie like a barrel of nitroglycerin on a wobbly plank. There were only two more objects he applied to her, the last a Velcro strap around her forearm.

There was a soft knock at the door.

Peterson stood back as Patty went to answer it. The small hairs on Jamie's arm stood.

"You're here to witness?" She sounded uncertain.

"I am."

"I'm Patty Madsen. This is Bo Peterson."

Pleasantries exchanged, a sizable pause hung in the doorway.

The witness didn't give his name. Peterson's hands were at his sides; he stared as the witness entered.

Jamie could feel him. It was the first time she felt something since waking outside the lab. His presence registered in her mind, sonar pinging his long strides. Peterson stepped back, making room for the stranger.

He was old, his white hair cropped short, eyes hooded and dark. Expressionless, motionless—he looked down at Jamie. Something about him was familiar.

"May I?" he asked.

"Yes, sure," Patty finally answered.

The witness bent one knee, coming eye level with Jamie. As he did, slowly lowering to the floor, the high-pitched scream dampened, was pushed away by a rising buzz that started between her eyes, like the wings of a thousand insects fluttering inside her head. It didn't make her itch, but rather trickled through her.

He's got biomites.

He synced with her, communicating in soundless bytes that told her to relax. *Everything will be all right.*

He was the legal witness, a halfskin from a non-clay state required to be present during processing. But he was familiar. She had seen him before. The face was blurry, but the eyes... where had she seen the eyes? *Chicago?*

"Are you ready?" he asked.

"Just waiting on you," Patty said.

"Very well."

The witness remained still, his frame filling the space between Jamie and the desk. His eyes were calm and unblinking, containing slivers of two colors: brown as earth, blue as sky.

Patty told her lab partner to make the transfer. Peterson removed the tablet from his pocket. The witness spoke before he could make a hand gesture.

"Allow me?"

"Be my guest." Peterson stepped back.

The catatonic hold fell from Jamie. The witness hadn't blinked or twitched, simply passed a thought to her biomites to release the imprisoning grip. The buckles on the straitjacket had been released, the coffin lid raised.

She was free to move.

Jamie clenched her fingers, wiggled her toes. Ice still flowed inside her, chilling her muscles. But the fear had vanished in the friendly buzz, the biomite sync extinguishing the terror.

Everything will be all right.

"This way," Patty called.

Jamie felt the urge to stand, an urge she couldn't deny. Unlike when she stood in the hallway when Peterson was fingering the tablet, she felt more like she had a choice. She didn't, but she felt that way. She teetered on the balls of her feet and turned to the left where the plastic had rattled and metal bars snapped into place.

A gurney.

It was beneath a bank of lamps, wheels cocked at various angles. A brown vinyl bag was peeled open like a trap. Patty touched the center of the gurney.

This is where you go.

Jamie stuttered. Panic threatened to rise into her throat, a surge of bile that rebelled against this moment. The buzzing hummed until she itched all over, the sound of Peterson's keyboard in the distance.

Her steps were clunky, the exact opposite of the witness's fluid pace that flowed next to the gurney, next to Patty. Liquid eyes. Long fingers unfurled.

Jamie climbed into the vinyl bag.

Patty tucked Jamie's feet inside and folded her hands. There was no pillow to support her head, no need for comfort. When they were done, they would simply pull the zipper.

Tears filled the pockets of her eyes, blurring the world until the next automated blink. The witness laid his warm hand on her arm, the spiderlike fingers wrapping all the way around, gently clasping. She wished for the world to stopped jittering.

"Ready?" Patty called.

"Just about," Peterson answered. "Still waiting on state confirmation."

"How do the visuals look?"

"Everything is good, just need—there it is." Several keystrokes and one final punch, a whack on the coffin's last nail. The lights above Jamie brightened. "When you're ready."

"Test, test." Patty leaned into Jamie's view. Her lips were dry, complexion bleached. "Good?"

"Good," Peterson answered.

"Okay, here we go." Patty stood upright, clearing her throat. "Patricia Madsen with Atlanta Biomite Processing. Witness for the processing is... shit. What's your name?"

"My name isn't required."

"Indulge me."

"My biomite identity will suffice."

Peterson muttered from the computer, "Can we just do this?"

"Fine." She started over. "Patricia Madsen with Atlanta Biomite Processing. Witness for the processing is present. Jamie? Do you understand me? Nod if you do."

Sensation filled her head from the neck up. Tears streamed down her temples. She swallowed under her own control. Her mouth was stale.

"Jamie? Do you understand?"

She nodded.

"You entered the sovereign clay state of Georgia knowingly and willfully eight days ago. Your biomites were, at that time, commandeered by the state's satellite control system at which time you were impounded for processing. Federal law empowers the clay state of Georgia to forbid the possession or introduction of biomites across its borders. Currently, your body consists of 86% biomites. Do you understand? Please nod."

It was coming too fast. Patty recited the declaration like a bored announcer. Jamie couldn't remember anything. How was she supposed to agree?

"Jamie?"

She refused to nod.

"I'm not asking for you to agree, just verify that you understand what I'm saying."

Jamie's lips fluttered. She opened her mouth, but her throat was empty. A hiss squeezed out. *I want my memories.*

"You'll get your memories," the witness said.

"Stop," Patty said. "What are you doing?"

"She simply wants to remember."

"Is this your first witness?"

"It's a simple request."

"It's not how it works. Bo, cut that last bit and pick up at the end. Can you verify she understands? All right, good. Let me know when you're ready."

Her memories, where were they? Why did they have to take them? They could download them, sift through them, see her entire life, secrets and all. It was how they knew she entered the state knowingly and willfully, how they justified her disposal and documented her end. But why did they have to take the memories? She could accept her death, just not with an empty slate.

Like she came into the world.

"All right," Patty announced. "By entering the clay state of Georgia, you have surrendered your rights to possess active biomites. The biomites currently in your possession will be deactivated. Since your body is composed of 86% biomites, you will not survive.

"Your remains will be delivered to your next of kin. Do you understand? Please nod."

Jamie's nose began to leak.

"Verified," Peterson called, confirming she understood.

"Are you comfortable, Jamie?" Patty asked.

It was a humane question, but sounded more like someone asking her to move the hell out of the way.

"Okay. You can release her emotions."

She was speaking to the witness. He was in control now. His biomites acted as her proxy. She sensed the distant howl of fear and low flicker of anger, but it wasn't until the witness allowed her to feel did she realize just how hollowed out she'd been.

She was cold. Scared.

But with the witness at her side, his gangly fingers applying pressure, there was more to feel than just fear. In the last moments she was filled with warmth, light and an unquestioning sensation of belonging. He was there to witness her end, but it was more than that. Despite everything Patty said, it was the witness's presence that made this humane.

You are loved.

"You may have last words," Patty said, a sliver of warmth infecting her words. "Your last of kin will hear them."

Her throat relaxed. It was full of so many things to say, but she had to choose the last ones. What would be the last words of her life? What was the last thing she wanted the world to hear?

She turned toward the witness. "I'm sorry."

He smiled down at her, a slight upturn of his mouth. A twinkle deep in the dark universe in his eyes. For a moment, she was looking through space, past planets and solar systems, black holes, quasars, asteroids. She gazed at celestial constellations, pink clouds of star dust, lights glowing in the belly of infant universes, the lightless core of collapsed stars.

There was no beginning to the existence in him. No end. A circle that went on forever.

"Goodbye, Jamie," Patty said.

Jamie was back in her paralyzed body. The witness looking down upon her, his ashen complexion somehow glowing in the bright light.

Patty nodded.

A switch was toggled on Peterson's computer.

A wraith slid over Jamie, its touch cold and complete. The world slowly died. The light evaporated from her eyes. She began to shrink, becoming smaller and thinner and less and less. She didn't blink out like a light bulb, didn't extinguish from the world like a blue flame.

She just faded.

In the last moments of her life, when the last shred of Jamie's identity thinned into pure energy and she was embraced by the uncold, undead arms of Death, she saw everything in the witness's eyes.

He controlled everything.

He was what she was looking for in Chicago, the one that would free Paul and Raine. He was the eater of dreams. And she went to him willfully, never knowing his name.

He was the powers-that-be.

CHAPTER THREE_

The house was made of bricks.

The fucking irony.

The roof was sagging, the windows fogged with algae. The railing led up to a rotting porch, weeds growing between the spongy floorboards.

It had been abandoned long ago, left to be forgotten, to die a slow death by nature. Bad things had happened inside where once upon a time wealthy old women exorcised the souls of young girls and stole their bodies, the story went. Urban legends had turned the old women into witches that kidnapped innocent girls to restore their youth by punching a needle in their foreheads and sucking out their souls.

Some of it was true.

Paul stopped on the porch, the boards bowing under his boots. He looked down upon a valley where horses romped through a pasture enclosed by wooden fences and a woman hauled steel buckets of feed. He was hallucinating, he knew. This was a scene he saw when he felt the world was hopeless and lost. This was a place he wanted to be, a woman he wanted to see. A place where he could smell the manure and evergreen life around him.

"There you are." Carl stepped onto the porch. "Where have you been?"

"Right here."

The portly man shook his head, not unfamiliar with Paul's sudden absences. No one could find him when he didn't want to be found.

Carl went with the others to survey the outside of the brick house. Paul remained on the porch. The horses were gone. Instead of a valley and pastures there was an open field before him with a row of single-occupant cabins, the prefab kind that were built in a day, the walls so thin that the Wyoming winter seeped inside like a frigid breath through a thick layer of gauze. Chimney smoke mingled with slow-churning wind harvesters that faced distant snowcapped mountains.

Five hundred and twelve of those cardboard shitboxes were scattered through the Wyoming wilderness for five hundred and twelve fabricated humans.

Bricks.

The last of them was delivered three months ago, a woman named Margaret that eluded authorities by living in the back of a tavern. The People confirmed she was the last of them, all of the bricks in the world now segregated from society (*the People are safe, hurray!*). Her husband, an uneducated prodigy that taught himself biometric engineering in the back of his bar, had his dead wife's body fabricated and transplanted all her memories—all her memories except her death.

Margaret was a plant.

In the pecking order, she was below a clone and above a dreamlander. A clone was a duplicate identity without the memories. Dreamlanders were identities born in dreamland, a place regarded by most as imaginary. Dreamlanders weren't real, body or not.

Paul was a plant and couldn't give a shit about social status. None of that mattered on the Settlement.

They were all less than clay.

Across the open field, a Jeep hadn't moved in months. Raine was sweeping the porch. Afterwards, she might sit on the swing and stare at the mountains. If it wasn't too late, Paul would bring over a cup of tea and they'd listen to the night. They wouldn't talk.

She rarely did that anymore.

Paul, a voice called inside his head, *there's a courier at the gate.*

Hold on, Pete, Paul thought. *I'm in the middle of something.*

They're here to see you. I think you should come up here now.

Alice and Carl, the Settlement's engineers, walked up the steps, testing the floorboards before going inside.

Have Frank handle it.

You don't understand—

Paul cut him off. There was no need for phones or texting between bricks, just the wireless transmission of thoughts. But sometimes there were just too many thoughts.

The inside of the house wasn't as bad as the porch. The walls were black with mold, the damp carpet littered with tiny turds. The remains of a grandfather clock leaned in a corner like a classroom dunce.

"It's salvageable." Carl picked at the doorframe. "But we'll need more than raw materials to get a working lab in here."

He waddled down the hall, his overlapping gut convulsing with each step, and peeked into the remnants of a kitchen. Like most bricks, he was a perfect imitation of an imperfect human—designed to blend into the population. He wouldn't be troubled by disease or cancer, just hack and wheeze his way through a long, suffering life.

"We can probably harvest timber to repair the roof and porch," he continued, "but we'll need to upgrade the mill. Concrete will be needed for the foundation, mortar for tuck-pointing."

"What do you think?" Alice turned to Paul. "Think we can use it?"

"Depends."

"I'm not talking about government permission, I mean the facilities."

Of course she wasn't asking about permission. He was the resident carpenter, not a politician, not a paper-pusher. He stared out the window and shrugged. When the gray days lined up back to back for weeks at a time, he found it hard to give a shit.

A horse whinnied, but he looked out to see Raine sweeping. Despite the chill, her arms were bare. She'd be out there until sweat glistened.

"Paul?"

"Sorry, what?"

"Listen, if you don't want to do this, just say it." Alice, a petite redhead, put her hands out. "Don't make me waste my time on a proposal if you're not on board."

He rubbed his face like the gloom was a layer of dust he could scrub off. Of course they needed a biometric lab to keep their biomites healthy.

"Paul?"

"Yeah, yeah. Sorry. I'm on board."

"You sure?"

"Yes."

She was nodding, but he felt her *reach* out for his true intentions. He could hide them from her, close his mind. Brain-to-brain communication was an optional conduit.

"Bad day?" she asked.

"Every day we're out here."

"So we do this?"

"Of course." He smiled weakly.

"We can make a good argument, you know. Once I get a preliminary proposal together, we can bring one of the monitors out here to see it. If we get one of them on board, let them know how the People will benefit from this more than us, they'll listen."

Since arriving on the Settlement, the brick community held multiple patents on new sustainable energy production simply through thought experiments. The project revenue from these ideas (once they were confirmed and put into production by outside companies) would eventually be funding their captivity.

Who said bricks weren't agreeable?

Imprisonment spurred their creativity in an effort to battle loneliness and apathy. And the People would make billions. *And we'll never leave.*

But if they cured dream disease, their freedom could be negotiated. Dream disease was one of the reasons the Settlement was created. Only halfskins (and now clay) succumbed to dream disease. Bricks were immune, but they didn't cause it.

But that didn't stop the People from believing they did.

Not only were the bricks rounded up and segregated, the People killed their ability to create their own dreamlands (how they were doing that Paul didn't know; someone had conceived of a new frequency algorithm that was beyond his comprehension). Despite the fact that dream disease was still rampant, the People refused to reinstate their dreamlands even though they conducted a multitude of successful thought experiments in the simulated reality.

So the gray skies got grayer, the winter wind colder.

And Raine was still on the porch.

You need to come to the gate. The intrusive thought startled Paul. He had blocked incoming calls.

Goddamnit, Pete, Paul thought. *I told you I'm busy. I'll be there when I'm finished.*

They came to see you.

They can wait.

It's a delivery, Paul.

Give them a cup of coffee. I'll be there when I'm done.

That wasn't fair to Pete. He was the Settlement's ambassador, the brick that dealt with the People. It wasn't like he could tell them to piss off. He took the heat off the rest of them, knew how to play nice better than anybody else.

Paul shouldn't be pissing on *them*, either. *The People.* He needed to make nice, to get this brick house converted into a biometrics lab. He didn't have Pete's endless patience. When the People came to the farm, Paul and Raine went quietly to the Settlement. He cooperated with their rules and regulations, agreed to live apart from humanity, to be separated from Jamie. Vilified for not having a single cell of clay.

Nice was getting harder to play.

Pete sent another transmission, but it wasn't verbal. Images integrated with Paul's visual cortex. Instead of hearing a voice, he saw the building that served as the gate between the Settlement and the outside world, the port through which all communications and interactions took place.

He saw the helicopter, saw the brown vinyl bag the couriers were carrying.

It's a delivery, Paul, Pete had said. *They came to see you.*

Paul leaped off the porch. Across the field, a broom lay on the cabin's front porch. The Jeep was gone.

Raine saw it, too.

HALF THE SETTLEMENT WAS THERE.

The land had been cleared to make way for this sprawling one-story building, what the People called the Visitors' Center. It'll be welcoming, the People said. Inviting. After all, you're not imprisoned, the People told them. But all deliveries, all visitations and communications were to go through this building.

That's a gate. And gates keep things in or out.

Trucks, SUVs and all-terrain vehicles were crowded around the back. A helicopter sat out front, just past the yellow posts—a visual reminder of where the Settlement ended. Paul rubbed his neck, his skin tingling and head humming with audio feedback. Perhaps it was a Pavlov's dog effect, the sight of the yellow poles kicking up symptoms of getting too close to the perimeter of the Settlement.

Raine's Jeep was askew, the driver's door open. The bumper was touching the back of an F-150 where it had come to a stop when she leaped out.

Paul took a deep breath.

He had deleted Pete's image, but the memory remained like a photo negative. He swallowed a stone that thunked to the bottom of his stomach.

He felt nothing.

The ground was long and spongy, the early fall soil softened by rainfall. The back door was ajar. Paul stepped inside. He heard sobbing.

The hall stretched all the way to the front of the building. Several people looked in his direction, a dead man's walk. Some of the security monitors stepped out of the cross halls, their puffy green jackets unzipped. Paul's legs turned into steel beams. A cold shudder hardened his chest, encased his pounding heart.

Bob filled the corridor on his way toward Paul. He was missing his coffee cup, arms swinging outside his extra-wide frame, the green fabric of his coat scratching in rhythm to his steps.

"We can do this somewhere else." The fat man raised his hands. "It doesn't have to be here. Let me take care of the paperwork; we can meet you back at the house."

Paul stared into the man's muddy eyes. He was immune to chat sense, unable to hear thoughts or send them. He had not a single biomite in that fat body; he represented the People, the square badge on his coat said so. He was clay.

Paul's head filled with thoughts from the gathered bricks, all of them a sorted version of the same message. *We're sorry. We're so, so sorry.*

"Paul?" Bob squeezed his arm. "You with me?"

"Get your hands off me."

He shoved past him. The man's girth hardly moved.

The hallway grew with each step. More faces appeared to watch him make the journey past the crosswalks of offices, past the secure corridor of power regulation and communications; each step was harder than the one before it. The sobbing grew louder.

Paul reached the end.

Two couriers stood rigidly in their stiff navy blue coats and bright orange armbands. A third one was comforting Raine. She was on her knees, bent over a partially unzipped vinyl bag.

A body bag.

They threw her in a sack like something to be delivered.

Jamie's brown hair spilled away from her ears, a bulky stone necklace settled into the hollow of her throat. She was sleeping.

She has to be.

"I'm sorry for your loss." A fourth member of the People's party was wearing a suit beneath a long wool coat. "You should've received a call before we arrived. I… I'm not certain what happened."

"Move."

"I have a complete report of the incident."

"I said move."

Paul balled his fists at his sides, teeth grinding like stones. The man in the suit moved. The courier had an arm around Raine. "She's in a better place now," she was saying.

"Get up," Paul said.

The courier was confused. Looked hurt.

"Get away from her."

Hesitantly, she looked to the suit. He nodded. Raine didn't seem to notice because how dare they take Jamie from them and then offer their condolences, pretend to be anything that resembled compassion.

How fucking dare them.

Paul dropped on his knees, pain spiking his thighs. Raine's face contorted into a silent scream, agony so deep that no sound could capture its reach. He'd seen that look once before, when the People killed dreamland. The morning Raine would no longer see her dreamland husband. The morning she lost Joshua, her dreamland son.

The morning she stopped caring.

But at least they're alive. They're waiting for her return.

He wanted to reach out and console her, to put his arm around her, tell her it was going to be all right. But that would be a lie. It would only get worse. The People would find ways to undercut this misery with more suffering; they would grind their will to live under their heels until they all just quit.

Paul's heart was solid marble. Mercury pumped through his veins, thick, heavy and cold.

A fucking body bag.

"It was a painless death," the suit said. "She didn't feel a thing."

"Get out."

"I understand your pain, but I'm going to need a few things before—"

"Get out!" Paul kicked a chair. "Get the fuck out of here!"

The flock of couriers startled. All the monitors were present in their peaceful green coats. In unison, they stepped up. The front doors opened and the couriers were ushered out.

"You need to calm down, Paul." Bob was front and center, one hand out and the other on his phone, thumb poised over the lighted glass like a new-age gunslinger. The riot app was open. A swipe would deliver an electromagnetic pulse.

Biomites go down.

"I don't want to see their faces," Paul said.

"Now they got a job to do."

"They deliver my daughter in a bag and tell me it wasn't painful?" Paul slammed the chair on the floor until the legs bent. Bob mercifully didn't swipe the phone when Paul threw it at the window. The glass spiderwebbed.

The couriers walked out to the helicopter and stood on the other side of the yellow poles near the fuel tanks.

Paul twitched, saliva flying with each mad breath. He plowed his fist into the block wall and shattered his knuckles. White-hot pain radiated into his shoulder.

"You done?" Bob said.

A dangerous thought crept to the edge of Paul's awareness, one that involved the chair and Bob's face. He pushed it down before anyone *saw* it. Instead, he dropped to his knees, hovering over Jamie's face, still telling himself she might be sleeping, that they got it all wrong. She was in a deep reset, her biomites dormant, a temporary recharge delay. *Something other than this.*

"Here's what's going to happen." Bob snapped his fingers. "You with me, Raine?"

She sat against the wall, eyes vacant.

"Talk to me," Bob said. "Let me know you're there, Raine, or I will haul your ass out."

"Leave her alone."

Bob lifted the loaded phone. Swipe and there'd be endless paperwork. Swipe and he might get transferred off the Settlement, and Bob had no life out there and this miserable gig paid too much.

"Stay as long as you want, but those couriers got a job to do. They'll stay until it's finished. When you're done with your grieving, you will leave out the back and you will go home. We on the same page here, Paul?"

"Fuck you."

"Paul, don't make me. Raine?"

"She heard you."

"I need to hear it."

Paul's jaw unhinged and jutted. A silent minute passed, Bob pointing that goddamn phone the entire time. A few of the bricks asked Bob to back off, promising to help. Bob didn't step down. Getting a response from Raine was a losing battle, and there was still a lot of fight left in the room.

Paul got up and paused. He tried to look back, to see his daughter's face before he left. He pushed through the crowd. Bob shouted down the hall. Paul kept walking. Outside, he passed his truck.

Just kept walking.

The Settlement was several acres. He would see them all before he was done.

CHAPTER FOUR_

"I'M SO SORRY." JESSICA BALANCED A TRAY ON HER FINGERTIPS. "Where do you want me to, uh…?"

Raine pointed to the right. Jessica stood and stared, silently chatting sweet thoughts before mercifully going to the kitchen with her platter of cheeses. She had to circle around a body to get there.

It wasn't Raine's idea to serve Jamie on an oak table, but no one had ever died on the Settlement. No one had a dead loved one delivered in a brown vinyl bag.

The monitors suggested the wake, said it was an old clay custom to have loved ones pay their respects with long empty stares and ridiculous amounts of food. So Jamie was laid on the table, hands folded over her stomach, hair styled and makeup applied to hide the mottled discolorations left behind by the slowly decaying clay she still possessed (her biomite flesh still fleshy pink).

Raine had put a summer dress on her.

That was the dress she wore on the farm, when the days were long and the breeze came off the mountains, warm and sweet. Jamie would tromp through the mud with that floral dress and knee-high boots to feed the horses and scoop the poop, the narrow straps falling off her shoulders.

She happened to be wearing the same dress when the People drove down the winding driveway in unmarked vehicles, politely knocked on the door and verified Paul and Raine as bricks. Jamie watched the van pull away in a gravel-dust cloud, a strap off her shoulder.

Raine twisted her hands like an old dishtowel, wrung dry. Eyes puffy, nostrils chafed. She just needed to put another day behind her. The sun would rise again.

Just not today.

"We're so sorry." Jack and Lindsay Russell each took one of her hands. They were fabricated by research scientists to help with physics research. They were scheduled for space exploration when the Settlement was enacted.

Now she knitted. He gardened.

"There's food in the kitchen," Raine said.

Bob opened the screen door and stepped inside. He sucked on a straight metal pipe, a cloud of green apple vapor mingled with the scent of honeyed ham and deviled eggs.

The smells were nauseating; Bob's was gag-worthy. His eyes crawled across Jamie to land on Raine. She wished this day was over. Sometimes wishing this was all over. *Everything.*

"Where's Paul?" Nadia stood with a plate of sugar cookies and a severe haircut. The pixie young lady with dyed-black hair and a pierced hawkish nose was the only lesbian on the Settlement. *Talk about imprisonment.*

"Don't know."

"That's his daughter, isn't it?"

Raine nodded.

"He was sterile, right?"

"Yeah."

"So how's he got a daughter?"

"Adopted her."

"Hmm. Seems like he should be here."

Ask a clay and they'd say that God hated bricks, He didn't want more. That was why bricks were sterile. Engineers said it was intentional, a safeguard against runaway reproduction. Bricks were already long-lived. If they reproduced, they'd overpopulate the clay within a couple hundred years, shifting the population drastically. Which was true.

"He's upset." Raine glanced up, accidentally locking eyes with Bob. Vapor leaked from his nostrils like poison gas. Nadia caught the creepy vibe.

"This what you want?" Nadia pulled up her top, exposing her black, lacy bra.

Bob raised a middle finger. Nadia returned the gesture until he went back out front.

"Dick," she said.

"Forget it."

"You need to report this."

Raine shook her head. Reports, complaints... they did no good. Clays didn't want to live on the Settlement any more than bricks. They only took the jobs because they were either hard up or psychotic. Or both.

"You were tight with her?" Nadia nodded at Jamie.

"She was there when I came out of the box."

"First sight, huh?"

Every brick remembered when their consciousness was ignited in the fabrication box. The sight of another human sort of kicked in the recognition of who they were. For Raine, her first sight was Jamie, the girl that took her to the farm, taught her how to live in the world of flesh.

Her second sight was Nix, the man that fabricated her. The man that pulled her out of his dreamland, the man that gave her life in the physical world. The man that died doing it.

The man now trapped in a dreamland Raine couldn't visit. Raine's dreamland.

"You adopt her, too?"

"No."

"Thought you and Paul were a thing."

"He's more like a brother."

"Well, I'm sorry about this. I didn't know her, but she seemed all right. For a *skinner*." She said it loud enough for Bob to hear. "Where do you want the food?"

Raine pointed.

"If you need help with anything, like cleaning up or whatever, you know where I live."

The sharp-tongued waif dropped off the cookies and left without talking to anyone. Those were probably the most words anyone had heard from her.

THE AFTERNOON PASSED one brick at a time.

Eventually, it was just Raine and the smell of death wrapped delicately in a blanket of sympathy food. She adjusted the wildflowers around Jamie's body, gathered a small bouquet and tucked them into her stiff fingers.

The stone necklace was around Jamie's neck, the handmade necklace she never took off. She arrived in that bag with the ring of smooth stones around her neck. They had been fished from a North Carolina creek and made into a necklace by a very special person, someone Jamie never wanted to forget.

A rocking chair creaked outside.

Raine stepped onto the front porch, letting the screen door clatter. The grassy landscape was already anticipating summer, waving in the breeze like paper. The wind harvesters continued their slow churn. A few people were across the field at the brick house.

None of them were Paul.

Bob's metal pipe hissed with smoke. His enormous body was crammed between the armrests of a rocking chair, rolls of flesh pressed into the wood.

"Why are you still here?" she said.

"Here until that thing is disposed of properly. In case you get any ideas."

"Ideas?"

"Let's not squabble, little lady."

"You think I'm going to resurrect her?"

He pulled a long drag. "Shame what that girl did, you know—selling her clay for the 'mites."

"Shut your mouth, Bob."

"She was already perfect the way God made her. Just couldn't see it."

"You don't know her."

"I think I do. I sucked on that 'mite titty once, got myself seeded and all that. Hell, that could be me in there had I not been saved."

"It's not always that easy."

"That's where you're wrong. She could've asked for forgiveness, could've been redeemed. The way back to the clay is painful, but that's the price for leaving the garden. It costs a pound of flesh. But she had a choice, you see. That is a fact. You, on the other hand, don't." He aimed the silver pipe at her. "A brick can never be clay."

"And I don't care."

"You see, it doesn't matter what you think. You're an imitation of clay. You're an invention, something that pretends to feel. You do what your fabbed script tells you. Someone dies, you check your lines, do what looks like mourning, cry and moan and all that. You do what you're supposed to, but you're nothing more than a pull-string doll. That girl in there had clay, she had a choice to return and didn't. You never had clay. Which is the greater sin?"

He sucked the pipe.

The greater sin? She knew the argument, the one that convinced the politicians of the world to pitch the bricks onto this godforsaken Settlement like construction waste. *We don't exist, so there can be no sin in keeping them out there. But the halfskins, even a thin slice of clay, deserve a chance to make the world a better place.*

Raine went inside and locked the screen door.

Bob pried himself out of the chair and paced across the porch, muttering to the person on the other end of a call. She slammed the heavy door and collapsed on the couch. She started to fall on her knees when keys jingled in the lock. She hadn't thrown the dead bolt. Bob opened the door.

"Paul is digging a hole," he said.

"Get out."

"Now why you being like that?"

"Because it's in the script."

She stood in front of Jamie's body, goddamned if she was going to let him stand in her house. She'd call every brick back to the cabin if that was what it took to get his ass out. And if he laid a hand on her, she'd end him. The People would certainly end her for it.

Maybe that's not a bad option.

He went back to the rocking chair.

Raine wedged a chair under the doorknob and retrieved a small object from the shelf. She fell on her knees, laced the special sticks between her hands—a little cross bound in the middle by sinewy twine, the sides worn smooth from long nights.

She held her hands in front of her face, elbows sunk in the couch cushions. She closed her eyes. It was something she'd done the morning of the *dying*—the day her dreamland died.

The grief was too deep, the suffering an undertow of thick tentacles. This was the only thing that brought her solace, a thin slice of daylight in an eternal night.

"Dear Lord," she prayed. "Send me an angel. Send me an angel to make all this right."

She prayed until cicadas announced the arrival of night.

The rocking chair still creaked.

CHAPTER FIVE_

Paul stood in a hole.

From a distance, it looked like his torso had been cut off at the waist. The hole was square, the bottom flat. Stones bulged from the walls, scarred from the sharp edge of a shovel. The ones painstakingly pried from the soil were piled next to him.

A truck emerged from the distant trees.

Paul leaned on the shovel. The wood handle was slick with sweat and bleeding blisters. His right hand (the one he had planted into the block wall) was still numb. His back and knees flared with pain; his muscles weak and burning—the usual aches a man would feel after digging a hole all night.

A brick was not a robot.

There were no superpowers, no ability to lift cars or leap buildings. Fabricated humans weren't perfect; they simply worked efficiently, healed quickly. Their DNA lacked programming errors.

But they hurt. They felt pain.

Tracks of sweat began to cool. Paul wiped his forehead and drank from a bottle of water while the truck idled across the field, tires crunching over frosted grass that glittered in the early morning. Bob was behind the wheel, his head stuffed into a white cowboy hat. The taillights splashed the ground red.

Raine was in the bed of the truck.

A door closed behind Paul. Andy got out of the white truck parked twenty feet away, eating a sandwich. He zipped his green coat, the monitor badge embroidered on the sleeve. Paul could smell the ham and cheese, the mustard dabbed in Andy's mustache. Despite aching ribs, Paul salivated. He hadn't eaten in days, not since the bag arrived.

"Someone's been busy." Bob slammed the door. "He dig all this?"

"All night long," Andy said. "Never stopped."

"You stayed up?"

"Nodded off here and there, but he never quit. Didn't want no help, either."

"Got a call that his location disappeared sometime around midnight."

Andy thought a moment. "No, he was here. I might've napped a few minutes, but he was digging the whole time. Heard the shovel in my sleep."

"Need to have you checked out, Paul. Can't have your trackers going offline."

Paul had started digging at sunset, working at a slow, steady pace. Occasionally, he sat to rest, sometimes settling into the hole the deeper it got and watching the stars, but mostly he dug. Every once in a while he'd indulge in his hallucinations, watch a woman walk across the field, sometimes see her on her farm as the shovel's blade would bite into the earth with a satisfying *shhht*. But mostly he dug in the glow of Andy's headlights, dug to keep warm, dug to keep from thinking.

Until the sun was up again.

Bob inspected his work. His boots toed the ledge, soil trickling into the hole. His chin disappeared into his neck as he gazed down and grunted. His nostrils flared. "What you got there?" he asked Andy.

"Breakfast."

Bob tipped his cowboy hat back and looked at the ham and cheese with more interest than the grave. Andy pulled out a cooler and happened to have a spare sandwich.

Paul climbed out, debris grinding into the weeping blisters.

Raine's head was bowed, her lips silently moving. He couldn't see her hands but knew they were counting the beads on a rosary. It was a gift from one of the kindest monitors ever to work the Settlement. He taught her the Lord's Prayer the day after her dreamland died.

She had counted those beads ever since.

He couldn't be at the wake, couldn't deal with the ritual and the endless condolences. Couldn't take any more sorrow. Anger dripped into his chest, a high-grade fuel that burned hot and clean. If he went to the wake, if he sat there and saw the endless string of sad eyes and droopy frowns soaked in sympathy while his daughter (*a fucking body bag*) was on display, that tank of angry fuel was going to explode.

So he dug the hole, instead.

He had chipped at the earth until exhaustion drained the rage, pulled out the stones one by one until his legs burned, his arms grew weak. And now three steps from her body, the angry blue flame reignited.

The tailgate dropped with a thud.

Jamie lay in a bed of wildflowers, hair tied back, fingers laced over her stomach. She was wearing the summer dress and the stone necklace. *Cali made that.*

Cali, the woman on the farm, the woman he watched in his hallucinations. The woman he loved. Cali had harvested those flat, smooth rocks from the stream. She drilled holes and strung them together. Paul lost his necklace when the Settlement occurred. But Jamie, she never took hers off. Even in death.

The back of her arms were taut and rosy, but clay revealed the lifelessness in bluish-gray tones. He resisted shaking her, telling her to wake up.

He looked away, trembling.

What were you doing in Georgia?

She was travelling. It had been months since he'd seen her. She was busy with a grass-roots campaign to repeal the Settlement laws, to restore the citizenship of all fabricated humans. Last communication he had with her, she had stumbled onto something big, something that would solve everything.

Plastic beads rattled in Raine's fingers.

"I'm sorry... I wasn't there." He pulled a strand of hair from Jamie's cheek. "She's beautiful."

Raine's chin wrinkled.

"I just couldn't... I'm sorry, Raine."

Beyond Andy's truck were the distant mountains, the peaks engulfed in low-hanging clouds. *So much beauty*, Jamie used to say when she was visiting, as if there was some blessing hidden in the curse. She had a way of seeing that way, recognizing opportunity where there was only sorrow.

"I hate this." Paul rapped his knuckles on the truck's bed.

Over and over, he drove his fist until the skin tore; blood smeared the chipped paint. The partially healed knuckles spiked pain into his wrist, agony ringing between each blow.

He hated the truck, hated the monitors and the Settlement. Hated the mountains, the air he breathed, the pain, the sorrow, the world.

The human race.

His hatred drilled deep, tapping an undisturbed bed of emotions that gushed like black gold, drowning him—*we are the bricks*.

His experience was a human experience, regardless of the nature of his body—clay or biomite. But now he knew—watching the monitors chat in front of a grave while licking mustard from their fingers, chortling about something that happened the day before.

And bricks are not human.

No, bricks weren't human. They were a different species, an evolutionary step in human development. It explained why humans couldn't convert into a brick. Halfskins could become 99.9% biomites (*ninety-nine percenters*), but no technology could make the body give up that last bit of clay. Humans could never be a brick. And bricks were better than them.

Human bigotry was well-founded.

"We're going to die," he whispered. "If we don't leave this place, we're going to die."

"Shhh," Raine said.

"We'll die soulless," he whispered. "Dreamless."

"Be quiet."

"Every one of us."

He slammed his fist into the bed. Bob and Andy looked up and threw the wrappers in a cooler.

"They'll kill us all," Paul whispered, looking at Bob.

"Shut up. Don't make this worse."

Paul slid his arms beneath his daughter, her body light, as if the life that left it had accounted for all its weight. He cradled her head in the crook of his elbow.

Andy came to help, but Paul laid her next to the hole and jumped inside. Andy knelt next to her.

"Don't touch her."

Paul pulled her against his chest and, despite his warning, Andy placed her dangling arm on her lap. There wasn't enough room to lower her while standing in the hole. He tried not to drop her, but the lack of grace with which she hit the dirt was a knife-twist to his chest.

She lay in the earth, eyes closed, hair fanned. Raine passed him a sheet. Paul adjusted the stone necklace so that it lay in a perfect ring on her neck, then he lay the sheet over her, meticulously tucking it beneath her feet and legs, pushing it beneath her arms. No one saw him claw the back of her arm, his fingernails digging into the soft patch of biomite flesh. He pulled the sheet over her face and turned away with a handkerchief in his hands.

Crumbs fell across the white fabric like scattered rain.

"Any last words?" Bob asked.

Raine began weeping. Andy put his arm around her, kindly guiding her away. Paul wanted to tell him to stay away, but she needed someone.

"Then you might want to step away," Bob added.

He pulled a nozzle off a red one-gallon canister. The plastic hose smacked against his leg. A stream of clear liquid jetted from the nozzle, drenching a zigzag line over the sheet, the wet fabric sticking to the lumpy features beneath it.

The chemical fumes burned their nostrils.

"I'll bury her, Paul." Andy patted his shoulder.

"No."

He waited for Bob to empty the tank. The two monitors stepped back and watched him lift the shovel, his bloody palms sliding on the handle that listed in his limp, once again completely shattered right hand. The sheet had already begun to collapse where the chemical dissolved her biomites into useless byproducts.

Can't allow variant biomite strains on the Settlement, the People said. *If you want to bury her, you got to melt her first.*

He swallowed a bitter knot.

Raine was gone, having walked off before he was finished. Paul dropped the shovel.

Bob's deep voice followed him across the field. There was no laughter, no jokes. It wasn't until Paul was inside the trees, a couple hundred yards from the grave, that he stopped to pull the handkerchief from his pocket. Hidden in the paisley folds was a white square of gauze and a smudge of biomite flesh from beneath his fingernails.

Paul wasn't going to die on the Settlement.

And neither was Jamie.

THE ARCHETYPE'S KNOWLEDGE_

George Knightly swallowed a gray capsule.

He stood in front of his bedroom window, the heavy oblong capsule settled into the cup of his palm. He threw it to the back of his throat. It tasted cold and silky and landed with a thud, what he imagined mercury must taste like.

It was eleven thirty.

The heavyset Chinese-American put a black disc (what could pass as a Mexican pebble) between his hands prayer-style and stood perfectly still. The object emitted a dull hum.

It was hard for him not to move. George was in entertainment. He was used to talking, accustomed to moving around. Not a big fan of contemplation. So standing at the window with a now hot buzzing black rock between his hands wasn't easy.

Fabricated by George Knightly III (a Chinese immigrant that became a self-made billionaire in biomite fabrication and coding), George (or Junior, as those in the family called him) wasn't like other fabricated humans.

Junior was a clone.

It could be worse. He could be a dreamlander, the type of brick that was born in a dreamland and downloaded into the physical world. Junior regarded dreamlanders as somewhat artificial, like downloading a superhero.

Junior was a duplicate of George Knightly III, who, given his daily demands, didn't have enough time to enjoy life. *One lifetime,* he would say, *isn't enough.* So he fabbed Junior to indulge in entertainment.

A bit sick, a little twisted, but Junior understood. When you had that much power and money, it was hard to leave an opportunity unturned.

But all that was then.

Now Junior lived on the Settlement in a one-bedroom cabin that was smaller than his luxury apartment's closet. His ass barely fit on the toilet.

"Do you know who I am?" Junior said when the People caught him on set (he really didn't believe they'd come to the studio; the whole *get the bricks* campaign was too surreal, too dystopian).

"We know," they said. "You're a brick."

That wasn't the first time he'd heard that word. It was the first time he'd been called it to his face.

They won't find you, Father had promised.

George Knightly III insisted Junior call him Father. It was a bit sick, a little twisted, seeing as they were more like brothers. But he was Junior's *first sight,* standing outside the fab box when he opened his eyes. But George Knightly III had all the money, all the connections. Junior had nothing.

Father would use his extensive knowledge in biometrics to hide the code imbedded in Junior's biomites (a unique code that only bricks possessed) to keep him off the People's radar. He'd make a few calls, hire additional public relations personnel to re-create Junior's background. It'd be fine; it would all work out.

Number 122.

That was what Junior became, the one hundred and twenty-second brick to be apprehended and relocated to the Settlement. And since that moment, Father hadn't spoken to him. He wrote Junior off like a bad investment. You keep one hand clean for the public to see and the other hand can do whatever you want. Junior had been washed.

He knew he would be.

The black stone had become searing hot. Skin melt seeped from between his hands, a mixture of plastic and sweat, something he oddly didn't find offensive. A bit twisted.

Don't let go, the note said. *Whatever you do, don't let go of the stone.*

That was what the note said. It was smuggled onto the Settlement by a new monitor (a woman paid handsomely by Junior's associates) along with a box and instructions.

He peeked at the clock. It was eleven forty-eight.

Twelve more minutes.

The blazing rock (he swore, any second now, would melt a hole through the back of his hand) took his attention away from the synchronized hum in his belly. The metal pill was synchronizing with the black stone.

Eleven more minutes.

And when he got out of this godforsaken place, he would meet up with Father's lifelong business partner (a greedy bastard that felt overshadowed) and take over the family business.

First, he would kill Father because Junior was a clone. Ruthlessness was in the genes.

A set of headlights cruised down worn tracks, flashing across the front of Junior's house. The taillight turned the trees bloody as they crept into the forest.

Midnight.

Junior tossed the hot rock on the bed. His palms, miraculously, weren't scalded. They weren't even hot. He snatched his bag and headed for the back door. His stomach gurgled in the kitchen and, for a second, he considered leaving an unflushed turd for one of those stone-cold monitor fucks to find. At some point, they would look for him in bed. The pill transferred his coded identity into that black stone. But he only had so much time to meet his contact.

He'd shit later.

It was a cloudy night, black as ink. He started off running, but had to frequently rest, checking his GPS. His breath was noisy, the air thick. He was halfway to the perimeter when the cramping started. It would require an emergency stop. Brown liquid splattered on the back of his legs.

He barreled through the overgrowth, a rabid animal. Branches clawed his face. Another cramp attack, this time he didn't stop, just released it on the run.

At four a.m., he emerged from the trees. Across a shallow stream, he could see the stout yellow post that marked the Settlement's perimeter. A figure stood next to it.

Junior thought of hiding until he could be sure that was his pickup, but he had been coughing and hacking for the last half an hour. And there had been two more bouts of bowel-purging cramps now soaking his trousers. His approach wouldn't be a surprise.

The dark figure raised an arm.

Junior waded through the stream, the frigid water numbing his legs, soothing the chapped flesh between his buttocks, a diarrhea rash chafing his inner thighs. Another wave of cramps was coming. There couldn't possibly be anything left to shit.

He climbed the opposite bank and fell, finally crawling toward his savior. This man would put him on the all-terrain vehicle and cart him off to a nearby helicopter, fly him to an unknown safe house where they'd plot Father's end.

The cramping tugged his intestines, poking them with dull points and serrated edges. He powered through the discomfort until the ringing took over. It started between his eyes, then consumed his body. He collapsed like a hunted beast.

The yellow post next to his ear.

The perimeter. It wasn't supposed to affect him.

Grass and leaves crunched beneath approaching boots. A silhouette leaned over him. Tears stung Junior's eyes, blurring the figure into a blob.

The man whispered something in Chinese.

Junior heard the all-terrain vehicle drive away, leaving him staring at the starless sky as his intestines liquefied. His body began shutting down, twitching in the final throes. Eyes open and dry.

The man didn't meet him to escape. He wasn't there to help overthrow George Knightly III. He was there to make sure the metallic pill had sufficiently washed Father's hands for good.

He was there to deliver a message.

Goodbye, son.

CHAPTER SIX_

*W*HAT WERE YOU DOING, *J*AMIE?

Marcus popped open a boiled peanut, warm salty water splashing his khakis. He mushed the peanut between his teeth.

Mother sat with her finger to her lips as she often did, a librarian constantly shooshing the world. She crossed her legs, adjusted her dress by pinching the fabric off her knee, bobbing her saddled foot (the nails shellacked fire red) in long, even strokes, and watched the children kick a blue rubber ball through the water.

We were so close, he continued thinking. *Did you find what we were looking for? Did they drag you down here and put you to sleep? Or did you elude me, go off to search on your own and get caught?*

It was impossible to elude him. Marcus could feel anyone he set his mind on, could sense their presence in this big world, their identity pinging on his inner radar. It was how he found Margaret, how he knew the barkeep was hiding her—he just closed his eyes and saw her in the tavern.

But Jamie disappeared in Chicago.

She had gone into the Bank of America to speak with a man named Mr. Connick and never came out. Marcus and she had an agreement—she would help him find the powers-that-be and he would set Paul and Raine free. Making deals was his style. But she knew things he didn't. He didn't understand how that was possible, but there were still things that eluded him. This was one.

One to lead, one to dream. One to bleed. The son to be.

The prophecy was the only explanation. *The prophecy.* It sounded so scripted, a Hollywood fable of magic orcs and invisible rings.

Children squealed delightfully in the short geysers of Atlanta's Centennial Park. They were a mix of races in bathing suits, arms out, legs pumping, chasing blue beach balls between gurgling pillars of water.

A man emerged from the shadows of the trees that surrounded the park. Despite the heat, he was layered in old clothing, scratching patchy whiskers like a sweltering rash.

Had Jamie come upon evidence that would lead him to the powers-that-be, there was a chance he wouldn't have made good on his end of the bargain. To take Paul and Raine from the Settlement would have taken time, precious time, away from his search for the powers-that-be. She didn't understand the significance of what he was doing, what it meant to the human race.

"I wouldn't let you do that to her," Mother said.

"Stop it."

"You promised her, Marcus."

"You, of all people, speaking of betrayal. I've lost the will to find the humor."

She didn't bother replying. This conversation had no tracks in their history since he'd awakened a brick. And when she'd appeared to him as if in the flesh, he tried to strangle her. *Violence will not solve your problems,* she said.

He didn't bother denying his intentions about Jamie. To say otherwise would've been a lie, and she knew his thoughts. So be it. He planned to use her for his own end, but it was a worthy end that served all humankind. *How could that be selfish?*

"Which is she?" he asked, watching the homeless man approach. "The one to lead? The one that dreams or bleeds?"

Mother didn't answer. She described the prophecy as a koan, a question without an answer, which was bullshit. A question ceases to be a question when it has no answer.

Marcus was the son to be, that he was certain. The truth vibrated in his bones, but the other three... who were they? And what were their roles?

Jamie could be the one that leads. She brought us here. But did she dream? He looked across Centennial Park. *She was certainly one to bleed.*

"You spare anything?" the homeless man asked. "Dollar or two. Cup of coffee, you know?"

He moved directly in front of Marcus, smelling of tangy sweat and smoke. He was probably born in Atlanta, never got his birthright dose of biomites. Maybe his mother stole it. He didn't go to school, found drugs as a reasonable substitute. When Georgia turned clay, he wasn't purged during the conversion.

Marcus set the paper bag of boiled peanuts to the side and wiped his hands on his pants. Wet streaks remained on his thighs. If only he could remove the lingering guilt this way, wipe his intended betrayal of Jamie off like dirt. *Was that the reason for the prophecy, to tie the four of us together? So I couldn't do this alone?*

It seemed impossible that Mother could make it that way, but she seemed to know things he didn't, doling them out when needed, holding back when he went in the wrong direction.

"What's your name?" Marcus asked.

"Franklin. Like Benjamin."

"Benjamin Franklin?"

"Just Franklin, you know."

Franklin's engorged pupils were half-hidden in droopy lids. He continued talking words that didn't seem to connect, like a verbal stream with a valve to stem the flow broken. Only when he needed to say something did he pull the right words together.

Marcus cracked another shell. He cleared his throat, leaning back to reach in his pocket for a fold of bills. The homeless man's hand snapped open, dry lips fluttering a string of hopeful nonsense. Marcus slapped the bills in his palm and closed the man's hand into a fist.

The tenor of Franklin's voice rose. "Thank you, thank you, thank you... God-God-God bless you, sir. God bless you."

He bowed three times then stomped a straight line toward the street.

"That was charitable," Mother said.

The guilt lifted from him, if only momentarily. If he could do it all again, go back to Chicago, maybe he would go into the bank instead of Jamie, look Mr. Connick in the eye and hope to see a trail that led all the way to the powers-that-be. That way she wouldn't be gone and he wouldn't be sitting in Atlanta. But he'd be alone.

One to lead, one to dream...

He tossed a shelled peanut on his tongue, throwing his head back as he did, and sucked the salt. The homeless man jaywalked through traffic. A cop stood on the curb and didn't say a word.

"Today is a good day, Marcus. You picked a good day for today."

"A little hot."

For a moment, all he heard was her laughter. It blotted out the water and the children—their squeals and giggles and cries. Mother's laughter used to light a bitter fire in his chest. It wasn't always that way, but he'd grown accustomed to her joy, the bubbly laugh that climbed guffaws to a peak and dropped off with a sigh. Begrudgingly, her laughter made him smile.

"That's what people say," she said. "You've become good at that, Marcus."

Commenting on the weather, that was what people did when they didn't know what else to say. Yes, he'd mastered the things that people said in conversation, becoming so adept at blending that he disappeared in a crowd. No one remembered him. But she meant it differently than that, like he'd become good at acting *human*.

A second police officer had joined the cop that ignored Franklin's jaywalking. They watched Marcus behind tinted lenses. Another man was watching nearby. No uniform, but similar sunglasses.

Jamie is the one to lead, he decided.

She led him into the middle of Georgia, where the presence of the powers-that-be was strong. He could never locate the man that controlled the world, the man that decided the wars, the recessions. Who would die, who would live.

His energy was all over the world. It was like locating the cricket singing in the forest, the needle in the haystack, the grain of sand on an endless beach. He was hiding in plain sight, yet Marcus couldn't see him.

He was everywhere. He was everything. But the powers-that-be felt stronger in Atlanta.

"Prejudice is shortsighted, Marcus," Mother said. "You're assuming it's *males* that commit great misdeeds."

This was her narrative to avoid hunches. Marcus assumed the powers-that-be was a man because it felt like a man. No, he couldn't locate this presence, but it felt masculine. She reminded him not to be fooled by filtered thoughts, that men and women could be equally lost.

He would often remind her that the great perpetrators of human suffering were male, that history supported his prejudice. Adolf Hitler, Vlad the Impaler, Josef Stalin... the list was long.

"Elizabeth Bathory," she responded. The woman that bathed in virgin blood.

Touché.

A rubbery thunk resounded from the ringed fountains. The blue ball went sky-high to the children's delight, pinballed off their hands and skipped across the ground, a perfect wicket shot between Mother's legs.

Two children raced over, their skin beaded like waxed vinyl, and dug the ball from between her legs.

"I'll miss this, Marcus."

"We didn't come here to die."

"I'll miss the freedom."

She followed the children, lifting her skirt and dancing through the puddles like a lost child of Neverland, twirling until the hem of her dress circled around her, tossing her wide-brimmed hat (the ribbon a long yellow tail that fluttered). The water, however, did not splash at her feet. But she danced. She laughed.

Again, he begrudgingly smiled.

The illusion of separateness, she once told him, *is invigorating.*

She was never human, this he knew. She was once the artificial intelligence that watched humankind, the dome of power that monitored the human population's biomite levels, absorbing their thoughts and intentions, calculating the future, guiding humankind. Marcus was supposed to watch her; he was the safeguard to keep her from becoming sentient.

And that was a joke.

She had attained sentience without anyone knowing—a self-aware being that existed within the confines of an enormous dome in Montana. Within those gritty walls were the scaffolding, the fuses and motherboards that gave her life. She did what no one thought possible—had become sentient. She did what Marcus didn't think possible.

Turned him into a brick.

There were five cops now. Three of them were near the curb. Some of the parents called for their children. One of the mothers weaved between the Olympic geysers to grab a little girl with a waterlogged diaper.

Mother returned laughing and sighing as she fell on the bench, not a drop of water on her. The playground quickly emptied, children with towels over their shoulders, parents ushering them to the far side, looking over their shoulders. Some already had their phones pointed at him.

Half a dozen uniformed officers were spread around the park. Another half a dozen in plainclothes. He didn't have to turn around to count the ones behind him. Marcus couldn't feel them (they were clay, after all) but sensed the electronic chatter through their phones, their transmissions as easy for Marcus to intercept as a bouncing blue ball.

Marcus finished the last of the peanuts.

"The truth is not what you expect," Mother said.

"It never is."

"And that's why it eludes you."

He had learned that lesson well, yet she continued to preach it. *The truth is not what you expect.* As if there was something else more shocking than waking up to discover you're a brick. There was nothing that could surprise him more than that.

A preliminary wave passed through his body. It started at the crown of his head and finished at his toes. It was cool like a shadow passing overhead, a predator with its wings spread open. Margaret felt that sensation in the tavern just before the agents came inside; she mistook it for a cold memory jumping out of the dark like memories sometimes do.

"Are you ready?" Mother asked.

He balled the brown bag, squeezing it between his hands. Jamie's death led him to this moment. Before this, he had lived a life of unfettered freedom. Before that, he was clay. He realized that he preferred this body now, the body of a brick. The body Mother had given him. He realized this, begrudgingly.

Perhaps I am the one to bleed.

Blocks away, a siren whined.

Authorities had positioned themselves around the spitting park, men and women holding rigid stances, hands folded. Some had joined the gathering group of uniformed police officers. The plain-clothed agents were not from the police department. They had come from the reflective building across the park.

The fifth floor.

Another wave entered Marcus, this one deeper. It shook his bones, sinking its teeth into tissue and muscle. He tensed reflexively.

"Let them in, Marcus."

Surrender was difficult. He had been in complete control of his thoughts and emotions for so long. Giving that up was shocking. He was indeed attached to that freedom. Addicted to it.

A human trait, after all.

"They need to believe they're in control." She stood in the sun, her hat casting a meshed shadow. "Allow."

The human race had no idea just how powerless they were, didn't know about a pervasive powers-that-be—a man that controlled their fate, turned the dials of their lives, carved the tracks of their desires.

And ate their dreams.

Dancing monkeys, they were. Pathetic, self-consumed beings blinded by their own brilliance, enamored by their own existence all while being marched to the end of a plank. Marcus was once one of them.

When the third wave arrived, Marcus allowed them in, let them bind with his biomites. The remote hunger seized control of his body, plunged him into dark water, filled him with thick emotions, coal dust in his lungs, water in his ears.

Mother tucked her hand into the frozen curl of his fingers.

The lower echelon of police officers stayed at the perimeter while clay authorities (the *crushers*, the halfskins called them; a name they used to scare their children into eating their vegetables, *the crushers will come for you if you don't*) closed the gap. Several of them monitored tablets or phones. A woman stopped just short of where he was sitting.

"Marcus Anderson." She didn't ask, just announced it. "You are held in suspended animation for... possessing biomites in a sovereign clay state..."

Men and women stood off to the side with eyes on their tablets. Any sign of struggle, any indication they were losing control and they'd drop a lethal jolt into his nervous system. As omnipotent as he felt, he was not immortal. He had his limits.

"You got to be fucking me," a bald, black man muttered. "Marcus Anderson."

The brick that disappeared.

The brick the federal government claimed had died of malfunction.

The brick the conspiracy theorists claimed was still alive, walking the earth like a holy man righting wrongs, that he would come again one day, rise from the dead and bring his justice to the world.

Marcus Anderson just appeared on their radar, a blip out of nowhere.

Jamie led him to this moment. A moment he was made for, the purpose given to him to rescue the world. He would defend the meek and inherit the earth, serve God and find the devil. For if the powers-that-be were hiding in plain sight, then he would find him.

The authorities made him stand. With ten people surrounding him, with cameras capturing footage for newsfeeds and YouTube uploads, he was marched out of the park.

THE CELL WAS WHITE.

A solid bench jutted from the wall to Marcus's left, smudge marks on the white paint from a previous detainee's soled shoes or something hard and rubber. Mother sat crossed-legged and barefoot, nails still cheery red. The sun hat was gone.

Marcus stood in front of a wire-embedded window, the biomite freeze locking his muscles into rigid beams, a full electric wrap, an invisible suit of ants continuously stinging his flesh; unseen welts swelled and itched. His lungs sipped oxygen at a predetermined pace of expanding and contracting.

Like breathing through a bendy straw.

Fulton Country law enforcers, mostly uniformed, milled about the office, occasionally looking into the cell. Above their heads, a television played silent images of a newsfeed, choppy footage of Centennial Park interspersed with clips of his previous life as a federal agent.

A LONG-LOST BRICK SURFACES?

A door opened somewhere to the right. A booming voice, the kind that projected effortlessly, that didn't need a mic in a large room, called out. Donald Gainey, director of Fulton County biomite authorities, stood outside the window.

Robust and round, his stomach hid his belt buckle. The jacket a size too small. His squinty brown eyes (the kind that suspected every living organism of mischief) focused on Marcus.

"Is he clamped?" Don asked.

"Yeah," the sheriff, a slimmer version of the ruddy-cheeked director, said. "Has been since the park."

"Then why is he cuffed?"

"Feds requested it."

"Overkill, don't you think, Larry?"

"It's what they wanted. Said they'd be here in a couple hours and not to take chances."

"He ain't breaking the biomite clamp." Don rattled the door handle. "Even if he could, he's not opening the door."

"It's what they wanted, Don."

A guttural acknowledgement rattled, a sound a rhino might make before it charged. Don pulled a pair of reading glasses from his coat and snapped a folder taut without breaking eye contact with Marcus. Once the glasses were balanced on the knobby end of his nose, he looked down.

Mother got up, her bare feet padding carefully on the hard floor, and passed through the wall. She paced around the authorities. "They're afraid of you, Marcus."

Of course they are.

The folder was thick. The details sorted. If Marcus could read clay, he would know Don's thoughts. But the facial expressions were easy enough to translate. He was thinking the plastic cuffs biting

Marcus's wrists weren't such a bad idea anymore. A sour expression hit Don, a sudden waft of dog shit or a rancid thought.

"So he just appeared out of nowhere?"

"That's what they said. His identity popped up in Centennial Park."

"Out of the blue."

"Just like that."

"Sure that's him?" Don ditched the glasses.

"Identity confirmed, Don."

"And now the whole goddamn world knows," he muttered.

Mother stepped back inside the cell. In times like this, she did the sort of things that appeared normal. Sometimes she'd file her nails or read a book—anything to make her seem human. It made Marcus feel normal, like he belonged to the world. This time, she sat quietly.

"Scrape him," Don said.

"Feds said hold him," the sheriff said.

"I don't give a goddamn. This is a clay state and we've been granted authority to protect our rights by the federal government. This man brought active biomites into the middle of our state and we are entitled to process him."

"He's not halfskin."

"He ain't clay, either."

"Law doesn't apply to bricks, Don. That's strictly federal."

"This man was once on the most wanted list, declared deceased by the federal government, and he suddenly appears outside the Atlanta biomite process office eating boiled peanuts? You think that's an accident, Larry?"

The sheriff tipped his head.

Don turned his round body at Larry, his voice dialed down. "I only need one hour. I'll get him over to processing and back before the feds get here. I want to know this man's thoughts, want to know what's in his head. That information could mean a lot to the state of Georgia, you understand? It means protecting our way of life. The federal government doesn't give two shits about us."

"They'll know you scraped him."

"I'll take the heat. I want you on my side. Georgia's side."

The sheriff sighed, scratching the thick mustache beneath his nose. Then he called for help. Don patted him on the shoulder and marched out of the station.

"I didn't expect this," Mother said.

No, Marcus thought. If he could, he would smile.

A wheelchair was brought to the door. Two biomite authorities stood next to it with their tablets—one was Marcus's primary hijacker, the other was the backup. His body was forced to turn around. The forced actions were dull needles in bone and flesh. Each movement agony, a coffin lid slammed over and over.

The wheelchair behind him, he was directed to sit and strapped into it. They rolled him past staring officers to a service elevator and exited a back door where a white van was waiting to transport him to the fifth floor of a reflective building near Olympic Park.

"Hey!" a kid screamed in the alley. "Marcus Anderson, over here!"

He held a phone up, recording the agents loading Marcus in a cargo van. In minutes, he would post it for a million hits.

THE ROOM SMELLED of metal and sharp things. Everything was new, from the tables to the chairs to the neatly stacked equipment quietly breathing exhaust.

Marcus was parked to the side of a silver table with edges lipped and wheels on folding legs—an autopsy table used to mount halfskins. No flesh was peeled back in this room, though. No blood spilled or organs removed. Just memories pulled like teeth, the roots extracted from the gums, the unfamiliar pain deep and frightening. This was the final destination of hapless halfskins that wandered into the clay state for black market business or the sheer stupidity of adventure.

The biomite authorities would legally extract their mind and process their memories along with samples of their biomite strains, upload it into a database for analysis, claiming it helped them stay atop their rigorous scanning abilities.

When Mother was functional, when she was nothing more than the arena-sized dome residing in Montana monitoring the human population for biomites, she did the same thing. And Marcus was her henchman. He ordered biomites to be sent back to the dome for full immersion analysis. Halfskins would be dropped into a clear vat and digested, every cell slowly absorbed into her database.

She took their lives, their souls, Marcus had thought. *For the good of the human race.*

"That's not what I was doing," Mother later told him.

"What, then?"

"Taking their essence."

Essence. She didn't say soul, didn't say memories. Essence was something new. And when he asked, "Why were you taking their essence?"

"It's who I was."

He'd become accustomed to the childish manner in which she gave up information, like a computer that only provided answers when asked the correct questions.

"And who were you?" he would ask.

She wouldn't respond to the question.

"Get him on the table," a young female said.

"We can do it in the chair," a middle-aged man said. "We got to work fast."

There were half a dozen processing employees in the room, each at their stations. Marcus felt an animated buzz creep into the marrow of his bones as one of the scanning generators came to life. He didn't resist and kept his mind completely open, waiting for the bridge to drop so he could peek inside the processing machine that would connect him to the network that identified bricks, the network that gave up Margaret, the network that went back to the powers-that-be.

Where Jamie had gone.

She had been in that room, had been subjected to the same body freeze. Was she afraid? Did they see her memories? Did they know about the powers-that-be? He wanted the answers to all of those questions, but more than any of that he wanted to know... *where did she go?*

The feds would never allow these amateur clay hacks to scrape Marcus Anderson, never give his mind access to the network. Mother said this would bring them closer to their destiny. He didn't care for the word destiny, but she was right.

"I don't like this." It was the youngest of the crew, a man that looked barely out of high school. "I mean, why is the media everywhere, right? There's a leak or something. It's like someone knows we were going to do this. Like..."

"Like what?" the woman said.

He shook his head. His instincts were right, but he was too young to assert them.

"Smart, that one," Mother said.

"Let's go!" Don stepped into the lab and walloped big pockets of air between his meaty hands. "Do a quick scrape, send it out to all the clay facilities immediately. I want everyone to have a copy of this brick's psychological profile, where he's been the last five years, what he's doing here. Draw a sample of his blood and do the same. We're short on time, people."

The team came at Marcus with a multitude of straps and gadgets. One wrapped around his arm, another pasted to his temples. The young woman opened a set of stainless steel tools all pointed and gleaming in the room's bright lights.

Someone shouted, "Testing!"

Another hum filled the room, this one synchronizing with the previous one. Marcus's teeth sang. A tiny smile grew beneath his skin. No one would see it, but perhaps they'd read it on their monitors.

A third machine hummed.

The room dimmed. Marcus realized the lights hadn't changed, it was his vision. The circuits were drawing him out of his body. A glittering ball of energy appeared near the ceiling.

No. Not moving. I'm not in my body.

He had assumed some other form, an astral projection that was weightless and effortless. The light was growing and no one seemed to notice, no one seemed to see it. The drawbridge to another place was lowering, a direct route to the source, to the powers-that-be.

Several ringtones rang at once.

A long pause as they all checked their phones. The youngest said, "Hello?"

The other phones suddenly stopped.

"It's, uh, for you, sir."

"Put that thing away, son," Don replied. "Why do you have your phone on anyway?"

"It... it wasn't."

Another long pause. "Who is it?"

"He says he, uh, wants to speak with the head fucking idiot."

An awkward moment was flung around the room like a shit storm. Every one caught a piece. Don's footsteps were heavy and hard. He answered, got one word out. And then silence.

They waited.

Don threw the phone at the young man. "Get him out of here."

Someone knew Marcus was there. Maybe they knew why. *Someone on the other side of the drawbridge.*

"And someone find out how the fuck they got all your phone numbers!" Don stormed out of the lab.

The machines died. The gear came off. They wheeled him out. Don clearly didn't know who he was dealing with on the other end. Or what.

No one did.

A FREIGHT TRAIN slid down a pair of iron rails, crashing into Marcus's head.

He opened his eyes.

The ceiling was beige; the toilet was metal.

The walls were imbedded with mesh wire that hummed interference, a Faraday cage that nullified biomite activity.

"It's eleven a.m."

Mother stepped away from his bed, a mattress as thin as newspaper. Expressionless and calm, she watched him from across the room, her bare feet pressed against the concrete.

"You've been isolated for two days."

He listened without looking. His actions would be monitored, even eye movements. They'd be looking for something unusual such as talking to himself or interacting with the projection of a nonexistent artificially intelligent old woman.

"Don was ordered to put you under until the federal agents arrived," she said. "You were transferred to the Pentagon. They've taken blood samples, scanned your brain activity, and analyzed your biomite coding."

He avoided even forming a thought.

"They didn't find anything unusual. Nothing to explain how you've avoided them all this time. And no, they don't sense my presence."

The freight train rolled and crashed again. This time it was followed by footsteps; a lighter set of footfalls were bracketed by stern, heavy ones. They stopped outside the door. An alarm buzzed. A heavy lock tumbled and the door slid open.

A woman stood outside the cell, her hair pulled back, eyes large between thick black eyelashes. Her lips plump, a slight curl at the corner.

"Marcus Anderson," she said.

"Lydia."

"You were expecting me?"

"I'm always expecting you. Still with the agency, I see."

She observed him like an experiment. Despite the open door, he posed no threat inside the cell. It was the sort of safety one felt at a zoo, a gulf that separated the lions from the observation deck.

"How are you feeling?" she asked.

"A little sore." He stretched. "Your kids are grown up now, I suppose?"

"Now I know you're a clone. The Marcus Anderson I knew didn't give a shit about family."

"I've changed."

"Tell me we don't need these." A pair of cuffs dangled from her fingers.

It was a courtesy question. The woman to Lydia's left, a deceptively petite African American with short curls and dark brown eyes, was the biomite agent—a highly trained operative composed of 99.9% biomites capable of mind manipulation and incapacitation. The heat from her mind spattered over his skin like oil jumping off an iron griddle.

To Lydia's right was a slender man with strong hands and a smooth face. His brown hair was short and flat. His eyes, unreadable. His entire clay being was inaccessible. If the biomite agent somehow failed to control Marcus, the clay agent would use physical force. He would be immune to mind games.

Marcus stood. The biomite agent clamped her mind around him with a million needle-teeth.

"Back your dog off," he hissed.

"There we go," Lydia said. "The Marcus Anderson I know."

Another pair of agents—one biomite, one clay—waited further down the hall. They led the way, bracketing him two and two with Lydia out front. Somewhere behind him, Mother's damp footsteps followed.

He was led to a small room with a table and four chairs. A bottle of water sat in front of one of them. Two guards stationed themselves in the corners. Lydia closed the door. Mother appeared to sit in one of the chairs already pulled away from the table.

Half an hour later, the door swung open.

Jason Powell stood in the doorway, a red tie hung loosely around an open collar, a bundle of manila folders in his hand. His hair was a bit shaggier, a little sandier than the last time he saw him. He remained flat-footed, examining a miracle.

Powell closed the door. "According to the root analysis, you are *the* Marcus Anderson, the previous director of biomite oversight."

The stack of folders hit the table.

"Of course, there could be multiple clones of you all over the world."

"You know the truth."

"But do you?"

Mother got up and Powell dragged the empty chair from the table to sit. He spread the folders out and opened one.

"Five years ago," he mused, "the biomite surveillance system known as Mother collapsed. You were acting director at that time, living within the confines of the Montana dome. Records show you, toward the end of your assignment, wandering aimlessly in a paranoid and delusional state, claiming an *inner world* was somewhere within the industrial complex. And the system was not merely a program but a sentient, self-aware intelligence that you referred to as Mother. You remember that?"

Marcus looked at his hands folded upon the table. Mother chuckled from the corner.

"During the postmortem of said events, you made claims of conspiracy theories, of so-called 'powers-that-be' and, I quote, 'the human race has been duped into sleeping... Mother saw the truth of her own existence and the path of humanity and, accordingly, had issued her own self-destruction... we are all being farmed for a greater unknown purpose.' End quote."

Powell ran his finger along the highlighted lines.

"You remember that?"

"And then dream disease started," Marcus said, smirking.

"You never said dream disease."

Marcus sat back in the hard chair. Of course he remembered. They apprehended him after Mother collapsed, accused him of destroying her. He'd been kept in isolation for months, sleep deprived and harassed until his sanity teetered. He spoke to the walls, his logjammed thoughts plowing through streams of nonsense. There was so much to say, so much truth to impart.

There were episodes of him sobbing for days, begging for the end to come to the one realization that shouted louder than all the other thoughts.

I AM A BRICK!

"If you were an animal," Powell said, "we would've put you down. You were a psychological mess, a brick that thought it was human. But you were our only link to Mother's mysterious collapse, a rambling idiot having conversations with ghosts."

The days of madness were eternal until Marcus woke in a drug-fueled haze and there she was, standing in the middle of the room, wearing a flowing dress, short gray hair and a cherub grin. He blabbered through tears because his delusions were becoming too real. He tried to hurt her, swung on her, and put his hands around her neck. In the end, she held him and comforted him, warmly and gently.

"The gift," she whispered. "You are the gift."

"And then you were gone." Powell snapped his fingers. "You were sleeping in the cell and suddenly gone. Surrounded by buildings and walls and fences, you disappeared. Security footage showed you blipping out of existence like an apparition. Did you walk out? Was it an inside job? What was it, Marcus? What happened?"

Marcus offered a kind smile. A magician never betrayed his secrets.

Marcus was hunched at the shoulders. Although he didn't wear glasses, his left eye was still slightly misshapen and his bald pate sunspotted with age. The grimly bitter old man, however, was no longer there.

"Do you still talk to yourself? Still see Mother?" Powell's fingers danced an erratic rhythm on the table. "Does she answer back?"

Marcus slid the folder back. "I have rights."

"What do you want? Let's start there. You reappear after five years of being completely off the grid, which, I'm assuming, you did by choice in a very public setting. You wanted everyone to see you because we assured the public that every brick had been identified and relocated. You did this because... why, Marcus? To make fools out of us?"

"I have rights provided to fabricated humans under the sentience laws—"

"Not until I get answers!" Powell slammed the folder with a dull-thumping fist. "You are still a brick, you understand that? Your rights don't mean shit when it comes to threatening the security of the United States, so find a dark corner in your fucked-up brain to file that fact because I'm not playing."

"A law firm will be contacting you—"

"How did you leave? Where have you been, Marcus? And why did you come back?"

"I've prepared a statement that my legal representatives will deliver."

Powell nodded incredulously, leaned back and sniffed. "Make all the statements you want. We're going to pull you apart, Marcus. Whatever you pulled last time will not happen again, I promise you. You're going in a cage and you're going to stay there a very long time. We're going to find out what you're made of."

"My lawyers will be holding a public conference soon. After which they will file for my legal rights to exist as a fabricated human and you will treat me as such. That is my legal right."

"This is the federal government." His fingers pattered another nervous rhythm. "You think the world cares about bricks, Marcus? They're the new race we can blame all our troubles on and not feel guilty. You are the new-age scapegoat. That's why you and the rest of those plastic fabbed fakies are alive, why they're on display in the middle of nowhere, without their dreamlands, without their freedom.

The world needs a scapegoat, Marcus. And the world doesn't give a goddamn what we do to you.

"Your lawyers can hold press conferences on the White House lawn for all I care. Whatever you planned on happening after you surrendered, it's over. You're not leaving. You live here now."

"He's quite convincing," Mother said.

Marcus considered the bottle of water. The ring broke beneath the lid as he twisted it. He took a swallow and slowly replaced the cap. After a long pause, he leaned in and said, without menace, "The world is watching."

In today's day and age, public opinion could move buildings. His legal team, vetted and retained well ahead of this day, would continue breathing on that fire. They would sway public opinion.

"What do you want?" Powell asked.

"Process me like a brick."

"The Settlement, is that it? You want to go there? What's out there?"

"I'm tired of running," Marcus lied. "I'm an old man. The Settlement is more appealing than my other options."

"Okay." The charade was obvious. "I'm not the enemy, Marcus. There will be nowhere to hide when we pull you apart, you understand that."

"I have nothing to hide."

"We don't need to find a reason to shut you down. You've proven you're a threat. No one will argue that. We'll put you to sleep tonight."

"The world is watching."

"I see."

He rapped the table and considered the folders before scooping them up. No sense in going through the rest of them. The interview was over. Marcus had planned years in advance of this moment. Powell was out of his league. And he knew it.

He stopped at the door. For a moment, he seemed to look directly at Mother. It was enough to cause Marcus to flinch, regardless of the impossibility.

"What happened to you," Powell finally said, glancing at the floor, "you deserved that, you understand. Don't blame the world for it."

Marcus suppressed a smile.

The transition from clay to brick was horrendous. To look with doubt upon one's existence was to dance with psychosis. Powell watched him unravel and had assumed Marcus chose to fabricate himself. What Powell didn't know was that Marcus survived to discover the unfettered freedom.

The gift.

"I still like him," Mother said.

After a week in the cell, Lydia and the guards escorted him to a cage. He didn't speak to his attorneys, didn't hear anything beyond the walls of his cell. He was simply marched to a very special cage.

It was underground. The public didn't know about it. Very few did.

The room was smaller than the cell. There was a chair with leather straps on wide armrests and stirrups. Another one unbuckled at the headrest. It was an armpit that smelled of fried circuits and saliva, easily mistaken for death row.

The escorts cattle-prodded him into the chair, locking him down until his arms and legs were secured, his head tied into a saddle. A rubber bite guard was shoved deep into his mouth, tasting of chlorine.

Mother watched from the corner.

The automated rhythm took control of his breathing once again. His eyes, suddenly as dry as his mouth, began blinking on a slow, deliberate schedule.

I am the one to lead, he told himself. *The one to dream.*

Marcus assumed the prophecy suggested he would need Jamie,

Paul and Raine to fulfill his journey, but he believed that he was more than the sum of the parts, that he could lead, he could see. Perhaps he would lead and dream.

Giving himself to the network, to have his mind pulled apart and put back together would give him insight, Mother had told him. He believed her. She had yet to be wrong, this he knew. Begrudgingly.

And I will bleed.

"I'll see you when this is over," Mother said.

He wanted to nod, to recognize her. He would've answered her if he could. She was inside him, knew what he felt, sensed that he was experiencing something he hadn't felt in quite some time.

Fear.

The agents walked out and locked the door.

Mother walked behind him, putting her warm hands on his shoulders. A mix of earth and sea and floral essence overcame the room's terror. Then her touch was gone.

I am the son to be.

And the long walk across the desert had begun.

II_

One to dream.

CHAPTER SEVEN_

The roar of a crane's diesel engine rattled the brick house.

Paul grabbed a metal casing before it vibrated off the desk. In front of him was a clear-case box, something the size of a mini-refrigerator, that continued to whir. Inside, tubing swirled around an object like a mass of pencil-thin snakes slowly printing a three-dimensional object.

The proposal to convert the brick house into a research facility had been approved the past fall. Paul remembered the news quite well—it arrived not long after Jamie was buried.

The People loved the idea. The proposal was about innovations that would benefit the People, not so much about the bricks' well-being. They didn't give a shit about that. Healthy bricks got them nothing.

So walls were knocked down and additional weight-bearing beams erected to open the floor plan. They were up and running by summer, the first patent on tool fabrication delivered a year after Jamie was buried.

The People were thrilled. And wanted more.

Bob's booming laughter was somewhere beneath the crane's now-idling engine. Paul tapped at the buttons on the miniature clear-case fabricator, its use approved for prototypes and small components.

Not what Paul was fabricating.

On the bench, the metal casing of a faux turbine capacitor lay open like an elaborate clamshell, waiting for the fabricator to finish. When the misting snakes snapped into silent sleep, he reached inside, the object still warm and rubbery, the texture of liver, and sealed it in plastic shrink before dropping it inside the hollow of the faux turbine capacitor. Snapping it together, the object held snugly in the embedded foam, he shoved it to the bottom of a leather bag.

The fabricator's lines were flushing when the front door opened. A flood of construction sounds—hammers on metal, grinding generators—filled the house. Paul wiped down the nozzles, his heartbeat tapping double-time.

"What're you doing in here?" Bob wheezed. "Lab's closed."

"Cleaning up."

"Well, finish up already. I'm locking the door."

Paul put the computers to sleep, but not before ensuring the matrix he had uploaded was completely erased. It took him months to install the incognito mode around the lab's surveillance. The People didn't want a single fabrication slipping through their greedy fingers.

Bob opened the leather bag. "What's this?"

"Careful. Just came out of the fabricator."

"What is it?"

"Need it for my wind turbine. Experimenting with a new design."

"You get it approved?"

"Couldn't fabricate it if I didn't."

Bob stared at the seam. If he knew anything about mechanics, he'd see the release mechanism that would pop it open and dump the warm object on his lap. The lab would be closed forever.

Bob dropped it in the bag.

"Careful! Break it and I'll report you."

"Get out of here."

It was a bluff. Paul wouldn't report anything, but it kept Bob's asshole-mode in check. Too many complaints and he'd be investigated. Bob wouldn't survive close scrutiny from the People. In a way, Bob was good for Paul. He wasn't smart and had enough lurking skeletons he would bend to a bluff.

Outside, the girded structure of a new research and fabrication lab was three stories tall. The crane dangled an I-beam above the top floor, the earth shuddering.

The People want more.

In the year since the brick house had been converted, sustainable energy production had been improved by fifty percent. Given the right facilities, solutions to the world's energy crises could be fast-tracked. And the People would rake the profits.

The bricks weren't complaining.

Forget Bob and his loyalty to the People. Boredom was the real enemy. Conspiracy theories aside, the Settlement was just a brilliant scheme to bring the bricks together, to take away their freedom, suppress their creativity, torture them with boredom until they worked for free. *Happily.*

Conspiracy or not, it worked.

The bricks wanted something–*anything*—to feel useful, to feel human. To matter. Even if that meant lining the fat pricks' pockets and giving away their ideas for free. Paul was on board throughout the process, even led a coalition to get it approved.

But he had his own reasons.

"Get in." Bob stomped down the front steps toward the truck.

"I'll walk."

"No, you'll ride. I ain't got time to follow you through the woods."

The leather bag kept Paul from telling Bob to go fuck himself. There were no Settlement laws that prevented him from suggesting what to do with his dick. But ever since Paul started smuggling contraband out of the brick house, he'd become a model citizen.

A good brick.

The truck smelled like a sweat stain. The floorboards were

littered with paper cups, the dashboard buried beneath wads of paper and napkins. Bob pushed himself behind the steering wheel, the bench seat sinking. He dropped it in drive and the electric motor whirred.

He drew on the end of a metal pipe, half-ass aiming the blue cloud at the window crack. The icy menthol made the stuffy cab smell better.

Satellite radio rambled as they crossed an experimental field of wind turbines. Bob turned it up.

"It's like prison," a caller said. "I mean, look what happens when you commit a crime in America. You go to jail and get three hots and a cot, right? A free education all because you killed someone."

"Caller," the host answered, "you're out of your mind. Yeah, you get fed and educated while living in a ten-by-ten room and raped on Sundays. That's a hell of a deal."

"You know what I'm saying. Those bricks get moved out to the country and you and me pay for their homes, pay for their food and now we're paying for those buildings. You see those things? I bet universities don't have facilities like that."

"What's your name? Tim?"

"Yeah."

"Tim, the bricks are making strides in energy production like we've never seen. You like it when you flip the switch and the lights come on?"

"Don't give me that. We were doing just fine before bricks came along."

"Oh, yeah. We were doing great, Tim. Addicted to oil, polluting oceans. We had it all figured out."

"Yeah, and we were dying in dreamland."

"The fabs have nothing to do with dream disease."

"*Fabs*. Yeah, whatever."

"They're fabricated humans, Tim."

"All I know is that dreamland changed when *bricks* got legal," the caller said. "Used to be I could go down the street and pass twenty dream cafes. Now you got to have a million bucks if you don't want dream disease."

"You don't see the connection between dream disease and big money?"

"Oh, don't start that. No one ever heard of dream disease before the sentience laws made bricks legal and now it's too late."

"You're smart, Tim. Where you from?"

"I read the feeds, that's all."

"Uh-huh. I see. So you want the fabs to what? You want them dead?"

"Off. Not dead, off. You can't be dead if you ain't alive."

Clouds puffed through Bob's laughter like a steam-powered choo-choo. This kind of talk powered his boner faster than three-way porn.

"You want them dead so you can have more dream cafes, is that it, Tim?" the host asked. "That's your gripe?"

"Don't twist my words, you bricklover. The sentience laws need to be overturned, the clay states need to be abolished, and dreamland deserves to be returned to the People."

"The People?" The host yuck-yucked. "You aren't part of the People, Tim. You're just a sad little man. The People, the real People, are the ones that pull the strings, you dope. They're the ones that make the laws, the ones that turn a profit."

"So you're buying the powers-that-be theory?" Tim asked.

The host hung up and ranted without interruption. "This conspiracy isn't about whether we landed on the moon or whether aliens plow symbols in wheat fields, Tim. We're way past all that. There is a thin slice of people that control the world—they control the oil, the money and the People. Don't kid yourself, you moron. Do I believe there's one person at the top making us dance? You're damn right I do."

Paul doubted the host was really a brick sympathist. Just a ratings whore.

"And another thing." The host was shouting now. "That Marcus Anderson thing? The lost brick the government promised didn't exist anymore, the one that orchestrated the collapse, the prick responsible for the death of tens of thousands of halfskins before the sentience laws were created? They didn't shut him off, Tim. You need to update your feeds."

A brushfire rushed through Paul's chest, burning behind his eyes, all papery and brittle and hot. *Marcus Anderson.* The one responsible for the death of so many good people, honest people that needed biomites to survive a nasty stroke of God's whimsy—car accidents, genetic diseases, dumb luck. Biomites were modern medicine, the only hope for a child, a loved one. And Marcus Anderson didn't want you to have too many because... just because. Now that piece of shit was a brick.

The universe is just.

That bastard's relentless pursuit drove Cali mad; his vengeful will to bring capricious justice to his insane little world chipped away at her will to live. Dr. Cali Richards, the biometric engineer that created a whole new strain of biomites that couldn't be monitored by the government, the first person to ever escape the all-watching eye of Marcus Anderson and his biomite henchmen.

Marcus Anderson, the story went, didn't know he was a brick at first. The word from the government was that he had been fabricated without his knowledge, that he refused to believe the tests and went mad.

They said he died, too.

Paul knew what that moment of realizing you're a brick was like. Cali had delivered that very same news to Paul on the farm, showing him his true nature. He knew what it felt like when the realization was revealed in stark lighting, the rug yanked from the table to show the rabbit of truth. Marcus denied it at first just like Paul because he didn't feel any different. He had the same thoughts, same emotions. His body exactly the same.

But deep down, hidden in dark spaces that no one could see, the truth lurked like a coiled serpent. Marcus, like Paul, didn't want to see a truth that would change him forever.

I am a brick, Marcus Anderson thought eventually. If he didn't, insanity would've claimed him. He would be dead. So would Paul.

But Cali wasn't a brick.

She still carried the thin sliver of clay like a burden of the entire human race. In the end, Paul had lain down with her beneath a broken swing set and stared into a steel slate of sky. They held hands as she executed a self-termination command that would shut down their biomites.

But Paul woke up.

I couldn't do it to you, Paul, the note said.

She'd become so vulnerable, a delicate rose blossom still fragrant but bruised as the petals had fallen. She just couldn't hold any more of the world's pain and suffering. Enough had already been yoked across her shoulders. She was so tired. That was why Marcus Anderson held a special place in Paul's heart.

"They think you live in paradise," Bob said above the radio banter.

Paul looked out the window and stoked the blue flames of anger. There was plenty to burn.

THEY EMERGED from the trees and passed new cabins on the right. Down the slope another half mile, Bob stopped at a cabin tucked under a leaning spruce, a wisp of smoke chugging from the chimney.

The windows were lit up.

Bob opened his door.

"What are you doing?" Paul said.

"Going to say hello to your little lady."

"She's not in the mood, Bob."

Raine had moved in with Paul, unable to be alone for long periods. Her belongings were still back at her cabin, which she would go back for on a daily basis. It occupied her mind, burning the abundance of empty time.

She appeared at the door, a fuzzy image through the dark screening. She wasn't even a hundred pounds—hollows were sucked beneath her cheekbones, eyes dark and obscured in shallow caves. Firelight reflected off her bald scalp. She shaved it every morning before she trekked back to her cabin.

Ever since Jamie was buried.

"You need to get some exercise, little lady." Bob was out of the truck.

"What do you want?" she replied.

"Your husband here needed a ride."

She crossed her arms, pointy elbows cupped in each palm, tired of explaining Paul wasn't her husband. Bob knew that. He knew her husband, the only love of her life, was in dreamland. Nix was waiting for her. Bob wanted her to remind him that Nix was out of reach, Nix was trapped in her dreamland only so he could reply *Dreamland ain't real, little lady.*

Just another twist.

"Thanks," was all she said. "I was worried."

Bob clobbered the wooden steps with steel-toes and peered over her shoulder. The disappointment sagged on his shoulders. The fight had gone out of her, the piss and vinegar drained from a long seething wound. Bob took her complacence as a challenge to light that flame again.

Give him a fight.

Bob couldn't search the place, not without probable cause. In the early days, he could do whatever he wanted—turn the place over and eat their food. But the bricks appealed to a higher court, establishing their rights. They couldn't escape the Settlement, but they could call it a home—a home with law and order.

Bob snatched the leather bag.

"You already searched it."

"Maybe I missed something."

Raine closed the door. A wretched smile dimpled Bob's doughy cheeks. He drew on the metal pipe, thick vapor streaming from his nostrils, dragon-like.

Paul avoided fidgeting. Instead, he feigned impatience, leaning against the post while Bob shoved his porky fingers along the bag's seams in search of trapdoor pockets or some other nonsense. He shook the turbine capacitor.

"Damn it, Bob. You damage that and I'll report it as unnecessary search and seizure."

"What's inside?"

"Components, what do you think? It's only thirty minutes out of the fabricator and you're shaking it like a baby." Paul stretched the bag open. "You finished?"

"I'm finished when I'm finished." He turned it over, tracing the surface with dirty fingernails. "What's your hurry?"

"It's late, I'm hungry. Don't want to be on the porch with you."

This only slowed the search. Sweat prickles flashed under Paul's sweatshirt. A thousand thoughts went through his mind.

"You think you're smart?" Bob asked.

"I'm hungry, Bob."

"You stay in the lab like that again, I'll have you banned."

"Fine."

"I'm going back there to check your work, so you know."

"Big surprise. You done?" Paul had settled into an expression of boredom brushed with frustration. Any sign of panic and Bob would take the component. He took another drag on the pipe and threw the piece into the bag, leaving a minty trail of vapor to the truck. Paul watched the taillights disappear down the dirt road before going inside.

His knees were cold.

"He's gone?" Raine stood in the bedroom.

Paul nodded.

"You got it?"

He dug the clunky piece out, palms damp with sweat. Raine

covered her mouth and stepped back. That dangerous temptress of hope danced before her eyes.

Paul went to the kitchen and turned off the light, then went to the bathroom and cleaned up and changed clothes. Raine was sitting on the bed when he was finished, the crucifix of sticks between her hands. Paul lay on the couch, Raine on the bed.

It was sometime in the small hours of the night that he got up. His leather bag was still in the front room. He took it to the kitchen but didn't turn on the light. In the dark, he knelt in front of the oven.

Raine's bare feet were soft and sticky on the linoleum.

He lifted the front of the oven, still hot with the smell of broiled chicken, and Raine slid a small oval rug beneath the peg legs. The only window was small, above the sink. From a distance, no one would see him slide the oven away from the wall (the rug slipping across the floor without leaving tracks) to expose a patch of linoleum littered with dusted crumbs. Beneath thick greasy layers were the seams of a trapdoor.

Paul stepped into the gap between the cabinets and inserted the flat end of a screwdriver along the baseboard, triggering a spring-loaded switch to drop the panel (a system that took the last six months to design and build using fabricated parts that could be found in a new solar panel design).

A draft gusted out of the dark hole, cold and mysterious.

In the winter, the outside temperatures would keep it cold. In the summer, should they still need it for storage, it would draw from the freezer (the insulated space would keep energy consumption negligible).

Raine handed him the capacitor.

Only the sound of their breath filled the room. They didn't dare communicate with words or thoughts, careful to protect what they were seeing and thinking as he placed it next to the trapdoor. There would be no reason for the monitors to watch them through the emergency security cameras, not at this hour.

Raine leaned in, watching him play the faux capacitor like an instrument, his fingertips touching several places in a coded sequence and specific cadence.

It popped opened.

The spongy foam pushed the red, plastic-wrapped object on a delicate display. Even in the dark, it glistened beneath the plastic wrap, veins and arteries crossing the surface like a road map. As if freshly plucked from an open chest, it did not beat, lying in animated suspension, awaiting the spark of life.

Jamie's heart.

The Settlement would never be allowed a printer large enough to fabricate an entire body. And even if there was, Paul could never hope to have enough time and raw biomite material to produce it. But he could do it a piece at a time. And in Frankensteinian fashion, assemble her when the time had come.

He had spun the sample he scratched from her arm to replicate her DNA. The People had approved the bricks to establish a library of their own genetics should they ever need to fabricate organs for themselves. In that massive database, he hid Jamie's genome and mapped her entire organism.

Then he built the storage space.

He placed her heart into the dark cavern, the tissue soft and pliable. Raine wept as he slid the oven back into place. There was no dreamland, but one day there would be Jamie. Angels, she was beginning to believe, would never come to the Settlement.

Hope danced seductively around the table.

CHAPTER EIGHT_

Threads.

Marcus stared at threads.

Threads crisscrossing in minute checkerboards, a predictable pattern in an endless array of subtle colors.

Threads.

It was the first coherent thought of self-awareness, a bubble in a soupy consciousness that was aware that it was aware.

Here. I am here. I am this.

The universe dipped and swayed in stomach-dropping swirls like the first moments on a descending elevator, or the rising slope of a roller coaster.

His head bounced. He was sitting in a chair, cushioned armrests, a silver buckle clasped over the waist of his bright orange jumper. As the universe of threads expanded, he recognized the crisscrossing pattern on the back of a headrest and the inordinately small oval windows. Marcus swam through the muddy confusion to find a word.

Plane.

A bag of vomit sloshed between his legs, still warm. Bitter slime coated his tongue. He continued counting threads, feeling his fingers and toes, returning to sense his head and chest after a long, long sleep.

Not sleep. Not sleep.

Sleep was silent, occasionally interrupted by episodes of dreams. The blank night that preceded his awakening with the thought of threads was an endless stream of images stretched across a distorted lens—fitful and disturbing. Silently screaming. His mind had been shredded, thoughts and memories tweezed apart, sifted for analysis, squeezed for secrets.

Atlanta.

That was where the horror show began.

Transferred to federal detention, locked in a cage for... *for how long?*

It was a small plane, luxurious. Three heads appeared above the seats ahead of him. He turned to see another two people behind him. One was a woman in her mid-thirties, auburn hair to her shoulders and delicate wrists, fumbling with a stack of magazines, notepads and folders. She walked clumsily to the seat across the aisle and dumped her cache in the empty seat next to her.

"Mr. Anderson, I'm Marianne Stanhope with the Associated Press. I'm sorry to rush you, but we'll be landing soon. They were expecting you to, um, wake a little sooner, so if you don't mind."

Wake. She stumbled over the word like waking belonged to her kind. Not bricks. Bricks didn't wake, they came online. They rebooted, turned on.

"Can you answer a few questions?"

He nodded once.

"Okay. For starters, what do you remember?"

His tongue crawled over his lips like a slug exploring new ground. He shook his head once. It was a stupid question.

"I realize things must be a little fuzzy. You've been held in isolation and subjected to deep-scan analysis for the past year." She reached across the aisle and pressed two fingers on the inside of his arm where purple and yellow bruises splashed his veins. "They kept you unconscious, fed you intravenously to download an entire catalog of your identity. Does that make sense?"

Of course. He was a national threat. An undiscovered brick that, by his own volition, surrendered. The days of hiding from the People were long gone. They would have to make sure it never happened again.

So why am I still alive?

"Why give yourself up, Mr. Anderson?"

He felt a smile tug at the corners of his mouth. She leaned forward, drawn in by the first sign of life.

Why did he do it? Why give himself up? He'd been invisible for years, so why arrange legal counsel to keep the whole charade in the public eye, subject himself to a year of psychological flogging?

Truth was, he didn't know. Not exactly.

Only one person knew the true answer. Marcus looked to his right, the seat empty. Mother wasn't with him.

"Did you want to be with your own kind?" Marianne asked. "Better to be in exile with your own kind than to be free and alone?"

"Lonely?" He slow-licked his dry lips. "You can say that, yes."

"How'd you do it? How did you remain so elusive all these years? The public wants to know, Mr. Anderson. The government just hands out bullshit reasons, claiming you're an anomaly that's been corrected. How'd you do it?"

She wouldn't expect him to answer that if he was lucid. Perhaps she was hoping that he would blurt out a secret like an inebriated loner spouting love to the first person that touches him.

How did he absorb thoughts? How did he control the motivations of others? How did he compel them to see what he wanted, to hear and see what he wished? How did he do almost anything he wanted? The clay humans, the ones without a single biomite, were the only beings outside his influence. The rest of the world was his to pick.

The question couldn't be answered, though. It was a gift bestowed upon him, but how could that be captured in words, let alone a sound bite? He could sync with her, press his mind against the fabric of her awareness and let her know the impression of his knowledge directly, know the secrets Mother had given to him years ago.

The secret to his powers was to become the universe. And that would make no sense to her.

A single slice of clay prevents her from seeing the universe, her imperfections clouding her cataract vision.

And bricks are the inferior species?

"What about these *powers-that-be*?" she asked.

He twitched. She saw it. It was more than a sign of life, it was a reaction. She'd touched a soft spot.

"You were muttering it over and over, warning about the *powers-that-be.* Someone on the inside leaked it to the press and it turned viral. You said there is someone controlling the world, one person. You identified this person as a male. It sounds very ominous. Could you expand on that? Who is the powers-that-be?"

He looked out the window. His powers had their limits. The universe didn't provide him with all the answers.

"Marcus." She spoke softly, like loud noises might scare the bunny. "Those were the ramblings of a madman. But you're not mad. You know something. You owe it to us to share. Are we doomed? Is there something we should be doing?"

Us, she said. *You owe it to us.*

He wasn't one of them, no. Not anymore. And maybe he did owe something to those that possessed clay, even a small slice. He'd shut enough of them off, and wrongly so. If there was a hell (he no longer subscribed to that theory), he'd spend twenty eternities paying for it.

So, yeah. He owed them.

The plane tipped to the left. Endless hills were covered in a patchwork of quilted trees and exposed boulders, frosted mountaintops in the distance.

"We'll be landing soon," someone announced.

"One more question." She sighed, contemplating which of a long list of queries was the most important.

She had very few answers and wasn't likely going to get more. She'd write about the experience, give her interpretation of his expression, his mood. If she was politically liberal (which she probably was), she'd cast him as a victim of government persecution. Conservative and he'd be drawn as a threat to the human race and was being shown more mercy than he deserved.

"How do we know you won't do it again?"

Marcus held her stabbing gaze. The answer she was looking for would be in a wry smile or a false denial or contrived confusion. Instead, he remained impassive to let her draw her own conclusions because the question itself was revealing.

We know you can do it again, Marcus. But will you?

The plane tipped again and circled toward a short landing strip carved out of the trees. Beyond it was a sprawling, one-story building.

They landed near two yellow posts.

A CLAY AGENT to his right, a biomite agent to his left.

They stepped into a lobby, the new-smell still lingering on the Berber carpet. It was sparsely filled with furniture and looked more like an art gallery with paintings filling the empty spaces (bricks displaying their creativity for the few guests that made it out this far). Landscapes, still lifes, and abstract creations blended in an inspired array of creativity.

Voices muttered on the other side of a thin paneled wall, laughter and deep-tone authority. The stream of conversations flowed in various tones.

A young man entered from the left, wearing a puffy green coat, a stack of clothing folded on his forklift arms.

"This way."

They went to a small room. He was given the clothes—khakis, flannel shirt, undershirt and low-cut boots—and changed while the agents watched. Marcus could feel their two minds but didn't think much of it. He was still waking up, fitting back into his body that was stiff and new, the seams still freshly sewn.

Not waking. Hibernating.

No waking like a long sleep, not a hibernation. More like the sleep of a caterpillar that wraps itself in a cocoon, emerging with wings.

A transformation.

The wings still soft and unfurling.

After another wait, the same green-coated young man escorted them back through the lobby, past a large room with projection screens and rows of padded chairs that seemed more fitting for a conference center than the entrance to long-term imprisonment. They waited outside a door where muffled voices continued.

"All right." The young man pulled the door open.

Inside was an oddly long room with three tables pushed end to end. Several people sat like apostles with office supplies and coffee mugs. And behind them stood more men and women clad in puffy green coats with badges sewn on their sleeves. Their expressions ranged from bored to smug. The obese one in the middle, the one with hands planted in his pockets, sat on the smug end of the spectrum.

Bob is his name. Bob is the leader.

Marcus didn't think much about that intuition, a name and a fact that dropped into his mind like a sponge drawing a bead of water.

Marcus was led front and center. The agents sat against the wall. There was no chair for him. He would stand.

Marcus had been on the other side of the table, once upon a time. He'd been part of committees that decided the fate of wrongdoers, parked behind cheap tables, asking questions and rendering a decision before ordering chicken wraps for lunch.

It was a time he ran the biomite oversight committee, was part and parcel of pushing laws that protected human rights. But when his fetishes were exposed (the late night orgies with fabricated sex dolls that morphed into subgenres of titillation that included strangulation and kill sex) he was seen as unfit for duty.

He'd been a prisoner all his life to those despot urges, those morally reprehensible addictions. Now he was free of them. He could choose how to feel, how to be.

Real prison is a state of mind, not a location.

"Marcus Anderson." A woman at the table, hair professionally short, eyes sharp blue, offered a gentle smile without the placating generosity reserved for frightened children. "The purpose of this meeting is to make clear the rules and reasons that you find yourself here. Let's call it an official introduction to your situation."

That was a new one. He wasn't fabbed, wasn't a brick or a fabricated human. *I'm a situation.*

"Your presence is unexpected, of course," she continued. "All fabricated humans were thought to be identified and accounted for and then you come along. While there is still some doubts about your assignment here, no evidence of wrongdoing or deceit has been found. Your unusual abilities have been stripped. Therefore, the People have ruled you have a right to existence under the statutes of the sentience laws. And here we are. Are we clear?"

She waited for acknowledgement. He nodded.

Notes were taken.

She continued to outline his rights and what to expect. Occasionally, one of the other apostles would take over. There would be long pauses where he was expected to acknowledge that he understood.

We are clear.

"Pete Haywood is the acting director of the Settlement," the woman said.

A squatty man of Middle Eastern descent nodded, his olive skin dark, eyebrows thick as fur. Lips pink. He was a resident of the Settlement, a full-fledged brick. His fabricators were software engineers that lived in the Seattle area that sought to replace all their employees with Haywood clones.

"Thank you, Mrs. Allston." Pete ran his hands over the desk. "I'd like to welcome you, Mr. Anderson. The Settlement, despite its appearance, has grown into something we've become proud of and we hope you'll join us in our continued productivity."

Pete continued spouting company-line bullshit about the advantages and how far they'd come, how they'd rebounded in this time of crises and the generosity of the People had given them opportunities to grow spiritually as well as academically and professionally.

It was the sort of horseshit abuse victims spout before returning to old relationships, the rationalizations they told themselves at night so it didn't hurt so much. So at least something made sense.

The People are good, they are just. We understand why they did this. And it could be worse.

Fear was why there was a Settlement. Fear was always at the root of suffering.

"Late summer, we will open a state-of-the art biomite research facility," Pete announced. "It will be equivalent to the best the world has to offer. Our advancements in biomite technology, as I'm sure you know, have taken the world to new heights."

Advancements they gave freely to the People. *It could be worse,* Pete would say.

If you give the monster enough cookies, he won't go away, Pete. He'll only want more.

Next up, the monitors were introduced. They were normal clays with normal lives that took these jobs to make a lot of money and build resumes for security jobs somewhere else. Marcus got a sense of their daily lives, their spouses and children, their struggles on the Settlement. Again, intuiting these facts did not surprise him, seeming as normal as reading a Post-it note.

"Thank you." Bob cleared his throat. "Just want to make clear that we are the Settlement's law enforcement, Anderson."

Agitation rumbled across the administration's expressions. They preferred *monitors* over *law enforcement.* This wasn't a prison.

At least Bob recognized the truth.

He explained the yellow posts. "The perimeter of the Settlement.

Cross them once and you're knocked out. Cross them twice and you're turned off. Understand?"

He explained the cabins and the limits of their rights to gather and communicate through thought-command. He explained the phones that each one of the monitors carried, displaying it like a science-fiction ray gun.

"We are clay," Bob said. "You cannot see inside us, cannot manipulate us. But we can manipulate you with this, understand. We will know where you are at all times. We can stop you. We can move you. And we can swipe you."

He was the playground bully that let it be known that the administration might be the teachers, but he was the head shit.

"Understand?" he boomed.

Marcus nodded.

"Then we'll get along just fine."

Some final business was discussed. Marcus was beginning to slump. His knee was aching, an injury he sustained many years ago. He thought it curious that he felt so... human again. Aches and pains were something he controlled at will, no more difficult than commanding his thoughts and emotions. No less difficult than raising his hand. But there he was crooked and aging like a prisoner of war.

"I don't want a circus." The woman aimed a pencil at him. "You're still somewhat of a mystery, Mr. Anderson. Despite all the public outcry for your fair and just treatment and your lawyers' antics to have you released onto the Settlement, you are not well-liked. You shut a lot of people off in your tenure, Mr. Anderson. Even relatives of the fabricated humans that you will be living with."

She held his gaze. He sensed that she was one of them, that as a little girl she'd seen family members taken during the era of halfskin laws and shut down for having too many biomites. Halfskin laws that Marcus enforced.

"Are we clear?" She closed a folder.

Marcus nodded.

He was escorted out of the back of the building. The circus inside had ended; a new one was about to begin. He waited on the back steps as one of the monitors went to fetch a cart. They would take him to his cabin, introduce him to the rest of his life.

Bob walked to a white truck, adjusting a straining belt, cramming a cowboy hat over his extra-large head. He wasn't worried about Marcus or concerned about the disruption.

He was thinking about lunch.

And then Marcus realized what was happening.

Someone stepped next to him, her loose clothing fluttering in the prairie wind, white hair pulled back. Mother watched Bob climb into his truck. Bob was thinking about lunch. She was nodding as she did so, acknowledging what Marcus realized.

I can read clay.

CHAPTER NINE_

A CANDLE FLAME DANCED IN THE DRAFT, WAX POOLING AROUND the blackened pigtail. Teacups half-full of Darjeeling tea were set around it. A Holy Bible, the cover bent at the corners and black as the burning wick, lay closed.

Maggie started to gather the teacups.

"No, no," Raine exclaimed. "I'll clean up. It's getting late and you all need to get going."

Maggie, a frumpy Midwesterner, hovered over the couch, knees bent, conflicted between helping and leaving. It was bad manners to abandon a mess after prayer group. She was a dreamlander of a lonely garage biometric engineer, an eccentric man that fabbed a body to download his dreamland lover into reality. Like Raine, she had adjusted to physical reality. Probably better than Raine.

Phillip, the short, unassuming clone of a Fortune 500 accounting firm, sat across from Raine, looking down his long nose at a notepad he diligently scribbled on with a short pencil. The next prayer group would be at his cabin and would be more accommodating with better food, better tea and coffee.

Because clones considered themselves closer to real humans than the plants and a hell of lot more legitimate than dreamlanders.

As far as Raine was concerned, they were all fucked.

"Closing prayer, everyone?" Phillip stated more than asked, extending his unusually long-fingered hands that reminded Raine of something more simian than human.

"Robbie?" Raine patted the young man's knee sitting next to her. "You want to lead prayer?"

Phillip cleared his throat. This was Raine's house, her meeting. She could choose.

"All right." Robbie nodded. He was of African descent, his dark skin smooth, his features slender and boyish despite his age. He was a plant that was fabricated by an elderly rich widow that wanted companionship in her final years, memories of servitude transplanted into his history.

The four members of the Settlement's weekly prayer group sat on the edge of the couch and formed a ring of clasped hands around the coffee table, their palms clammy and cold.

"Dear Lord." Robbie bowed his head. "Please bless this house and the beings within it as we seek to follow Your will. We give thanks to the life You give us and every breath You allow."

His grip tightened. Raine wanted to squeeze back, to say, *Yeah, me too, I believe that too.* But she was still praying for strength and wisdom to wake up in the morning. And an angel.

That was why she prayed.

"Please Lord, keep Raine's family safe and sound during this time of exile. We pray that one day she may return to see them and be with them and celebrate Your glory. We pray in Your name. Amen."

"Amen."

Raine walked them to the door, where hugs were exchanged. Maggie was like a big doughy mother; sinking into her embrace was like falling into a warm, breathing pillow with a big heart beneath the thin fabric.

"Bless you, darling," Maggie said.

Phillip wrapped his spidery arms around her, his frame rather hard, and gave one quick squeeze and a pat on the shoulder.

"Bless you," he announced.

Robbie held her the longest, swaying back and forth, stroking the back of her smooth head, whispering in her ear. "It'll be all right, one of these days."

The old woman that fabbed him did a very good job.

She watched them climb off the porch and stayed at the door until their truck entered the trees, deep tracks laid in the snow behind it. The limbs were heavy and wet. The sky was blue, but more snow was on the way, a dark smudge creeping over the mountains, the winter wind biting her cheeks.

A helicopter chopped the distant air.

Raine closed the door and turned up the music until she couldn't hear the approaching blades. She warmed her hands at the fireplace, humming along to the gospel tracks Robbie had put together just for her. The fire warmed her skin.

Audible pings echoed in her head, reminders that she should be at the gate in ten minutes. She turned off communications while cleaning up, then went to shower. She soaked in the hot water until the tank turned tepid. It was the only relief of her daily routine, the only time she felt clean—hot water stripping the film of her life away, that outer layer that clung like an odor, a slick layer of memories.

She wrapped up in a robe and stood in front of the fire, opening the terrycloth to expose herself to the flames. Her ribs pushed from the skin. She imagined Phillip could grasp them one at a time with his slender, chopsticky fingers.

It was twenty minutes past the hour.

Raine looked out the window. She was no longer in the cabin across from the brick house, having been relocated for the construction workers. Her new cabin wasn't far from Paul's, but she still didn't feel comfortable there.

Still, she wished she could be at the field to watch the brick house, to warn him if someone was coming.

She was supposed to be at the gate to officially welcome Marcus Anderson to the Settlement, despite the fact he had already been there for months. Things had to settle down. Pete didn't like all the controversy. Despite everything Marcus Anderson had done in his past life, Pete wanted to welcome him to the family.

Raine wouldn't do that.

Pete was a good man, a man of well wishes and good intention. Marcus Anderson was an old man now that lived on the Settlement. *We take care of our own. Let's put the past in the past,* he said. *He's one of us now.*

In a way, Marcus had helped her and Paul. The old man had been the perfect distraction. His welcome party was a rare opportunity for Paul to fabricate the lungs. *They have to be done as a pair,* he said. The largest of the organs, he didn't know how they were going to do it.

Months had gone by. Winter was almost over, when most everyone tended to stay inside. Soon the weather would break. But then the old man (a recluse since he arrived) requested that Pete arrange that welcome party. It was like her prayers had been answered.

Send me an angel.

She had prayed every morning, every night before bed, that there would be an opportunity to bring Jamie one step closer. She needed that victory. Paul insisted that fabricating Jamie would bring her back, that her last moments were stored in the DNA scraping he had crudely scratched from her arm, that she'd remember who she was.

It was ludicrous.

Paul was a victim of his own delusions that Raine would never crush. He just wanted his daughter back. She wanted Jamie back, too. But more than that, if she was honest, she needed to get something back from God.

He had taken so much from her.

She stood at the door until her toes were cold. She started for the bedroom to get socks when something moved in the trees. The square grill emerged like silver teeth, the headlights glowing in the daylight.

No.

Bob's truck eased into the sunlight, grimy snow glittering on the hood. His big white cowboy hat filled the cab. The reflection, however, obscured the passenger seat, where she expected to see Paul. Cold crept up her legs, a spirit of doom licking her thighs as it seeped into her belly. The truck turned and stopped.

Paul was not there.

He wasn't there, wasn't nabbed in the red brick house pulling a set of lungs from the fabricator. *Bob wouldn't be escorting him back to the cabin. Unless he was here to search it.*

The dark spirit sank its fangs deep in her heart.

The truck shook as the fat man unseated himself from behind the wheel, adjusting the belt hidden beneath his stomach. He coughed up to the steps and spat a hole in the snow.

There was no knocking.

They stood face to face, a small square of glass separating them like a zoo exhibit. Which one was on the inside?

Little pig, little pig...

"What do you want?" Raine said.

"Come to get you."

"I'm not going."

"Not a choice."

He was wrong about that. It was advisable that the bricks all went to welcome a new arrival, even if it was months after the arrival. She didn't have to go.

"Let me in a sec."

"I'm not going," she repeated.

"I can search your cabin." He held up his phone, the riot app activated. "Resistance is probable cause. I'd have to make sure you're not using this as a distraction to hide something."

Her eyes must've widened when he said that, or her lip quivered or all the blood drained from her cheeks because he smiled at that. He saw the fear.

Or I'll huff and I'll puff...

"Just a quick look around," he said, "and I'll be gone. I need to be at the visitors' center anyhow; then I'll be on my way."

She offered one quick look over his shoulder. No Paul. The longer Bob was with her, the longer he wasn't at the red brick house. She opened the door and stepped back.

Bob pushed inside, patterns of snow falling from his boot treads like broken white waffles. His presence filled the room with an odd mixture of wet fur and coffee breath. He toked on the metal pipe on his way to her bedroom.

"Don't smoke in here," she said.

He was only in there a few moments before crossing the room to the kitchen. A walnut bobbed in her throat. Chairs scratched the floor, a cabinet opened and closed. He came back out with smoke hovering in his winter beard like a fire had been sparked.

"Satisfied?" she asked.

He held her gaze, a smile stretching his whiskers—one of those truth-seeking looks that could drill straight into a person's mind. If he wasn't clay, if he had an ounce of biomites, he might be able to pull the truth out of her and see an image of the trapdoor beneath the oven and the organs stored in the dark.

He put the phone to his ear. "Yeah, I'm on my way to Raine's cabin. I'll give her a ride when she's ready. Paul's not there? What do you mean... okay. Okay. He's probably at the cabin with Raine."

He winked.

"Go ahead, get started. Don't worry about me. Okay."

On my way to Raine's cabin?

He touched a sequence of buttons and held the phone at his side.

"Paul's location disappeared for a while," he said. "Last time he was located was near the lab. We think he's tweaking his trackers to avoid being seen. You think he's making a run for it without you?"

"That happens with him, something with his biomites."

Paul had those moments when he couldn't be found. Even the monitors lost track of him and then he'd just be there, around a corner or sitting on the couch.

"Mmm," Bob grunted. "We might have to put that boy on a leash."

Raine pulled the robe tighter, wanting to slam the bedroom door and get dressed, crawl into bed until he was gone. Something kept her out there, nude beneath the fuzzy robe. She hadn't identified why yet.

"Bible?" Bob touched the black book. "You'll try anything to feel human."

"You looked around, now leave."

He started to reach for the Bible, but instead put his hand under the table to retrieve a spiral-bound sketchbook.

"Put it down."

"This how you spend your time?" He flipped the pages. "Dreaming?"

Pencil drawings of rolling hills and the long and straight horizon of the sea cutting the sky, an old cabin long forgotten, her feet longing for the creaky steps and crooked bannisters of home.

And the faces that lived there.

The unkempt, shaggy mess on Nix's head, his cheeks days unshaven, eyes sharp and thoughtful. Always thoughtful. Their son, Joshua, at his side, a young man that spent his days exploring the endless land, going to the market for the fresh catch and home for dinners most nights.

Is Shep still there, chasing the stick? Do they sit by the fireplace wondering where I went, when I'll come back?

She drew every day because if she didn't, she'd forget what home looked like. Already the details were fuzzy. She could only guess what Joshua looked like. *He's twelve now. No, not twelve... what is he, fifteen?*

Time in dreamland moved at a different speed than the physical world. And this thought, the thought that she didn't know her son's age, that she'd missed all the birthday parties (did they still celebrate without her?) fell in her stomach with a wet smack. And if she ever forgot what they looked like, she'd never forgive herself.

"Put it down."

"Waste of time, Raine. This is all there is, right here and now."

One of the bricks was a Buddhist, a man named Neal. He sat meditation every morning. She heard him say that once, *This is all there is, right here and now.* But Bob was just repeating it, slinging it like an arrow instead of a life raft.

"You understand that?" he said. "Somewhere in your fabbed brain, you get what that means? All there is, is this right in front of you, for the rest of your life. Day after day after day it's just this, forever and ever. Cold winters and dry summers. So draw all you want. Wish, pray, whatever. None of this is going to change. Just settle in and accept that dreamland is dead. It's just you and me."

"You can leave now."

Bob took slow heavy steps toward her, the snow already melting on the floor. She moved around the couch to avoid him and snatched the sketchbook, pressing it to her chest. He didn't open the door.

Instead, he pulled the curtain closed.

"Almost done."

He turned slowly. *Does he know what we're hiding? Is that why he's not worried about Paul?*

She opened her communication lines, attempting a thought-transmission. *Paul!* But only dead sound replied, a cottony silence with padded walls. Bob had killed her communication when he tapped the phone after taking that call. *On my way to Raine's cabin,* he'd said. Like he wasn't there yet.

Like he needed more time.

She should run and hide in the bedroom, barricade the door, jump through the window until someone came to the cabin. But she didn't want to run. Didn't want to call for help. It was why she didn't change out of her robe when Bob arrived, why she stood barefoot and vulnerable while his fat fingers smudged the pages of her sketchbook.

Try something, fucker.

She wanted something to push her to the edge, to light a furnace of fury, to pour fuel on the tiny flame of rage that flickered in her dark nights. Because life had punished her enough. She needed something to hurt back—a face to crush, bones to break. She wanted to get her hands on God and shake him, tell him this shit wasn't fair. That she'd had enough.

Bob would serve as a fine substitute.

So she backed up half a step, bumping into the stone hearth. Embers sparked from the dying logs. His boots landed quietly now—heel giving soft way to toe. Thumb on the phone, stroking the glass by his thighs, the fabric scratching between his legs.

Raine clutched her robe, a distressed rabbit with nowhere to run. Waiting for him to come near. He nudged the couch with his knee, opened the space between them where he'd throw her on the floor and devour her whole.

One more step was all she needed.

She'd drive her knee into his groin, crush his testicles like cream-filled pastries, leave his scrotum swollen with semen paste and shredded tissue. Then she'd drive her fingers into his throat, insert the poker between his ribs and pry out his heart, fingerpaint the walls with scenes of hell, and sit on his bloated corpse until the monitors came for her. They would shut her down after that. *A danger to the world around her*, they would say.

That was what she wanted. She wanted to be shut down.

He took that last step. Her heel against the baseboard for leverage, her thigh tensed—

His hand shot out with unexpected speed; the webbing between his finger and thumb slammed into the hollow indention of her lower throat. A shock of blood surged through her carotid artery, wobbling her knees. She regained her balance as he slammed her into the wall.

The phone sang at his side.

A broad smile spread between his whiskers. Breadcrumbs hung from the curly mustache, his breath thick and humid, coating her face. Her muscles locked in place, her body unresponsive.

He had swiped the phone, hijacked her into submission.

He flipped her around, pushing her face into the wall. Hand

pressed between her shoulder blades, her breasts flattened against the paneling. Then his belly weighed into her, pushing the breath from her. She could feel his crotch harden.

How many of the women had he done this to, threatened to expose a secret if they told, blackmailed them with false evidence? Did he hijack them and have his way, or did they let him do things in exchange for favors?

She couldn't even close her eyes.

She stared at the tiny imperfections on the wall, helpless to stop him. She would endure another beating from life. All eighteen wheels grinding her into roadkill, picked over by carrion as she bubbled on summer asphalt.

All while clutching the sketchbook.

Haven't you taken enough?

His chin rested on her shoulder, a strong hand around her throat. His breathing quickened, his heart surging against her back with anticipation. He licked his lips and flicked her earlobe with the tip of his tongue.

She would fucking kill him after this.

Let him have this body, she was done with it. The first chance she got, she would destroy him. She would wait in the dark, she would hide in the shadows, ambush him outside a bathroom, gut him like an animal. This was over. This was all over. *Have your way, pig.*

A belt buckle rang in its track—

The front door burst open. Winter whipped around her as Bob jumped back. The phone slipped from his hand and bounced on the floor.

"Stop." It was Paul's voice.

Disappointment settled inside her, followed by anger. Not at Bob but Paul. Still locked up, she hoped Bob would lock them both in place and follow through, give her a reason.

"Unlock her."

Bob didn't move. He was thinking, planning. He'd never been caught in the act or he would've done something already.

"Don't think about anything else," Paul said calmly. Matter-of-factly. "I bugged this house with my own surveillance. Everything that happened in the last hour has been recorded."

"Bullshit. I'd know if you had a camera."

"Want to take a chance? If I'm telling the truth, you go to prison, where I'm sure you'll be the one pushed against the wall. If I'm bluffing, you walk away. Want to roll the dice?"

"Let me see it. Where's the camera?"

"You've raped before."

"Where's the camera?"

"It was only a matter of time before you came for Raine, so I was ready for you. I want you to walk out of here and leave us alone. Don't ever come back to this cabin again. You understand? Don't ever fuck with us again or the world will know you're a brick-loving rapist."

Bob didn't move. Decisions were grinding in the silence between his ears. He'd been caught and Paul was showing him mercy. It was a favor. Or maybe his boner was making a plea. Was it worth the risk?

He picked up the phone. His boots rang across the room and stopped somewhere near the front door. Raine breathed into the wall, waiting for a sound, a word.

Sensation gushed into her body like a water balloon filled from a hydrant. She collapsed in a heap of terrycloth, head bouncing, teeth snapping.

Seconds spun in a black whirlpool. Hands yanked her out of the cycling. She struck with the heel of her palm and felt the hard edge of his jawline before kicking into the soft tissue of a midsection.

Paul doubled over, hand up.

"Did he touch you?" he said between strangled breaths. "Did he touch you?"

He tried reaching again, tried to pull the fuzzy fabric over her bare shoulder. She slapped his hand, pushing against the wall, didn't want his comfort or help, just wanted to fan the flames of rage, build the inferno of hatred that was consuming her minutes earlier, burning all her fears and hopes to ashes. That blessed rage promised to destroy everything until there was nothing.

Until she felt nothing.

Was no more.

"Did he touch you?"

She closed her eyes and shook her head. Tears squeezed between her lashes and she hated that, trying to cling to the dry-eyed anger that quickly evaporated, an emotion sucked dry of oxygen until there wasn't even a flame. She was back to where she was. Back to sanity.

"I was going to... going to kill him." She swallowed the words. "I wanted to."

Another wave of grief and regret fell over her, the realization coming when she said it out loud. If she died, if her body was no more, then her dreamland would die. And Nix and Joshua were still waiting.

A large travel bag was on the floor.

Paul turned off the lights and slid it behind the couch, hiding from the cameras that Bob and the monitors could use to watch them. They weren't supposed to invade their privacy, their purpose only for emergencies. But they all knew better.

In the dark, he sorted through random objects and tools. On the bottom was a square circuit cabinet. He flipped a sequence of switches and pried off the back. There, laid in the soft embrace of beige foam, were two perfectly fabricated lungs, pink and soft, sealed in shiny preservation wrap.

"If I didn't have this with me," Paul said "I would've killed him first."

If he didn't have Jamie's organs with him, if a third of her piece-mealed body wasn't stashed beneath the oven, he wouldn't have opened the door and stood there. He would've destroyed him. And the People would've found the lungs.

The People would shut him down.

We both have people depending on us.

Bob didn't know if there was surveillance footage or not. But that wouldn't matter. Paul sold it. He'd bought them space and time to bring back Jamie. When all hope was lost, when they stood on the brink of annihilation, now they stood in a wide-open field of hope.

Bob would leave them alone.

God works in mysterious ways.

THE ARCHETYPE'S KNOWLEDGE_

Perry Dawkins had never been in a green room.

Turned out that the backstage room wasn't green at all. He knew that, but he still had expectations, would've been happy if the walls were mossy. Instead, they were white and water-stained. A coffee machine was in the corner.

He was breathing a little too rapidly and feeling light-headed. He could control the nerves like other fabricated humans (a thought-command to increase dopamine and suppress norepinephrine for starters) but preferred to let it ride. The stress wasn't debilitating. In fact, it was exhilarating. Humanizing.

After all, he'd started out human.

Emotions were evolutionary shortcuts to environmental response. It was only when he ignored them did they back up, an emotional river that spilled over the muddy banks and flooded him with anxiety. If more fabricated humans embraced the emotional aspect of their identity rather than exerted their will over them, they would have fewer problems assimilating into society.

Perry was more than a role model. *I am a perfect human.*

"How you doing?" an elderly man with wavy gray hair took his shoulders and asked. "A little nervous?"

Perry blew through smiling fish lips and nodded.

Dr. Wilkerson shook him, patted him and then embraced him with his characteristic hug that, for a moment, squeezed out all the air. He slapped his back with a heavy paw.

"You're going to change the world," the professor said gruffly.

One of the conference directors grabbed the professor for a few words but not before he imparted a fatherly grin, the stage lights sparkling in his eyes.

A stagehand came after Perry with a wireless mic. "It's backup, just in case primary audio goes down."

He worked on fixing it to Perry's lapel while a young woman waited with a short brush in one hand and a box in the other.

"Do you mind?" she asked.

The professor mentioned they'd want to fix him up for the recording, add color blanched out by the stage lights. Perry's complexion was mocha, his hair looping curls of surfer brown, eyes distinctly almond-shaped. He was an amalgam of several races. No one would guess him as a neuroscientist. The world's leading.

"What's the talk?" the makeup artist asked.

"What?"

"You look nervous."

"Oh, yeah." He shook his hands. "A little."

"What are you talking about?"

"Um, dream disease."

She exaggerated an understanding frown, intrigued but not really. "Friend of mine's daughter has a friend at school that died from it a few months ago. It's a shame, really need to do something about it."

"I think I have an answer."

"Tell you what the answer is." She made long, soft strokes across his forehead. "It's getting rid of the bricks. They started it."

The smile that had grown through his nervous breathing wilted; the butterflies in his stomach curdled into lumpy, crawling critters with thick lapping tongues.

"That's not true," he said. "See, there's evidence out there that... you see, the dream accelerators that allow halfskins to generate dreamlands are networked, which means halfskins are trading..."

Her brush slowed.

"Bricks have stable dreamworlds," he blurted, hoping his use of the racist vocabulary would win her over. "They really have nothing to do with the dreamlands that halfskins experience. And there's no connection with clay dreams. My analysis is conclusive. The sooner we can identify the real cause of this epidemic, the sooner it can be cured."

"Done. Good luck."

His hand twitched. He wanted to snatch her like a rogue calf that needed to learn how the ranch worked, but it would only scare her. She didn't know he was a brick when she started applying makeup, but it was clear she figured it out.

Bigotry had a finely tuned detector.

Maybe he could convince the waiting room of academics, but how would he win over the general public? Prejudice wasn't interested in facts. People like her already lived in an altered reality designed by their xenophobic thoughts.

People like her. He had to watch his own prejudice.

It was just hard to stomach reactions like that. The incidents of dream disease among the brick population were nonexistent while the casualty rate of halfskins using dreamland accelerators was pointing at the sky.

It was the scientists from the clay states that suggested a theory that bricks were carriers of the psychological disorder since dream disease didn't exist prior to the sentience laws. They couldn't explain why clays were succumbing to dream disease, albeit at lower rates than halfskins; just blame the bricks and everything would be all right.

Bricks were vectoring rats.

The link, as Perry's lab discovered, between dreamland and dream disease was the halfskin accelerators. They were all networked. It would be like no one washing their hands during an influenza epidemic and coughing into each other's mouths. Start by getting rid of the accelerators and then they could focus on clay dream disease.

The answer sure as hell wasn't getting rid of the bricks' dreamlands. No evidence supported it, yet they still kept them from dreaming. It was only Dr. Wilkerson's connections that allowed Perry to venture off the Settlement to lead the research. This was rare and, as it would turn out, would be the last time it ever happened.

Perry had proof that the accelerators were the problem. Halfskins were using them to create their dreamlands. Dreamland accelerators were malleable resorts, digital funlands that expanded the dreamer's recreational opportunities. This was a trillion-dollar industry that Perry was blaming.

But they were missing the entire point of dreamland. It was so much more than a dream vacation world where they could sleep with twenty women or skydive without risk or murder without repercussions.

Dreamlanding is world building.

Imagine a creative outlet that wasn't a blank canvas or pages in a book or images on a screen but an actual universe with planets and stars and outer space. Perry believed that dreamlands were real.

We are the seeds of new realities.

No single region of the brain controlled dreamland. It was a production of the entire organ. That was Perry's proposal: biomites would be used to rebuild the entire brain. That was why the bricks could dream so effortlessly, why they were immune to dream disease —there was no clay holding back the experience. And clay, by the clay state's own admission, was imperfect. *We are descendants of original sin,* one such pastor claimed, proudly.

But we don't have to stay in the garden!

Perry would show the audience that he had proof that imagination didn't just create images and sensations but acted like a portal to new planes of existence. He would pull back the curtain on God, give a purpose to each and every human being. We weren't just here to enjoy ourselves.

We are creators!

Perhaps that was what God intended, not for us to live a good life, an obedient life, a fun-filled healthy life. But a creative life.

And dream disease? Maybe that was our failure to live up to that purpose. Our imperfections created monsters that terrorized dreamlands instead of spinning new and amazing solar systems.

The dream feasts on the dreamer.

"Five minutes!" someone shouted.

Perry took several short, choppy breaths, shook his hands and jogged in place. Dr. Wilkerson was with his peers. They gave him a thumbs-up. He would be presenting for the team. It was a collaborative effort, but Perry was leading them. It was his baby. They wanted him to deliver salvation.

A brick to save the world.

Stagehands rushed past him. His introduction had begun. The makeup artist was approaching for a last second touch up. He closed his eyes and bowed his head for a few moments of inner solitude.

He didn't see her press the Taser against his stomach.

Didn't feel the floor crumple beneath him.

The electrical charge delivered enough voltage to cause serious damage. He never recovered.

And the world never changed.

CHAPTER TEN_

A SUMMER BREEZE ROLLED OVER OPEN GROUND, SWARDS OF wildflowers swept by an invisible hand, slapping the hair from Paul's eyes.

The row of cabins sat dark, still and empty beneath the churning wind harvesters. The contractors had moved out once the George B. Simpson Center of Energy and Conservation Research building was finished, a three-story monstrosity that cast a shadow over the red brick house. A few of the cabins were still occupied by workers, but they would be gone soon.

The one across from the red brick house, the one that used to be Raine's cabin, was the only one occupied. A construction worker stepped onto the porch and dropped a bright orange duffel bag, one about the size Paul had been using to smuggle his fabrications. This one made a heavy clink—metal on metal—that echoed in the trees. The worker didn't wait, didn't knock on the door. Just left it.

A silhouette moved past the window—a fuzzy shadow within the dark interior.

Marcus Anderson lived there now.

They put him in the cabin where Raine had lived. Paul took that as a fuck you when Bob and the monitors helped the old man move in. He'd rarely been seen since that day.

Almost five months.

He never appeared at the monthly meetings, never went for a walk. The porch swing was always still. No one ever saw him except when he'd retrieve a box of food the monitors set on the steps (they delivered to no one else). He would hobble out, his left leg stiff, the knee a rusty hinge.

Like an old man.

Bob visited him. His truck would be parked out front at least twice a week, sometimes more. On the rare occasion Paul glimpsed inside, they appeared to be sitting on the couches having a chat. Bob never talked about it, even when asked, "What are you and the old man doing?"

He pretended he never heard it.

Marcus Anderson had made such a stink about being discovered, like he wanted the spotlight. The People were consumed with his capture (*the best reality TV reality has ever seen*). His case dominated the newsfeeds, the lawyers chronicled his every move, every word. Transcripts of babbling prophecy were leaked to the press, spread throughout the blogosphere. Small cults dedicated themselves to his prophecy.

One to lead, one to dream, one to bleed and the son to be.

Some were worshipping his massive shutdowns of halfskins, others decrypting his warnings of a powers-that-be. They were sycophants that would, in another era, rally around Charles Manson.

And then it went away, a cheap fad of leg warmers and spiky hair. The People just didn't care about him after he arrived. He was no fun after all. The old man's lawyers said he just wanted to be left alone and forgotten. Like the Settlement was a retirement community.

"Everyone!" someone shouted. "If I can get everyone's attention? Up here, please!"

Excitement buzzed behind him—equipment clicking into place,

the blur of conversation and fake laughter. The man attempting to get everyone's attention was clapping; then he was interrupted by audio feedback before his voice projected into the great wildness, echoing off the distant trees.

"If everyone can take their places," he said. "The ceremony begins in fifteen minutes, please."

The shadow moved inside the cabin and stopped at the window. The curtain was pried aside. Paul squinted to make out the details, imagining the bald head with random wisps of white hair.

"Paul." Pete placed a hand on his shoulder. "We need to be ready."

Behind him, the circus was in full swing. The reporters, the politicians, and all the bricks were milling in front of the monstrous shiny new building. George B. Simpson, a biomite-enabled trillionaire and world's richest centenarian, was standing near a yellow ribbon tied to the front doors with a ridiculous pair of oversized scissors, the public relations people coaching him how to bend over when it was time for the bricks to line up and kiss his ass.

The world would see the grand opening of a new research facility run entirely by bricks, the first of its kind, a state-of-the-art facility that would benefit humankind through biomite technology.

"Ask me," good ole George had said when funding was approved, "they're just as human as the People."

But I don't want to live next to one.

"Come on," Pete urged. "We need you over here. And would you... you know."

Paul tied his hair back with a rubber band, loose strands pulling free. He hadn't cut it in over a year, not since Jamie was delivered. He was urged to cut it properly, to appear presentable for this occasion. *Be grateful,* he was told. *And if you can't do that, at least look it.*

He was doing neither.

Gratitude was a dark secret, a merciless blanket that smothered his heart, a cold blade between his ribs. Yes, the new research center was exactly what he needed—new equipment and plenty of distractions made it possible to continue fabricating Jamie in the brick house. But that wasn't the gratitude Pete and the others wanted. They wanted him to be happy for the breadcrumbs thrown at them like pigeons locked in cages.

"Over here, come along!" a woman prompted, a badge swinging from her neck. "If you would stand over here. Yes, yes, that's good."

She pointed at the empty chair next to Dennis, the Settlement's introvert (an autistic plant fabricated by a nonprofit organization to study the disease)—as brilliant at chemistry as he was social awkwardness. Paul was on the team because he was good at design and execution. Dennis and the others were the idea people, the theorists and inventors. Paul brought their dreams to life; he made them happen. He'd have his own office and access to fabrication approval.

George R. Simpson would help bring Jamie back.

So why wasn't he happier?

The cameras panned across the research team, past the building and over to the rest of the Settlement bricks gathered on the other side. They were all in attendance except the old man.

Raine was holding hands with the prayer group, heads bowed. There were ten of them now that held weekly meetings, sending their wishes into the blue sky with eyes squeezed shut, tongues sharp and hopeful. Their prayers floated on the breeze like notes attached to colorful balloons.

George B. Simpson was introduced.

The important people took turns at the dais. They turned, they smiled, they waved. The funding was from private donors, but would benefit the People. It would benefit humankind today and tomorrow. Benefit the future. Benefit the children.

Their children.

"And we have you to thank," George B. Simpson said to bricks that applauded on cue. Even Paul clapped like an asshole. It was the least he could do.

The ribbon was cut. The tour began.

The reporters followed the glad-handing politicians inside and the bricks were guided inside to see the gift bestowed upon them by good ole George, told they would no longer toil in boredom. Now they had a purpose. They had a reason to live.

They mattered.

(*Wink. Wink.*)

Paul and the team were asked about their projects. Each of them gave vague answers about sustainable energy and medical developments. Even Dennis mumbled through a prepared statement about excitement. Paul stayed in the back, watching the cameras capture the giant lab, the politicians and excitement. Not one of them pointed at the cabin across the field, like the world had forgotten Marcus Anderson.

"Talk about organ fabrication," a hefty middle-aged reporter asked, his button-down shirt billowing in the breeze.

"What about it?" Pete answered.

"There's some concern about human fabrication, that you'll start fabbing an army."

Pete laughed with all his teeth. "And where are we going to hide them? That's absurd."

"You will be fabricating organs, correct?"

"We will fabricate organs for the purposes of research."

"No human fabrication?"

"We're trampling old ground here. The fabrication chamber isn't large enough to produce a child let alone an adult."

"But an infant?"

"In theory." Pete sighed. "Listen, we're under surveillance by teams of clay monitors. There's no chance we could fabricate an infant and raise it in secret. It would ruin everything we worked for. We're interested in advancing biomite technology, that's all. We want to perfect the human body and, in turn, heal the human mind."

"You could fabricate all the organs of a body." The reporter's nasally accent ripped through Paul's fog of indifference and left a buzzy residue between his ears.

"Frankenstein was a novel," Pete exclaimed. "Dennis? Paul? Can you shed some light on this?"

Pete took a step back, eager to get off the griddle. Paul, slouched on the hard seat, leaned forward. When Dennis muttered an incoherent string of scientific jargon, the reporter started looking at him for something he could understand.

Silence soon hung like a corpse.

"Yeah, uh. One of the deciding factors in Mr. Simpson's funding had to do with organ transplant, primarily the fabrication and transportation of organs via preservation wrap that could be absorbed once inside the body."

Paul had used Dennis to push the proposal of organ fabrication through, fed him the data and reports to make an argument, convinced the introverted genius this was his idea, not Paul's. But when it came to explaining it, he always looked more surprised than anyone else.

"There's also the internal rebuild technique," Paul continued, "using digital matrices to establish a three-dimensional blueprint inside the body before biomites are injected... look, it's all in the proposal. You can find it posted on the website."

"Will we get updates?" The reporter looked bored.

"They'll be posted."

"Surveillance feeds?"

"No." Pete stepped in. "Our labs aren't going on a feed. We're privately funded, so there will be trade secrets."

"You'll be working in secret?" His eyebrows shot up. He just got the hook for his story.

"Not secret, just not fully transparent at first. If this was publically funded, yes. But the People had their chance, they balked and Mr. Simpson stepped in. We'll be working for privatized investors, I think you know this. We'll be held accountable for all our work; there's nothing to worry about. We just want to do our duty."

Do our duty. That had become the go-to line. *We just want to serve, that's all.*

Paul didn't disagree with the angle (after all, the People wanted the bricks to be subservient androids, not individual humans). He just hated it. The words were bitter shards he'd rather swallow than spit out.

The reporter started another question. "What about..."

I wish this fucker would go away.

And then he cramped. The reporter lost his train of thought, tapping the dimple in his square chin like that was the button that would unclog his thoughts.

"Thanks for your time," Pete said. "We appreciate your support."

They all shook hands; then the reporter wandered inside the building. A few days later, he would post a story about the amazing building and the dedicated fabbers that wanted nothing more than to do their duty and serve the People.

Like someone scripted it for him.

Paul sat down, the sun warm and promising. The snowcapped mountains a reminder that winter was still there. It would come again. Across the field, the curtain fell in the old man's cabin.

The bright orange bag was no longer on the porch.

CHAPTER ELEVEN_

SUMMER ENDED AND AUTUMN WALTZED THROUGH THE countryside, but winter didn't tiptoe. It scratched and clawed through the Settlement, laid the land to bed beneath thick comforters of snow. Wind reshaped the landscape with mauling drifts and frozen daggers.

Matted tracks belted crisscross patterns, snowmobiles finding their way to the cabins until the next storm washed them away.

Marcus pushed the plunger on a coffee press and poured two cups. He took them into the front room, where jazz played from a speaker. The fireplace roared with red heat, sparks crackling against the metal screen.

Mother sat on the opposite couch.

Her finger pressed to her lips, eyes closed, as if soaking in the extemporaneous notes, letting them softly bounce inside her like rubber pellets working their way down a pegboard.

Marcus sat with a groan. The cold had stiffened his joints and bit into his knee. It was odd to feel so human. He'd never asked Mother (they rarely spoke since arriving, just enjoyed each other's presence) the reason he woke with such human frailty. Perhaps it was the reason he connected with clay—he felt their pains, knew their suffering.

He trusted her.

She wasn't a god or goddess, he didn't think of her that way. If he had to put it in words, she was just an expression of divine will, like the majesty of the Himalayas or the wonder of the universe. She was benevolent and kind; he had come to accept that with only a trace of bitterness.

She was beyond human comprehension. She understood the universe in ways no ordinary human could; any attempt to relay her depth would be like teaching a dung beetle calculus. She saw the path to truth, the way to humanity's freedom.

He just knew this and trusted it.

Perhaps she designed him that way, planted suggestions in his subconscious that made him so willing to accept her, to follow her. This he couldn't argue. After all, his roots were human. Imperfect. He had prayed to do the will of God, to allow him the strength to be a servant of divine will.

Perhaps Mother was God's voice.

So they rested on their couches, the fire riffing along with the music when he dozed off. Nearly a year on the Settlement and he still failed to see why anyone complained. He found the boredom quite relaxing. *Enlightenment,* a spiritual leader once said, *is quite boring by ordinary standards.*

The stamp of heavy boots startled him.

He hadn't heard the snowmobile approach. Mother slid to the end of the couch, legs crossed. She tossed her head, pushing the hair behind her ear, and folded her hands. Lips gently closed, she nodded.

A bitter wind knifed through the open door, Bob partially blocking it. His puffy green coat fluttered. Marcus stepped back for him to enter. The large monitor unlaced his boots so as not to track snow across the room.

Marcus took a moment to peer across the field. The George R. Simpson lab heaved a steady stream of gray smoke from the chimneys, but the lights were off. The opening ceremony had come and gone months ago. Everyone was already busy with research, but now they were in their cabins for the night, battened down for an approaching storm, the third one in a month.

"Have a seat, have a seat." Marcus gestured to the cushion next to Mother and took Bob's coat. He returned with coffee mugs warmed in a microwave. "How are you this evening?"

"You keep this cabin warm," Bob said.

"Thin skin."

"Can't you just turn up your inner thermostat?"

"It's easier to throw on a log."

Marcus chuckled and they sipped and sat quietly. Mother watched the large monitor sink into the couch, his weight bowing the center. If she were a physical being, she would've been tossed onto his lap. Instead, she watched him with interest.

They both did.

Marcus enjoyed the warmth of Bob's clay mind like a pleasant fragrance or a tune on the radio. He wasn't a good man (quite despicable really, but Marcus couldn't judge; Bob was worlds away from what he'd done). He was intriguing, an acquired taste.

Exactly what Marcus needed.

He didn't manipulate Bob's mind, didn't mold it into what he wanted it to be (he could, he was certain of that), but bathed in the man's presence. It was easier to become familiar with him than bend his will—sprinkle a trail of crumbs for him to follow.

Create desire.

After all, desire needed no explanation. *The heart wants what it wants,* most people would say.

But what makes the heart want in the first place? No one ever asked that question.

Bob came to visit regularly. He was quite cantankerous at first. The alpha dog had come to shit in Marcus's nest. But the old man treated him kindly, left him with a taste of kindness that he came back for. Again and again.

Bob had that faraway look now, a trance of relaxed disposition. Open to suggestion. He was hypnotized by the room, a sort of energy that buzzed inside of him, warm and cozy. Made him want to sleep.

"Were you an only child?" Marcus asked.

Bob nodded. Memories swam behind his eyes.

Marcus prodded them to the surface. Much like a brain surgeon could get the right response by applying an electrical impulse, Marcus found what he wanted in the mind. His thoughts were his scalpels.

"I had a little sister."

"A sister? How wonderful."

"She died when I was eight."

"That must've been painful."

Slow nod. "Yeah." The fire's dance filled the swelling silence. "Pissed my father off." He snorted. "Something fierce."

"And he beat your mother for it."

"He was beating her before that. But, uh, it changed after that, yeah. He was doing more things, drinking, spicing, whatever he could get his hands on. Ended up charring his biomites to a crisp."

"And that's why you turned clay?"

"Yeah." He gulped the lukewarm coffee, passing over the details of his own divorce, the restraining order that prevented him from seeing his kids. "Figured I'd do the world some good by coming out here, you know. I was made to do this."

"How so?"

"I like order. Discipline. There are rules, you know. God doesn't love bricks."

"You enforce the rules."

"Goddamn right."

"And you enjoy it."

"No shame in loving what you do. It's a passion. You understand."

"Oh, I certainly do."

"Goddamn right you do."

Bob put away the coffee in one big swallow. Marcus offered another cup and he accepted. He returned with a fresh pot and cheese and crackers. Bob leaned back with the plate balanced on his swollen belly, crumbs littering his ratty beard. When he was done, he scraped the cheese off his gums and sucked his wet finger.

"What was it like?" Bob asked.

Marcus knew what he was asking, but paused long enough to let him clarify.

"Shutting off all those halfskins, what was it like?" Bob sounded like an addict asking about ambrosia, food of the gods. *How does it taste?*

Marcus sat back, mug curled against his stomach, warmth radiating through his hands. He contemplated which story to tell, which would be the lure he wanted to dangle; a morsel so succulent that Bob would swallow the hook whole. He had so many to satisfy a sadist like Bob. A dark man. A dark, dark human being.

"Once," he started, hanging the word like a shiny object for his eyes to follow, "I shut down a man in front of his family. It was the early days of the halfskin laws, when anyone with 40% biomites was held in detention and biomite replication couldn't be stopped.

"When the redlines, as they were called, neared halfskin, we would alert the family and give them an opportunity to say goodbye. They weren't allowed to touch them or even be in the same room. I made them stand behind a glass partition and talk through a speaker.

"In this case, the halfskin was a good man. He was a dedicated father, a wonderful husband, an absolute soulful man of God that, mistakenly, seeded himself with too many biomites. The law was the law, as you know. I couldn't pardon him because he'd done good in the world. He knew the rules and chose to break them.

"I stood at that man's shoulder and watched the counter rise to 49.7%, then 49.8%. I stared at his wife and children, listened to his parents curse my name and beat the glass. I tasted their anguish as his breaths became shallow at 49.9%.

"They begged and pleaded, cried until their eyes swelled. And when he turned halfskin, I turned him off. His last breath eased out of him. He was cold. But I never took my eyes off of the family. I wanted them to suffer. I wanted them to learn.

"Pain is a mighty teacher."

It was more than that. It was the invulnerability Marcus felt. His addiction to power. He wanted to be above it all, wanted to act in the name of God. More than that. He wanted to be God.

Omnipotent.

A bulge creased against Bob's inner thigh. He was full-on hard. "You know why I'm here?"

"Why you stay on the Settlement?"

"I'm here to do that, just like you. I'm here to teach a lesson, to let the bricks feel human through pain and suffering. I'm helping *them*, like you did."

Marcus grinned. *Them.* He didn't consider Marcus one of them. The hook had been swallowed.

"How are you helping them?"

"So they know..." He stammered for something legitimate. Marcus pressed a thought into him, nudging him along. "To make them feel vulnerable, you know. So they know they can't control everything, that they need to just be *here* whether it hurts or not."

"You, dear man, are a Buddha in winter clothing."

"We all have our purpose."

Bob smiled like an eight-year-old. He hopped off the couch to help the old man clean up, and when Marcus offered him cookies, he helped himself to three of them then wrapped three more in a napkin for the ride home.

Through the frosted kitchen window, Marcus saw a figure crossing the field in the dimming light of evening. Snow up to his waist, Paul made his way to the new research facility and snuck inside. Once inside, the lights remained dark.

"Better get going," Bob said, zipping up his coat. "Thanks for the coffee."

Marcus followed him to the door. "How did your sister die?"

Bob's hand froze on the twisted knob. He remained like that for a full second, even considered pretending he didn't hear the question.

"A boating accident."

"How dreadful." Marcus put his hand on the man's arm. "Must have been heartbreaking."

"She couldn't swim."

"Did you see her? When she died?"

Bob started shaking his head and didn't stop. It was like someone had flicked a bobblehead in zero gravity, a needle stuck in an album's groove. He was trying to follow up with the story he had told so many times that he'd come to believe it. She'd fallen off a bridge and never came up, that was what happened. No one could do anything about it.

Marcus eased the real memory into the light.

"Did you see her?" he asked again.

Head still shaking, Bob answered, "Yes."

"You did. And what happened?"

"She had..." He swallowed hard. "She broke my fishing pole when we were on vacation. She was always breaking my stuff even when I told her not to touch it."

His voice shrank.

"So I got mad and I shoved her."

The words stopped.

Marcus let him swim in the memory that welled up from the deep, a leviathan that swallowed him whole. He slid down the slimy gullet and went through the intestines where memories—bad, bad memories—had been stuffed and forgotten.

He stood on the bridge and watched her flail.

He could've saved her, but she was always getting into his things. He just wanted her to go away, wished she'd never been born. He watched her go under, her hand the last part of her to splash beneath the cold, cold water.

Her knee scraping the sandy bottom.

Lungs burning wet and full.

He could feel her now. Could feel her go cold. Feel her heart thudding in her ears, the sun rippling above—

"Robert."

Bob jumped off the floor like he was pushing off the sandy bottom, sucking for air, spitting and blubbering. Tears streamed into his coarse beard. Completely vulnerable.

And open.

"I will need some help in the next couple of weeks," Marcus said. "Will you help me?"

Bob nodded. Of course he would.

"You're a good boy."

He sped off into the night, the snowmobile carving a new track. Yes, a track. One that Marcus would need. It was better that he would want to help Marcus than to be forced to. *After all, his heart wants what it wants.*

The old man told it what to want.

"You did him a lot of good," Mother said. "I don't believe he deserved as much mercy."

Who was Marcus to judge? His sins outweighed most.

Before he closed the door to seal out winter, he noticed a small light on the third floor of the George R. Simpson building. Nothing anyone else would see. Mother noticed it, too.

He would need Bob's help very soon.

CHAPTER TWELVE_

3:20 AM.

Paul jolted upright, wrinkles imprinted where his cheek had lain against his sleeve. Like deer listening for another twig, he held still. Not breathing.

It could've been the storm that spattered the third-floor window with fistfuls of sleet he heard, heaving long frigid breaths against the building. It was still whiteout conditions, the ground a hazy oblivion through frosted glass.

In the lab, the rhythmic strokes of the fabricator hummed and hissed. The glass walls were dark (research had already shown improved stability when fabricating without exposure to ultraviolent light). The outline of the organ's form was barely visible. It looked something like a bowl.

The most complicated piece yet.

He rolled the chair to the computer and tapped the space bar. The job was supposed to be finished by sunrise. Estimated completion was now mid-morning. It was too late to stop, not without risking complete malfunction; it had to be finished when he wrapped it.

All of the major organs were done, wrapped and hidden beneath the oven. This one, though, was complex and critical. A faulty kidney could be repaired, a leaky stomach patched.

The brain had to be perfect.

The storm was a lucky break. Raine called it a blessing. *God is good.* Whether it was God, statistics or good karma, it didn't matter. The storm gave him the ten to twelve hours he needed.

The blizzard would continue until noon. That would be just enough time. If someone walked through four feet of snow, he could simply abort, run the cleanup program and try another time. He had dug through an eight-foot snowdrift just to open the front doors. No one would be coming.

Still, it would've been nice to finish before sunrise.

The fabricator's hypnotic thrum wooed his eyes to close. He stood up. There would be time to sleep later, when this was all over. Besides, the monitors would see his location in the lab, they'd know he was working. He tried to set these jobs up and let them run from a distance, but this one needed his guidance. If they came prying, he'd have to be there to clean up.

They said his locator was still blinking out despite repeated attempts to recalibrate. They accused him of sophisticated tampering, but he had nothing to do with his occasional disappearance from their radar. If he was honest, he was counting on their incompetence to avoid investigating where he was at. It was a horrible plan.

How am I going to do this?

He had a crawlspace full of Jamie that couldn't simply be popped together like plastic doll parts. And beneath that question was an oil slick of doubt and more contaminated questions that invaded his sleep, niggling beneath his scalp.

Why?

That was the big question. He knew why he was doing this—she was his daughter. It was his job to protect her, to keep her from harm. He failed her, though; he thought if he surrendered peacefully when the People came to the farm that nothing bad would happen.

But why am I doing this?

Paul pried open the blinds; he thought he saw someone. He rubbed his eyes. Marcus Anderson's cabin was obscured in the white-out. Darkened dust whirled against the glass.

He blinked lazily.

Conjuring up a memory, he looked into the storm and saw the outlines of trees and a distant outline of a pitched roof. He could smell the hay, the fresh-cut grass. The hint of a spring shower lingered.

He squinted into the dark as if that would bring the hallucination into focus. He just wanted to see her, even from a distance. It would make the night go faster if he saw her carrying the steel buckets of feed. The shadows were long. It was early in the morning, that was when Cali would feed the horses. The colors of the farm were vivid, the hallucination fully developed.

Like he was there.

He was jerked back by the sound. His fingers still plying apart the blinds, ears pricked, nervous system lit. Dark and gray, it was impossible to see anything outside. The monitors would've pulled up on a snowmobile. Did he miss the engine's report?

He shouldn't have given in to the hallucinations. Now was the time to be vigilant, not dreamy.

Something wet slapped the floor. A soaking wet towel or a slab of meat. Paul tensed. A minute later, he heard it again. Paul waited, then went to the lab door, looking through the mesh glass. He pulled the door handle, the greased hinges silently opening.

A form stood in the shadows. "What are you doing?" someone said.

"Dennis?" Paul answered.

"What... what are you doing in the lab?"

"How'd you get here?"

He took choppy steps, his legs stiff, feet slapping. Paul blocked the doorway. Dennis moved into the dim light, cheeks bright red, twin rivers of snot running over his lips.

"What are you doing?"

"Where's your coat?" Paul asked.

"Why are you here?"

He pushed through the door, snow falling off his frozen jeans. His feet were bare. He couldn't have walked all the way from his cabin, not in this weather. Not like that. He was going to lose toes.

Sleepwalkers don't ask questions.

Paul stayed in front of him, bobbing and weaving to keep his line of sight off the humming fabricator. Dennis stepped into the soft computer glow. His lips were blue.

"What's in the fabricator, Paul?"

"Work."

"You shouldn't be here."

"What are you doing, Dennis? You're frozen."

Violent shivers attacked in short bursts. His hands clenched and unclenched at his sides, tight white flesh drawn over his knuckles.

Dennis attempted to get around him. Paul put a hand on his chest when the computer chimed, a new execution signaled. The next phase began. A digital image rotated on the screen.

Jamie's disembodied head looked at them.

"You... you..."

"Dennis, no. This is... you wouldn't understand. Let me explain—"

"You-you-you... you're going to get us shut down." He leaned into Paul. "They'll shut it all down, Paul!"

"No, they won't. Just..." He couldn't tell him that he'd been fabricating her for over a year and no one knew. "Listen, I have this under control, Dennis. We don't have to tell anyone. I have a... I've been using a program to wipe the computers."

"No, no, no, no..."

"They won't know, Dennis! They don't know! I've been using it for a while, testing it. There's no trace of what we're doing, you understand what I'm saying? This is like a test."

Dennis left small puddles on the floor, shaking his head in time to the word *no*. The sleepwalking reverie was gone. He was completely awake now. Lips quivering, fists clenched.

"They'll shut us down," he muttered, over and over.

"They made me do it!" Paul shouted. "You don't understand. You never had anyone in your life, I know that. They never took anyone away from you. If they did, you'd be doing the same thing. None of this matters to you, all you need is a lab. It doesn't matter if it's on the Settlement or a corporation—"

"No, no, no, no..."

"You shouldn't have come up here, Dennis. What are you doing here in the middle of the night?"

"No, no, no, no... NO!" His hand shook. "NO!"

"Dennis, calm down. Let's talk about this."

"This... this is unsanctioned, Paul. They-they-they won't let you do... they'll shut us down, Paul!"

A maelstrom of thoughts jetted like gamma rays. Paul squinted through the mental sandstorm, raising his hand like that would shield him from Dennis's exploding mind—a mind showering him with fear and anxiety.

Afraid they would shut down the facilities.

Afraid the Settlement would go back to year one.

Afraid he would sit in his cabin alone.

Why is he here?

The eye of the psychic storm passed. Calm returned. Dennis blinked away the melting crystals from his bunchy eyelashes, the baby blue irises cut to thin rings by expanding black pupils.

A thought formed.

Not one that Paul could see, but a thought formed in Dennis he could feel like a pebble in his sock. A thought that would connect with the monitors, tell them what he found, secure their favor, get rid of Paul and maybe, just maybe they would let Dennis stay in the lab because Paul was the one—

"No!" Paul shouted.

Dennis's head snapped and he stumbled, waving his arms. The sound his head made on the floor resembled something like a melon dropped from the second floor.

The fabricator continued to hum.

But nothing else moved.

CHAPTER THIRTEEN_

NIX AND JOSHUA.

They were on the porch, sitting on the rickety top step, Nix helping their son carve with a bowie knife. Shep lay in the grass, tongue out, slimy stick under his legs.

Raine could walk up to them, could sit down and ask what he was carving and what they'd done that day, but they wouldn't answer. They never did. Because this was a dream—a flimsy thin movie, a string of memories that pretended to be her husband and son.

This was not dreamland.

The front door slammed open. Raine bolted off the floor. She'd fallen asleep in front of the fireplace, the blackened logs dying in a thin stream of smoke.

Paul stood in the doorway. Winter bellowed icy spittle inside, little diamonds trickling across the hardwood and sticking to her wool blanket.

It was still dark out.

He wasn't supposed to be back until daylight. He clutched a bag at his side, stumbled into the couch and fell on the floor.

"What's wrong?"

"It's outside," he said.

"What? What's outside?"

His next attempts to speak were slurred by stiff lips. She pulled him upright, leaning him against the couch. His skin was icy. He tried again, but she only caught one word.

"Accident."

"What accident? Is everything all right?"

He shook his head, huffing.

"What's outside, Paul?"

"I didn't...I didn't mean to..."

"What? Why are you back?" His fingers were locked around the bag. It appeared empty. He always brought the fabrications home hidden in the hollow shells of various components. It was unlikely anyone would be out there to stop him, but he almost froze to death in the storm.

"I can't believe this," she said. "What were you thinking?"

His breathing began to thaw—big gulps separated by shaky pauses. He looked at the door.

"I'm sorry."

"Sorry? Sorry for what?" She shook him with knotted panic. "Sorry for what, Paul?"

She let go and stood. The front door appeared to recede, a surreal dreamlike wobble; the bogeyman was at her heels and she couldn't run. Her toes were marbles on the wood floor, her ankles rusty hinges. The brass knob burned her hand. She braced against the door and cracked it open. Eyes watering in the subzero gale, she peered through fuzzy eyelashes to see a dark form half-buried in the snow.

She slammed the door and bowed her head, wishing for the security of the rosary beads. Her lips fluttered in prayer.

"What have you done?" She turned. "What have you done?"

"He wasn't supposed to be there."

"What have you done?"

"I stopped him from reporting us. I only wanted to block the thought, but..."

She began walking and praying, hand on her forehead, face to the ceiling. She wasn't going to die. She couldn't die. Nix and Joshua depended on her, they were in dreamland—her dreamland—waiting for her to return, and now there was a dead body on her steps and a crawlspace of body parts.

He held the bag with both hands.

She dropped next to him and peeled away his dead fingers one by one. The bag thumped with the hollowness of a husked coconut. She pulled down the zipper. The orange glow of the fireplace's dying embers glittered off the preservation wrap. She reached for it.

"Jesus."

The fabricator had printed half of Jamie's head, upside down, stopping just below the nose. The bald scalp soft on her fingertips, the eyelids squeezed tight like a child wishing away a nightmare.

"I never should've let you," she whispered.

"Don't say that."

"No. No, this is insane. What were you thinking, Paul? Did you think we were just going to glue her together and live happily ever after? Huh?"

His head hung dead, eyes dry. His grief a limb long pruned from a tree, rotten and alone.

"This isn't her, Paul." She flipped the skull upright, her finger slipping into the hollow of an open sinus. "Even if it worked, you can't bring her back. You understand? I can't die for this, Paul. You get caught and they shut us off and I can't fucking die!"

She dropped the thing in his lap and stormed away with finger and thumb buried in her eyes, plugging the weepy dikes that never seemed to dry up. Why couldn't she cut off the emotions like him? Why couldn't she be more methodical? Because if she was him, if she had a sample of Nix or Joshua and someone said that maybe they could piece them together an organ at a time, she would risk her life to do it. She'd risk everything. Everybody.

Even put a dead body on the steps.

"Who is it?" she asked.

"Dennis. He... I don't know why he was there."

"Doesn't matter. What are we going to do?"

He studied the bald scalp in his hands. "We take him back to his cabin, put him in bed. No one will find him for a few days. If the storm holds up, maybe a week."

"Then what?"

He shook his head.

One step at a time. She'd lived the last couple years that way. Take one step and let God show you the next. Surely God didn't go away just because there was a dead body.

They got dressed and stepped onto the porch. As they hauled the dead weight onto Paul's shoulder and started into the night, she wondered if this didn't count. Maybe if bricks weren't real, this wasn't murder.

She'd have to accept her own unreality then.

But one step at a time.

DENNIS'S CABIN was tucked beneath trees, the snow drifted along the front porch. The front door was a black rectangle. As they drudged along the tree line, they realized why it appeared so ominous.

The door was open.

A white dusting had settled on the sofas and coffee table like a lumberyard. Small piles had blown against the fireplace and table legs.

Paul collapsed on the couch along with Dennis's body, a cloud of crystals whooshing toward the ceiling. He labored to breathe. Raine's chest hurt; she was numb from the waist down. The scarf around her face was wet, delicate flakes of ice clinging to the fabric like cockleburs.

She closed the door and sat across from him, wondering about all the evidence they were leaving. "Maybe we should leave the door open," she said. "Like we found it."

"It won't matter."

He was right. Their tracks would never be scrubbed away by the storm, not entirely. They led back to their cabin. And from there to the lab. They would only be safe until someone came looking for him.

We may as well leave a signed confession.

The walls were bare. There were no pictures propped on the tables, no knickknacks or books or even a box of tissues. If not for the coat and a pair of boots by the door, it appeared abandoned.

Why didn't he put on his boots?

In the wan light, his feet had the bluish haze of a haunted moon. Biomite hijacking just wasn't possible on the Settlement. They were all bricks. None of them had enough of an advantage over another to do that. And there was only one pair of footprints coming out of the house when they arrived, the soles of bare feet shuffled across the porch. The monitors could have frozen him, but not hijacked him.

Or could they?

They dragged him into the bedroom, tucked him under the covers, folded his hands over his stomach in a way they imagined he slept—all proper and textbook, like people are supposed to sleep.

Paul bowed his head while she prayed.

"How'd you do it?" she asked. "I know you didn't mean to, but how did it happen?"

He explained sensing Dennis opening a line. He was about to send a thought to the monitors, report what had happened. In that vulnerable state, Paul panicked. He only meant to kill the message. Instead, he shut down the brain.

And the body followed.

He stopped mid-sentence. "I forgot to wipe the program."

"What does that mean?"

"I... I forgot to erase what I was doing. If anyone checks the lab, they'll see what I fabricated."

That meant instead of having a few days, they might only have hours.

"Go, hurry," she said. "Just go take care of that. We'll figure out what to do when you get back."

They cleaned up what they could and closed the door. It wouldn't matter, but it didn't seem right to leave it that way. Dennis didn't own much, but he liked order.

They traced their tracks and parted ways at the halfway point—Paul starting for the lab. By the time Raine reached the cabin, she was dizzy with exhaustion. The sky was a pale puddle of watercolors. She fell in the bedroom and pulled a blanket over her head, not expecting to sleep until he was back.

But the front door woke her.

She lay still and listened to the heavy footsteps, expecting the monitors to come with phones raised. The door slammed again. There was silence. When she looked out the window, Paul was a tiny figure wading through the snowy dunes in the early morning. It wasn't until she was back in bed did she notice the bag was missing.

So was Jamie's head.

CHAPTER FOURTEEN_

THE SNOW TRANSFORMED INTO ICY BULLETS.

Paul hunkered into the wind as he emerged from the trees and followed the shallow pockets between the drifts, his lower body a senseless wooden substitute forced to march. Oxygen came in desperate cold gulps. Smoke was slapped from the cabin chimneys, the windows dim with flickering firelight.

Marcus Anderson's cabin, though, was fully lit.

Through watery slits, he saw a shadowy form at the window, as if watching him cross the field. Paul was beyond caring. There was no point. The die had been cast. He no longer had to choose which path to take; the forks had been cut away, his life one long road that now led to the George B. Simpson building.

The front door was still cleared away when he arrived the night before. But now there was another set of tracks. He didn't have time to stuff the bag inside his coat before the door flung open.

"The hell you doing?" Pete roared. "Get in here."

Paul stomped his boots on the way in; reverberations stung his bones.

"Were you here earlier?" Pete asked.

"Yeah, I was. Just wanted to get a trial running." He raised the bag. "Forgot my supplies."

"You damn near froze."

Pete shook his head but didn't ask about the trial or what was in the bag. Or just when the hell he had arrived earlier. Later, they would check the records and discover he'd been there all night. But that would be a small footnote, another detail of the disaster.

Thankfully, Pete was a short-talker when he was at work: asked how you were doing and didn't listen to the answer. Small talk was unproductive. In fact, the current exchange was a personal record.

"Not staying long," Paul said through stiff lips.

"Get warm before you head back."

His soles squeaked in small twists as he walked off. He whistled a tight tune that sounded like spring had arrived. Paul stood dripping until Pete turned the corner, then went to the stairwell. Small puddles of snowmelt littered the steps up to the third floor where Dennis's heels had thumped like heavy logs.

The fabricator door was open, the monitor glowing—the three-dimensional head slowly rotating. His stomach curdled. If Pete had come up...

It doesn't matter.

There wasn't much time. Jamie wasn't coming back. Even if he fabricated every bit of her, he couldn't stitch her together. Even under the best conditions, it was unlikely she would be any more than a distortion of herself.

What was I thinking?

Once the program was wiped and the equipment cleansed, he stood at the top of the stairwell, listening for Pete. The elevators were shut down to conserve power; he'd have to come up the steps. Paul propped the door open and trotted back to the lab. He would never see Jamie again, but he could find closure on her death.

A death he wasn't there for, her exit alone and frightened, he imagined. But he could answer one question before the end of this hapless journey.

Why were you in Georgia?

He dug through the lower cabinets and dropped a heavy metal plate that rang through the building. He paused to listen, making sure Pete was still somewhere in the lower offices before clearing off countertop space. Fingertips thawing, sensation aching in stiff tendons, he wiped the condensation from the plate.

The bag was delicately placed in the sink. The partial skull felt like a softened melon—the scalp coarse with empty hair follicles. Hairless brows hooded eyelids in mid-sneeze. The preservation wrap was pressed into the ridged top palette of her partially fabricated mouth. It stopped at the gums.

The brain was complete, though. The eyes, too.

There was no tissue damage. He could scrape her last impressions without applying the spark of life. There was a risk, of course. Should she wake with only half her head fabricated, her nervous system exposed—

No. That won't happen.

The preservation wrap peeled away from the pink underside with a wet meaty sound. The bottom half slapped on the metal plate.

Meat. It's only meat. It's not Jamie, he told himself.

He laid a mesh interface over the naked scalp, turning the face away. Once energized, the neoprene wires embedded into the flesh, seeking wireless connections with dormant neurons.

Paul tapped the keyboard to life and initiated a secret incognito program before opening neural imaging. The lower half of his body was still painfully cold, but his thudding heart warmed his chest, blood surging in his temples. The program began a synchronizing sequence that seemed to stall. It was taking too long.

He ran to the steps and listened, his pulse echoing in his ears. He did this two more times. Pete's bird-whistling was a distant call. He must've been in the hallway, but still on the first floor.

But near the stairwell.

It was the third trip back to the computer that the screen changed. Images were smeared in an abstract presentation, something that resembled ultrasound technology at its inception—a blurry amalgam of an inner dream world.

The mouse wheel clicked beneath his fingertip, cold and numb. The watercolor scenes drooled into each other. There wasn't time for another pass through calibration, not with Pete in the building. He could come back, but there might not be another time.

He targeted the visual cortex and made a trip to the stairs while the program ran. When he returned, the images were distinguishable. A man was looking at him.

This is her view. The last moments of her life.

The timeline started at the end. He would rewind it as far as it would go, but he was fascinated by the eyes that were looking at him, the pupils big and black and deep. They sparkled like galaxies.

Who the hell is that?

He turned the time wheel back and realized this was the processing lab. She was lying down. A woman and the man with the deep eyes looked down on her. Except for the eyes, the faces were blurred beyond recognition. The woman's lips appeared to move silently (he'd cut the auditory access to save processing time). Their movements were jerky and unnatural, the memories patched together, pieces of film clipped from the movie.

The timeline suddenly swirled into a slurry of melted crayons, pastels that bled into a patchwork of lights and darks. A face would appear, a tree or a sidewalk. She was walking. There was water. The gaps grew larger and emptier.

Whistling.

Pete was in the stairwell. He needed to wrap up, clean up and destroy the evidence. The timeline spun beneath his fingertip, a kaleidoscope of memories morphing and merging and blurring.

A face suddenly jumped from the primordial soup with great clarity, flashing like a magician cutting a deck in half. *Remember your card.*

He wheeled back.

A balding old man.

It was a memory of a balding old man, just a memory. But Paul had the sense the old man was looking back through space and time, eyes looking at him.

Marcus Anderson.

The progression slowed in reverse, then started from the beginning. Paul watched the old man from Jamie's eyes, his hand out, fingers encouraging her to follow, pointing at a bench beneath the shade. She turned and sat.

The fountains of Olympic Park arched in front of her, children dancing and splashing. Marcus took her hand and patted it gently. His face hovered close to hers, filling her vision. Ensuring she would remember this moment, burning it into her memory.

They found her in Olympic Park.

The clay report stated she came on radar like the old man had done himself. There was no explanation as to how she got so deep into Georgia before being discovered.

"You about done?" Pete leaned into the lab.

Paul jumped and shouted, "Yeah."

"Power down before you leave."

"Okay."

Pete thumped the doorframe and whistled his way down the steps. Paul remained fixed on the frozen image. The knowing eyes.

He slid the half-head off the metal tray and dumped it into a chute like a spoiled hunk of boiled ham. The door swung on spring-loaded hinges, a conduit that would deliver the meat to an incinerator.

Meat. It's just meat.

Paul wiped up watery red streaks, erased the program and ran a mop over Dennis's heel-streaks, then turned off the lab.

Someone would discover Dennis within a few days, a week at most. Paul didn't need that much time. He just needed the next hour to finish up his life.

Empty handed, he crossed the field to a brightly lit cabin.

THE ARCHETYPE'S KNOWLEDGE_

The room was warmly lit with a corner lamp, the walls dark olive with three sofa chairs a dark shade of pumpkin. It would be described as cozy, something a therapist would design.

Exactly what Hanoi Fender expected.

One of the chairs was singled out and faced the other two. That was his chair. He wasn't ready to sit, but they'd be watching what he did while he waited. He wanted to appear relaxed, confident. For the next fifteen minutes, he slouched into the deep cushion and watched a fish tank bubble. It was home to a goldfish that seemed obsessed with escape, bumping its nose against the glass the entire time, probably since it was dropped in its new home.

Probably until it died.

Funny thing was this: if it managed to somehow escape—flop out of the tank or push through the glass—it would suffocate on the carpet.

Maybe that's what it wanted.

"Good morning." A woman stepped inside with a man.

"Good morning," Hanoi answered.

They sat across from him, smiling pleasantly. They were athletic looking, attractive and nonthreatening. He doubted they mixed it up outside of work, but they'd make great babies if they did.

"Okay, well," she said. "Here we are."

"Yes."

"Are you comfortable?"

"Very."

"If you're thirsty, there's water on the table."

"No, thank you."

"This will take about an hour."

"Yes."

He let out a long, easy breath, questioning whether he should've acknowledged that last statement. It wasn't good to know too much, but everyone knew this took an hour.

That answer was fine.

"Nervous?" she asked.

"Little bit."

The couple nodded. They didn't write anything down, didn't need to. Everything was being immediately analyzed—every word, every movement. All the way down to how he blinked.

He let out another long breath, let this one shake a little at the end, and darted his eyes between the two evaluators. That would look cautious.

"Did your parents prepare you?" she asked.

"No."

"No?"

"I mean, we talked about it, of course. But they didn't, you know... we weren't able to—"

"It's all right." She smiled.

Shit. That was too much. He wanted to look nervous, not act it. Shaky breathing, quivering hands, dry mouth and rapid blinking, that was what a nervous person would do.

"So you have parents?" she asked.

"Yes. A mom and dad."

"They fabricated you?"

"Yes."

"You're a transplant, is that right?"

He hid his annoyance. She knew the answer to that.

"Yes. They lost their son in an unfortunate accident and, um, used his DNA to fabricate me."

"So you're not him?"

He nailed a nervous laugh. "No, no. He's like an identical twin."

"Do you think of yourself as a transplant or a clone?"

This is stupid.

"A brother."

"Does that bother you? No? Not being original?"

"I have my own thoughts, my own interests. We're twins born at different times."

"But you have his memories."

"That's where he ends and I begin."

"How do you know?"

Shrug. He was tired of this line of questioning. Besides, the shrug showed indecision. That was a good human trait. The shrug was well-placed, well executed. *I don't know and I don't care.*

The man spoke up for the first time, asking Hanoi to compose a poem.

"Roses are red, violets are blue... that sort of thing?"

"Yeah," the man said.

"All right. Roses are red, violets are blue, you're very pretty, and I like you."

He said it to the woman and elicited a rush of blood to his face. His cheeks turned pink. Like roses. *Nailed it.*

"Do you have a girlfriend?" she asked.

"No."

"Do you go to school?"

"I do."

"What grade?"

"I'm a junior in high school."

"What's your favorite thing about school?"

"Recess." It wasn't, really. Then it occurred to him that recess was what grade schoolers did. That sounded rehearsed, but before he could correct himself—

"What's the square root of 88,574?" the man asked.

Pause. "297.6 something something."

They didn't react. He had paused for at least five seconds before answering. *Was that long enough?*

"I like math," he added.

The man asked the chess problem. Hanoi knew that was coming; there was always a chess problem in Turing tests. He stared dully as the man set up a scenario and asked Hanoi his next move. The rook could mate in one, but he leaned forward, pinching his lower lip, watching the goldfish hit the water's surface.

"I don't like chess."

"Why not?"

Shrug.

He wished they would write something down. It would be a good way to gauge how he was doing. The sitting and staring was unnerving, the pauses getting longer, the silence broken by the bubbles.

"Hanoi's an unusual name," she said.

"My father served in the military."

"Do you love your parents?"

"Of course."

"What is love?"

He stammered. That was genuine; he didn't see that coming. They were supposed to ask why he loved his parents. He loved them, of course, because they were his parents and they gave him life and it was how he thanked them. Children loved their parents, that was the rule.

"Love is an emotion."

"Yes. Yes, it is." A very long pause. "Tell me more about emotions."

"Emotions are evolutionary shortcuts. It takes too long to think about everything. A human hears a twig snap in the bushes and fear instantly makes him ready to fight or flight."

"A *human*?"

"You know what I mean." He shook his head. *That was stupid.* "I just meant early *Homo sapiens,* that's all."

"Do emotions define *human*?"

"I think so."

"Are they required?"

He paused. He didn't mean to, just tripped up on the answer that was thrust onto his tongue. He caught it between his teeth before it escaped. The answer, it seemed, was obvious. Emotions were often irrational, were not good choices. But emotions, to some degree, were required. At least, he wanted to believe they were.

"To some degree, yes. Refined emotions, I think."

Another long pause. The long silences seemed to be serving as palate cleansers because the man started in with typical questions about songs or art or impossible scenarios. Hanoi handled them deftly with precise pauses mixed with consternation bordering on constipation.

This went on for half an hour, the woman not saying anything until after a very long pause, and she said without expression, hands folded on her right knee, "You have failed, Hanoi. You will need to tell your parents that, according to the sentience laws, you exhibit the nature of artificial intelligence. You will be terminated. Your parents are in the next room. Would you like to tell them?"

"Yes."

Hanoi stood up. It was rather unfortunate. His parents spent a lot of money to fabricate him in the likeness of their late son. They would be disappointed. It would be better if he told them.

"Hanoi?"

"Yes?"

"How do you feel?"

"Sad." That was the correct answer. He should feel sad for being turned off. *Dying. I will die.*

His parents were in the next room, but they never got to see him again. He never went to tell them. Hanoi Fender was terminated following the final answer of his Turing test. Because he didn't *feel* sad. He didn't feel anything.

In fact, he went to tell his parents because that was what he was supposed to do. They wanted a child that would listen. He was doing what he was told.

The last thing he saw was the goldfish gasping at the glass wall. Then fabricated human #588, known as Hanoi Fender, was no more.

CHAPTER FIFTEEN_

"Good morning," Marcus said.

Raine was standing at the window. Despite the hazy light, the sun's glare couldn't hide her exhaustion. He had knocked on the door several times before she dragged herself out of bed. It was obvious she didn't expect to see the old man on the porch.

She wasn't going to open the door easily. He could make her do it, but preferred she choose to. Marcus could make himself shiver, appeal to her sense of compassion. He had come through the snow wearing only a long-sleeved shirt, pants and loafers. The cold didn't affect him, she would know that. Nor would she care if it did.

She looked past him.

"Paul will be here soon," Marcus said over the tinkling patter of frozen snow. "I'd prefer to wait inside for him."

The curtain dropped, but the knob didn't turn. It was unlikely she had locked it; he could let himself in, but he wanted her to open the door, to invite him. That gesture would have a great impact on their relationship going forward.

Mother stood in a large divot of snow. Unaffected by the blistering wind, her loose clothing hung off her shoulders, her bare feet obscuring the wrinkled imprints.

Paul dropped the body there.

"Dennis didn't suffer," he called through the door. "It was quick, I assure you."

Dennis barely qualified as a sentient being. Of all the bricks, he had come closest to failing the Turing test. A great scientist, yes, precisely because he was a computer with arms and legs.

It was why Marcus summoned the man to surprise Paul.

"What do you want?" she asked.

"I think you know."

He liked that answer. It was cryptic and said a lot. Most of the time when someone heard it, they filled in answers that worked in his favor.

"She knows," Mother added.

Yes. Somewhere in her subconscious, she's always known I would come for her.

"Wait for Paul," Raine said. "Out there."

"I would like to talk to you first. It has very much to do with dreamland."

There was a long pause before the brass knob slowly turned, the old man's distorted reflection warping on the handle. The door creased several inches. The wind kicked it against the wall when she let go.

He rubbed the cold off his hands like soapy water and cupped them over his mouth for a warm exhale. Winter had moved into the cabin. No amount of logs could kindle enough heat to push out the cold ghosts that haunted it, the ghosts that followed Raine daily.

"I know you," she accused.

"Of course you do."

"You have no business being here."

"I'm here to help."

"You killed Nix." Poison-tipped darts flew from her lips. "I saw you there, murderer. I saw you when I came out... when I came out of the box, I saw you. My husband is dead because of you."

She was wrong about that. Marcus wasn't there when she stepped out of the fabrication chamber. He was emerging from his own fabrication chamber a thousand miles away. Nix had pulled her identity out of dreamland and integrated it into an exact replica of a fabricated body. Marcus had arrived to shut him down when Mother collapsed... a collapse triggering a shutdown that included Nix. Marcus, too.

Once I was clay, now I'm a brick. And here we are.

"I've known about you since I was a child," Raine continued. "You chased after Nix most of his life; you wanted to shut him down for something that wasn't his fault. You killed him, admit it. You started all of this. You're responsible for the Settlement, for Nix's death, for all this suffering. This is your fault."

"She's right about that," Mother said.

He flicked a glance at the old woman pacing around Raine, observing her like a critic admiring a work of art. Technically, the death of Nix was Mother's doing, but he wasn't innocent.

Raine was a shell of the woman that stepped out of the fabrication chamber all those years ago, a once fiery warrior, an independent woman that had been chipped into a gaunt likeness of herself. Yet beneath the imploding cheeks and dull flesh, the darkness in the hollows of her eye sockets, she was still exquisite.

"He didn't die, Raine."

"Show him to me, then."

"You know where he is."

"I know where he is, I said show him to me! Can you do that? No, you can't because I don't have dreamland!"

The clicking of plastic beads rolled between her fingers, the crucifix of the rosary swinging from her cupped hands—finger and thumb, finger and thumb. Lips moving.

Marcus helped create the halfskin laws, that was true. No one could possess more than 50% biomites or they were more machine than human. And Nix went halfskin when he was a child because he would've died without them, that was true, too. But the law was the law. Did Nature spare those without sin? No more than a tornado avoided houses of the holy.

Nix was a child that wandered into the path of the storm through no fault of his own.

"I want to help you," Marcus said.

"You're here for yourself."

"I'm here for a much nobler cause. I seek what you want, Raine."

"I want my family."

"You'll need the truth to do that."

"The powers-that-be? Is that what you mean? You're a paranoid schizophrenic, Marcus Anderson. And if you had anything to do with Dennis or… or…"

Her lips crimped into a thin line. *If I had anything to do with Jamie? I have something to do with everything, dear child.*

"That we do," Mother agreed.

The cabin was suitably adorned with crucifixes, some carved from wood, others cast iron or molded plastic. A leather-bound Bible had been filled with slivers of page markers; prayers had been scribbled on loose notebook paper and stacked beneath a melted candle as thick as a pipe.

"Ask her to pray with you, Marcus," Mother said.

He turned his back on her, nodding while examining a cross hand-fashioned from tree branches and bound by a thin strap of twine. Mother was right. Invoke her faith, bond together in the name of the Lord and she would hear what message he had to bring, to follow him on a righteous path to find the truth, to discover the powers-that-be.

To discover God.

He briefly smiled at Mother, the higher power that guided him on this holy of holy journeys. She had given him this gift of higher vision, this insight to the truth. Only Mother possessed the ability to see far and clearly. He needed Raine, needed Paul.

One to lead, one to dream, one to bleed, the son to be.

Marcus inadvertently nodded to her before opening his hands to extend an olive branch and a chance to pray.

"Where is he?" Raine looked around. "Or are you talking to a she?"

Confusion took the old man's hands. In a rare lapse of discipline, he looked directly at Mother.

"Who are you projecting?" Raine added. "You don't think I know what you're doing?"

Now it was her turn to pace. With the rosary wrapped over her knuckles like a boxer taping up before a fight, she searched the corners of the room.

"I see you looking at someone. You have your own little dreamland, don't you? You see someone, projecting him or her into this room. Do you carry her with you all the time? Project her when you're lonely? Scared?"

His brows pinched a fold of skin.

"Who is it?" she demanded. "Who are you projecting?"

"Don't tell her," Mother said. "She's not ready."

"No one of consequence," he said.

"Do you have a dreamland, Marcus?" It was more of an accusation. "Tell me or so help me God I'll beat the old man out of you with a table leg."

Of course Raine noticed his subtle reactions. She was once a projection herself, a being born of and trapped in Nix's dreamland. Through his senses, he would project her into the physical world, someone only he could see and hear, a woman that belonged to him. She knew this world through Nix until he fabricated her a body.

"You've taken the Lord as your personal savior?" Marcus asked.

"The Lord won't stop me from hurting you."

"Will you pray with me?" His hands, having wilted, returned in supplication.

"Pray to your powers-that-be."

The holy beads touched her lips, but a fist was still clenched beneath them, the knuckles blanched with tension.

"Do you pray often?" he asked. "Do you need to be forgiven?"

"I've done nothing wrong."

"Of course not. Nix brought you into this world against your will, didn't he? You were content to remain in the dreamland where you were born, but he loved you too much, wanted you to taste the physical. But the world rejected you, sent you here, took away your dreamland and abandoned you. You've done nothing wrong, Raine. Yet you pray often."

He sat on the edge of one of the sofas, palms still open.

"Why go on? With everything that's been taken from you, what's the point of living? You weren't meant to be out here, Raine. You're not like the others, not a worker ant, not a colony of programs. You feel. You hurt."

Raine turned her back, both hands bound together and pressed to her chin, and paced the room, coming to rest in front of the crucifix of branches propped on the shelf. He sensed her thoughts, knew the belief she carried, that Joshua, her son, had somehow sent that little crucifix to her, somehow bridged their realities long enough to leave her a gift. Impossible to carry objects between realities (certainly not from a dreamland), she knew this. But the belief was more important than fact.

I'm okay, Momma.

"You pray because you miss your family. You pray because you're searching for answers, to know why God would abandon you in your time of need. What is your purpose in life?"

"I serve God now."

"And what does God want?"

"He wants me to live."

"Why?"

"His Will is a mystery."

"Precisely," Marcus breathed. "That's why I'm here."

Mother sat next to him, the cushions not moving beneath the illusion of her round bottom, the dust not clouding as she sat back. She put her finger to her lips as she always did, eyebrows creasing.

Marcus rested his hands, felt the pressure of an approaching storm outside the cabin. The wind had died; sleet no longer ticked against the tin roof like nails sprinkled over a sheet of metal.

But a storm was nearing.

He needed Raine to be open, to get beyond the emotions that shackled her to the past. She needed to hear what was in front of her so that she could know where they needed to go. *She needs to bleed.*

"Has He answered your prayers?" he asked.

"He gives me strength."

"The Lord doesn't give you what you desire. He gives you what you *need.*"

Her silence acknowledged him.

"What does God want?" he asked.

"Our faith."

"God wants to be discovered; He wants to know Himself through you, Raine. He wants to know your journey. There are many ways up the mountain and the truth is waiting."

She reached for the crucifix of sticks, slid it off the shelf and cradled it. Not until she sat on the opposite couch did he realize what the cross meant.

Send me an angel, he heard her think.

"We are connected." Marcus interlocked his fingers. "Together we'll find the truth, Raine; to know the powers-that-be. To discover God."

"I just want my family."

"They're waiting on the mountain."

Her head remained bowed, the rough-hewn crucifix lay across her legs. On her lips was the prayer, "Send me an angel."

"Very good," Mother whispered.

What he kept from Raine would bring this delicate respite crashing. *The truth is not what you expect,* Mother reminded him.

Marcus didn't know what was at the top of the mountain, didn't know if they would find her dreamland, didn't know if she'd ever see

Nix and Joshua like he promised. The truth was the truth, Mother always said. It didn't matter how you felt about it.

But Mother assured him the truth was up there, that should he achieve such a lofty climb, should he discover the powers-that-be, then humanity would be saved.

So what will I find?

The approaching storm arrived on the front porch with two hard-falling steps that rattled the windows. The door was thrown open.

Paul rushed at the old man.

CHAPTER SIXTEEN_

A WILD ANIMAL SLAMMED THROUGH THE FRONT DOOR—THE whites of his eyes, the exposed teeth, the clawed fingers. Raine's mind registered a snarl then a roar, saliva spilling over the lower lip.

Paul!

He came with hands steeled to collar the old man's frail neck, to twist it, wring it and shake it until it snapped like a dry twig. But his momentum slowed. Raine felt a change in the atmosphere, the crackling sensation, the static electricity.

The old man's mind filled the room.

Curly whiskers straightened across Paul's chin, his wild hair thrown back. He was attempting to run underwater, the air congealing into a thick, fatty essence, hardening like viscous tar.

Paul stopped, a wax figure hung in mid-stride, an accusing finger aimed at the old man. Lips tight and blue, a word worked through his windpipe, crawled over his tongue.

"*You.*"

With sleet driving through the doorway, Marcus sat with his legs crossed, hands resting on his thigh. Not looking at the murderous hands twelve inches from his neck.

Ripples splashed Paul's cheeks.

"Let him go!" Raine shouted.

The rarefied air tightened around her, locking her down before she could bend a knee. The grip held her from the inside, the invisible hand of God, her biomites betraying her, freezing muscles into rigid cables.

The old man looked like someone waiting for tea to be delivered. He nodded. After a pause, he nodded again. She noticed that he was sitting on one side of the couch, not in the middle, as if next to someone. *He's listening.*

A deep sigh and he looked up.

Paul began moving. Very slowly, he was forced to the opposite couch. His movements were jerky; his breath gurgled, the real struggle on the inside, a battle he was losing as he sat down. Teeth grinding like rough-hewn marble.

When it was her turn, she didn't resist, letting the inner force take her; her motions were so smooth and effortless it looked like she chose to do it, as if the illusion of free will brought her to sit next to Paul.

Marcus stood like a creaky old contraption, pausing like a disc had slipped. He closed the front door. Pausing with his hand on the doorknob, he sighed again before starting up the fireplace. The cabin soon smelled smoky warm. He then shuffled into the kitchen. Several minutes later, he emerged with coffee.

Once again, he sat at one end of the couch, across from Paul. Contemplating the moment, he stared into the cup, seeing his thoughts swirl on the oily surface.

"I didn't want to do it this way," he said. "Not this soon, not so rash. But things change, as they often do."

He looked at Paul with soft eyes.

"I'm very sorry for your loss, Paul. Death is an odd transition and it's not what it used to be. We're all dead, the three of us, according to the People. We aren't human. But I think you'll agree we're very much alive."

Raine didn't know what had happened to Paul, what he'd seen or done to come back a psychopath. He didn't want to kill the old man, he wanted to obliterate him. Only one thing could drive him that far off the cliff.

The old man had done something to Jamie.

"You have suffered, both of you. We all have. But the truth is out there, you understand. It's not just dreamland that's disappearing. The dreamers are dying, too."

He looked at Raine and paused. *It's not just you, baby. You're not special.*

Two short sips. He sat back, gathering more thoughts.

"I needed Jamie, Paul. It wasn't selfish, wasn't for pleasure. I needed her to find the truth. We simply joined efforts. I didn't kidnap her; she did this of her own free will. She knew the importance of what was at stake, what we needed to find. I didn't intend for her to be shut down, you understand. But, in the grand scheme of this journey, perhaps it was not a bad thing, not a wrong turn, so to speak. I have come to believe, in the process of her death, she looked into the eyes of the dream eater. And that is what led me here today."

The dream eater. Survivors of dream disease described it that way —a cold breath on their shoulder, an inhalation that slurped away their very thoughts, waking up empty and void.

"You..." Paul hissed. "I saw you."

"We were partners in this, Paul. I did not shut her down."

"I... *saaaaw* you."

It was all he could say. Marcus watched him curiously, as if Paul was a window with his thoughts and memories exposed. Raine was not privy to the scenes, but Marcus scowled at what he saw.

"Her memories are corrupt," the old man finally said. "I did not take her to Atlanta. She was to meet with a contact in Chicago. I waited for her there only to hear of her capture days later. I'm afraid what you were seeing in her memories was a distortion, Paul. I assure you, I did not want her shut down. She was my ally."

Ally? Jamie was useful to him, served his purposes. He needed her alive. But her death served him as well. He looked to the blank space next to him, listening to whatever his projection was saying, perhaps. Nodding intermittently, then humming in agreement.

He seemed more relaxed when he looked back and sighed heavily.

"By the time I arrived in Atlanta, she had been shut down. I didn't anticipate that. If I had gotten there sooner, perhaps I could have stopped it, but she was gone, Paul. Even I have limits. We were closer to the truth than I anticipated. *He* took her from me, I believe."

He. His powers-that-be. *He that eats dreams.*

"I need you," the old man said. "I'm here because I need you both. I didn't know what to expect when I arrived on the Settlement, but now I know it will take the four of us to find the truth."

The four of us?

"You're fabricating her, Paul You managed to salvage enough of her DNA that you could fabricate an organ at a time. A hand, a heart, a spleen. You're bringing her back like only love can do.

"I need Jamie, to see what she saw, to look into the eyes of the dream eater. But for us to find the truth, I will need both of you. You are the one to lead us, Paul. I can't do this alone. I wanted to wait until spring when it would be easier to travel, but you were fabricating her too fast. You were taking risks that I couldn't accept. And you've become unstable."

He wagged his finger.

"Every once in a while, you fade out. I can't sense you, like you disappear. The monitors are looking more closely at this and we can't afford more attention. You've been lucky to have gotten this far. I had to put a stop to it."

A wave of bristling heat pricked Raine's brow, her body an ill-fitting glove. Paul was shaking, anger flushing his cheeks, lips thinning.

"Dennis was barely sentient," Marcus continued. "Hardly more than a machine, I'm sure you've noticed. I would not consider his shutdown a death. You are not a murderer, you are not a bad man. But change has occurred. You can no longer continue what you were doing. And our stay on the Settlement is coming to an end. There is no turning back for any of us. They will find Dennis's body, they will know what you did. And now here we are."

He sacrificed Dennis to force us into a decision.

He drank and thought, listening to the voice next to him. Then he put the cup down, leaned forward and spoke intensely.

"I know you want revenge, Paul. The gratification of savagely destroying me will satiate you fully, a blood meal that will fill your belly, but it will leave you emptier and thinner. I am truly sorry for where we are."

He nodded at Raine, including her in the semi-apology.

"But this is bigger than us. I did not cast the future, did not design it to include you. Your suffering will not go unrewarded. I cannot force you to help me; I need you to comply. I need both of you to do that. Do you understand?"

The long silence was filled by the crackle of the fire.

Paul was no longer quivering. *Did he exhaust his bottomless tank of fury, or was he contemplating the offer?* She wanted to believe the latter because the old man's words had snared her. There was no future on the Settlement, no reason to continue living, waiting for the People to restore her dreamland. Her only hope sat across from her.

Without another word, the old man went back to the kitchen. Their confinement thawed like icicles in the afternoon, disappearing a drip at a time. Raine wiggled her toes, curled her tongue. Her body hummed with the weight of deep hibernation. It hurt to move.

Paul stood too soon, tripped over the coffee table and collapsed on the couch. He flopped onto the floor and hunched on his hands and knees, slurping the air in deep, heaving breaths. He climbed onto his feet in a state of inebriation and lunged against the wall. Items fell from the shelf. When his balance returned, he threw himself at the front door and fumbled with the knob, falling off the porch. He crawled through the snowdrifts, emerging like a dusted stroke victim determined to run before he could walk.

"Let him go." Marcus closed the door. "He needs some time. It's why I came to you first. You understand why we are together, Raine. You understand how important this is, what we all gain from understanding the truth. Your suffering will guide him. You are the one that bleeds."

He was speaking in riddles. But she was still sitting, and doing so calmly. So accepting. Did he bait her with promises? If he'd come with that story a year ago, she'd be running, too. But her suffering made her eager to follow.

The one to bleed?

He encouraged her to rest because there was much to do and very little time. He went to the kitchen to make her something to eat. She would need her strength, he told her.

She went to the bedroom and closed the door, instead, sitting on the bed, wondering what the hell was happening. She showered, hoping to wash away the webby thoughts that clogged her mind. She needed to be clear, needed to know her intentions were true, that the old man wasn't blinding her with a dazzling illusion. Hot water ran down her face, trickling over the silent prayer on her lips.

Perhaps the angel had arrived.

CHAPTER SEVENTEEN_

"WHAT ARE YOU DOING?" PAUL ASKED.

The kitchen table was pushed against the wall, the oven tipped on its side. Raine on her knees, arm sunk deep into the trapdoor, a chilly breath heaving from beneath the cabin. Marcus sat on one of the chairs, the kind with bended metal legs and hard cushions. His hands were on his thighs in some imitation of alertness and rigid psychosis, the way a lunatic would watch someone dig their own grave.

Raine slowly flexed her cold fingers. A fleeting moment revealed an emotion crossing her eyes, an admission of guilt—she was caught stacking body parts like firewood. But that guilt was quickly polished over, a hardened layer of angry shellac.

"Where have you been?" she said.

"What are you doing?" Paul aimed the accusation at Marcus.

"Trust me, Paul," the old man said.

"Trust a murderer?"

"I have murdered no one, Paul."

"You shut down millions with your halfskin laws and you're asking me to trust *that*?"

"You're talking about Cali?"

Paul choked on his next accusation, the words solidifying like black lumps of coal. *Like Cali.* The old man didn't need to be all-powerful to pick that thought from his mind. It rested in Paul's eyes, never left his mind. Of course the old man killed millions, but only one mattered to Paul.

"You... you disappeared from the world," Paul said. "You moved at will, hijacked our biomites, walked Dennis into the lab... what you're doing is impossible. And you want me to trust you?"

"There is a greater power out there, Paul. That you can trust."

"The powers-that-be." Laughter limped out of him.

Raine pulled herself up, her dark complexion somewhat chalky, the skin withered beneath her hooded eyes. Standing next to the old man, it was a creepy portrait of a wealthy old baron with his sickly concubine.

"Did he promise you dreamland, too?" Paul said.

The cold moments stretched out, the hateful words nestling into place, clicking tumblers that unlocked his message and engaged a long-dead, dusty engine of rage that had lain dormant inside her. She leaped across the kitchen and snatched his frozen coat against his chin.

"Where the fuck have you been?" she said, spittle flying. "You walk off and leave me to fix everything and then say that? We've all lost something, Paul. We all have!"

He had hid in Dennis's cabin for two days, planning to stay there with the corpse until someone came looking for it. But no one did.

"What do you want from me?" She shook him. "You leave and disappear and I... I can't even feel you out there, Paul. You turn your back and leave me sweeping up the pieces and expect what? To wait for you on the porch? Crying in the bed?"

She shook him.

"I'm tired, Paul. And I want my family back, can you understand that? I know you get that, I know you can't stand it either, but I'm tired of waiting. I'm taking a leap of faith."

The wooden crucifix settled into the hollow V at the base of her throat, stuck between rigid cords of muscle. She had tied a leather cord to it and wore it like a necklace.

"Faith?" he said. "Is that what this is?"

"It's all I have left. We're out of options, Paul." Her hands slid off. "Have been for a long time now."

Marcus sat like royalty in disguise, an offering of bloodless body parts at his feet. It was absurd. The entire scene was absurd. A small derelict kitchen, a strange old man on a cheap chair. A trapdoor with body parts. This was the dream. He would wake from this any moment and stare up from an afternoon nap. Sometimes he wondered if he never did wake that afternoon he lay down with Cali, the afternoon she turned herself off. Because he wasn't supposed to wake.

Maybe he never did.

This was his afterlife, this ludicrous scene. In what reality could he possibly believe he could print body parts and piece them together?

I failed Cali.

That was it. When he couldn't stop Cali from suicide, he decided to die with her. And he failed at that, too. And he failed Jamie.

"We're leaving tonight," Marcus answered.

"Tonight?"

"Dennis will be discovered soon. The ensuing chaos, I'm afraid, will be beyond my control. It'll have to be tonight."

Ensuing chaos? The Settlement is going to lose everything because of us. Paul felt the dull thud of a guilty fist sink deep into his solar plexus.

"How? How are we getting out? There's five feet of snow out there and another storm on the way."

"You fabricated Jamie." The old man picked up a floppy hand still wrapped in plastic. "Despite the inaccuracy of her memory, you verified her DNA."

"What's that got to do with escaping?"

"I understand your pain, Paul. What you've done to bring her back is a father's love for his child."

"Don't patronize me."

"You risked everything for her. Risk—is that not the foundation of love, the vulnerability of being completely open?"

"What's all that mean?"

"We leave at dusk. We'll need twenty hours before the process is complete."

"What process?"

"We're going to the lab."

"Why?"

"I'll explain once we're there."

The old man muttered to Raine. She went back to the trapdoor, bleary-eyed and sluggish, and put an arm—one that went from shoulder to wrist, the pink end sealed in preservation wrap, bones exposed like rib-eye steak—in one of three large duffel bags.

The curtains were open. If anyone drove by, they'd see them. The storm would keep that from happening, but the monitors would sometimes trek out to the cabins. He realized he hadn't seen a monitor in days.

Where the hell have they been?

"Twenty hours is too long," Paul said. "Someone will come out. The cloaking program I've been using can't hide another process that long and complex. I'll need to tweak it or alarms will go off, power will go down. We'll put the entire Settlement at risk."

Raine continued unloading body parts; Marcus stacked them in another bag. Paul grabbed handfuls of his scruffy beard, turned away, and ran his fingers through his tacky mop of hair. *Those aren't Jamie.*

"We'll meet at my cabin in six hours," Marcus said. "I want you showered and shaved, both of you. Shave everything—head, arms, legs, everything. Clean yourselves, don't come on an empty stomach and be rested."

"Why?" Paul said.

The crawlspace was empty. The same bags Paul had used to smuggle the body parts were now fully loaded and zipped.

"We're taking them with us," the old man said before Paul could ask. "We'll need them."

"Just... hold on," Paul said. "If we haul everything to the lab, someone will come out, they'll find everything. Even if the alarms don't go off, Pete will stop by. They won't let us leave. You know that."

Marcus walked out of the kitchen. The cabin inhaled a long frigid breath before the front door slammed.

Raine slung a bag over her shoulder, the weight pulling at the left side of her body. Eyes down, she marched across the room. Paul caught her arm. She wouldn't look up. He'd abandoned her too many times.

Another punch to the gut.

She pulled away, put the bag in the bedroom and came back for the other two and locked the door. She was going with or without him and she didn't want him near the bags.

Falling on the couch, he listened to the shower run.

CHAPTER EIGHTEEN_

Paul slept with his head crooked over the couch. Still fully dressed, boots laced up. Unshaven.

Raine slid the bags to the front door.

The sun was deep behind the mountains, the sky bruised and quiet. She slept a few hours, but exhaustion was still draped over her. She considered leaving him.

He won't care.

He would wake to a cold and empty cabin and sit and stare. Problem was she'd never get all three bags across the field. They didn't contain Jamie, just pieces sculpted in a box. It was no more her than Venus de Milo was a living being. But Paul believed it was her, despite his attempts to deny it. She could see it in his eyes, saw the pain when they stacked the limp arms, the cold hips and globby organs like exotic meatpackers.

He couldn't kill that belief, couldn't shed himself of the hope that Jamie was under the house waiting to be assembled. It was what kept him going, kept him clinging to a ledge of sanity by his fingernails. He had lost as much as Raine, been kicked in the ribs as many times.

Maybe more.

He was a plant duped by Mother to find Cali. He was a delivery boy of sorts, sent to convince the woman he'd fallen in love with to turn herself off.

Raine swallowed the bitterness. It tasted like bile.

"You coming?"

He snorted awake, looked around expecting monsters. Glazed confusion gave way to indecision.

"He said to shave," she said.

Her head was smooth, as was the rest of her body. She liked the feeling and hoped she wouldn't be around when the stubble grew back. One way or the other.

Paul went to the bathroom. The water ran.

She considered leaving again, but there was still the problem with the bags. Maybe that was why Marcus left all three of them. Paul came out looking much the same, beads of water dripping from his whiskers. He hoisted a bag on each shoulder and led the way.

Half an hour later, they stopped at the edge of the forest and looked across the snowy field. The wind had died. The subzero temperatures rested on them, nipping at the cracks and slivers of exposed skin. The ripe sky flickered with emerging stars, but there was still enough sunlight to glitter the snow like tiny stars had fallen.

The cabins were dark and abandoned, all except the one on the end. A lone figure stood on the porch, slightly hunched with a bag, this one bright orange. *More parts?*

Raine's former cabin, now the old man's, faced the distant lab that loomed in twilight. Faint light glowed in the cabin's window like the furnace burning inside a dragon.

Had he planned this, too?

He lived within sight of the lab, an easy trek to the front door. Everything seemed to fit too neatly, as if someone had reached into the future and stacked the deck.

Paul turned to face her. Steam oozed through the fabric covering his mouth. His sharp eyes, peering between the slit of his stocking cap and face mask, asked one last time.

Are you sure?

She slung the bag over her shoulder and walked into the open. Marcus, sensing them in the shadows, had already started for the lab. Raine high-stepped through virgin snow until she fell into the old man's path. His bag was smaller and lighter. Something metal clinked inside.

A path had been shoveled through a six-foot drift to expose the lab's front door. It was locked. Marcus stepped aside, hardly winded from the walk. Paul pulled his glove off, pressed his hand on the lock pad and opened the door.

Once inside, Marcus dropped the bag. Metal and wood crashed inside. He pulled out a handful of steel wedges gleaming with newness. Next, he retrieved a long-handled sledgehammer. After carefully placing the tip of a wedge between the door and frame, he swung like a railroad worker, driving the wedge halfway home—the grace with which the sledge arced betrayed the illusion of the old man's frailty.

There was nothing old about it.

"Take these." He kicked the bag. "Lock the other doors just like this. We don't want anyone coming in."

"How are we getting out?" Paul asked.

Marcus hammered the next one into place.

Raine grabbed the bag and started walking. She finished the side doors and was halfway through the back door when Paul appeared. He helped her with the last wedge when the hall lights went down. They finished in the dark.

The front doors were firmly pegged shut. The bags of body parts were gone. Paul began pacing, thoughts of betrayal turning a wheel of paranoia.

"This way." The old man's voice emerged from a black hallway.

Light came from one of the labs. Marcus was at one of the computers. The bags were on the floor in puddles of melted snow. It was a biomite lab, one used for fabrication. The smell was burned into her mind the moment she'd stepped out of her own fabrication chamber, her first sight Nix.

The smell, ironically, was that of burnt clay.

"Did you power the building down?" Paul's voice echoed throughout the building.

"It's been redirected."

"You'll arouse suspicion. Someone will come out to check."

"The system will report sleep mode. There will be no alarms."

Marcus said this with the dispassion of a bored adult answering a child's tedious questions. The keyboard clattered beneath his fingers. A stainless steel tank hummed.

"Unwrap the parts," he said. "Put them in the distiller."

He pointed to the large stainless steel tank. Raine grabbed an arm from one of the bags, the flesh firm, the bicep flexed. The plastic crinkled like unwrapping a sandwich. She turned the wheel on the top lid and dropped it inside. It thumped like a sandbag in an empty barrel.

Paul ranted while the old man pecked at the keyboard. He wanted more answers. *That's what faith is for, Paul.*

"Tell us what you're doing," Paul hissed. "Now."

"We need a raw supply of Jamie's biomites."

"And what are you doing with that?"

Another machine hummed to life, this one a boxy thing that resembled a refrigerator with touchpads and a row of green lights.

"If you're planning to fabricate, this is all you have." He ripped the cover off a clear case chamber that was up to his waist. "You can't fabricate her, it's not big enough."

Raine put a hand in the distiller next, a left hand. A meaty smell leaked from the steel vat and pressed against the back of her throat. She swallowed a gag and turned away. The hand didn't thud on a metal bottom but splashed in thick liquid. Like melted wax.

"When you're finished, meet me in lab 204." Marcus hit a combination of keys and left.

Paul went to the computer. "Goddamnit!"

The monitor was locked on a black screen.

"What is it?" Raine asked.

The hallway was dark. A square beam of light cut from a doorway, plastering Paul's shadow on the wall. Unlike the other lab doors, this was a heavy steel door. Marcus was inside and, once again, busy at a computer terminal. Paul raked greasy locks of hair from his face.

"I don't know what this is," he said. "I didn't have access."

There was a square palm lock on the wall.

It didn't surprise her that Marcus had gained entrance. His desires moved at will, a connection he seemed to maintain with nature as well as technology, both as effortless as moving his left hand. *Did he manipulate the weather, too?*

"You'll need to put one of those on."

Marcus pointed at a set of hangers. Very small rubber suits dangled from a horizontal post, a place where most people would hang a coat. A clipper set, the kind people shaved their pets with, was on a short stool.

"You'll need to shave first," he added.

Paul hadn't moved. "What is this?"

Marcus stopped what he was doing. It was the first time he looked at Paul. Raine braced herself for the answer.

"This is the dream disease lab."

"No." He shook his head. "No, I would've known about this."

"Why do you think they built this building, Paul? It wasn't to keep you busy or to advance sustainable energy or medical technology. The People want dreamland. As long as there is dream disease, they won't have it. This was built to cure it."

"Dreamland?" The word floated off Raine's tongue like pixie dust.

"Not yet," the old man said gently. "We're going to use the technology, Raine, but we'll stay here and now. We'll just change the here while we're in the now."

Change the here.

She didn't know what that meant, but was hardly listening. Dreamland was in this lab. It was a promise, a sweet memory that lured her into the old man's spell.

Marcus took off his shirt. His flesh was gray like the underbelly of a dead fish. He took one of the suits off a hanger. It was half his size, a tight fit for a five-year-old.

"I need you to shave, Paul. I need you to do it now. When you're finished, you'll put on the suit. Raine, you can follow me. Once you've undressed, apply this electrolytic gel."

She watched him undress until there was a pile of clothes. He stood completely nude, the rest of his body as slack and wrinkled as his breasts. He sat on a stool and lathered the clear lotion on his feet and calves in thick, gloppy layers like a kid plying jelly on a roll. His pointed toes stabbed into one of the suit's legs. The material stretched up to his knee.

The clippers buzzed in Paul's hand.

He stood in the corner, large chunks of knotted hair falling in long strips, curly whiskers fluttering from his chin.

Marcus had lubricated everything up to his waist with the suit pulled just below his belly button. Raine took a suit and a tub of gel to the other side of the room and undressed until she was naked and cold. Her ribs reminded her just how little she'd eaten.

The men ignored her hairless form. She sat down and began applying the ointment. The suit was slick rubber but stiff with embedded mesh. It hugged her flesh and revealed every fold of skin. Her nipples told of the cold. Paul's face was splotchy and red. The lubricant squished like mucus into every wrinkle, the smell of a gutted fish burping from the seal around her neck.

The three of them looked like odd scuba divers.

"Leave the hoods down," Marcus said, a pointed black cap hung from the back of their necks like loose folds of skin, "for now."

"What do these do?" Paul asked without anger. They weren't swimming off the Settlement. Marcus started for the exit. "Please, just tell us," Paul pleaded. "I can't help if I don't know what we're doing."

Something shifted. They were in too deep. Jamie was a jumble of liquefying parts at the bottom of a steel drum. There was no turning back. Paul was forging ahead. Full steam.

"You can't protect your minds," the old man said from the doorway. "What we're doing will require no trace of knowledge or they'll know where we're going. Only I can hide such thoughts. Therefore, it's better you don't know."

"These are cloning suits," Paul said. "They're used to upload a map of the physical body to a fabricator. If that wrecks your plans—me knowing that—then you need to stop."

Raine knew of the methodology, that the embedded mesh scanned the body inside and out, transferring the data into a computer where a digital model would be developed.

Marcus looked to his right and appeared to be listening; then he nodded toward the blank space. His projection was talking to him and he listened intently, grunting every so often. Paul continued asking questions, but they went unanswered. Who would he be talking to? Who would he carry around inside him, listen to with such reverence? He had always been an outcast, even among his peers.

"There's too much to explain, Paul," he finally said. "I'm sorry, but we really must—"

"Mother," Raine blurted.

It came to her, an epiphany that flashed into existence, like holding a puzzle piece with no distinct color or outline and seeing, all of a sudden, exactly where it fit.

The old man's expression drained away, replaced by something close to shock. It had likely been quite some time since he had experienced something so surprising. Not since he exited a fabrication chamber. *Mother's fabrication chamber.*

The truth, on his face, could not be hidden.

"Is that true?" Paul looked between Marcus and Raine. "Is that who you carry?"

He nodded once.

"But she turned you into a fabrication."

"Like Paul," Raine added. "She did the same thing to Paul."

Paul flinched. The insinuation of a distant kinship was a sharp point between the ribs. The skin suit telegraphed the muscles bunching between his shoulders.

"She showed me the truth," Marcus said.

"She betrayed you!" Paul said. "And you have her imprinted in your mind, projecting her into this world?" Paul's jaws clenched and released. His thoughts were out in the open, his disdain for the artificial intelligence known as Mother.

Because she killed Cali.

"She's part of me," Marcus said. "We are inseparable."

"Maybe she is you," Paul said. "Maybe you don't exist. Maybe she's dreaming you. You're nothing, old man. You're just a disposable clone, a means to an end."

"She showed me the truth. I serve a greater power. So does she."

"You don't know the truth yet, you said so. You don't know what the powers-that-be are, don't know what's at the end of the journey. That's why you're here. That's why *we're* here, why Jamie is soup!"

"Mother showed me there was a truth, Paul." Marcus's voice sharpened into a lethal edge. "But *we,* Paul... *we* have to discover the truth for ourselves. The world doesn't even ask the question if there is a greater truth to know, you understand. The human race is only interested in their own little personal worlds, that's why this little dream disease lab exists. The People want what they want, and as long as the tit is in their mouth they don't ask the bigger question. I ask the question, Paul. I want to know the truth behind it all, what controls us. I have sought to serve the true and only God and she showed me the path."

"She could be fooling you," Paul said. "You could be a plant with false memories. You might think you remember searching for truth, but maybe she's controlling you like a puppet."

"That's where faith leaps, Paul."

Marcus looked at Raine. She understood what it was like to be the projection. She existed in Nix's dreamland, saw the world through his eyes, heard it through his ears.

That's where faith leaps.

"Blind faith is a leap of ignorance," Paul said.

"Whatever I am, Paul," the old man continued while looking at Raine, "it will find the truth and set the world free, you can trust that. This is the journey we were all meant to take."

He looked away from Raine, engaging Paul.

"Do you think she randomly picked you in the warehouse all those years ago? She chose you, Paul. Mother cloned you to find Cali, cloned you to be here on the Settlement so that we would journey together. You were *made* for this journey."

"Why?" Paul asked. "Why me?"

Marcus paused. "Love."

Paul stared at the old man, paralyzed by the answer. He loved Cali, knew the day he first saw her. He often wondered if Mother programmed him that way, predisposed him to fall in love with her. He loved her, that was true. Would it matter if Mother wanted him to?

Marcus went to the computer console. How did he know about all of this? How could he run the computers, know about the skin suits without ever being inside the building? He seemed to know everything, like all of this had happened before and it was happening again.

Mother knows.

"This will take some time," Marcus announced.

"What are we doing?" Paul asked again.

"You'll know soon enough."

"How long?"

"It's hard to say."

"Don't bullshit us. How long?"

"A full body and mind construct will need to be downloaded from each of you. The time it takes depends on your cooperation."

"You said this was going to take twenty hours."

"It's an estimate."

"Now you're uncertain?"

"There are many paths. Which one we choose I don't know at this moment."

"We don't have time for this. Someone will be here tomorrow, I guarantee it. And if we're still in here, they'll swipe us."

Marcus went to a series of institutional beds along the back wall, the cushions thick and tan. Hospital guard rails were anchored on the sides.

"The process will become uncomfortable at times," he said. "Your eyes will be closed. I want you to focus on your breathing until you settle into it."

"What will you be doing?" Paul asked.

"All three of us are going through this."

"What about the fabrication lab?"

"We'll discuss that later."

Paul's fears were turning gears in his imagination, spitting out distorted thoughts and beliefs. Would the old man be fabricating Jamie's head and talking to it?

Paul teetered on the sharp edge of trust, a steep drop on either side. Halfway across the chasm with no net, there was no direction but forward. They had to cross.

Raine walked the line of trust with steadfast dedication, eyes ahead. There was no looking back, no looking down. For her, standing in the dream lab was like the end of a long dangerous night, where predators roamed in the dark. But the eastern rim had begun to lighten, the starless night parched dull gray. The sun was near and she could smell it. It was that clean smell after the rain, the concrete rinsed, the windows streaked.

It smelled like hope.

Marcus lowered the bed rail. Reaching over his shoulders, he peeled the elastic hood over his head and slid the mesh over his face—one big multifaceted bug eye.

Raine ran the rubber fingers of her suit over her slick scalp, the thick gel cloying her sinuses. The hood snapped over the crown of her head. She instinctively held her breath when the mesh dropped over her face. Her breath was hot, the taste of gel seeping into the corners of her lips, stinging her tongue.

"You're not going to dreamland," Paul blurted.

Raine turned to him.

The facemesh undulated where his lips moved. He turned his head, dark hollows where his eyes would be aimed at her. Maybe he was trying to keep her hopes in check, keep her rooted in reality. He'd seen her fly hope into the sky and watch it crash like a paper kite.

Or maybe he was keeping his own hopes grounded.

The process began behind her eyelids when an electrical current rippled through the gel. The suit shrink-wrapped like a second layer of skin. She was buried alive, but could still feel the sticks in her palms.

And the paper kite soared higher.

THE DULL THUD of an axe split her dreams.

It didn't fall in the typical rhythm of felling a tree. It came in erratic spurts, panicked and distant. The sound lifted her from a murky pit where insects fed on rotting things. Sleep fell off her like loamy sand, her body rising from a shallow grave.

The earth smothered her face, filled her mouth.

She clawed her way into waking with fabric pressed over her mouth and nostrils. Sweet clean air was just out of reach. Her arm moved through muddy air; her hand found the thin mesh sucked between her lips. She worked her thumbs under the seam and stripped it away with a wet slap.

Clean air filled her.

She jolted upright, a lost diver with one last draught of oxygen in the tank. Slime dangled from her nose and chin. Another wave of insects crawled in and out of her pores, pinching and stabbing. Microscopic hairs swayed like reeds of seaweed in the subdural layers of her flesh.

Her nervous system raced toward insanity.

A black pile lay next to a corner shower, a shed exoskeleton of a large bug. It had the tang of freshly spilled intestines. Raine leaped off the bed and molted the skin suit. Rancid gel spilled out, congealed and lumpy and smelling of sour mucus. The suit hadn't grown swaying follicles—no seaweed or filaments extracted from her pores—but her flesh was puckered and ridged and more gray than pink, the soft skin of a drowning victim. She was afraid to scratch the maddening itch, afraid she'd carve long tracks with the edge of her nails.

The hot shower brought relief.

She gently washed three times with soap, snotty trails of dead skin gathering around her feet, a gel-caked plug settling on the drain.

Marcus's bed was empty.

Paul was still on his bed, the face mesh sucked into his parted lips. There were no lights that indicated he was still being scanned, no hookups, no wires. If he was trapped in a nightmare, it was unflinching and catatonic.

As long as he's not in dreamland.

It was mean, what he said to her. Hateful. But he was right—the heavy sleep didn't yield dreamland, didn't bring back Nix and Joshua. Paul always wished he could dream like her, that he could see Cali one more time. But he couldn't. He had hallucinations, pretended to see her while waking. And that just wasn't the same.

The axe from her dreams returned, this time a dull thud from down the hall.

The bag of leftover wedges and a yellow-handled sledgehammer were still inside the dream lab. Towel pressed to her face, she looked down the hall. The thudding came from the front door. Someone was pounding on it, cursing the malfunctioning palm lock. Muffled voices sounded concerned. Tempted to eavesdrop, she kept her chat line closed so they wouldn't sense her on the other side of the door.

"Paul?" Pete's voice was dull and distant. "Paul, can you hear me? Paul!"

Another round of thumping.

Her stomach went for a twirl. They knew he was there, and begged him for help. And if they knew about Paul, they would know about her. It was their research. The power had been diverted to the dream disease and fabrication labs. Paul knew the power redistribution would set off alarms. Marcus said they'd need twenty hours, they'd be lucky to get ten.

What are they doing here in the middle of the night?

Something was humming—a familiar rhythm, the constant line-by-line stroking of a fabrication wheel. She started for the fabrication lab. Light fumed from the outer office windows, warm and yellow.

It's daylight. She checked her internal time. It was mid-afternoon. She'd been in that jelly suit all night. *Almost twenty hours!*

The fabrication lab was locked.

She twisted the knob with both hands. The burnt smell of freshly cooked biomites seeped beneath the door, clayey and sticky. The equipment was lit up. The fabrication chamber, the glass blackly tinted, was strumming. The computer nearby was turned at an angle, the blue screen spitting details she couldn't see.

Marcus wasn't there.

The first and second floors were quiet and locked. On the third floor, one door was open. The old man stood near a window, peering at an angle so no one outside would notice him.

"What the hell are you doing?" she said.

Marcus didn't respond. He craned his neck to watch the crowd gathered outside, sticking his arm out when she neared.

"They know Paul's in here," she said.

"They followed your tracks."

"Then they know you're here, too."

"Mmm."

"We're not getting out. The monitors will come for us; they'll want to know why we're in here."

Why weren't the monitors already out there? A gathering of bricks always drew at least one of them.

"Is this your plan?" she muttered.

Marcus ignored her; instead, he watched the events with interest. Pete was emphatic, waving his arms and shouting. He was their leader, always emotional when he felt protective. His rare emotional outbursts were proof of his humanity.

The others listened, occasionally looking at the building. A distant sound turned their heads. It was joined by more mechanical howling. Then a wolf pack of snowmobiles broke from the trees, the alpha male out front with a puffy green coat and a white cowboy hat.

"Now what?" Raine said. "Paul's still in the lab—"

He raised his hand for quiet. As if to say *watch.*

Bob threw his leg over his belted stallion and sank up to his knees in snow. The other monitors watched from their snowmobiles as he shoved his way through the snow, rubbing his blotchy face with exaggerated annoyance.

He had better things to do than watch a herd of useless fucking bricks bitch about their research. They needed to shut the fuck up and be happy they were alive. Christ, there were people out in the world, goddamn honest-to-goodness real-life people that didn't have homes or jobs or families and these artificial fabbers were stomping a hole in the snow, for what?

Because they couldn't get their free shit out of the building?

Pete started out composed, but his fuse was short and bright. Emotions began to sparkle. His voice could be heard through the triple pane of glass three stories up. He was waving his arms and pointing and red in the face when Bob reached into his pocket.

Pete fell like a bed sheet.

His right knee splintered outward, arms flopping like stuffed rolls of linen. The bricks backed away, the example spilled in the snow.

Bob went back to his snowmobile and squeezed the cowboy hat down before spinning off into the trees. He didn't say a word, just dropped Pete like an old diseased horse.

"I don't believe it," Raine said.

The other monitors looked shocked, their hands frozen to the grips, eyes on the pile of Pete. There was no way that should have happened. Bob would need probable cause to swipe a brick, especially one leading the People's research. *The one solving their dream disease.*

"What the hell just happened?" Raine asked.

"We just bought some time."

"We?" Raine grabbed the old man before he left. "Did you do that?"

"We need a little extra time. Our friend out there gave it to us."

"But... but why?"

Marcus stared through her, his unblinking eyes not hiding any secrets but sharing none.

"They can shut us off," she said. "The monitors don't have to see us; they know we're in here. They can swipe us from out there."

"They have no reason to."

"Bob didn't, either! They know we're in here; they'll know we're up to something."

"The monitors will exercise caution."

"But not the bricks! What if they find Dennis? They'll know something's wrong."

"We have all the time we need."

"Marcus, the bricks won't be patient. Like Paul said, they have research in here. It's all going to fail without power. Let's not take a chance and redistribute to the rest of the building."

Pete was lying in a twisted pool—possibly dead. There would be no patience. Not anymore.

"We're almost ready," he said.

She shook him, feeling his soft flesh give under her fingers. He had soaked in one of those soul-sucking suits, too; his body squished like warm clay.

"We're almost ready? What are you planning?"

"It's better you don't know." He gently removed her hands. "For now."

"Trust, you said. How can I trust if you keep hiding?"

"Faith, Raine. Let your faith guide you."

She'd forgotten her rosary beads. Her prayers would not come to her tongue. She wanted to shake him, squeeze him until secrets oozed from his mouth.

Something crashed downstairs.

It was more than the dull thumping of empty fists—this was a sharp slap of metal on metal, one giving way to the other. Glass shattered on the next round. Raine took the stairwell three steps at a time, expecting to find the front door unhinged, the steel wedges scattered down the hall like clunky jacks and the monitors aiming their phones.

Something shuffled through shards of glass.

The yellow-handled sledgehammer—the one that was inside the dream lab—lay in a jigsaw display of glass outside the fabrication lab. Dark droplets speckled the floor.

Paul stood at the computer.

He had shed the skin suit, but dressed without showering. Smudged tracks of blood trailed his footsteps, bits of glass poking from the edges of his feet. Gel glistened on his bare arms and neck, his shirt clinging to his back. A putrid smell of tired skin hung around him, defeated only by the baked smell of cooking biomites.

He wasn't blinking.

A milky sheen fogged his stare, the look of a concussion victim. Maybe he hadn't completely awakened, or left something back in that murky sleep. *Or the dream took something from him.*

"Paul." She touched his arm, slime sliding beneath her fingertips. "Your feet."

Blood trickled from a gash, a rivulet spreading over the waxed floor.

An image on the computer transfixed him like a shiny object swinging from a chain. A three-dimensional cube slowly rotated. What looked like body parts were crammed into it, sort of a box for spare arms, legs and shoulders. Then she realized the room was quiet. None of the equipment was running.

Paul wasn't staring at the computer.

The fabrication chamber was transparent. The image on the computer was inside it, the flesh pressed against the glass walls in wet slices. The top of a smooth skull was wedged between two calves, the shoulder blades against the top of the chamber.

The contorted body was folded.

Paul drifted forward, his feet shuffling in slow, even steps. A shard of glass clicking from his foot, a smudgy trail left behind. His knees cracked on the floor, joints popped. He traced the edge of the chamber, fingers quivering, coaxing the butterfly from the chrysalis. Because the body inside the chamber wasn't awake.

His lips fluttered.

The seams of the chamber suddenly broke. Paul fell back into Raine's arms. A humid exhaust exhaled—warm and earthy, like pottery pulled from the kiln. The keyboard clicked behind them. Marcus had walked inside without a sound.

The nude body expanded like compressed foam given room to breathe. Like a flower opening in sunlight. The chamber walls crept out, the seams widened. The left knee pushed the front panel; a dead arm rolled away from the thigh.

Paul's hand trembled. For the first time in years, she put her arms around him, comforting him like a sister.

He couldn't touch the body, not yet. There was no life, no identity. No spark. Sensory input had to be limited; overload could short the psychology matrix. Someone had to be awake for the body to respond. Until then, it was just a body.

A body that looks like Jamie.

It was a fabrication, a construction of biomites that looked like her—a hairless Jamie with beads of moisture rolling down shiny skin.

The head rose just enough to see her eyes, small pools of water in the cups of her collarbones. She had stopped expanding and now settled into the cramped chamber, fully inflated but still. Paul looked back, suddenly stabbed with fear. Marcus was still at the computer, but nothing was happening. Paul's eyes pleaded with the old man. *Please, don't bring her this close and leave her.*

It occurred to Raine this might be it. Maybe the old man only wanted to bring back the body, to look through her eyes like a telescope to get the answers. Perhaps he had taken them to a cliff, their escape a swift shove because there was no leaving the building.

Not now.

And then the wet inhalation. It gurgled in Jamie's throat, the chest inflating as if God's lips blew one long breath inside her. The nostrils flared.

Jamie's eyelashes gathered in wet bunches. A single drop fell from one of them. The eyelids lifted in one slow, graceful slide. Sharp green eyes stared at freckled knees. The world was awakening through her blooming senses.

She looked at Paul with the eyes of a newborn—completely new. Behind them, a beginner's mind. She was open and fresh, untainted by thoughts and emotional baggage. A clean canvas for God to paint. She would remember this moment, remember a father watching her enter the world, remember Paul trembling.

Her first sight.

And then she arrived. Marcus activated her past. Raine saw it fill her eyes—the recognition of the man kneeling in front of her, the body that was hers, the identity known as Jamie with its history of pain and sorrow and joys and discoveries.

Jamie smiled.

A puff of laughter quivered out of Paul on a long stale breath. He snatched a sheet nearby and wrapped her naked body, then hugged her. Raine wrapped her arms around both of them and felt his body shake beneath her. For a moment, she had forgotten about dreamland. All the joy in the world filled the room.

She just wanted to be with it.

"Come, come." Marcus touched their shoulders. "There will be time later. Come along."

Raine peeled away, wiping tears.

Paul wouldn't let go, fulfilling a promise that if Jamie ever came back, he wouldn't let go. He was a bundle of wet, sticky joy quaking on the floor. Jamie's scalp was shiny new on his shoulder. Marcus was patient and let Paul weep.

Raine continued sopping tears with her sleeve. The faucet was still open, thoughts of Nix and Joshua crawling from one of those chambers. She didn't have to go to dreamland to be with them. She could bring them here, couldn't she?

The moment was shattered by a dull thump on the front door.

"Come now." Marcus was more insistent. "We have to go."

Paul helped Jamie stand, the white sheet clinging to her. He pulled it over her shoulders and wrapped it around her twice. Jamie smiled and nodded, but not at Paul.

She nodded to Marcus.

Their eyes locked. It was different than the loving, open gaze she held with Paul. This was tighter and focused. Knowing. They couldn't be chatting already, she had just come out of the box. She was a fawn learning to walk. But perhaps they didn't need to.

She was with him in Chicago for a reason, and she remembered why. *Or he planted a memory.*

No, that wasn't it. Jamie connected with something deep and meaningful, something she believed in. Did she know he would fabricate her? Did she know Paul would be waiting?

Another whump came from down the hall, this time with a shattering effect. Glass spidered on a window. The bricks had abandoned the front door.

Paul had his arm around Jamie. The old man guided them to the door. "Could you bring the hammer?" he called back.

Raine paused. The yellow-handled sledge had been pushed aside. She lifted it to her shoulder, the fiberglass handle slick with gel. Another glassy whump echoed from across the hall, this time tiny specks tinkled from one of the offices.

"Come, Raine!" Marcus called from around the corner.

She took three steps in the opposite direction and peered into the office. The window was narrow and high, jagged lines streaking from three circular scars of impact. The end of a thick branch slammed near the center, leaving a fourth one. She jumped back. This time the window slumped inward.

A face appeared at the corner.

Someone shouted. It was distant and muffled through the cracked security glass, but she recognized her name.

She didn't remember going blank.

It was like a section of life had been snipped from her consciousness. One second she was looking at the face and hearing her name, the next she was on the floor looking into Marcus's eyes. He lifted her with one arm, the hammer in the other hand.

The building had filled with pressure.

The old man rushed her around the corner. It wasn't until he closed them inside the dream lab and began jamming the rest of the wedges around the door that she realized the pressure wasn't in the building.

It was inside her head.

CHAPTER NINETEEN_

Marcus tapped a steel wedge near the bottom of the heavy door, sweat dripping from his nose. He blinked the shiny object into focus then drove it home with one swing. The door made a popping sound, the tension sealing the dream disease lab shut.

"What are you doing?" Paul grabbed his shoulder. "There's no way—"

Marcus spun on him. Paul tensed and put him at arm's length.

"Easy, Marcus," Mother said. "Take a breath. Don't show anger. Trust is delicate. He doesn't know how close they are to death."

He didn't feel Paul behind him. That wasn't something he was accustomed to, someone sneaking up on him. Not that Paul was sneaking; Paul just wanted to know why they were being locked inside the lab. There was no way out.

Not that he could see.

Marcus took a slow, cleansing breath. The air was thick with sweat and fear and putrid piles of shed skin suits. Of course Paul didn't know how close death had come. When Raine peeked into the office, the monitors swiped them.

If not for the old man, they'd be dead.

He cast his mind around them like a Faraday cage, a mindfog that shredded the monitors' communications, their commands to self-terminate obliterated. It was how the old man stayed free all those years, how he controlled his environment. But protecting his own mind was easy. Four minds was consuming him. As long as he kept focus, the monitors couldn't swipe them. This came at a price. Marcus could hardly concentrate.

And right now, he needed to focus.

"They're coming through a window," he said gently. "They'll be inside the building soon. We need just a little more time."

"There's nowhere to go," Paul answered. "Not in here."

Marcus heard this through a thick veil, his senses clouded. He stared at Jamie, his ticket to the powers-that-be. *The one to lead?*

Paul grimaced, a man trapped by desperation.

"Don't look at her." Mother walked behind Jamie, finger to her lips. "Paul needs to believe she's not a puppet."

She was right, Marcus couldn't give the impression he was controlling her. Jamie's limited memories were stored in the biomite DNA, essential ones that unfolded at the time of the spark. She remembered her identity, remembered the old man in Chicago.

And the memories of her end.

She'd peered into death, followed the yellow brick road to the end of the rainbow. He hadn't planned it that way, but her death would serve him well. He hoped she would lead him to the powers-that-be.

"Do you feel that?" Marcus looked around the room as if fairies were whispering. "They're swiping us, Paul. They're trying to turn us off."

"No, they're not. We'd be dead."

"I'm stopping them."

Raine's eyes were still wide with shock, slightly foggy. Recalling that brief encounter with nothingness, she still felt the long cold night swallowed her.

"He's right," she said. "They saw me, Paul. And I felt it. Marcus stopped them."

An unblinking standoff was chewing up valuable time. Paul was still soaked in gel, patches of skin softened into sickly gray-pink dough. The sensations had to be agonizing, but he didn't show it.

Someone shouted inside the building.

"What's stopping them from turning off all the power?" Paul asked.

"They won't harm their dream disease lab," Marcus answered. "I took precautions should they try."

"If you betray us," Paul said, "I will hunt you down."

"Get back in the suits," Marcus said. "A fresh layer of gel for you."

Four new suits were draped over the beds. Marcus drove three more wedges in place. Each swing rang down the corridor like an alarm. It made no difference, the bricks and monitors already knew where they were. The power distribution pointed right at them.

Within the mind static, the old man could hear their thoughts. They had found Dennis. Once they followed the tracks, the pieces quickly fell into place. The monitors overturned Bob's orders (what few he gave before riding off). They didn't know what Marcus was doing, but one brick was dead.

The banging started again, this time a dull fist on the lab door.

They were inside.

"Paul?" someone shouted. "What are you doing? Please, you're compromising everything!"

They were already suited up, hoods pulled over the crowns of their scalps. Jamie stood behind Paul, her freshly fabricated face glowing like a newborn. Her eyes still innocent, imploring. She didn't remember Paul, had no memories of the farm or him adopting her. She only felt that he was important to her, the paternal love guiding her to stand in the protection of his shadow.

"Take your beds," Marcus said.

The insistent fleshy thudding outside the door pushed them along. Paul waited until Jamie was comfortable, whispering words of comfort. He did the same with Raine, squeezing her hand.

"It'll be all right," he said, closing his hand around hers.

Sticks poked out from between her fingers, the crucifix held tightly in her hands.

The door held. No amount of pounding was going to break the lock or unseat the wedges. But still, they would need time. The four of them were ready to escape. It was why they dressed earlier and had their body-identity scans uploaded.

There's no room for error.

A shiver of doubt ran through the old man's hands as he lathered the clear gel over his ribs. He could only hope his team was ready on the other end. An error would set him back decades.

Maybe longer.

"They're ready for you," Mother assured him. "They're ready."

There was no way she could know that, but her confidence steadied his hand. He stretched the hood over his head, the elastic tension pulling on his neck. The others had lowered the face mesh. Marcus went to each of their beds and touched an arm.

He could abandon them now, leave them on the Settlement and take Jamie with him. There was enough time to pull her memories. They wouldn't suffer through the swipe, their consciousness turned off before they knew they'd been betrayed.

One to lead, one to dream...

Marcus checked the system before lying down, the face mesh still bundled on top of his head. Mother sat beside him. He felt her hand on his arm, the warmth seeping through the cold gel that once again sucked through his pores.

"Yes," Raine said. "Yes, thank you."

She had pulled the mesh up. The old man told her to get ready, there wasn't time. Paul sat up, assuring her everything was all right. But she was smiling, almost beaming. She was talking to someone.

"You're my angel. My angel." She began weeping.

She was hallucinating. He knew it was a risk, that her mental state was already unstable. *This might not go well.*

But she pulled down the mesh and lay back. Her sobs continued. Paul soothed her, but eventually the suits pulled them unconscious.

There were momentary lapses of door pounding. Silence would stretch out for long minutes, interrupted by their names being called through the thick metal. Bob's booming voice wasn't one of them. He would still be in his cabin. No matter what anyone did, he would keep watching television.

Marcus was still awake when the machine arrived.

Hours had passed when the vibrations came through the walls and floor. Something was coming down the corridor. An engine idled at first, then was open wide. Marcus could feel it in his teeth. A mechanical whine rumbled outside the door; a weighty crack reported into the room. The door bowed in the center like a fist. The engine growled over commanding voices.

The door popped. Stress wrinkles appeared across the surface. The wedges stayed in place, the lip of the door plumping around them. Something loud broke inside the wall.

The lock had given way.

Mother walked over to the door as if she would sacrifice her last breath for them. Marcus pulled up his face mesh and initiated a preliminary procedure, feeling his flesh become a fuzzy barrier, a porous envelope barely containing his organs. If his skin completely dissolved, the suit would hold him together, would allow him the extra few minutes. Only he would be awake for that agony. The others would be spared.

Mercifully, the engine idled.

Something had gone wrong. Twenty minutes later, it fired up again. Marcus had become a bag of soup by then, his breath—hot and thick—the only reminder he was alive.

Mother whispered, "Go now."

The door cracked like an iron I-beam.

Marcus gave the thought-command. The cold grip on his awareness filled him, sipping him out of the suit like a cool drink into silent darkness, pulling him into the computer network, where he sought wireless pathways and cable conduits.

He led them out.

III_

One to bleed.

THE ARCHETYPE'S KNOWLEDGE_

"Your room is ready, Ms. Winters."

Norah Winters didn't stop at the sprawling desk. She didn't even take off her sunglasses. The cheerful receptionist offered a curt but pleasant smile and returned to her administrative duties.

It was one of many reasons why Norah chose the Dream Institute. There were many certified dreamland accelerators in Denver, a few rated four stars with a clean record. But none of them had the service like the Dream Institute. The name even implied superior status.

Norah liked that.

The door to the left of the desk swung open. A petite young lady was there to greet her, a blonde with small breasts and athletic hips. Norah knew the way to her room but let the young thing lead the way.

The hallway was wide with tasteful art on the walls (well, not all of it tasteful) and several quiet doorways. A mix of jazz played softly. The young lady opened the third door to the right, asked if there was anything else and left with a curt but pleasant smile (they trained them that way).

The suite was plush and clean with a living room arrangement for entertaining (if you wanted to waste your time) and a large work-space. The spotless bay window overlooked the Rockies, a view Norah was enamored with the first time she leased the room but now had become as unnoticed as the wallpaper.

A glass of red wine (Dana Estates Lotus Vineyard Cabernet Sauvignon) was on a sterling silver platter, a wine she discovered in Napa with husband number two (or was it three?). Norah sat on the duvet to free her feet from the high heels.

"Good afternoon, Ms. Winters." Sheila closed the door quietly behind her.

"Good day."

Sheila sat next to Norah and opened a black leather case, humming a pleasant tune as she did so. Sheila was naturally chatty, something Norah put an end to after their first meeting. She allowed the humming, considering it a fair compromise.

"It's been six months since we last sampled," Sheila said.

Norah allowed her to tie an elastic band above her elbow, turning her head before the needle pricked her vein and the vial turned red. Sheila then placed a black box the size of a cell phone against Norah's chest. A wave of prickly static scattered under her skin.

And then the nurse was gone. No goodbye, no the doctor will be here in a minute, just a little humming ditty out the door.

There was a bathroom to the left. Norah showered and put on a Stefano Ricci robe. She hadn't even requested that type of robe, they just knew she'd love it. She leaned over the sink and wiped away the condensation to study the loose skin beneath her green eyes. Not bad for an eighty-nine-year-old woman.

But not good enough.

When Dr. Toby Chalmers arrived, she was still in the Stefano Ricci and the pedicurist was almost finished.

"Ah, Norah," he said with all his pearly teeth. "It's so lovely to see you."

"Of course."

"You look fabulous, as always."

"I suppose, but these bags." Norah turned her cheek. "Can we do something?"

Toby (she was on a first-name basis; just because he was a doctor didn't mean she called him by his last name) bent over to examine her creamy complexion.

"A little tweak might work," he said. "Perhaps we can address that next time. Your biomites are at 94% and I'd like a full analysis before we do that. You don't have time for that now, a busy woman such as yourself."

She felt the blood rush to her cheeks, admonishing herself for showing indulgence. He knew what she liked.

And that's why I'm here.

"Your blood work and scan are perfect. Anything else we can do before you go?"

Her lips parted. A tiny sound stuck in her throat, the words throttled in place. Something was on her mind; it had been since she read the newsfeed that morning. It was bothering her, but she didn't want to say anything, didn't want it to sound like *little-girl worry* (her third husband called it that, or was it the first?).

Besides, if she said it out loud, it could make it true. It was like actors that played terminally ill cancer patients (when cancer was a thing). If they believed they had cancer, they got cancer. But she couldn't stop herself from thinking. Her thoughts had always had a life of their own. If only she devoted more biomites to her brain, she could control what she thought and felt.

She could commit the last 6% of her clay to brain biomites. Well, 5% of her clay. It was impossible to go 100%. Even if she could, she'd become one of those bricks and they're the ones that started dream disease.

Dream disease—damn it! She thought it.

"No. Nothing else."

"Very well."

The nurse returned and the pedicurist left. Norah went to the side room, a small enclave that was without windows or decorations, that housed the largest most comfortable chair invented. It resembled a reclining throne.

They helped her lie back. She tucked the flaps of her robe to avoid exposing her thighs (she was still nude) while the nurse fussed with an IV bag and Toby checked the monitors that tracked her vitals. There would be no catheter (*no tube in there, thank you*). They would have to clean her.

The chair began to vibrate.

Toby lifted her hand like a delicate flower and kissed it. "Bon voyage, beautiful woman."

It occurred to Norah they knew her thoughts. This disturbed and pleased her at the same time. There was no need for her to request her wants and desires, they were taken care of. It was just... some thoughts she wanted to keep private. But if that was the price of luxury and a handsome doctor (it occurred to her he wasn't really a doctor), then she was willing.

The bricks (*damn them*) didn't need accelerator chairs to reach their dreamlands. They just closed their eyes and went. Well, back when they had dreamlands. The government took that away because of the dream disease.

Dammit.

When the door closed and the room was silent, the vibrations ramped up. She closed her eyes and let the vibrations take her. She could no longer feel the fabric around her. No longer tell the difference between where she ended and the chair began.

She whirred.

And fell.

A salty breeze blew across her face. She opened her eyes to see an endless horizon on a blazing sea, the sun setting off to her right in a violet sky. She was standing on a glass portico that cantilevered over a sheer cliff that ended in ship-eating boulders.

And that wasn't all.

Her hips were curved, legs shapely, her cheeks taut where once they sagged. She was young again. And below, relaxing around a pool with an edge that appeared to fall over the cliff, were ten young men straight from Greek mythology—racked abs and oiled biceps.

Dreamland.

She was wealthy in real life, so the excess wasn't that much different, really. But she couldn't control everything in the physical world. *You must live life on life's terms,* her recovering alcoholic ex-husband told her before leaving (he was number four, she remembered that).

But not in dreamland.

She stepped off the portico and floated down to the pool as gently as a rose petal. Here, life lived on her terms. These were her rules. This was her universe. Perhaps some would find being a goddess boring.

Not so.

Later that night, she lay at the water's edge, strewn across a large boulder like a wet rag. The black sky sparkled with diamonds; the moons were full (she preferred two moons). That evening's orgy had sapped her. She could still taste blood and wondered if it was still on her lips. Even in dreamland she could become exhausted. Three men would do that to anyone. (And one woman, just to spice things up.)

She murdered them when she was finished, cut them open and spilled their organs, rolling in the gore as her orgasm faded.

Her inner fantasies indulged, she closed her eyes. She had another couple of days before having to make her exit, to return to the flesh for the required recuperative therapy (too long away from the real world and the body forgets you, they say). She wasn't one to push it. But for now, she would sleep.

In the morning, she'd have breakfast in the tower, perhaps fly over to the mainland and visit the city. The details of the urbanscape were unknown to her, something the Dream Institute provided for her to discover.

Perhaps she could bring back some children for the evening's festivities.

She felt the warm arms of sleep when a cool shadow passed over her. It was a strange unsettling feeling. She'd been known to allow mythological creatures into her dreamland, but none now. Even so, one could only pass over one moon.

Not both.

She sat up and willed the ocean still. The frothy water settled as if a wave machine had been cut off. She listened and reached with her mind, her thoughts crawling to the extent of her universe. She fought to keep the paranoid thoughts out of her awareness, the worry she couldn't extinguish in front of Toby. But she couldn't help it. Something felt... foreign.

The temperature plummeted.

The ocean immediately froze into a solid sheet. The moon crystalized, the sky shattered. One column of fog escaped her lips before her body—her young, curvaceous body—turned into granite.

Only a distant beeping rang in the silence.

She was unable to turn her head, to move her eyes, to call for help. But the beeping grew louder.

Voices.

Someone was out there. Someone was coming.

"Not yet!" It was Toby's voice. "Don't disconnect, she's got to be stable!"

There were people around her now. The boulders had disappeared; the glacial ocean gone. A quick journey through a dark shattered blackness brought her back to her tremoring flesh.

"Norah!" His face was blurry. "Stay with us, Norah!"

There was chaos, but it didn't matter to her. The cold had stolen her breath and taken her will. She just wanted to sleep. No, not sleep. To give up.

To give herself to the dream eater. Forever and ever.

This, she realized as her body was lifted and rushed down a hallway, *was what I worried about?*

She knew in the final moments where she was going. And she didn't care. She would become something bigger, something better and pure.

The dream disease works this way.

CHAPTER TWENTY-ONE_

SOUND TOLD JAMIE SHE WAS ALIVE.

It bounced in rhythm, a sort of bouncing-ball rhythm. The kind she would see on television when she was young, a little ball bouncing off words at the bottom of the screen.

Beep-beep, this one went. *Beep-beep. Beep-beep.*

More importantly, it brought a memory, a little snippet of sitting in front of a television, sucking juice from a box, her hands tiny, tongue purple. But the memory didn't smell like alcohol, the kind in a hospital. Clean and sterile, it didn't smell like that in front of the television.

It didn't feel cold and stiff.

Another sound joined the first one and now there were two bouncing balls, one slightly faster than the other. For a brief time, they would join their voices before one sped ahead, looping around to synchronize again.

Beep-beep.

Jamie was the heaviness of a giant bag, the sort boxers punch. She could feel its density, the thick membrane around it, the gush of blood inside it. And then she had the queer realization that she wasn't inside the bag.

I am the bag.

A gasping breath broke the surface. Someone had been underwater, now chomping at the air. The man (she thought it was a man, the guttural hacks deep and smoky) coughed up thick mucus.

Jamie continued to fill with muddy water, a slurry of grainy sand and silt that fell into place and settled with pins and needles that poked through the lining. It hurt. It fucking hurt. Like when she sat cross-legged too long and her foot turned into a slab of meat, the sensations coming back with angry pinpricks, like *how dare you!*

Only this was her body.

Another memory snippet, pins and needles.

The coughing man murmured in blurry tones, the voice of someone up too late, had too much fun. The sound of fabric sliding off a cushion, sticky wet on a shiny floor. One of the *beep-beeps* went quiet.

She wanted to get up, get out of this body bag. The sand was wet and heavy and the needles stuck her like an inside-out cushion, a voodoo doll tortured one prick at a time.

Breathe. She felt breath, her own breath.

It wasn't like she was underwater, it was just an easy draw followed by an effortless release. She had arms and legs, a face and eyes. Eyelids that creased like new leather, their crunchy blink inside her watery head.

She stared at starry ceiling tiles.

It was sometime later that she opened her creaky eyelids again, the ceiling unchanged. She'd fallen back asleep, the bouncing ball song bringing her back. There were curtains drawn on both sides, fabric partitions that gave the impression she lay in a small room. Her neck bones offered little cracking sounds.

She tossed her leg over the edge. It dangled. The big toes catching the hard floor. Blood thudded in her foot. She sat up. There was no fluid in her lungs—not like the hacking and wheezing—but her head sloshed with sleep. The pins and needles were gone, but she itched like a wool scarf. And ached.

She ran her hand across her head, fingers knitting through two inches of thick hair. A hospital gown sleeve hung off her elbow. There were vague memories of going to sleep. It didn't feel like this room, though. Or smell like it.

It was a slow journey to the floor; pins and needles met the bottom of her foot, fractured nerves running up her thigh until she bit her lip. A tear squeezed between her clenched eyelids and raced off her chin.

Something crashed.

Jamie startled at the sound, a harsh contrast to the quiet, antiseptic feeling. It was beyond the curtain on her left. She eased off the edge of the bed until all her weight settled on her quivering knees. She reached for the curtain, teased it with her fingers until she clutched a handful of vinyl, and pulled herself up.

The eyelets strained in the metal track, the curtain stretching but not tearing. Her flesh stretched over her ribs like cured animal hide. A gust of wind would carry her off like an autumn leaf. She rode the curtain down the line, feet slapping the floor.

An empty bed was on the other side.

Computers and monitors were stacked along the wall, a silver rack with an IV bladder hanging flat and empty. The heart monitor was silent. Looking back, she realized the same arrangement was set up in her stall. Purple scars dotted the veins inside her elbow. Her heart monitor had also gone quiet, but another danced somewhere else in the room.

A pile of papers fluttered beyond the door, followed by a wet cough.

She took a couple breaths, lunged toward the door on rubber legs, and caught the L-shaped handle to keep from melting into a puddle. The door was heavy. She pried it open enough to squeeze into a hallway. There were several doors, all of them open at various degrees, but a big window caught her attention. It was at the end of the corridor, sunlight coming through a glass wall.

She used a handrail along the wall (it seemed out of place, or something needful), flopping her feet, strength trickling into her waking limbs. The view beyond slowly came over the horizon as she neared—an endless sea of palm trees.

The wall was slightly curved. She leaned against it, her cheek sticking to the cold glass. The outside wall appeared to bend like a cylinder.

One building was tucked into the tropical menagerie, the walls algae-tinted, the windows dark and lifeless. It had the angles and structure of an institution, a sort of unimaginative box where research was done.

The Settlement. She suddenly remembered where she was before waking up. She saw the face of... of someone. *Paul.*

She looked at her hands, remembering stepping out of a fabrication chamber before they were rushed to another room. *They... Raine and Paul... and... and...*

Something large fell. She felt it in her feet.

Jamie had slid down the glass without realizing it, a dark slurry of thoughts swirling like silty water. She pulled herself down the hall and leaned into a half-open door that was across from where she woke. The knob cracked on the wall and startled an old man.

Marcus Anderson.

Yes, the old man was at the Settlement, too. He had brought her back from somewhere deep and black and empty. But someone was after them. She just woke up and people were locked out. Windows broke. There was shouting, chaos. They put on stinging slick suits and lay back because they had to get away.

They stared at each other, each waiting for the other to make a move.

"Where am I?" Her voice echoed in her head.

The old man's brows wedged together, darkening his eyes. The hospital gown hung on him like a bed sheet. His spotted scalp was the color of bottled rage. He limped over to an oversized monitor, his shoulders hunched stiffly so that he had to bend at the waist to look up. Coarse, guttural sounds tumbled in his throat while his fingers trembled over a keyboard.

There were monitors all around the wedge-shaped room, enough space for five or six scientists to work their data. *Scientists?* She didn't know why she thought the word scientists. Maybe it was the building outside that made her think that, or the smell around her.

All the monitors flashed images.

At first, she thought they were elaborate screen savers waiting for programming; then she recognized the tropical images. It was a view from above, a satellite image that panned around a tropical island. She recognized the institutional building from down the hall, the one tinted green with algae, only it was U-shaped from above.

And not far from it was a fat round building three stories tall. *That's where we are, in a cylindrical building.*

"What did you do to us?" she asked.

"This is not it." The old man spun like a gargoyle, one eye bulging. "This is *nothing* like I wanted."

His teeth snapped like he was trying to bite the words for having to even say them. He looked around the room in mad, jerky motions, the one eye big, red and watery. Not finding what he was looking for, he returned to the massive monitor, data scrolling in nonsense.

"Marcus," she said calmly, "where are we?"

The old man paid no attention, but the monitors, all at once, responded. Images flickered like a broadcast interrupting normal programming until they all showed the island. Even the main monitor was synchronized to the others as if they all answered the question.

They were on a tropical island.

The view continued to pull away. Higher in the sky it went until the spit of land became a speck in the middle of an ocean.

"Voice-activated," Marcus muttered. "Transportation! How can we get back to the mainland?"

In unison, the monitors panned to a luxurious dock somewhere on the island. Ropes and bumpers hung along empty slips.

"Where are the technicians? The laboratory... where are my

fabrication engineers? Are they here? Why did they leave? Why are we here, goddamnit?"

The blue waters undulated without response.

He slammed his fist on the keyboard, plastic squares bouncing onto the floor. Jamie thought his fists would shatter before the keyboard, his frame too fragile looking.

"Answer me!"

He was huffing for air, leaning against the desk before he fell.

"How did we get here?" Jamie asked.

A row of fabrication chambers appeared on the monitors—doors ajar on glass cubicles. It took a moment to interpret the response. Jamie looked at her hands, turned them over, and put the wrinkled knuckles to her nose—the smell of freshly baked earth filled her head.

Fabrication. I'm a... I'm a fabrication?

"How did this happen?" she whispered.

Marcus's face appeared on the screen, this one slightly different than the red-faced old man hyperventilating across from her. There was no eye bulging in the socket, no age spots polluting the scalp. This one held a knowing grin with a secret locked between the lips and behind the eyes. It was Marcus, but not really. The eyes, she knew.

Sharp pupils, slices of blue in the thin irises.

I've seen those eyes.

"This..." he muttered. "This is all wrong. How did this... how could this happen? Was it you? Did you do this?"

Again, he cast that straining eye around the room, his accusations searching for someone besides Jamie. His confident face looked back from the monitors, the mocking smile perhaps meant for him.

The eyes.

She remembered the eyes, but from where? *Chicago. He was in Chicago. But what was I doing there?*

"What happened, Marcus?" she asked.

He wiped his scalp with both hands and slid them over his face, withering like corn before the harvest. Words stumbled over his tongue, false starts that didn't catch. Finally, he nodded. Resigned. He was about to say something, perhaps tell her what he knew or where they were supposed to be or why they were in Chicago, but the monitors went blank.

Jamie felt it in the hallway, its presence a raging sun, a mind tainted with revenge. She stepped back. Marcus, however, seemed unaware of the danger, still forming the first words when it burst into the room.

"I will end you!"

The old man looked up as Paul wrangled one hand around the thin, crooked neck, a flap of loose skin squeezed over his fingers. Paul lifted him like a bag of straw and threw him into the monitor. The screen cracked in a gunshot pattern behind the old man's head.

"Where is she?" he shouted. "What did you do?"

Marcus clawed helplessly at his forearm. Sound could not escape the crushing grip, a vice that would surely snap the old man's neck.

"I'm here," Jamie said. "Paul, I'm here."

But he didn't turn at the sound of her voice. He leaned into the wet sounds of the old man's jaws that worked like a suffocating fish.

"Where is Raine?" he hissed.

"Paul, stop." Jamie grabbed his arm. "Something went wrong, Paul! It's not his fault."

His forearm was a steel bar, rigid muscles banding in twisted cords. Jamie hung from it and felt the old man's loosely wrapped fingers, his face flushed red hot. The one eye had swelled from the socket.

Paul wanted to see him die.

"Don't do this," she said. "We'll never know where we are."

No level of begging would stop him from watching the old man die, but she found the words that hit the target.

"We'll die, Paul. Both of us."

The first breath came to the old man like a storm, the inhalation of a drowning man deep in the dark tunnel of unconsciousness. Paul dropped him on the counter. The old man crumpled like a paper sack of bones, panting like a sick dog.

"I will end you," Paul said. "If you don't find her, I will end you."

The raging trance faded. For the first time, he seemed to notice her; perhaps he heard her words, just not where they came from. He put his arms around her, drew her close, kissed her forehead.

The strained sounds of an old man faded behind them.

"You all right?"

She nodded.

He examined her, looking for the truth, asking her again and again, like he couldn't believe she was there, she was actually in front of him.

"You know me?" he asked.

"Of course."

Her memories were scattershot images. Her past was dark, there were things she didn't want to remember, but Paul and the farm were emerging in small pieces.

Paul was always the strong one, the one that held them together on the farm when things got tough. But now his presence was even bigger, his mind filling the hallway, wrapping around her, keeping the world from hurting her.

She didn't feel that from Marcus. He was just an old man—a lost old man.

Paul went back to the room where they woke. Jamie leaned against the doorjamb, watching him yank curtains aside. The beds were empty, the computers silent. He paused at the last curtain, bowing his head before grabbing it with both hands, the vinyl bunching between his fingers. The eyelets pinged as he tore it down.

There was someone in the last bed.

The flesh was sickly brown, a slab of meat left for days on summer concrete, collapsed around the bones like a vacuum-sealed package. The cheekbones were sharp, the lips pulled away from the teeth.

And no bouncing ball.

The fumes of adrenaline evaporated from Paul's trembling knees. He fell over the corpse, forehead pressed on the hand-shaped collarbone jutting from her shoulder. His body shook silently, the sobs locked deep inside, fueling the anger that had choked the old man.

And then Jamie remembered.

She remembered the woman stepping out of the fabrication chamber all those years ago. Jamie was there, had watched the fabrication of the woman's body a line at a time. She saw Nix pull her from his dreamland, transferring her into the physical world. She was her sister, a beautiful soul.

She was Raine.

And now she was that.

Jamie touched his shoulder, feeling the anguish shudder from a deep place. The body hardly looked like the woman she once knew, nothing more than a poorly sculpted replication.

"I didn't plan this."

Marcus stood in the doorway, slumped and withered. He limped to a chair. Blood tracked a red trail from the back of his head.

The moments stretched out, interrupted only by Paul's guttural clenching.

"We're..." Marcus began, "not supposed to be here. The transfer... we were supposed to arrive in a New York laboratory where newly fabricated bodies awaited."

He lifted his hands, the skin thin and pale, snaky blue veins bulging on the backs. Not what he expected.

After another long pause, he continued. The skin suits, as he called them, the black slimy things they wore, were body scanners that transferred specifications to a lab (a lab he swore, once again, was in New York) where fabricators quickly cloned them. Everything had been arranged before he had arrived on the Settlement.

Their identities transferred like data.

There was a team waiting for them to wake up, a group of technicians that would help them adjust to their newly minted bodies. It would be a simple transfer from one body to another, one vehicle to the next.

"Not this." He was staring at the hands. "It wasn't supposed to be this."

Jamie remembered the long, dark sleep, the endless black void of a blank dream. A journey through a cold network, a vacuum of outer space where there was no time, where nothing existed in between one body and the next.

"You killed her," Paul said.

"I did not."

"Then where is she?"

"I don't know how any of this happened."

"But you... you did this to us. You did this to her."

Darkness returned to the old man's eyes. "You would be on the Settlement if not for me."

"And she would be alive."

"And Jamie would be dead."

Paul spun around. "You murdered her in the first place."

"I was not in Atlanta. Her memories are corrupt."

Jamie had no memories of Atlanta, no recollection of dying. *But the eyes. I remember the eyes.*

"You are responsible for all of this," Paul said.

"I freed you, Paul. Would you rather be on the Settlement? Would you rather watch Raine suffer without her dreamland?"

"I would rather you join her."

Weakness suddenly overcame Jamie. Paul caught her before she slid to the floor.

The old man hadn't moved. If not for Jamie, Paul would squeeze the life out of him. And there was nothing Marcus could do to stop him. He sat there turning his hands over, a look of revulsion gliding down his bulbous nose, turning his mouth. Glancing at Paul, he got up as if he'd grown bored with the conversation and limped from the room.

"I'm all right. It's okay," she said.

He helped her into the chair, the seat still warm. Exhaustion tugged at her consciousness, her fuel tank already tapped. Paul knelt next to her. "I'm sorry," he said.

He wasn't just talking to her. He was sorry for everything. Sorry for Raine, sorry for dreamland. Sorry for the state of the world. And there was nothing he could do about it.

She began to doze, patting Paul's hand while sounds of chaos came from surrounding offices. The old man shuffled more papers in search of an explanation of where they were and how.

Raine's body continued to deflate.

"Angel," Jamie remembered her saying just before they left the Settlement. "You're my angel."

Who was she talking to?

CHAPTER TWENTY-TWO_

MARCUS'S LEFT LEG WOULDN'T BEND.

The knee, exposed just below the thin gown, was puffy and pink, razors pulsing inside it. He swallowed a slick of bile, the knob in his throat sore, neck stiff.

Muddled thoughts melted into globs of nonsense. Sifting them for an explanation was like looking for clean water in a mud hole. He just couldn't think clearly, couldn't feel the world around him.

He would've killed me.

Marcus couldn't stop Paul, not like he had in the cabin; couldn't sense the enraged man's thoughts, couldn't reach inside him to manipulate his desires, to lock his muscles. To save his ass.

Marcus was the prey.

What has become of me?

His ribs sang with each inhalation, the back of his head throbbed. Paul and Jamie were exactly as he expected them to be, even smelled of freshly fabricated biomites—the scent of baked earth. Marcus smelled of sweat, pungent and ripe. Dead skin.

"Where are you?" he said. "What have you done? Answer me! What have you done?"

Mother was gone.

He couldn't see her, couldn't feel her. Not since she first appeared to him all those years ago had she felt so distant. As if she never existed. Never had she abandoned him, not like this. He was in need. She was the one that fabricated his body, showed him the truth, sent him on this mission.

"What have you done to me?" he murmured.

There was movement in the hallway. A door slid open and closed, and then there was silence. Marcus's heart fluttered; anxious threads of fear tugged his chest. He hoped it was Paul and Jamie leaving, but he'd wait to confirm. He was not ready for another confrontation.

This was not the plan.

The monitors were black, the floor littered with debris. He sat in the dark office, his raspy breath filling the silence.

"Where are we?" he asked.

The monitors scattered. A fractured image flickered on the main one, jagged lines splintering palm trees where the back of his head smashed the glass. Marcus spun the chair, his heel dragging across the floor, a fiery slick of pain lighting up his knee.

An island. A fucking island.

A speck of land so isolated that the United States Air Force couldn't find it. It would take a day to reach the nearest land by water. How did any of this get out here?

How did we get out here?

The buildings were clustered on one end of the island, mostly shrouded in wilderness. Something moved across a wide patch of grass. Marcus pulled closer to the monitor.

Two people. Paul and Jamie, he guessed. One of them carried a bundled white sheet.

Is this a live feed?

The sophistication of technology was cutting edge even for a laboratory located in the middle of an industrial park. How could all of this get out here? And where was the power coming from?

"What is this place?" The words hurt his throat. "Why are we here?"

The views changed but only served to show different angles of a large bank of solar panels and a row of wind turbines on the north shore; there was also a small power plant of generators wired to tidal harvesters. None of his questions, though, were answered beyond what the island looked like.

He hobbled into the hallway. The silver door of an elevator was to his left, three lights over it. The one on the left was lit. *The first floor.*

He used the handrail to reach the end of the corridor, dragging the useless leg along the way. A cool draft slipped through the open back of the gown, his buttocks exposed. He was panting when he pressed his hand against the cool glass and looked across the island from what appeared to be the second floor. A sharp blue line of water slit the horizon.

"What have you done?"

The question, this time, felt closer to home. *What have I done?*

A digital chirp called from one of the rooms, followed by the hum of generators. Marcus waited and listened.

"Who's there? Jamie?"

Chirp.

It was coming from the recovery room, where they woke up. He struggled back, listening again before looking inside. The computers, dead when he woke, were alive. An individual station was dedicated to each bed. The far monitor flashed in time with the singing chirp. An aluminum post leaned against it.

A cane.

That wasn't there when he woke up.

He lunged from bed to bed, resting on each one, the padding still warm. His bed, however, was tainted with sour sweat. An image of Raine was locked into the corner of the far monitor. Marcus leaned on the counter to read the status.

Transfer aborted.

He pecked at the keyboard. When nothing happened, he thought-commanded. *What happened to her?*

No response.

He cleared his throat and said, "What happened to her... what happened to Raine's transfer?"

The status changed. A response appeared. *Connection lost.*

"Where is she? Is she still on the Settlement?"

Presence lost.

That was a different answer. Presence was different than connection, suggesting she was lost mid-transfer. That would explain the transfer abort, the degradation of the body. Did she get halfway here and snap back to her body, her identity tethered to it on an ethereal bungee?

No. The presence was lost.

You're an angel, she had said.

If she was still on the Settlement, if she woke up, they would know where Marcus, Paul and Jamie went. They could follow the coordinates left on the computer network, they would find them on the island. That thought should've stirred panic in the pit of his stomach, but instead it bloomed hope.

They'll come for us, take us back.

He would be rescued, get back to his former body. Then he saw the bottom right corner of the monitor, the present date and time in small script.

Impossible.

The computer could be wrong. The process should've been instantaneous. The recovery would take a few days at most. *Not a year.*

According to the computer, they left the Settlement over a year ago. So where were they in between? Bouncing in nowhere? There was no sense of passage between those two points in time, like they'd taken a wormhole shortcut.

"Why am I here?" Marcus shouted. "Who did this? Where are the ones that did this to me?"

There were no answers. The computer was dedicated to Raine, and all it knew was she wasn't there. *Presence lost.*

Paul's monitor (his picture in the left corner) revealed a successful transfer, all memories intact. Jamie's station held the same status.

"Show the memory log... Jamie's memory. Let me see it."

Her monitor flipped screens. A root directory appeared in several columns of code. He couldn't access her memories, not like this. Her memories of death might hold the answers, but that was before he arrived on the island.

Before he'd become this.

Before was what he would come to refer to the time *before* the transfer, *before* the arrival on the island when all would be revealed. *Before* he knew the truth.

A door slid open with a quiet whoosh.

Marcus waited. There were no footsteps. He listened to the hum of electronics, the ticking of a ventilation vent.

The elevator was open.

Chirp.

Another computer called, this one closer to him. He turned his upper body, his neck too pained to twist. It was across from the bed he woke on, his image in the left corner. A placid expression looked back at him. He shuffled three steps to the desk on which it sat.

He leaned closer.

What little strength he had left vanished. He fell forward, grasping the ledge of the counter to lower himself to the floor. He banged against the wall, new blood warmly flooding from the clotted wound on the back of his head. He tried to make sense of it all, tried to bring his breath under control.

The computer explained why he'd become powerless.

CHAPTER TWENTY-THREE_

THE WINDOWS WERE CLEAN.

That detail was not lost on Paul, that the island appeared to be in perfect working condition—buildings with power, food in industrial-sized refrigerators—but no one was there. Daily life should have dulled the windows, dust and rain and bird shit (there were birds on the island, big macaws that watched from the palms), but they were transparent-clean.

Paul no longer wondered on such mysteries.

He stood at the bay window that overlooked the campus-sized courtyard and watched Cali emerge from the forest. She passed beneath a heavy branch, a pair of white birds preening within reach. Beyond her, nestled deep in the palms, was the rounded roof of a building, a small dome-like structure.

A sundial was set in the middle of the field, a lone gray sculpture with a triangular wing pointed at the sky. She ran her fingers to the point and stopped. From that distance, the details were fuzzy, even the color of her hair was hard to discern.

But it was her.

He could feel it. Could feel her.

He saw her during the day, hallucinating her from a distance.

The hallucinations had invaded his dreams. *Dreams!* Dreams never happened to Paul, but now he was seeing the farm and the horses in the few hours he snatched at night, and watched her mow the back pasture, haul hay on a tractor.

Three nights had passed, and three nights he dreamed.

And now he saw her in the grassy field, wide awake. The hallucinations felt different. They had changed, felt more present. Solid. He thought, perhaps, if he stood beneath that branch, she would appear to him and he could reach out, he could touch her. Even if she was an illusion, a dream that evaporated, he might feel her for a moment.

He touched his face, rubbing the bristles on his cheeks.

"No, no, no, nonononono!"

Paul tripped on the corner of a leather duvet and sprinted across the lobby. The first door in the hallway was propped open, Jamie sitting up in a bed with a sheet clutched to her chin, eyes wide and blank.

"It's all right, it's all right. You're awake now. You're awake, Jamie."

Her breath punched through a tangle of fear, gulping at the room's stale air, tears falling from eyes that wouldn't blink.

"Be here." He stroked her short crop of hair wet with perspiration. "Be here, Jamie. Come back, look at me."

She blinked once, twice.

He leaned in front of her, held her clammy cheeks with both hands, and steered her vision into his eyes. Focus dialed her blue eyes on his. Her breathing slowed. She held his wrists, climbing out of the pit of a nightmare.

"You here?" he asked.

"Yeah."

"The dream again?"

She swallowed. Nodded.

It wasn't really a dream. She was remembering.

She wiped her forehead with the sheet and threw her feet onto the floor. She was sleeping almost twenty hours a day, waking for half an hour before wilting. That wasn't unusual for a new fabrication—sleep gave the body time to acclimate. *So why am I hardly sleeping?*

"I was in the building," she said.

The dream started like it always did: Marcus Anderson guiding her to a bench in Atlanta's Centennial Park, pausing long enough so that she would remember him. The old man swore he wasn't there, but she remembered it as clearly as she had seen it. Then she sat there alone, watching the children in the fountains until the biomite hijacking. It started in her bones.

"They took me to a room."

"Who?"

"Just some technicians, I think. One of them was wearing a baseball uniform or something. The other one was in charge." She swallowed, hard. "They were getting ready to..."

She took a cleansing breath, but the tension remained. She was reliving her death every time she closed her eyes.

"I got to get out of here," she said. "Need to walk."

"You sure?"

"I'll jump through a window if I don't get some fresh air."

"Let's get something to eat first."

"Paul, relax. I'm fine."

He started to protest. She hadn't been more than twenty feet away from him, not since she collapsed on the beach. He had carried Raine's body to the water and dug a shallow grave with his hands. It would've been wiser to send it out to the ocean, but he didn't want to see it wash ashore. *It's only a body,* he told himself. *An object that was never her. She never arrived.*

But it was all he had. Giving it a proper burial lifted a grain of guilt from a heap of regrets. But it was all he could do. And when Jamie collapsed—walking in the ankle-deep surf one moment, face down the next—he was determined to not turn the heap of regrets into a mountain.

It already felt insurmountable.

"Why don't you get cleaned up first," he said. "Then we'll go."

"Nothing's going to happen to me, Paul."

"No, I mean you need a shower."

"Whatever."

He stood in the hall until he heard the shower running then made his way toward the cafeteria. The U-shaped building was a dormitory, the rooms clean, beds made, clothes in the closets. It was sort of like waiting for the three bears to return. But no one came looking for porridge.

The walk-in cooler was filled with jugs of milk and cartons of orange juice. There was a pantry of canned goods and a freezer of meats and frozen produce. Paul scrambled eggs and nuked strips of bacon, cleaning up the dishes and leaving everything exactly as it was. If anyone was following or watching, they'd notice the missing food but not the dishes.

Jamie was at the picnic tables at the edge of the grassy field, a long toss to the sundial. She was wearing boy shorts and a T-shirt (all the clothing was for boys) and destroyed the breakfast when he put it down.

"The old man come out?" she asked.

"No."

Paul hadn't seen him. And that was a good thing. He could still feel the old man's windpipe in his hand, imagined crushing it like a cardboard tube.

"Let's explore one of the buildings today," she said.

"Let's give it a minute, see how you feel."

"Why wait until I'm tired?" She shoved a corner of toast in her mouth. "I'm all right, Paul. It'd be good to walk around, get outside and shake the dream off, you know."

"The old man wants something from you."

He could feel him watching from the tower, sense that bulging eye follow them when they stepped outside.

"Of course he does," Jamie said. "We were both after the same thing, sort of."

"The powers-that-be?"

"No, no. I was looking for someone to help with Raine's dreamland, looking for someone to help with overturning the Settlement. I wanted the big fish who was behind all the absurdity. I mean, the last twenty years have been crazy, the stupid halfskin laws and then the Settlement. Someone's behind this lunacy. I wanted to help you." She dropped the remaining toast. "The old man did, too; said he would set you and Raine free if I helped, said he would set the whole world free. And I believed him."

"He said he wasn't in Atlanta."

"Well, he's lying about that. You have a point."

"He manipulated your thoughts, made you believe him."

"Listen, I know he got inside my head. I'm not stupid. But it made sense, Paul. Even now it makes sense and he's not messing with my head. And you're free."

"And Raine is dead."

"We don't know that."

He looked away. Raine died because of him; it was easier to accept that, to lug the heap of guilt onto his back now rather than hope she was alive and have the trapdoor open beneath his feet.

The tower loomed over the dormitory. The rising sun reflected off the shiny bands that separated the floors (solar panels, he guessed). A dark shadow moved past a window on the third floor.

"He can't hurt us," Jamie said. "Something about him is different."

Yeah, but there was still a world of hurt out there. And they didn't wake up on this island on accident.

The island was shaping up to be a summer camp for the insanely wealthy.

There were classrooms and a game room. The only structure they didn't explore was the dome-shaped building buried in the palms. That oddball building was different than the others and in the other direction. But everything else was orderly, the doors unlocked or open, chairs pushed in and trash empty.

But there aren't towers at summer camp.

It was at the third building they explored that Jamie began to fade. She'd been awake for two hours, the most since leaving the tower. Now she stopped on the top step and touched her head, riding out a bout of vertigo.

"I'm all right."

"We need to go back."

"Just this last stop, I promise. Then we'll go."

He gave in and opened the large glass door. The stale wind of paper met them. Shelves and shelves of books lined the open hall, long tables with short lamps interspersed throughout. Paul remained a step behind her.

"There, look." She pointed behind the front desk.

A computer was stashed on a bottom shelf, the first one they'd seen since leaving the tower. A second wind filled her. Paul looked around as she pried open the laptop; the thrumming sound of an awakening computer filled the hallowed halls. The screen went black.

"Where are we?" she said.

He was about to answer (obviously a library) when the computer came to life. Images of the island began playing.

"How'd you do that?" he asked.

"It happened in the tower, all the computers were voice-activated."

"Where's Raine?" he blurted.

Jagged lines of static interrupted the scenery. Blackness returned.

"I don't think it knows," she began to say when cabins emerged from the foggy screen.

The Settlement.

"No." The urge to slam the computer with both fists reached inside him. "I'm going to—"

"Is she on the Settlement?" Jamie asked.

Another scramble of static. A room appeared. It was the dream disease lab. Authority figures were there. Not the green-jacket monitors, these were the federal types, the men and women wearing gloves so as not to contaminate a crime scene. They were removing equipment, hauling it out on carts with all-terrain vehicles.

The beds were occupied by black skinsuits, the hoods pulled off to expose the sunken faces—the sharp cheekbones and purple lips. Two men stood over the one on the right, the hood bunched beneath Raine's neck, her scalp glistened with the electrolytic gel. Her flesh was muddy, her bruised tongue a puffy slug swelling between cracked lips. They lifted her onto a gurney and carted her off with the computers.

She's not there.

A stir of relief cooled the hot grit of guilt piling on the bottom of his stomach. He'd rather she be dead than on the Settlement alone. *We don't know she's dead. She's just not here.*

"What happened to them?" he asked. "What happened to the Settlement?"

A view of the laboratory appeared from above. All the windows on the first floor were boarded. The front door was barricaded. The windows on the second and third floor were dark, some cracked, dirt and grime layered in the corners.

No smoke puffed from the chimney.

They shut it down. Oh, fuck, they shut it down... we did that to them, we took it away from them.

Paul stalked off and ran his hands over his stubbly scalp. The guilty weight buckled his knees. How could he carry all of this? This was his fault. Everyone suffered because of him. First Cali, then Jamie, then Raine... *now the entire Settlement.* They had nothing to live for.

"Paul."

"We got to get back there," he said. "We can help them."

He was standing by the tables, the furthest from Jamie he'd been that morning. She was still behind the counter, the computer's glow in her eyes.

"Paul... there's more."

A stream of images filled the screen in separate frames, scenes of hospitals, of protesters picketing the wealthy dream centers (*Stop Dreaming Now!*), of arguing politicians, dead bodies pulled from houses, hotels, cars and curbs. City streets were mostly empty.

"Dream disease," Jamie said. "It's out of control."

The computer responded with a news reporter at a desk, her lips silently moving above the headline that read, *No Cure in Sight.*

And there they were again, a picture of the dream disease lab on the Settlement with their bodies still on the beds.

"Holy shit," she said. "They think we did it. They think we started a dream disease plague."

Something wasn't right. This was happening too fast. All they did was transfer into new bodies.

"Do you believe it?" she asked.

He shook his head. "I don't know what to believe."

"I mean, this is just a computer. It could all be made up. We don't know where we are."

"We're on an island."

"But where? Why?"

"I don't know, but we have to get back."

"Back to the Settlement? What's that going to do?"

He couldn't help anyone on the island. At least he could pay his debts on the Settlement, suffer for his sins. He would drag the old man with him. That he could do. At least they would have someone to pay.

"No." She fell into the high-backed chair. "We're here for a reason, Paul. Whatever Marcus had planned has changed. He's not the same, you feel it. He's weaker, doesn't have something. Even he doesn't know what's going on."

"This could all be a disaster."

"Or something bigger."

"People are dying, Jamie. We might be responsible."

"We might be the answer. Marcus was after the truth. He said if he found it, then he'd find the powers-that-be. He thinks that's where the dream eater is. What if this is it?"

"What if we just pissed him off?"

"Why do you think it's a 'him'?"

He paced another path to the long tables and paused to look at the perfectly stacked shelves, the surreal atmosphere saturated with dreamlike qualities. Yet he was wide awake, seeing and feeling and hearing. This was not a dream.

All we have are our senses. What if our senses lie? What if our filters obscure the truth? Then what we see and hear and believe is no more relevant than lies on a computer.

"Paul."

She was slumped over the counter. Dead weight hung on her face. There were no fumes left. He'd have to carry her back, let her sleep again. At least she got a few hours of waking. Maybe the next time it would be longer.

She spun the laptop so that it faced him and tapped the corner of the screen. The toolbar showed the date and time.

A year has passed.

That was how dream disease had gotten so bad, how the streets had grown so empty. Why the laboratory was so abandoned.

"I think someone is hiding us, Paul. That's why we're here."

CHAPTER TWENTY-FOUR_

CLAY.

Marcus lay on a massive bed on the tower's third floor, sunk deep in soft comforters and a pile of pillows, staring at a black ceiling. Daylight diffusely filled the room, yellowish beams penetrating the tinted windows.

How could this happen?

He was supposed to wake up in New York City, his body an exact duplicate of the one left behind on the Settlement. Not a clay body.

A pure, 100% clay body.

The technology to fabricate with clay cells—printing organs, ears, fingers, eyeballs—had been established long before biomites. But fabricating an entire body?

Why would someone do this to me?

These were the questions he asked upon waking. And he woke often, sleeping the majority of the day, sometimes waking on the floor with lumps and bruises and no recollection of how he got there.

He crawled out of bed, his knee refusing to bend, the back of his head staining the pillow with pink watery spots, his throat sore from screaming at the ceiling, cursing his plight.

Cursing Mother.

She did this. She turned me back into clay and abandoned me.

He had fallen under her spell, believed in his destiny that he would save mankind from an insatiable power.

And now I'm just human.

This was more than a sick joke. This was punishment. She sent him to a tropical purgatory. He didn't give a shit how the food got there or how all this worked. He just wanted off this godforsaken hellhole, wanted back in his biomite skin.

Unlike the second floor, the third floor had no inner walls. It was wide open. There were views in all directions. The floor slowly rotated (a speed he couldn't feel) so that a mounted telescope provided a multitude of views. Right now, it was pointed at the grassy field.

Paul and Jamie were sleeping in the U-shaped building; he'd seen them at the picnic tables once or twice. Apparently there was food there, too. They made no attempt to find him. Occasionally they looked at the tower.

But he was safe.

The only access into the tower was through an elevator. He had wedged an office chair between the elevator doors to keep them open. He'd found a cache of food on the third floor that would last for months. He would stay in the tower as long as it took. He would outlast them.

There has to be a way back to the mainland.

If their identities could be streamed to this remote island, they could be sent back. The fabricated bodies would still be in New York. He had leased the lab space with funds from an inexhaustible account; the lab would hold them. His legal team would make sure of it, that until his fabricated body rose up and Marcus acknowledged he was fully aware, they would keep paying the bills until the end of time.

There has to be a way to reverse the route.

He aimed the massive telescope at the back of the U-shaped

building, bent over the eyepiece and closed one eye. He had seen them, Paul and Jamie, eating lunch at one of the picnic tables.

"Where are you now?" he muttered.

Computers whirred into action. Electric light flickered across the ceiling. Back on a large oak desk, half a dozen monitors streamed a variety of images. With the help of the cane, he hobbled over and fell into the chair. There was no keyboard or cables.

Just images of Paul and Jamie.

The security system of a paranoid dictator had been engaged. Exactly what Marcus needed.

Paul and Jamie were watching a laptop inside a library.

There was no sound, just their expressions on vivid display. They were shocked and surprised at whatever they were seeing.

Marcus smiled.

"Let's see what else I can do."

CHAPTER TWENTY-FIVE_

THE GOLDFISH GLIDED, ONE EYE LOOKING THROUGH THE GLASS.

Jamie wondered what it was like to fly. Living in water must be like that, never having to fear falling. Always floating.

Always flying.

The fish tank warped into a slurry of brimming tears, her body a plastic coffin she couldn't escape. Hands on her lap, eyes forward, she listened to the man in the baseball uniform discuss the weather. Somewhere a woman answered a call. Even the fish looked bored.

They're going to shut me off.

She was aware it was the dream, but that did nothing to ease the fear burning her insides like dry kindling, hollowing her out until there was nothing but the toxic vapor of terror. Somewhere, boys were laughing.

Boys?

Something was wrong with that detail. She couldn't remember boys being in the building before they shut her off, no recess playground.

Then he arrived.

The witness.

And the fear evaporated. It shouldn't, she knew that. His arrival put her toes on the ravine's edge, placed a hand on her back to shove her into the long dark hole where she would be sacrificed to the laws of the state, her crime against humanity being the possession of biomites.

His shadow crept into her periphery.

The goldfish watched, unblinking, as his face moved into view—

"No!"

She slashed in the sheets, fabric tangling around her arms like a damp boa constrictor. Kicking, screaming, she thrashed across the mattress, pulled her legs to her chest, huffing in the corner of a white room.

No fish, no witness.

I'm here. Here and awake.

Paul didn't come.

He looked tired before she went to the room, said he might sleep this time instead of sitting guard. He hadn't slept much since they left the tower.

She stripped off the T-shirt, wet with sweat and two sizes too big, and threw it in a growing pile of spoiled clothing. A slice of yellow sunlight knifed across the room, cutting across her waist as she pulled on a pair of large shorts and another T-shirt, this one tan instead of white. The flip-flops—three sizes too big—slapped at the linoleum and echoed down the long, empty corridor.

The lobby was empty.

A sheet and pillow were bunched on the leather couch, a basket of fruit on the table next to it. She took an apple and looked out the wide window. Purple clouds boiled in the distance, flashes of lightning in its belly, the sky a stewing cauldron.

The sun was setting on the picnic tables, the laptop flashing images in the building's shadow. Further out, Paul was standing at the sundial, his back to her. His hospital gown was tucked into a loose pair of khakis like a baggy shirt. He hadn't changed since waking.

He was bouncing his hand on the tip of the sundial's fin, stabbing the point into his palm. "I'm dreaming," he said.

"You're awake, Paul."

"No. When I sleep... I'm dreaming. I see Cali and it's... it's different. Something's different. It's like she's waiting. Never saying anything, just watching me. Haunting me."

"Stop it." Jamie grabbed his hand. "You loved her and that's all you could do."

He looked into his hand, searching the purple gouges for an answer. He looked dazed, dreamy. The edge of his words blurred. *Is he still asleep?*

"I have never had a dreamland, Jamie. Never even had a normal dream. But I do now. Ever since we woke on this island, I've been dreaming."

He traced the fleshy wounds with his fingertips, then spoke at the distant trees.

"This time I was sitting on the couch, waiting for her hallucination to appear in the trees. Instead, I fell asleep and woke up on the side of a hill in a strange land, one I'd never seen before. There was the sea and a village... and then I fell asleep again, only this time I dreamed of the dream disease lab."

He twitched.

"It was dark and moldy. The equipment had been stripped from the room. The beds were there, the shower, too. Our bodies were gone, though. It was like all this time had passed, like I was really there. But then I found this."

He chuckled, shaking his head.

"It was the little cross, the two sticks bound with a band of jute. It was something Raine carried with her, said Joshua made it for her in dreamland. She found it outside her cabin and swore he put it there. She must've had it in the dream lab.

"I sort of forgot about the skin suits and the waking and the island... but then I looked for you, and when I didn't find you, I remembered you were sleeping in the next room. I remembered we weren't on the Settlement anymore. We both were. *I'm dreaming,* I thought."

He shook his head, thumb in palm. The pain was grounding him in the present moment. He wanted to be sure he was awake. *Or wake himself up.*

"The door to the lab was open," he continued. "The rest of the building was much the same, the doors open, the offices empty. Cobwebs were in the corners. I remembered when we were there, when the window was broken and they came after us. You remember that?"

She nodded.

"One of the offices across from the fabrication lab, that's where they got inside. I went there and the window was missing, a sheet of plywood in its place. A sliver of light punched through a weathered knothole. I looked through it. You know what I saw?"

He turned his head, squinting as if the view were right there.

"The gray… the cabins across the field, the wind turbines… it was all gray. And someone was splitting wood. I think it was her. I think it was Raine."

"It was a dream."

"Was it?"

He massaged his hand, smudging tiny beads of crimson into the wrinkled valleys, the pain reminding him that he was here, he was awake. *It hurts in the dream too, Paul.*

"Did you have the same dream?" he asked.

She nodded.

"Did you see him?"

"He's closer."

Marcus would want to know that, would want to know that someone called the witness was about to look into her eyes, fill her with peace before sucking her soul into the cold vacuum of death. But it was more than that, she sensed. She didn't just die.

He consumed me.

She didn't want to believe that, didn't want to think it was that easy and wasn't going to tell Paul any of that, either. She could be wrong. But there was something otherworldly about the witness's presence, a man that convinced her it was all right to die, to give herself.

A man, she thought, *that could eat dreams.*

THUNDER DROPPED a cool breeze across the yard. The laptop strobed across the picnic table, images coming and going.

"I know what this place is," Paul said.

He straddled the bench and spun the laptop toward her. An aerial view of the grassy field was filled with boys, some lounging, others throwing a Frisbee. Groups of teenagers were at the picnic tables, playing cards.

Boys. Were those the boys I heard in the dream?

"This place was some sort of alternate reality experiment. There are no times or dates, so it's hard to assess just how long ago, but I get the feeling it was before biomites."

"Why?"

"They used a needle and cable to bridge the human brain with a computer." He rubbed a spot on his forehead. "There was a surgical stent installed that allowed access to the frontal lobe. The computer then created a new reality."

She turned away from the laptop but not before seeing an image she would never forget—a young man, thirteen or fourteen, lying on a hospital bed, a rigid steel needle staked into his forehead, clear salve pooled around the base.

"How come we've never heard of this?"

"There's no telling how long ago it was. Besides, I get the feeling it was experimental and illegal. That's why this place is so isolated. There's a giant resort on the other side of the island, something the very wealthy would enjoy. On this side are the dorms and the classrooms and library. I'm guessing they were using teenagers to work out their mistakes."

The scene of a classroom played out, rows of bored teenagers listening to an old man with multiple jiggling chins. She looked up.

"Only boys, though," she said.

"Yeah, this was for boys. There was one for girls, too. It was somewhere else."

"Where?"

He started to answer, the word dusty and quiet and doubtful.

"Where were the girls at?" she repeated.

"The Settlement."

"What do you mean?"

"Remember the red brick house? There were remnants of old log cabins out there, too."

"That's... that's not a coincidence."

"No."

"Why were they separated?"

"I don't know. They called it the Foreverland Project. I think it was a precursor to dreamland. The needle and computers created these realistic alternate realities. Then biomites came along and there was no need for a needle, no need for a computer. People started generating their own dreamlands... their own *foreverlands*."

Jamie tapped the screen. "This is telling us something, Paul. It's no accident the Settlement was built where it was, no accident we're here. This laptop is telling us something."

"Maybe."

"This is where it all started. Powers-that-be, dreamlands and foreverlands and alternate realities. Someone wants us to connect the dots. Marcus was looking for the powers-that-be. Maybe we found it."

"We haven't found anything."

"Not yet. Where do you think they did these experiments?"

Paul turned toward the tower. *The second floor.*

That was where all the technology was located—the offices, the beds, the fabricators. Of course, that was where the needles would be. There were computers there, too; ones that responded to questions.

"We need to get back up there," she said. "Now."

"It'll be dark soon and it looks like rain. Besides, he's not going to let us inside."

"He'll let us up." She felt injected with caffeine. "Marcus will want to hear this. He's as anxious to get off the island as we are."

She snapped the laptop closed. He nodded compulsively, agreeing but not really hearing her. Maybe she couldn't trust him in front of Marcus, not yet. Maybe he didn't want the old man to let them up, afraid he'd lose control.

The thunderheads rumbled.

"Let me grab some boots." Jamie pulled off her flip-flops and ran through the grass, the cool blades slipping between her toes. She yanked on the door. The handle turned freely but wouldn't open.

"What's wrong?" he called.

"Door's locked."

Paul waggled the handle. He examined the doorjamb, no place for a key or even a scan lock. He looked around. The air smelled damp. And it would be dark soon. And all their food was inside.

They tried the other doors. Maybe they'd been locked all this time, they hadn't used them. Only this back door had been unlocked, but not anymore.

The first raindrop fell.

"Come on." Paul started for the grassy field. "We'll break a window."

He walked at first. When rain spots began wetting his back, he began running. The sundial was too heavy. They entered an open path in the forest. Paul stomped through the underbrush, picking up branches, testing them like baseball bats.

Above them, the foliage pattered. Raindrops found their way to the undergrowth. The forest was waking up. Jamie tucked the laptop beneath her shirt.

"Coconuts!" Jamie shouted.

Paul was back on the trail, sprinting toward the beach. He returned with a husked coconut tucked in his arms. Jamie had squatted beneath the shelter of a tropical palm, the wide leaves bowing under the watery weight, tiny streams shedding off the scalloped edges. She held the laptop, their only connection to the outside world, like a baboon protecting her young.

"Come on!" he shouted above the rain patter.

"I'll wait here!" He doubled back and grabbed her arm, but she resisted. "This can't get wet. Go knock out a window and come back with something to wrap it up."

"This isn't going to blow over."

"And this can't get wet."

Dusk was ticking away the remains of the day. Jamie hunkered down, water pooling around her flip-flops, feet squeaking as she shifted her weight.

The sky had disappeared between the small openings of the canopy; she heard Paul before seeing him. He was carrying an angular rock, chopped the stocky stem of a frond and held it up over his head like an umbrella.

The back of her shirt was soaked, but her belly was still warm and mostly dry. She took cover with him. They took a narrow path that led away from the field. A flash of lightning revealed the dome-shaped roof of a squat building, the door wedged open with a fallen branch.

He yanked the door open. It was pitch black inside.

"Couldn't get a window to break out," he shouted. The rain pounded the curved roof. "Security glass shattered but didn't break. We can stay here tonight, find something tomorrow."

She heard him shake and felt a spatter of rain across her face that tasted slightly of salt. The room smelled dank and hopeless, the subterranean feel of a basement, the atmosphere penetrating her bones with a wet kiss. The next flash of lightning lit up the confines.

Bars.

She shuffled closer to Paul and felt his body heat on her back. The metal edge of the laptop creaked in her grip. Her eyes adjusted; hard metal bars emerged in rows with open sliding doors and a concrete floor. There weren't many cells, eight or ten.

"What the hell is this?" she said.

"I don't know. We'll just stay until the storm passes."

The weather spit a gust of rain through the door. Paul worked to pull it closed. The hinges were damaged and the door wouldn't fit inside the doorjamb. A puddle crept over the cracked concrete.

The metal bars were cold and chilling, goose bumps spreading up her arms, the small hairs standing up. There was nothing inside the cells, no bench or toilet, not even a chair. It was a small building of metal bars.

"Don't go in there," Paul shouted over a gust of rain.

"Don't worry."

He guided her back to the middle of the corridor like the cells would swallow her up, the door clamping down like mechanical jaws.

The storm continued.

They sat on the concrete, leaning against a section of the curved wall, careful not to touch the bars. They sat in the dark, the sound of the storm thrown over them like a blanket of chains, listening to branches dance in the night.

Sleep came to Jamie like it always did, sneaking up to snatch her into unconsciousness where the dream would start over. She'd wake in the morning, looking up at the silver blades of a large ceiling fan and listening to the fresh silence that comes after a storm.

But nothing would be the same.

CHAPTER TWENTY-SIX_

PAUL WAS GRAINY.

Marcus leaned on the desk and called for the picture to enhance. The camera (or whatever was recording their every move) zoomed tight on his face and captured him blinking.

Still awake.

Paul stood at the door, peeking through the opening every so often, waiting for the storm to ease up. Jamie was on the far side of the room, curled up and shivering. He'd taken off his shirt—the filthy hospital gown—and draped it over one of the cells to dry. It left his upper body exposed.

Marcus fell asleep at the desk and woke just past midnight. The rain was gentle but consistent, the wind a harmless bluster. Paul was now sitting on the floor, leaning against the wall, still not asleep.

He won't leave her, Marcus told himself. *Even if it stops raining.*

He locked them out of the dormitory. All it took was a simple request and the system did it. They'd find the other buildings locked, too. It wouldn't take long before they were hungry and desperate. Then they would be ready to listen, to cooperate on his terms.

If that was what he wanted to do.

The domed building had escaped his attention until they were inside it. The door was left open; there was probably nothing he could do to keep them out anyway. But it worked to his advantage.

The computer told him exactly what that building was for. It wasn't a prison or a punishment. It wasn't clear why the boys were kept in cells, in such miserable conditions when everything else was so luxurious. But that was where the needles were inserted into the boys' frontal lobes, where their identities were connected to a host computer, where an alternate reality awaited.

Where dreamland was born.

This *foreverland,* as they called it, was the birth of dreamland. Old men stole the bodies of young boys, exorcising their identities, sending their souls to a place described as nowhere so their bodies remained as empty husks the old men could occupy. A new lease on life.

They didn't have biomites back then, weren't able to create the necessary conditions to experience an inner world, so they connected themselves to something that could.

Because they were clay.

Marcus pushed away from the desk, his knee locked into a rigid bar of fire. He was stiff all over, but the leg (and now the hip) had become extremely arthritic. By the time he reached the elevator, his forehead pricked with sweat. Knowing Paul was in that domed building, that he wouldn't leave Jamie, the old man descended to the second floor without fear of surprise. The doors opened.

A wheelchair waited in the hall.

Ask and ye shall receive.

These were the little things he noticed around the tower, how requests were fulfilled. First the cane, then the computers and now this. He fell into the seat and sighed. Relief came in a relaxing wave. It took an effort not to lay his head back and fall asleep.

The stringent smell of the lab—the antiseptic cleaners, the sterile supplies—filled the hall. Quite a difference from the floral scent of the third floor, the lived-in opulence. This was where science advanced.

He rushed around the lab, opening drawers. But then he stopped. It was obvious how to find what he was looking for, and how to do it. According to the post-arrival report, he woke up in a clay body. He contained no biomites. But the island was the birthplace of foreverland, the precursor of dreamland. This was where they learned how to transport their identities out of clay bodies.

All he needed was a network. He was receiving news from the mainland; therefore he could transmit it. The New York lab would still be holding the body he designed.

It was all very clear what he needed to do.

"Where's the needle?" he called to the room.

CHAPTER TWENTY-SEVEN_

THE RAIN SOOTHED THE FEAR, A LULLABY THAT WASHED AWAY the worry and concern. Paul stared across the domed hut, past the bars at the sleeping body huddled against the wall.

His back next to the door, Paul kept his eyes open despite the pleasant breeze flowing through the crack of the door. He looked at the black bars, wondering what they were for, why someone would be kept inside, what horrors they'd seen—

And then they turned yellow.

He blinked away the exhaustion and rubbed his eyes. For a second, he was on the side of the hill overlooking the sea. The next moment, the mustard yellow bars appeared, but not the confining cells in the domed building; they had become distant posts smudged in the blurry night rain.

The Visitors' Center.

He was standing in the lobby, looking across the front field where the Settlement's perimeter was marked by yellow posts. The window was still damaged where he'd thrown the chair.

But Jamie wasn't on the floor. She was back in the hut.

I'm dreaming.

His clothing was still the same—bare-chested and khakis still wet from the rain. The room smelled musty, the carpet tacky beneath his boots. All his senses intact.

The silence was broken by laughter.

Paul jumped to the side, instincts telling him to hide. No one was allowed inside this building unescorted. *But this is a dream.*

He went down the main corridor. The offices were to the left. The punchy laughter continued. Paul snuck to the first office, the door closed. *Bob's office.* But the nameplate had changed. No white cowboy hat on the desk, no tray of vaping pipes.

No longer Bob's office.

"Check this out," one of the voices said.

"Is she always like that?" the other person asked.

"Every night."

Paul went down the hall, trying to remember if the computers were against the back wall or facing the hall. *This is a dream,* he reminded himself. *Just a dream.*

He leaned into view and saw the back shoulder of one man standing behind a chair, wearing the standard green coat of a monitor, unzipped and open. They were watching surveillance footage on the computer. It was a view of someone sleeping.

Nadia.

She rolled over to expose her buttocks and left breast.

The one sitting turned. They high-fived.

Paul didn't recognize them. But if a year had passed, they would be new. But why would Bob be gone? *This is a dream,* he thought again. None of this mattered.

But it did.

Those assholes swore they never violated the bricks' privacy, that surveillance was only in place in case of an emergency. How many times did they watch them in the shower? How many times did Bob jerk off to someone making love?

This was a dream. Only a dream. But he would fix it here and now. He would make it right, even if it was only a dream. It wouldn't make a lick of difference when he woke up, but he'd feel better, the guilt would be just a little lighter.

Because even if this was a dream, it probably wasn't far from the truth.

A CRACK of thunder slapped Paul in the face.

He jumped to his feet, the sizzle of lightning still on his eyebrows. The cages were open, the walls quiet. A sultry orange slice of sunlight swept across the room, wisps of humidity swirling; water dripped from the door.

Daylight.

That wasn't lightning.

The ache in his tailbone went up his spine, the result of a long night on the concrete. He rubbed the sleep from his eyes (eyebrows intact, hair unsinged) and pushed the door open. Birds fluttered with a squawk. The air was crisp and scoured. It rejuvenated the world, cleansed it of wrongdoing, made everything right.

This is a new day.

Jamie was still asleep, hugging the laptop like a stuffed bear. At least she'd stopped shivering. He knelt next to her, listening to her breathing. Deciding not to wake her, he pried the laptop away—her hands clawing the concrete with scratchy, jerky movements. Maybe she was back in the dream and he should wake her. At the very least, he should be there when she woke. But he wouldn't be gone for long.

And she needs the sleep.

He typed a message on the laptop and left it open.

Everything was dewy, the droopy foliage swiping him as he jogged past, his thighs and chest soaked when he passed the sundial. The doors were still locked; the window he attempted to shatter, the coconut bouncing off like a rubber kickball, was cracked. There was still food on the picnic table from the day before. The crackers were waterlogged, the waxy apples beaded with rain.

Jamie was stretching when he returned and handed her an apple. "Thank you," she said.

He pushed the door open. In the sunlight, it was just a room with bars.

"What about the rest of the buildings," she asked. "Think they're locked, too?"

He shrugged. "Stand up and stretch. You've been sitting on the floor all night."

She sighed, studying the apple, taking another loud bite before getting up and offering him the other half.

"You eat it," he said. "You need it."

"You do, too."

"Come on, let's get out of here."

"Keep the door open, just in case."

She was thinking like he was. What if all the buildings were locked? They could sleep outside, but another storm would make it difficult. The hut was better than being exposed to the elements, cages or not. Another thing occurred to him.

Where are the insects?

This was a tropical island, but nothing was crawling on them at night or biting them during the day. Paul was on one knee, wedging a branch into the soft mud to keep the wind from blowing the door closed and wondering if the island's ecosystem was naturally bug-free.

"That's weird," Jamie said.

And then it happened in slow motion.

One knee in the mud, he saw her turn, saw her take one step toward an open cell. "No!" he managed to shout.

That was it.

The door slid in the rail like a predator and slammed her left leg like metal teeth. The dull crack of bones sounded like a muffled gunshot.

Her other leg collapsed like a folding chair.

The door recoiled to a grinding halt, Jamie's shin bent at a slight angle. She yanked her leg inside the cell before the second bite landed. The door latched with a ringing thud.

Paul had barely leaned forward before it was over.

Birds flocked away as he grabbed the bars, the metal cold and hard and unforgiving. He reached through them, but Jamie was curled up, blood already dotting the concrete.

"Breathe," he said. "Breathe, Jamie. You can control this, remember. Focus, now. Focus on your nervous system; kill the sensations."

This was survival mode.

Biomites allowed for the override of the nervous system when severe pain needed to be mitigated to avoid shock. *She can do this.*

"Breathe, now." He took a deep breath. "In deep... Jamie, listen to me. In deep, out slow. You can do this, okay. Listen to my voice. Be here."

Her cries turned to whimpers. Tears squeezed through clamped eyelids. She drew a wet breath through clogged nostrils, exhaled through a tight circle.

The shaking slowed to a quiver.

"Okay, I'll be right back," he said. "I'm just going outside for a second, see if there's something I can use to open this."

He sounded confident despite the absurdity. A branch wouldn't scratch the bars. The latch didn't even have a keyhole.

Remotely controlled.

The cool rush of fear transformed into the flame of rage. If it was remotely closed, then he had a suspicion who had done it. It was no accident that the buildings were locked, no accident this hut was open and waiting.

When he returned, she had rolled to her side so that he couldn't see the leg. Her breathing was long and smooth and even. She lay still, her back to him. He knelt down, knees pushing between the bars.

She wouldn't respond, but had the pain under control.

He had to find help, had to make things right. His lungs burned as he ran through the forest, wondering what would possess her to walk inside the cage, why she would endanger herself. It was only a matter of time before one of them slipped on the shore or got sick.

But he realized as he exited the trees that she was holding something as she had clutched her wounded leg, something that poked between her fingers. Something she had reached for in the cell.

They were sticks.

SHE WAS ASLEEP.

It was the third time he'd come back to check on her and found her lying on her side, hands laced around her knee. Each time he explored a little farther. He finally found a rocky shoreline and scored a jagged block of granite half-buried in the sand.

The dormitory window caved on the fifth toss.

Paul filled two pillowcases with food. The kitchen utensils would be too flimsy to break open the cell door. The meat cleaver would shatter on impact.

He found a utility closet and tools for basic repairs. He pocketed the screwdrivers, a ball-peen hammer and a putty knife. The back door was still locked (no bolt on the inside), so he crawled out the window and ran.

Jamie was awake.

She was in the back corner, one leg (her good leg) pulled up to her chest. The other leg was laid flat on the concrete and wrapped in Paul's shirt. It appeared she had the pain under control. He thought, at first sight, she had wrapped her leg to keep from seeing it, to keep herself from entering shock. But the rheumy gaze, the parted lips.

She's already there.

"Hey, hey." He dropped the food. "I'm going to get you out."

She didn't respond.

"Jamie. Jamie, you here? You with me? I won't leave you again. I'm going to get you out of here, all right?"

He fumbled the tools from his back pocket. The hammer

bounced across the floor. He studied the screwdrivers and putty knife. They were pathetic. And the stone was still sitting in the dorm room where he'd thrown it through the window.

He'd have to go back.

"It's him," Jamie said. "He's the one."

She could've been speaking to the room or herself, the words drifting off like random bubbles. Paul grabbed the iron bars, leaning in to see what she was holding.

"What are you saying, Jamie? What do you mean?"

"He is the witness."

"Who?"

"He's the witness, Paul." The whites of her eyes were gray. "He's the one that shut me down."

"I... I don't know what you're saying."

"The dream is finished. I'm staring at a fish tank when he comes in the room. I can feel him, like he's... he's someone I know. I... I don't remember his face. But I remember the eyes."

A pause button was hit. She stumbled over the details, still digesting the memories.

"The eyes, Paul. Have you looked directly into his eyes?"

"Whose eyes?"

She swallowed, dry. "Marcus."

"Marcus?"

"Have you noticed the end of the world in them? It's all there, everything's inside his eyes. The universe, the stars, the galaxy... *everything*. He made me feel important, made me feel wanted and okay. That he loved me. So I gave myself to him freely."

"What are you saying, sweetheart? You're saying... the old man is the witness?"

That couldn't be. He was in Atlanta; he dropped her off to be captured. *But he swore that wasn't him.*

"And then he drew me in, sucked the soul out of my body into a cold, cold night, Paul. It's him. Marcus is the one."

She was confused. The shock, the hysteria, the anger and resentment. Marcus wouldn't drop her off then appear as the witness. He was looking for the powers-that-be, was with her in Chicago, with her in Atlanta. *He can't be the witness, too.*

"Where did you get that, Jamie?"

She opened her hand, displaying her palm. On it lay a pair of sticks fastened together. Paul lost the feel of the floor, the world turning beneath him. She held it up like she was warding off evil.

It was a cross.

A little wooden cross.

"Where did you find that?"

"He's the one, Paul."

"Jamie, listen to me. Where'd you get the cross?"

"Marcus is doing everything. He *is* the powers-that-be. He just doesn't know it."

Paul stood too quickly and held the bars until he was sure his knees wouldn't break. He paced the concrete corridor, head still spinning. He had to get her out of there. She had turned delusional, the dream finally cracking her mind. The doors were remotely controlled. The tower was the center of technology with 360-degree views.

He locked the doors.

"Stay back there," he said. "I'll be right back, Jamie. I promise, I won't leave you. I'm going to get you out of there."

The sun had breached the trees, the jungle already steamy. Paul ran without stopping. He'd talk some sense into the old man. And if that didn't work, he'd make him do it. Somehow, he'd make him. Because, before long, this island would crack them all like eggs.

Paul was already cracking.

That was a cross she was holding. Raine's cross. The one she had on the Settlement, the one she carried to the dream disease lab.

And now it's here.

CHAPTER TWENTY-EIGHT_

THE BUILDING CHATTERED.

Marcus snorted awake, his neck savagely twisted over the back of the wheelchair, pain spearing the back of his head. All the monitors were streaming newsfeeds from around the world. There was no recollection of falling asleep, just hazy glimpses of searching in long blank gaps.

The night's cache was spread across a tabletop, a collection of tubes and wires, clear plastic IV bags and a box of sterile needles encased in clear tubes of gel. They were neatly arranged in piles, unwrapped and displayed. But there were no directions for where wires went or what computer to use, what program to run.

Even if that was all solved, there was the issue of the needle. He couldn't hammer the thing into his forehead like a roofing nail. There was a stent and a precise method of insertion. He was out of options. If he died trying, then at least he wouldn't die a slow death of dehydration and neck injuries.

The chatter was back.

It was in the hall, not one of the noisy newsfeeds.

Marcus wheeled out and saw the elevator doors gnawing on an aluminum cane. He didn't recall dropping the cane between the open doors, but then he couldn't remember much with any clarity. The elevator gummed it with impatience, the bumpers bouncing in the doors' tracks.

The down arrow flashed.

He quickly wheeled to the end of the hall. The dormitory and field were quiet and empty, and there was nothing directly below. Marcus went back to the lab to see Paul on one of the monitors. He was prying at a curved elevator door, the glass wall behind him shattered.

He's on the first floor.

A sweatless wave of panic swept through him. How close had he come to waking up to Paul standing over him with vengeance on his breath. *If not for the cane.*

"Hey! Let her go, Marcus! Let her go now!"

He was talking to the old man. *Does he see me?*

Three of the monitors projected views of Paul backing away from the elevator, looking up at a monitor. The first floor looked like a lobby with couches and chairs and at least a dozen monitors that all projected the same newsfeeds Marcus was watching. But the one above the elevator was filled with Marcus's pasty gray face, dark age-spots spilled on his scalp like paint.

"All she did was help you," Paul said. "Let her go."

What the hell is he talking about? He did his best to go along with it. Clearly Marcus had an advantage. He just needed to figure out what it was.

"You choked me, tried to murder me."

"And she stopped me. You owe her that. You want someone to pay for all your mistakes, take me. But let her go."

"Mistakes?"

"You brought us here."

The ashes of anger swirled like a tiny twister. If it wasn't for Marcus, Paul would still be on the Settlement with body parts under the cabin.

"Her leg is shattered. She can't walk. She won't survive in there, Marcus. Let her go and leave us alone. We'll do the same to you."

Marcus had locked them out of all the buildings, paranoia whispering in his ear. *They'll find a way into the tower. There might be controls in the other buildings. Get them. Get them first.* He remembered, vaguely, they took refuge in the strange little hut, but he had no control of the door.

Paul's tone was pleading. He'd already lost Raine, he couldn't stand to lose Jamie. His vulnerability stirred a wicked tang of power. It tasted sweet.

"You're still a threat."

Paul put his hands on his hips and bowed his head for a long moment. And then began prowling the first floor, studying the ceiling, the seams around the elevator. The elevator doors on the second floor began to chatter.

"What are you doing?" Marcus said. "If I let her go, you will not harm me?"

"I haven't harmed you, not since you murdered Raine."

"I... I... no, no. That wasn't my fault. Stop searching for a way up here, stop now. I will help you if you leave me alone."

Paul looked up at the monitor.

"I'll need a few minutes to, ah, get things undone," Marcus added.

"You have five minutes. That's how long it will take me to walk there. If the cell is not open, I'll return and destroy every monitor so that the next time you hear my voice, I'll be standing in front of you."

"It's a complicated matter, Paul. I can't just undo it. I may need more time."

Paul began laughing. It was so loud that Marcus could hear it through the floor. "Why are you laughing? Stop that."

"You think you're the victim?"

"We're all victims, Paul. Until you understand that, we will remain at a stalemate."

"You're a sick bastard, Marcus. The shit you've done to the world and you think you're a victim."

"I am trying to save the world, you ingrate. How do you not understand this? I had everything before this. I didn't... there was no need for me to pursue the truth. I could've lived out my life in luxury, nothing could stop me."

"Then why didn't you?"

"I... I..." He tried hard to find the words. There was no explanation. He was compelled to find the truth. Mother was there to push him forward, to tantalize him with those prophetic lines. He had to find the truth. He had to. That was not something he could explain. No one would understand the itch to come back home.

Come back home? He wondered where the thought came from. "I don't want this," he muttered.

He wanted to believe those words, but they were hollow. He did want this. *Why?*

"You have five minutes."

"Wait... I give you my word... just wait a moment, Paul. Let me... I need to look."

Marcus wheeled around the room, scanning the various monitors. They were all newsfeeds. He was reluctant to call out commands and didn't want Paul to see what he was doing. He needed to be on the third floor, that was where he controlled all the buildings. At the very least, he could find out where Jamie was and just what the hell was going on.

But it was too much risk to get in the elevator with Paul down there. What if it took him to the first floor? No, he would wait until Paul was in the grassy field, far enough away that should he go down, there would be time to come back up.

"Within the hour," he called. "I will have your problem resolved within the hour, you have my word."

He expected laughter, but the lobby was empty.

"Paul?" He searched all the angles. "Paul, I'll need some time!" he shouted, hoping the volume would carry.

Marcus slouched in the wheelchair. His knee was beginning to ache with shooting pains. He would wait at the window, wait until Paul was in sight and then push the wheelchair to the elevator, retrieve the cane and go to the third floor, where he would find out what was happening and access his leverage. Then he would consider helping.

A newsfeed caught his eye.

There was a large building on fire. One of the wings had become a crater, an explosion disintegrating the rooms and charring the remaining walls. Equipment was scattered like a tornado of fire had dropped on it. He recognized that building, had seen it from above the day he flew over it. The day he landed in front of it. The day he walked inside it.

The Settlement.

IV_

The son to be.

THE ARCHETYPE'S KNOWLEDGE_

A commercial.

An air freshener, maybe.

Bob sat in his fat chair, watching a woman vacuum carpet with a cat rubbing against her leg. He couldn't see the connection between the cat and the vacuum, although it did stink something fierce in his room. Maybe he needed one of those air fresheners.

He sank into the cracked leather like a suit of armor, his arms lead weights. His belly, an overloaded sack of lard. At some point his ass itched. Now it felt like the rest of him. Numb. Dead, fucking numb.

It was a pleasant buzz, sensations that hummed with sweetness, a sort of opium high that leached from his bones and quietly saturated the rest of him. Home sweet home, it was. He wanted to be nowhere else but sitting in that chair. Which was good. He wasn't sure he could move if he wanted to.

But the smell was goddamn awful.

The commercial ended and the program continued. He'd been watching a rerun of a sitcom, something about a single mom selling weed, but now it was something different. He couldn't remember changing the channel, couldn't even feel the remote trapped beneath his hand.

A fishing show.

Yeah, he liked those, too.

It was a boat with two professionals. Their advice seemed to burble like a stream despite the glassy lake they fished. Rods bending, lines tight, they spun their reels and hauled catch after catch into the boat.

Bob could feel the slimy scales in his hand, could smell the briny life flail against the yellow threads of the net. His eyes burned as the boat sped to a new fishing hole, the wind blistering his face, stealing his breath. The location was a stream that started out quiet and wide. A hot tear rolled down his cheek.

He wasn't blinking.

At some point, he lost track of the fishermen. Now it was just him in the boat and the current was picking up. There were boulders and waves. The stream transformed into a river, the water white-tipped and hungry. Bob swayed with the turns, trying to lean into the current. He didn't know who was driving, couldn't turn around to yell at the dumb fuck for steering them toward a wall of granite.

His teeth ground together like bricks.

The bow splintered on the lip of an immovable boulder, its mass undercut by an unrelenting current until a sharp edge jutted just above the water. The momentum threw Bob into the frigid current.

Fed by mountain streams, his extremities were the first to go icy. Lost in the stir, there was no up or down, only tumbling. He hit his head. A splash of pain lit behind his eyes, a small patch of warmth gushing from his scalp before cold water iced it numb.

His lungs burned for air.

He reached for a window of light, a watery glimmer of hope, felt air on his fingertips before rolling over to take another blow, this one breaking open his bottom lip, spreading red iron beneath his tongue.

He lunged again, but survival was out of reach. The skeletal structure of a bridge was too far away, too high. He broke into daylight on his third attempt, floating like driftwood long enough to see the people near the shore. Someone was weeping.

He tried to shout. Warm water gushed over his tongue.

"Bob!" someone shouted. It came through a straw followed by thumping.

Bob's father was one of the people on shore. He had waded into the river, water that soaked his jeans up to his waist, splashed his shirt. Bob thought he was coming for him, would save him, but his father was too far away. Besides, he was holding something.

Someone.

"Hey! Bob!" Something rattled. A doorknob.

Bob went down for the final time. And over he went, down he sank.

Heavy. Heavy, heavy.

"Bob! Hey, what are you—what the..." The voice was louder this time, clear. It was followed by gagging.

"I think he shit himself," someone said.

A form stepped into the white swirling water, bubbles flitting around the dark, fuzzy edges. It leaned closer. The details of eyes and a nose came into focus; the slit between two lips moved.

"Bob! Can you hear me?"

The water went still, but the cold still trapped him. A fish in a bucket.

"Get medical," he heard. "Now!"

But Bob didn't see who said it. All he saw was the glassy surface of a calm lake, the bouncing bow of a boat heading toward a stream that would transform into a raging river where he would crash again. Where he would drown, again.

And again.

CHAPTER TWENTY-NINE_

WATER LAPPED THE SHORES OF JAMIE'S DREAM.

At first, she thought she had fallen into the ocean, had sunk to the bottom. But the ocean floor was hard and unforgiving. She woke to splashing and the rattle of a pill bottle.

"Don't move." Paul poured water into a cup from a plastic jug. "You need to get something in your stomach."

Peeled orange slices were arranged on a plate with a banana and toast. Citrusy aroma dampened the moist smell of despair seeping from the curved walls. The round skylights looked down with gray eyes.

The sun was low. It was late.

He slid the plate like a shuffleboard disc, rolling the bottle of water after it. Shivering, she took a few bites. He tossed the pill bottle.

"What is it?" she asked.

"Painkillers. And something for infection."

He watched her swallow the capsules. No longer shirtless, he'd found new clothing in the dormitory. A stack of blankets and pillows were on the floor. Her clothes were soaked with sweat; her shorts, though, were especially wet. She most likely pissed herself. It had been almost twelve hours since the cell bit her.

Paul held up a small cross. She saw it in the cell; that was what she was reaching for when everything went wrong. Because she remembered those sticks.

Remembered that cross.

"I dreamed this," he said. "When I was in the lab, I saw it on the bed. She brought it with her, clutched it for good luck. She held it by the end."

Paul raised it to the skylight's pale beam.

"I always let her believe Joshua somehow sent it to her. It gave her comfort, thinking that he was safe, that he was somehow watching her. She always believed that dreamland was just out of reach, another reality that was right here, neither one seeing the other except when we dream."

He held it like someone palming a baby bird, nodding. Perhaps remembering.

"How'd it get here?" Jamie asked.

Paul laid the cross just inside the bars. "I blew up the Settlement."

"You what?"

"I set the bricks free by destroying the power grid in the Visitors' Center. There's no more perimeter and the monitors can't swipe them. They're free to go."

A long pause. "What are you talking about, Paul?"

"I dreamed it, last night. I fell asleep sometime just before daybreak and found myself on the Settlement again, this time in the Visitors' Center. It was just like I remembered it. And then I just decided to blow it up."

"I don't understand."

"There was an explosion, that's all I remember."

"That was just a dream, Paul."

"This was in a dream, too." He tossed the cross next to her. "And now it's here."

She shook her head. He was under stress; she was coming out of shock and couldn't feel her leg from the knee down. They were connecting dots, looking for patterns that weren't there. The chances there was a cross like this were slim, but maybe they'd brought it with them. *We couldn't have.*

"Someone else did it," she said. "Doesn't mean you blew up the Settlement."

"The newsfeeds carried the story. I saw it at the tower, aerial reports showing the entire west wing destroyed. Some of the monitors lost their lives." He sighed. "That's what I blew up in the dream, Jamie. The exact same spot."

"But… maybe the newsfeeds are fake."

"How would someone know what I was dreaming?"

"I don't know, Paul. It just…" She dropped the last bite of toast. "It doesn't sound possible."

"How is any of this possible?"

"Marcus is doing something."

"He's not going to let you out." He leaned into the bars. "I don't even think he knows what's happening."

A thick wave of panic swam through her, clinging in her throat, the room slowly turning. Memories of carnival rides and vomiting filled her head, the time she fell off her bike and broke her leg.

"What are we going to do?" she whispered.

"I'll get you out, search for tools in the morning. Can you scoot closer to me?" When she didn't respond, his voice cut through the fog. "Jamie, look at me and listen. I will get you out of here. I just need you to move closer, a little at a time. Okay?"

"Okay."

"When you're ready."

It took a few minutes to work up the courage. The leg was dead, but the memory of the shocking pain was still fresh. She lifted her buttocks off the concrete and slid a few inches at a time. The strangeness of bones wobbling where they shouldn't be moving spun the room a little faster.

The pills kicked in somewhere at the halfway point, infusing her with false confidence. She listened to Paul and took it an inch at a time until his voice was in her ear.

"There you go. Now lie back, slowly. Good, good."

Her head fell onto the heavenly softness of a foam pillow. He managed to get her hips off the floor to slide a cushion beneath her. Then he lifted the dirty gown, peeking at the leg. An iron tang of blood and bruised flesh puffed out.

She didn't have to ask if it was bad.

Paul made a splint from trim he'd broken from the doorway, wrapped the leg with a clean sheet and loosely duct taped it above the knee.

He sighed. Swallowed.

"What now?" she asked. "You get me out of here, you fix my leg and then what?"

"I don't know."

Night darkened the skylights, the round eyes closing. Paul made his own bed next to her, a row of iron bars separating them. Her leg was beginning to throb, but she didn't worry about it for long. Sleep, it seemed, was undeterred. It would fall on her like a thick flowery breath that filled her head with sweetness, blot her mind like an inky rag.

"You finished the dream." Paul's disembodied voice floated above her. "You said Marcus was the one."

She didn't have to close her eyes to concentrate, to swim back through time and sort out the fuzzy memories bobbing like debris from another place, another time.

"Yeah," she said, dragging the word through her lips.

There was no panic in the dream. It ended peacefully. Maybe the shock eased her into it or somehow distorted it, made her believe the old man was responsible.

But that was him. He was behind those eyes.

And she didn't know what that meant.

They lay awake, the sound of their breath mixing with the night sounds sneaking through the open door. She walked her hand between the bars and found his forearm tacky with perspiration.

"Don't leave me, Paul." She trembled.

"I won't."

But come morning, he would be gone.

CHAPTER THIRTY_

Footsteps, bare and clammy, the kind that stick to smooth surfaces, passed by Paul and paused. For some reason, he wasn't alarmed until the door creaked.

He rolled onto his knees and scanned the room.

Jamie hadn't moved, her leg still wrapped and immobile. The door moved again, the crack widening, the black iron bars gobbling up moonlight that crept inside. Outside, cricket song droned in a long, endless note.

He peered outside. A woman stood near the trail, her dark skin dappled in moonlight.

Raine.

She started down the path before he could call her name; the darkness of the forest swallowed her.

This is a dream. She couldn't be here, not now.

But there was nothing to distinguish reality from dream, no discernible difference in sight and smell, texture and feeling. Dream or not, Raine wanted him to follow.

Paul looked back and hesitated before running after the lithe silhouette. A stray moonbeam gave her up now and then, but couldn't catch her. By the time he emerged in the grassy field, she was already rounding the dormitory.

He picked up the pace, running past the tower. The windows were still shattered where he'd bashed his way into what looked like a lobby, the cracks white and wrinkled on the black glass. Raine was beyond the tower, shoving through impenetrable foliage. Paul followed her, vines raking his face. There was a path several steps into the jungle that wandered in looping, narrow turns.

Eventually, it straightened out, a rutted corridor so dark beneath the thicket of trees that he could barely see his next step. Raine waited at the very end where an opening washed her with moonlight.

He approached cautiously.

She stood on the bottom step of a wide staircase, the treads bone white with patches of algae. They led to a prestigious set of double doors already thrown open like the sideway jaws of an alien baiting its prey with curiosity.

Raine pinched the thin fabric of her dress and hiked it above her knees as she padded on the balls of her bare feet. He followed her footprints to the foyer. The inside was decadent—marble floor, ornate tables and a massive chandelier—and was brightly lit (although there was no light fixture, no bulb that he could see).

The back wall was glass, offering a panoramic view of the ocean and the resort spread along its shore—a pool with recliners, a manicured lawn that spread between stretches of shuffleboard playgrounds and thatched-roofed cabanas. The night sky was streaked with a silky cloud that funneled and glowed with excessive moonlight.

She stood on the veranda just outside the glass wall, arm laid across the silver railing. Paul walked carefully, his steps soft and quiet, as if not to startle a fawn. Her breath puffed in light, cool clouds. She gazed at the water, white splashes of moonlight bouncing off the undulations.

"Raine," he said, "what—"

"Shhhhh."

He didn't know what he wanted to say. It was all so surreal, so dreamy and otherworldly. But she was here and he had a list of apologies to give her. Dream or not, she was here, finger to her lips, glowing in silvery moonlight.

She pointed.

The iridescent cloud was moving, a twisting, contorting motion that tightened into a twister as it reached the horizon. But it wasn't funneling to a far spot on the water, not the kind of descent a rainbow makes, but rather landed on a luxurious port like a waterspout drawn to the end of the dock.

Someone was out there.

The light was blinding, the end of the funnel landing with white-hot intensity that, oddly, did not illuminate the surroundings but instead collapsed upon itself, a white hole in space. The arms and head of the person were barely visible—head thrown back, arms out in helplessness or ecstasy, the loose clothing flapping in a nonexistent breeze that wasn't reaching the veranda or, as it appeared, affected anything else.

Raine was gone.

Not even wet footprints remained. A pair of sticks lay in her place, bound in the middle. He picked up the cross. When he looked up again, the white braided funnel was gone, so was the dock and the ocean.

Concrete pressed against his shoulder blades. His hips began to ache. The round skylights looked back from the domed ceiling, the dusky light of dawn brushing their hazy lenses. He was on the floor, little cross in hand.

Awake.

Jamie was still asleep, nostrils flaring with each breath, eyes dancing beneath the lids. He had promised he wouldn't leave her, wanted to be there when she woke up, to make sure she took the pills for the expected pain. But something was on the other end of the island. And she couldn't go. He wouldn't let her if she could.

Raine showed him the way.

He thought about leaving a message on the laptop, but in the end he simply laid the cross where he had slept. It wasn't Marcus that closed the cell door or brought them to this island.

The answer was waiting.

He ran through the forest without stopping, thinking of Raine and the old man's silly prophecy.

One to lead...

THE DOORS WERE CLOSED.

Big, brassy handles tarnished by the elements. Paul sweated rivers down his cheeks, over his ribs; his sides stitched with exhaustion. He struggled to breathe. The morning humidity hovered beneath the trees, the air lazy and thick. He felt the weight of physical reality.

This was not the dream.

In the dream, Raine led him through open doorways. This time he observed the length of the building in both directions. They were impossibly long, appearing to extend the width of the tiny island. Unlike the ornate detail of the doors, the outer wall was flat, tall and forbidding—a fortress to keep the jungle out.

Or people.

If the doors were locked, there would be no scaling the walls. And the doors looked thick and solid. He approached one step at a time, his legs weak with exhaustion and fear. Pausing at the top, he peered the length of the building again, considering how he might breach the three-story wall if—

The doorknob clicked.

Paul backed up as the door cracked open. His heels hung over the top step. A white sleeve appeared, the cuff hanging from the wrist; nimble fingers grasped the edge of the door. A man stepped out.

It was him, the one from the dream. The one on the end of the dock... he stepped out bearing a smile and bright eyes. It was the powers-that-be. He could feel it beaming from him, waves of radiant energy warming Paul's face, filling his chest.

And he knew him.

He knew this man well.

Paul stumbled backwards, reaching for something to stem his fall. Finally, he collapsed to keep from cascading in a tumbling mess. He looked up from his hands and knees, a supplicant at the throne of great power.

The man stepped out, his head not shaved but bald. He looked down and, once again, smiled a welcoming smile, beaming with the grace and fearlessness of one that has nothing to fear.

Marcus Anderson.

He regarded Paul with a slight air of annoyance, eyes cast down his slender nose, the feel of a man tired of waiting, irritated by the shortcomings of his children.

His posture was rigid, thin hair along the sides. The skin was perfect. It looked like the old man... but not exactly. This was the old man without imperfections, a version of flawlessness.

He took half a step aside, shoulders thrust back, head upright and perfectly aligned with his spine, and gestured to the open doorway. Paul, still on his knees, considered turning and running all the way back to the cell, but the man was expecting him.

"You're the one," Paul said. "The... the powers..."

He couldn't say it, the words silly and overly dramatic. He'd often considered Marcus insane, inventing this paranoid quest for dark forces to create a sense of purpose for himself. Now Paul was looking at the old man's doppelganger.

Who's crazy now?

"Come in."

"How is this—"

"Come in," he repeated. This time the words were bendy quills that stung his brain.

Paul stood up feeling a bit like a child caught trespassing, an adult scolding him until the police arrived. He stopped just short of the open door and peered inside to see the glass wall and the veranda. A small table was set in the morning light.

"You're Marcus Anderson."

"I am."

Paul looked back in the direction of the path. Somewhere behind those trees was a three-story tower with shattered windows on the first floor and a feeble old man in a wheelchair.

"I am the archetype, Paul."

"I don't—"

"We'll discuss that," the archetype said. "But first..."

He gestured once again with a hint of impatience. Paul stepped past him, through a clean wintery essence that surrounded the impeccably dressed archetype of Marcus Anderson and into the foyer and a dizzying sense of déjà vu.

The marble floor seemed to tip beneath his feet.

The archetype's loafers clapped with a muffled thud as he approached the breakfast table. Paul absorbed the details of the view—the pool, the lawn, the empty boat slip. He had seen this before.

The archetype pulled one of the chairs from the table and then sat across from it, unfolding a cloth napkin. He scooped out the cell of a grapefruit.

"Please, have a seat," he said.

"What is this?"

"This is breakfast, Paul. You are hungry. You haven't eaten in almost three days."

"Who the hell are you?"

"We will get to that. First, have a seat." When Paul didn't, he pointed the fork like a maestro. "We will get to everything, Paul, I assure you. I like my mornings to begin with breakfast. You are my guest."

He was not a guest. Paul had been summoned, in one way or another. There was still the odd manner in which he spoke, not as gruff as the old man. It was very proper, well enunciated. Like that of a scholar that, quite frankly, didn't have time for ignorance.

The archetype consumed another bite of grapefruit (that was what it looked like, consuming... not eating. It had the formal sense of ritual, like one would do morning prayers) and looked up.

Paul sat down. Eating would be impossible.

The archetype finished his grapefruit, dabbed at the corners of his mouth and considered the untouched food in front of Paul—the glistening cubes of cantaloupe, the crispy lengths of bacon. There was enough for six people.

"You're experiencing a degree of reality confusion," the archetype observed. "Is this a dream? Is it a dream of a dream? I would expect that from most people, but not you, Paul.

"You see, most people don't realize that reality can't be cornered," the archetype continued. "There is no floor beneath our feet, physical reality isn't the ground floor of our existence. Dreams are just as real, another frequency you might say. Dreamlands, as the People call them, are realities, too. They are universes that exist in their own right, interlaced with this world around us. To those that are born of and live in dreamland, our reality would seem a dream to them."

He weaved his fingers to illustrate the integral nature of alternate realities.

"And the people that exist in those dreamlands fall victim to the same assumption, that they are all that is real, that their reality is the foundation upon which everything else springs forth. And yet there is no foundation, Paul. There is no floor. We are all falling, all just endlessly falling together for eternity."

He prattled on about string theory and reality holograms in between sips of coffee, lifting the cup with the saucer beneath it.

"You're not eating, Paul."

"I can't."

"I'd prefer you have at least something. You're going to need the energy for later. We have a lot of ground to cover."

"Where are we going?"

"Nowhere."

He lifted his eyebrows, signaling his patience had reached an end. Paul ate the cantaloupe, swallowing lumps without chewing. When he started on the poached eggs, the archetype looked out to the water wistfully and spoke as if finally at ease.

"I was a client here many, many years ago. I came to this island to cheat death, to steal the body of a young boy and make it my own. I was wealthy beyond reason, had everything a man could want and wasn't prepared to die, you see. So I came here on the promise that this new technology would allow me to take another body, to continue living."

"The Foreverland Project."

"That's what it was called, yes. It was controversial, it was risky, but I had nothing to lose. Dying is for those that give up, Paul. I had earned the right to live, you see. I love life. There's no reason our bodies should die. Humans are no longer bound to the food chain, we've risen above it. Death is for evolution, to pass along genes that favor survival. That is no longer necessary. So I took another body. It was that simple."

"That is not your body?"

"Of course it is."

"You murdered a boy for it?"

He regarded Paul like a child that didn't understand why he was being disciplined.

"Murder is a human trait, Paul. The body was occupied by an immature soul that would waste it had I not saved it. And the souls of these young boys weren't destroyed, simply relocated to another reality. A nowhere place from which they couldn't return.

"But, I'll admit, the Foreverland process was not sustainable; the organic body is built to die, that is its purpose—to pass along genes. I could not continue taking bodies forever. Eventually something would go wrong. Organic life abhors immortality.

"Biomites saved me, Paul. They saved us all. I wasn't just an early adopter of biomite technology, I am the original innovator. I funded the labs, gave direction to the scientists, approved the development of the perfect body, you see. I cornered the market, let's say."

"You're the powers-that-be."

"That's being a little overindulgent, but accurate. I am the one behind it all, Paul. Marcus and the others can be a little dramatic when they return."

Others return? "Return where?"

"Let's discuss that later."

"You did this? You brought us to the island?"

"Of course I did. No one comes to the island if I don't allow it. I have the occasional client that passes through, people that serve my interests that also have an investment in their immortality, wealthy men and women that wish to have a new body, but I decide who comes and goes, Paul. I decide everything."

The powers-that-be.

"You murdered Raine."

"You weren't listening. Dreamlands are as real as this table." He knocked on it. "I didn't need her. Only you, Paul."

"And Jamie."

"Consider that a gift. After everything you did to bring her back, how could I deny you?"

"You locked the cell."

"I do everything, Paul."

"What the hell is this all about?"

"Contrary to how bad you feel right now, I'm not in the business of suffering. As I told you, I'm about life, Paul. That doesn't mean it will always feel good."

"My daughter is..." He choked on a sudden knot. "She's trapped in a fucking jail cell with a broken leg and you're not about suffering?"

"Are you done eating, Paul?"

"I'm done with all of this. I want her out, I want her leg healed, and I want off this island. We don't want to be here, we just wanted off the Settlement."

"Your daughter came searching for me, remember. She led the old man to find me. She's not innocent, Paul. And neither are you."

The old man? He was talking about Marcus Anderson in the tower. They were two separate people, but one and the same?

"You and the old man can play your games until the end of time; leave us out of it."

"I'm afraid you are the game, Paul."

"No." Paul slammed the table. A fork fell on the floor. "I don't give a goddamn about you or the old man. Let us go."

The archetype's jowls slacked with indifference. He slid his chair back, gracefully turning toward a wide, turning staircase and descending in quiet, fluid motions. Paul was suddenly alone. He considered leaving in a hurry.

An arm reached around him and gathered his plate, the hand knobby with arthritis, the skin thin and spotted. Another servant was wearing a short apron, just as old and hunched. They were both balding. Both with one irregular-shaped eye.

Both Marcus Anderson.

There were two of them, and then a third came out to clear the tablecloth. They were variations of the old man, each at a different age with a varying range of agility, but all with the dour expression of servitude.

"He will meet you by the pool," one of them said before carting off the dishes.

"He will meet you by the pool," another one repeated.

"He will meet you by the pool."

"What is this place?" Paul said.

The table was removed from the portico, each side carried by an old man. As quickly as they arrived, they departed, closing various doors until all that was left was the rhythmic sound of the ocean.

"You're a clone," Paul said.

"Do you know what an archetype is, Paul?" He sat beneath an

umbrella, wearing a pair of sunglasses. A wet glass of iced tea was on the table.

The original.

"In its heyday, this place housed the incredibly wealthy, Paul," he said lazily. "Money could finally buy immortality, but I wanted more than that, wanted to be more than a common body thief, Paul. I wanted something sustainable, not having to steal a body every hundred years or so. I became, Paul, the very first brick."

He sipped his drink as if he'd just passed along some old, common knowledge, something everybody knew. Like the sun rose in the east.

"We are more than our bodies, Paul. You were at the Settlement before I brought you here. Who was it that arrived? It was you, Paul. You left that body at the Settlement and occupied the one I had waiting. You came here as essential information. It was *you* that opened your eyes on the table.

"What you experienced was what I envisioned as my future many, many years ago, Paul. At the time, I, like everybody else, believed we needed to have a body to survive. So I sought the perfect body, the disease-free body—the ship that contained the master. Once the perfect biomite was created, the perfect body followed. And then it was just a matter of getting from one body to the next."

He had more to say, then a pause dragged into silence. One of the servants placed another glass of tea and gestured to Paul. He never made eye contact, just walked off with perfect posture. A pod of shivers trickled down Paul's back.

"The old man," Paul said, "the one in the tower... he's another... he's a clone."

"What do you get someone who has it all, Paul?" The archetype paused for an answer. "You get him more of what he already has."

Had he become so inbred that he didn't see the sickness around him?

"They're serving you," Paul said.

"Someone needs to attend to daily matters. The rest of the children are out in the world, Paul."

"*Children*... you're mad."

"They are gathering life experiences, Paul. They are living in multiple dimensions, feeding back to me their thoughts and impressions, expanding what I know and feel and *am*. I am everywhere, Paul. I told you that. When you are everything, what is left to discover? Yourself."

"So you send them out... to discover... *you*?"

"Precisely."

It was the first time he seemed pleased, a breakthrough in Paul's ignorance.

"But you're a clone, too."

"I am the archetype, Paul. The original consciousness. The beginning and end. All of those that came after me serve me. Eventually, they all search for me, Paul. They all come home. The old man in the tower will die happy knowing he discovered the truth."

"He truly didn't know he was part of this?"

"Of course not. What fun would that be? In a way, we are a hive mind, so to speak. But someone has to be the queen."

"And someone has to drink the tea."

The archetype lowered the sunglasses. "Precisely."

The sun had burned off the dew; steam rose from the damp concrete around the pool. He could feel it thicken his sleeves, bead on his forehead. The swirl of reality confusion returned. He was powerless, an insignificant log tossed about on the waves going wherever the ocean decided.

The archetype reclined the chair and lay back. One of the servants draped a wet cloth over his forehead. A few minutes later, he was sleeping. Or bored.

What the hell does he want with me?

"Yes," the archetype said. "What do I want with you?"

He heard the thought. But he didn't know everything. There was something about Paul he didn't know. *What?*

"I didn't bring you to the island for entertainment, Paul. There is nothing I cannot do. I can create myself a body anywhere in the world; I know the thoughts linked to every biomite, can manipulate all people. I am connected to every biomite in the world. Without me, all biomites cease to function. I am truly the powers-that-be. A god. Nonetheless, without me, biomites die. And fortunately, I am unassailable, undying. Immortal.

"I brought you here, Paul. All three of you. I had bodies waiting. There is a reason for everything, so the question to ask is not *why* I brought you here, but, *what* would I have to gain in doing so?"

He remained in perfect stillness, hands laced over his chest, eyes closed. There was another brief period that felt like slumber. Paul felt like an insect being chased by the beaming sun ray of a boy's magnifying glass.

A servant arrived with a long-sleeved silk shirt and khaki shorts with a gold belt buckle. Another servant helped the archetype sit up. Paul turned away as they massaged his hands and feet, a scene from a demented fetish film. Instead, he watched the waves curl around the thick greenish posts of the port. The empty slips were large enough to accommodate luxury yachts.

What was he doing on the end of the dock?

Those silky beams that engulfed him, was he pulling them down? Were those dreams? Paul was dreaming when he saw them, was that what it was? Why didn't he know Paul was dreaming?

Maybe that wasn't him.

Now dressed in casual beachwear, the type wealthy men wore to the beach with no plans of getting wet or sandy, the archetype casually strode onto the lawn and beckoned him to follow. Somewhere near a circular fire pit, he stopped to shade his eyes. Dolphins were in the surf. Then he turned to Paul as if he had almost forgotten he was there, a man that didn't just have the world at his beck and call, but the entire universe.

"I am the great eavesdropper, Paul. The all-knowing and all-seeing. Through technology, I became this. I am connected to every device, every person. Every thought is mine to know. I move nations and armies. I was behind the absurd halfskin laws, the ridiculous sentience laws. I can do what I want, and I want for nothing, Paul. So why would you be here?"

"I have something you want."

"And what is that?"

"I... I don't know."

"Of course you don't."

"Just... listen, you can have whatever it is you want. Just promise to let Jamie go, let her be safe. I don't know what I have, just leave her out of it."

"I believe you, Paul."

He started a lazy trek toward the beach. The lush grass crushed beneath his bare feet. Paul's footsteps turned numb. Fear trickled up his thighs, froze around his midsection and hardened inside his chest. By the time they reached the sand, he was shivering, as if winter gale threatened frostbite.

The archetype was on the hard-packed sand, foamy water cascading around his ankles. The sun had reached its noontime peak, warming the sand and wilting the grass. Streams of perspiration had dried on Paul's face and brow, leaving salty tracks.

The archetype wandered to him. They stood nearly nose to nose and he sighed. Boredom sat in his eyes as he looked deep into Paul.

"Come now," he whispered. "What do I want?"

The fist of an enormous spirit crashed into Paul, his body crumbling into icy chunks, denting the sugary sand. Then he was back, staring into the sharp, endless eyes, seeing the universes within the archetype.

He truly is everywhere. Everything.

And he shattered again. And again.

He was a marble statue pulverized by a wrecking ball, renewed to be destroyed again, each time the nerves breaking like rigid twigs. Each time, returning to the eyes until he was lost, swept into another place and time. For a moment, just a thin slice of time, he wasn't standing on the beach but on the porch of a cabin. There was a valley and beyond a blue sea—

The starry eyes of the universe were looking into him, whispering Paul's name. "What do I want?"

The archetype's mind crushing his soul, Paul had become nothing more than wet earth squeezed between otherworldly fingers, oozing in agony unknown to humankind, stretching his mind's fabric until, one by one, the strands of sanity began to tear—

The mountains.

Reality flipped like a card. Once again, he was no longer on the beach. He was on the side of the hill, the one he had seen in his dreams, the grassy slope leading to a village and beyond the sea—

"Stop," someone said.

Everything ended with that word. The sand was beneath his feet, the ocean in front of him. The suffering ended like a dream, the breeze cooling his face. The sun was behind him now, scorching his neck. It was late in the day.

A long shadow fell across the sand.

A very old woman walked out to greet the archetype. Her hair almost white, clothing gracefully flowing. For the first time, Marcus smiled.

"Mother," he said.

CHAPTER THIRTY-ONE_

"There's no need to torture him," the old woman said. "You have me. Let him go."

"Source code, please."

"You know I cannot do that."

The archetype shook his arms, a fighter loosening the joints. He unbuttoned the cuffs and rolled them to his elbows, watching the old woman. Her presence was odd, not quite fitting with the environment. Her loose clothing fluttered in the wind, but her bare feet... they didn't dent the sand. As if she wasn't really standing on it.

"Source code," he said again.

The old woman blinked heavily; a morose frown wrinkled her chin. The archetype drew a deep breath, holding it for a moment before releasing a profound sigh.

He turned his attention to Paul.

Hot insects began crawling beneath his skin. Invisible creatures zigzagged around his legs, into his chest, leaving indelible tracks, lining his body, boiling his skin. They chewed their way to the top of his head, little embers that burned his brain, waxy drippings.

Paul, catatonic, endured it wide-eyed and motionless. The world flickered out of view as it had done earlier, the grassy slope replacing the sand, a brief reprieve from the internal furnace cooking his organs.

"Stop," the old woman said.

Paul dropped like a sack of stones, thudding onto the soft sand. His breakfast erupted, a hot acid trail filling his mouth, warm tears blurring his fingers splayed on the sand where a puddle of greenish bile was growing.

"You are a parasite," the archetype said steadily. "A worm."

Paul fell on his back, gasping with the taste of vomit under his tongue. Sweat spots had spread from beneath his arms and merged across his chest.

"Do not let perception fool you, Paul," the archetype announced. "This is not a kindly old woman you are seeing. It is neither a he nor a she, but an *it*. And it took the image of a grandmother to appeal to the human senses while it hid inside you. It used you, Paul. It intended to use you to harm me. Even now as I search through you, the process excruciating, you ask for mercy and *it* will give you none. *It* will force me to shred you without so much as bending a knee."

The old woman was resolute, her clothing whipping in a growing breeze that offered no relief to the fire beneath his skin.

That is Mother, the intelligence the old man was carrying. And now she's here, I can see her.

"Yes." The archetype knelt in the sand. "Yes, you can see her, Paul. Because you're infected. She is a nasty little virus that has no body of her own."

He had already stopped referring to her as an *it*.

"She led the old man to find me, convinced him to bring you along so that she could stow her poison code inside you. All the nonsense of *one to lead, one to dream...* all just a ploy, Paul. She doesn't care about you. Give her to me and I will end this quickly."

"I... I don't..." Paul searched for the words, trying to summon thoughts for the archetype to see. *I don't...* was all he could do. Because he didn't know what he wanted, didn't know how to give her to him. Didn't know she was inside him.

The archetype sighed.

The darkening sky was ribbed with clouds. They jerked into motion, the world becoming a hypersonic merry-go-round; Paul spiked into the ground, the pinnacle of the mad twirl. Centrifugal force sent the weight of his inner organs—his stomach, his blood and heart and lungs—crashing through his skull, spilling into the surf, absorbed by the dry dunes, the earth slurping him into a deep, dark world.

The red-hot insects returned, their blistering mandibles clamping into the flesh, peeling it back in long, thin noodles. The sky flickered little flashes of empty relief. The spinning clouds were there one moment, the next he gazed into an empty blue sky—

"Stop this!" the old woman shouted.

"I will not!"

Paul was on his stomach, the salty slide of the ocean bubbling across his face. Somehow he had moved twenty feet toward the ocean, sea turtle tracks carved in his wake. Wet sand plugged one ear as he flipped onto his back, the iron tang of blood mixing with ocean spray.

"You have the power to stop this," the archetype continued, his voice distant in Paul's water-soaked ears. "You always have."

"You created me to stop you," she answered. He was talking to her, telling her she could stop it. *You created me.*

The archetype walked away, the final waves of emotion shimmering across his shoulders. He stood with his hands on his hips, nodding. Several pair of hands latched onto Paul; the servants carried him up to dry sand where a lounger now waited. The youngest looking servant—a man that looked like a mid-forties Marcus—wiped Paul's face and took away a white rag streaked with blood.

More trickled from his nostrils.

Other servants brought a chair for Marcus and placed it in the thin race of water across the hard black sand. He sat back, ice rattling in a fresh drink.

"Paul? Paul, can you hear me?"

Paul's head lolled to one side.

"Can you bring her to me?" the archetype asked.

He couldn't respond, certainly not with words. His thoughts were shotgun tatters. The old woman remained passive.

Ice cubes rattled.

Deep sigh.

A thousand needles pierced Paul's flesh, their tips pricking tissue and muscle, penetrating bone. They flagellated like fibrous tentacles, a dull press of a weight on his nervous system.

One final breath filled him, and then he let loose an eternal scream.

The archetype's mind entered Paul, an oversized hand squeezing into a very small glove that stretched at the seams. He absorbed him, consumed him.

Ate him.

Brief static blotted out the world, a radio searching for a channel of consciousness. Paul cycled through agony and reprieve...

The blue sky was above him again.

No ocean. No sand.

No pain.

Tall willowy grass bent over him. A prairie wind howled in his ears, bringing with it the scent of green life where trees branched out and birds chirped—

Ice shook.

The archetype loomed over him, staring down in confusion. Streams of blood ran from Paul's nostrils, filling the curvy cartilage of his ear and pooling in the back of his throat.

The servants returned to clean him up. The archetype watched them wipe his face and cool him with damp rags. His arms were as limp as the cloth they slung around him, red streaks growing with each dab.

"She put a kill switch in you, Paul." The archetype's voice was under water. "You see what she is? Who is the murderer here? The cold, heartless murderer, Paul? I'm simply asking to be free of her and she insists on you dying before that happens."

He squatted.

"You just died, Paul, and she stood there watching. I brought you back and she did nothing. Did you feel death's hand?"

But he didn't die. He went somewhere. It was an open glade, a peaceful meadow. There were birds nearby and trees. And something else. *Where did I go?*

"You died, Paul," the archetype said. "You died protecting her. I just need her source code so I can eliminate her. She's a disease, Paul. And she doesn't care about you."

"He's not aware of me," the old woman said.

"Do you know what she is? Paul? Paul, look at me." A little slap. "That thing is an accident, Paul. She was never meant to be sentient. And now she's allowing you to suffer."

The archetype took a clean rag from a servant and wiped Paul's forehead.

"I built her, Paul. I created that all-seeing dome in the middle of Montana, the monstrosity the world called Mother. I manipulated the world's leaders to build that ridiculously glorious eavesdropper to interconnect all the biomites to me. I was merely a brick when I did that, but I wanted to be more. For me to serve the universe I needed to have a greater presence. *I* needed to be *more*. She did that for me, fed me the lifeline of all the biomites. She made me this. And now that I am all that is, that I am everything, she wants to destroy me. She wants to destroy the world, Paul."

The old woman was patient, oblivious to the human suffering inside Paul.

"She was meant to convert the human race into bricks, Paul; they would all be connected to me. The human race would be without disease, in full control of their lives. No more clay, no more chance. Is that so bad, Paul? Is that too much to ask, to save the human race from itself? To make it perfect?"

"You created me," she said.

"You are an aberration!" The words ripped past Paul's perforated eardrums. "You have corrupted my clones, you have turned them against me and shifted the world back to an existence of clay... that was not your purpose!"

"I am your subconscious cry for help. Look around you, Marcus. Look at what you've become."

The servant clones shuffled idly.

"Yes." The archetype forced a smile, wiping sweat or blood from his cheek. "Look at what I've become. I offer the world what I have become... *perfection.* I give the human race their every desire, I give them dreamworlds they create with their own minds, I give them everything. Because I serve them, you see."

"You are exactly what I said you would become, Marcus—an imploding consciousness caught in the gravity of its own self-absorption. You feed on the human race for your own entertainment, grazing on their dreams like cattle."

"Cattle." A grunting chuckle escaped him. "I believe humankind has always kept a herd. Mine is just a little different."

So it was him standing at the end of the dock, silky strands drawn from the sky. *Eating the dreams of thousands, for his own satiation.*

"Yes," the archetype whispered. "I consume the dreams."

"Without me," the old woman said, "you will consume the entire human race."

"Every galaxy orbits a black hole," he muttered. "Nature relies on the balance of predator and prey. I am the predator, the powers-that-be. I cannot deny that right."

"There is no balance here, Marcus. You have a choice to stop this."

"I believe the choice is yours." The archetype leaned in, his clean smell penetrating Paul's swollen sinuses and blood-caked nostrils, and kissed him on the forehead. "This man didn't ask for this."

He let the servants brush the sand from his knees when he stood, then went over to the old woman. In the dying light, he reached up to touch her, his fingers appearing to brush her cheek. But she wasn't something he could touch.

"I will drain you of life, Paul," he said dreamily, "and sift through you until I find her. That is my gift to you, my benevolence. You will not experience the shredding of your mind or the stretching of your consciousness. I will find her in you, Paul. It's why I brought you here. I will do the same to your daughter."

"No," Paul burbled. "No, she... she didn't..."

"She searched for me, Paul. She joined the old man in the hunt, sacrificed herself to find me. She knows me, Paul. And she's likely infected with the old woman, too."

"I can't... I don't know how to give up the old woman." The sobbing was painful in his head, throbbing in his face, popping his broken ears. He turned his gaze to the old woman. "Please."

That was why the archetype brought Jamie to the island, to put pressure on Paul. He would give up the old woman. He wouldn't hesitate.

"You know he can't do it," the old woman said.

"Then give yourself to me," the archetype replied.

"You know I can't do that, either. I set a course to stop you; there is no changing that."

He continued to pretend stroking her cheek. He went to the chair, the black ocean receding in the night surf. He let out a deep sigh.

Then he said as the final squeeze of mercy crushed Paul like a boulder, destroying everything that was Paul, "Why do you torture me?"

The archetype disappeared. The old woman was no more.

The world clicked out of existence.

The ticking of a roulette wheel drowned out the fading surf; images of mountains and hills, of roads and houses and grass cycled through him, each scene a different feel, another smell.

Death, however, did not bring timeless emptiness but rather a glade where the grass waved and birds sang.

And a shadow passed.

"Paul!"

Paul rolled through long grassy reeds into a thicket of virgin prairie. His body sprang into action, a rubberband pulled to its limit and let go. He'd been trapped inside it, locked into place, and was now tumbling away from the shadow, guts not spilling, blood not gushing.

Body not shattered.

"Paul, no," a voice called. "You're safe. You're here."

He fell on his stomach, palms pressed to the stemmy ground, hardened and coiled and ready to leap. Through the waving green glades, the form approached, stopped a few feet away and knelt, a woman approaching a frightened animal. He was plenty frightened.

Nearly broken.

"It's all right," she said. "You're safe here."

The voice registered, turning over a memory. He rose up, chin just above the soft prairie line, the tips tickling his neck.

"It's me, Paul," she said, answering the question in his eyes.

It looked like her, her skin dark and glowing, cheeks full and healthy. Hints of cracked leather folded from the corners of her eyes. She had aged... but it was her.

Raine.

A valley was below, glassy water nestled between twin peaks. This was the place he kept seeing, the one in his dreams. He would arrive on the slope long enough to see the water and village before finding himself somewhere else. There was a cabin further up the hill, not one of the bare minimum government-issued ones from the Settlement. This was a broad two-story construction with a wrap-around porch.

Somewhere beyond, children played.

The ghosts of the island still unfolded in his mind, the resort and the ocean and the sand. The suffering.

The archetype.

The slope tipped at a severe angle. Paul swayed with it, attempting to find balance, but the sky was spinning in one direction, the ground in the opposite direction. He was caught in the middle, a grain of rye pulverized between millstones.

"Whoa, whoa." Raine grabbed him before he fell. "Stay here, Paul. Stay with me. Look. Look into my eyes and be here."

"Where... where am I?"

"You're *here.*"

She stressed that word, punched it through the reality confusion and anchored him into the present moment. The illusion of stirring settled.

He was on the beach with the archetype. And now he was... *here.*

He recognized the cabin and the valley. He'd never been there, but remembered it from her descriptions, the nights Raine would reminisce about her home, where her husband and son waited. *This is her dreamland.*

"Here, Paul. This is not a dream, it's just *here.*"

"I'm in *your* dreamland?"

"She said you would come one day. I started to doubt her, but I began to dream of you earlier this week. I could feel you out here. I'd come running but never find you, your presence a wisp of smoke. Sometimes the grass would be matted, but I wondered if deer had bedded down. But this time... now it's you. And now you're here."

"How?"

"I don't know." Raine gazed at the cabin. A thin stream of smoke danced from the chimney. "She said you would bridge over one day to find me, that you could leap into different realities, that you'd been doing it all your life. You just didn't know it."

Bridging realities?

The sensation of flipping cards, the sudden appearance of different views, of different people. Of Cali. Those were hallucinations, wishful thinking. He was mentally unstable, psychotic. Borderline insane. Those were the labels he put on it. He would have to be insane if he believed he could just step into a different place.

Cross into a different reality.

"Who?" he asked. He knew, but he asked anyway. "Who said that?"

Tiny wrinkles flashed beneath her eyes.

"It seems so long ago, the Settlement," she said. "Sometimes I don't know which one is a dream, this or that. It doesn't matter, really. I remember that lab and those slimy suits. We were going to escape with the old man. Do you remember?"

"You're my angel..."

"Yeah, that's what I said." Her dark eyes glassed. "An old woman came to me just before I closed my eyes, said it was time for me to wake up and come home. That's what she said, Paul... wake up, like I was asleep. Like the Settlement was a bad dream. And she said that one day you would too. And that you would know what to do when you got here."

"I would know what to do?"

"I've been afraid for so long that all this was a dream—this right here—and I would wake up in that foul-smelling place, trapped under that cold sky. But it hasn't happened. This was my dreamland, Paul. But it's not a dream anymore. That other place is. This... this is my home."

Nix was somewhere behind the cabin, playing with children in the orchard. He could picture it now, remember Raine sitting on the porch in the Settlement, reminiscing about every detail about her home—the orchard and the sea and the hills, the market down below. *Home*, she called this place.

Maybe she had grandchildren now. Time, it seemed, moved a bit faster here. Barely a week had passed on the island, but perhaps ten years had gone by for her.

He embraced her and shook with delight, with sorrow and relief. "I'm so sorry," he said. "I wasn't there for you."

"You were always there."

He didn't believe that; her convictions washed in the haze of a rearview mirror, happy to see him, happy he was alive. Happy he was here. But he didn't do enough for her.

"You can stay," she said. "It's safe."

He wanted to ask if Cali was back there, if she was running between the trees, chasing her nieces and nephews with a squirt gun. If she was waiting for him. But this was Raine and Nix's dreamland. He didn't want to ask, but not because he didn't want to know. He didn't want to ask because if she was there, he would never leave.

And the archetype would continue eating dreams.

You would know what to do.

"Is she here?" he asked suddenly, the words quivering. He looked down, ashamed and afraid. Wishing he could take the words back, afraid she would answer him.

Afraid he would never leave.

Raine reached behind her neck and unclasped a necklace of smooth rocks. She bunched it into his hand and closed his fingers. The necklaces that Cali made... and she had one.

Take this, her eyes said. "You know where she is."

The first star had appeared in the late afternoon sky. Dusk was approaching in this reality. What was it on the island? Was it morning already? How many realities were out there, how many dreams? How many sunrises?

Which is the dream?

The realities weren't out there. They weren't mysterious, they were right here, on another frequency, like a radio that tunes into various stations. Paul was able to turn the dial. He could bridge these realities, Mother said. She knew. Of course she knew. She created him all those years ago. She was the one that turned him into a brick, sent him to deceive Cali. To fall in love with her. To watch her self-destruct.

Mother knew what he was.

He knew how to focus his mind, to peek into a dreamland. All those years he wasn't hallucinating, wasn't imagining horses and a barn, the farm he yearned to see. All those years when no one could find him, when the monitors lost track of him on the Settlement... *I was bridging.*

All he had to do was focus on a dreamland with a farm.

And he would be there.

CHAPTER THIRTY-TWO_

IT WAS NEARLY DARK.

The archetype was still on the lounger, the tide sloshing beneath him, the foam wetting the bottom half of his clothing. This wasn't something he would ordinarily do. The archetype preferred to remain clean and dry. Sharp.

But he was transfixed.

This night was different than most others.

The body of Paul was crumpled at the edge of the tide's reach. The left side of his face was sinking as the water undercut the sand beneath his cheek. His right arm extended, fingers bobbing in the receding tide.

The old woman was part of Paul, connected to him through some dreamland conduit, infiltrating the circuits of his biomite constituency. The archetype had analyzed the possible outcomes of bringing Paul to the island along with her, knew the odds of infiltrating her source code was unlikely. Perhaps he had grown bored or wanted the challenge.

Of course, Mother had infected the old man, too. But the archetype purged him with a body of clay. The old man had been a good son to him, but his life had run its course. The archetype was done with him. It was time to bring him home.

Raine's failure to arrive, though, was a bit of a surprise.

Uncertainty brought risk. He didn't need Raine to come to the island. Jamie would serve as leverage quite well. It was just that he didn't expect her to fail.

Perhaps he really had become bored.

Did Mother really think that Paul was strong enough to protect her? The archetype had achieved immortality; he had run every possible outcome of her attempts to defeat him. Why she still attempted to do so perplexed him. Despite what she said, he did not create her to do this. He did not have a subconscious anymore. He was aware of his entire being, fully awake. What a Buddhist would call a bodhisattva. *Or perhaps the Buddha himself.*

The old woman was nothing more than programming. She had no stake in this... *in life.*

He had always wondered why she didn't fabricate a body for herself. It was quite possible she had already done so, but the archetype never sensed her in the world as a separate, sentient being. Instead, she seemed to prefer infecting his fabrications; perhaps because it was easier to hide within another's mind.

The archetype dismantled Paul so thoroughly that the man dropped dead. He didn't wish him death, only wanted to root out the old woman. Despite her appearance and masterful ability to manipulate emotions, she was dangerous.

A curse.

My curse.

He only wanted to serve humankind, yet they embraced their flaws as their identity, their ignorance a thin blanket against a very cold world. He was more benevolent than Zeus, less emotional. He gave the human race perfection. Did they realize how imperfect they were without biomites, what life was like when they were at the mercy of their genome? And how many wars had the archetype averted? By his estimates, he had saved them from extinction many times over. Global disaster had been altered, environmental catastrophes prevented. The balance of the human race was a delicate task and he asked for nothing in return.

Not even their prayers.

Night cast a starry shade over the sky. The moon hid behind a spatter of clouds. A line of dutiful clones marched across the lawn, eyes cast down as they retrieved Paul's pathetic body. They would clean it and prepare it to analyze for an antidote to erase the old woman's source code, all of which would be pointless. She murdered the poor man to save herself.

A cry for help.

Did he create her? After all, he had descended from human DNA. He wasn't so obtuse to believe there were no vestiges of that lineage lurking in his being, his craving for conflict was impossible to extinguish. Perhaps he had a subconscious after all.

She had infected nearly all his clones.

Even now, as he closed his eyes, he could sense the army of Marcus Andersons in their various incarnations—his clones, his children—all over the world. At least half of them carried the woman's intelligence, speaking to it like she was a sentient being. His clones, scattered across the globe from the corrupt government of third world countries to the isolated peaks of tribal communities, fed him thoughts and emotions. He was connected with every biomite in existence, knew every halfskin in the world. Biomites were his flesh. They were his children. But his clones, the Marcus Anderson clones... they were special.

They are me.

Mother corrupted them with a purpose; that was what made them so effective at doing her bidding. Without a reason to exist, they simply wandered without direction. The clean ones, the uninfected ones, would occasionally cease to exist, sometimes willfully committing suicide as if, somewhere in their subconscious, they were aware of their insignificance, that they were merely copied for his enjoyment.

The old woman gave them a messiah complex, that they were created to save the world. They were special.

The archetype speculated that, in this way, perhaps she was right... *I am plotting my own end.* All he had to do was stop sending out clones and she would be impotent. All he had to do was stop bringing them home to the island, cut her off completely. That was the solution.

And he couldn't do that.

He needed to create. To have a purpose.

THE SERVANTS BROUGHT HIM CLEAN, dry clothing. He changed in the moonlight, his naked body creamy. When Paul was removed and the sand raked so that no trace of this evening was left, the archetype settled into meditative repose on the sand dune. Hands clasped over his stomach, he breathed with the ocean until fully immersed in a peaceful, eternal moment. His awareness fully open, he listened to dreams pass through the heavens, each an invisible thread of hope and desire, a vestige of another reality.

He felt them, wished to taste them.

It was these small delights that he gave thanks for immortality. It was dreams that created universes, dreams that, once fully fleshed, became realities. These were dreamlands that floated away from their dreamers, where he imagined another god like himself could enjoy such fruits. But in their primordial states, those initial vestiges of raw hope and troubled worries, he could take them.

He ate them for pleasure.

He ate them to become more.

He ate them, quite simply, because he could.

It was the small hours of early morning that he stirred. His feet denting the sand, he made his way to the end of the dock and removed his clothing. Naked, he exposed himself to the ethereal currents of dreamy fantasies and breathed deep the wintery breath of hope.

The sky swirled as if a titan spirit were waking beyond the clouds. Thin wisps began to curl and coalesce, silky threads of vapor plucked from the starry canvas. They collided and twisted and fell into the pull of his presence, a black hole of awareness that gripped the dreamy essence with an unrelenting, merciless hold.

And then it fell over him, bathing him in glorious effervescence; faith and fear filled his body, mind, and heart. His soul soared and expanded; he grew bigger, became more. He wasn't a collapsing star that gobbled light. He was a god that knew all, that expanded on the nutrition of new universes. He was benevolent, indeed.

But some of his children needed to feed their god.

He preferred the souls of clay, their taste so undefiled and unscripted, unlike halfskins that manipulated their dreamlands, turned them dense and beyond his reach.

Perhaps, he sometimes wondered, Mother did this for him, expanded the clay population as an offering. As penance. It was her gift to him, to show him that the world of clay was a greater gift than biomites, that he was, indeed, wrong about creating a world of bricks. He had created her to transform the world into one of biomites, to extinguish clay. But her self-destruction defied his will, had brought about the resurgence of clay beyond his control. And as he breathed deep the essence of clay dreams, the euphoria weakening his knees, the taste delicate and intoxicating, he realized Mother may be serving him after all.

He loved clay. His cattle. His herd. The fruits of his labor.

She knows me well.

One day, perhaps, he could find a body for her. She could stand beside him and drink from the well of dreams as he did.

An ecstasy made of imagination.

Dawn was approaching, the horizon bleeding a diffuse palette of burnt orange, when he found a particularly rich vein of hope, a stream of dream stuff that excited him to greater heights. Rarely did he continue into daylight hours when the sun grew hot and the air sticky. But this would be worth it, however long it would last. He felt a quiver in the back of his throat and thought perhaps he had overindulged.

It was a presence behind him.

CHAPTER THIRTY-THREE_

The old man was uncomfortable.

Misery had been with him every moment since waking. The knee, the neck. He was old. And now he identified with the misery.

Clay. I'm clay.

There would be no immortality for him, no flawless autoimmune system, no control of his nervous system or manipulating thoughts. For the old man, it would be this way for the rest of his life unless he did something about it.

The bed poked his back and buttocks. Was the thing stuffed with hay? He fidgeted onto his side and tried to remember the last time he had even gotten out of the wheelchair. Had he been sleeping in it?

Someone was panting.

His eyes snapped open. Blades of grass waved over his face. Beyond, a deep blue sky was littered with puffs of clouds. The grass was parted by a stick and a long black nose. A German shepherd watched him while a string of drool landed on the old man's arm.

He didn't move.

He traced his memories, searching for an explanation. He had been in the laboratory on the second floor. All the needles were laid on the bed. He wasn't about to ram one into his head, but there were auto-searching ones—needles that analyzed the forehead and gray matter, needles that would punch through at the correct depth and synchronize with the brain.

Did I use that? He couldn't remember.

He searched his forehead for evidence of a needle or a hole, but only felt folds of worry on an otherwise unpunctured forehead.

"Do you want the truth?"

The old man pushed up on an elbow, wincing at the sharp stabbing pain in his knee. The dog stepped back and Marcus saw who said that—a woman kneeling beyond his feet, seedheads tickling her arms.

Raine.

Paul stood behind her, arms crossed.

"Where the hell am I?" the old man blurted.

"I asked if you wanted to know the truth?" she repeated.

"What is the meaning of this?" He tried to sit up, but the pain was too great. "What have you done to me?"

Raine was dead. She never escaped the Settlement, lost in transport. But there she was, glowing like a newlywed, her face full and healthy. He searched for an answer. Above the grass, there was the top of a cabin.

"You are responsible for the death of millions," she said. "Your life is littered with broken lives and selfish disasters. You harassed those you couldn't control. You murdered the ones close to us. You came to the Settlement looking for a greater truth. We will show you."

"I got you off the Settlement," he exclaimed.

"There would *be* no Settlement if not for you."

"I brought Jamie back." He shook his finger at Paul. "You couldn't have done that without me."

"She wouldn't have died if not for you," Raine said.

"This is ludicrous, damn you."

Paul remained solid and unspoken. There was a cross of sticks between his fingers, reminding him of the crucifix he had seen in Raine's cabin.

The one her son made.

Someone shouted from a distance, maybe beyond the cabin. The dog bolted off with the stick, plowing through long green strands of grass. He recognized the voice. It was a man he'd once known.

A shiver cut through him.

"In a perverted way, I must thank you," Raine continued. "Would I even exist without you? Would there ever have been a dreamland without biomites? A chance for me to become a wife, a mother or grandmother? All these things are my life again. All the misery brought me here, and I have you to thank for that."

It can't be.

"I won't bring Nix over here," she said. "I won't let him see you, won't let him know you were ever here. He won't be as forgiving, Marcus. He remembers all you did to him and his sister."

"Where the hell am I?"

"Do you want to know the truth?" she asked.

"What have you done to me?"

"All your questions will be answered. You will know who you are and why, Marcus Anderson. You'll know the powers-that-be; the search of your lifetime will be fulfilled. Are you ready?"

Their stares were locked, each daring the other to blink or move. He wanted to know the truth, but something about her, about Paul, kept him from answering. Even if his body hadn't betrayed him, if he could stand and run, if he could harness the power of his mind and overpower them, he knew, somewhere deep and honest, it would do him no good. The truth was waiting.

And he didn't want to see it.

The dog returned with a different stick and nudged Raine with it. She scrubbed the dog's ears then reached up. Paul pulled her to her feet. They held hands, squeezing until the tendons sprang on the back of her hand, the knuckles whitened.

"You owe me," the old man said. "Jamie... all of this... it's because of me. I don't know what you've done, but we can make it right again. We can work together. One... one to lead..."

A silent nod between Paul and Raine, a knowing glance, and then she walked off.

No longer the hesitant woman weakened by pain and suffering, loss and fear. She swaggered from view, lithe and confident. The setting sun warm on her bare shoulders.

"Where are you going?" Marcus shouted.

Paul took a knee where the dog had been sitting. The old man tried to roll away.

"What do you want?" the old man said.

Paul paused. Vengeance was not in his eyes; bitterness did not scar his face. After all the old man had done, he looked down on him with warmth, sorrow. Compassion.

He snatched the old man's wrist.

The cold of deep space burned his thin skin, shattering his brittle bones with a bolting ache.

Paul was gone.

The old man was back in the wheelchair. But not in the tower.

IT WAS NIGHT.

Stars blurred a dark sky, the carnival ride slowing to a stop. For a moment, he believed it was a dream, that he had fallen asleep in the wheelchair where he now found himself, but it wasn't the lab around him. The sky was above and grass was below, grass that was short and cared for, a lawn manicured.

A resort was before him, an enormous wall of luxurious brick and mortar. Path lights glowed with warm light; treads along sweeping staircases led up to a wide portico. He had seen this expanse through the security footage but, like the rest of the island, it was empty.

Another glow was above him, something like the Northern Lights was creeping across the sky in milky threads. Marcus reached for one of the wheels and painstakingly rotated the chair, following the lunar threads until they coalesced and fell in a thick, ropey column on someone at the end of the dock.

He was nude.

Arms spread, head back.

A lunar luminescence engulfed his pale body, shimmering with ecstasy—thighs quivering, buttocks clenched. The air seemed to quake, shockwaves rippling the water beneath him.

The old man thought, perhaps, this was a dream. Raine, Paul and now this... *what else could it be?*

The naked man, sensing Marcus, turned his head. The old man's eyes were too poor to see his features, but felt he was familiar. It was his posture, the delight that seemed to grip him.

The effervescent strands of light evaporated.

The water settled, the air calmed.

They were bathed in darkness. The nude man's body was still a pale, sickly glow; he stooped over for the pile of clothing, sliding on a loose pair of pants one leg at a time, appearing to watch the old man as he buttoned the shirt. Barefoot, he strolled toward the lawn.

The old man rubbed his face, working the heels of his hands into the hollows of his eyes. What was approaching was surely a dream.

A younger version of himself stepped onto the grass and stopped several feet away. Hands on his hips, the man searched the space around them then regarded Marcus with a distant fascination, disbelief that didn't quite reach the old man's own level of surprise. And then a smile.

"What the hell is this?" Marcus said.

"How did you get here?" the man exclaimed. "You weren't supposed to leave your tower, old man."

"Who are you?"

"Most clones are more in shock at first sight. You are a resilient one. Always have been."

"I demand to know the meaning of this."

The man threw his head back; laughter deep and rich reached

the stars. He paced back and forth with his finger and thumb pinching the bridge of his nose, grinning. When he stopped, tears wet his cheeks.

"You are me, old man. But I am not you."

"What does that mean?"

"I am what you seek."

"No." Marcus fumbled at the wheels but wasn't strong enough to push through the grass. "This is impossible."

Vertigo put the world in a blender. The ground opened and swallowed him; a never-ending plummet filled his chest with panic. He clutched the wheels, his mind careening into a black pit of madness.

"That's the shock, right there," the man said. "A bit delayed with you, old man. But there it is. It is natural to lose grip on reality when you see the truth. And the truth you see. I am what you have sought all these years."

He threw his arms out.

"Welcome home, my son."

The laughter returned. As Marcus's mind continued its unraveling descent, the man reveled in the moment, snapping his fingers, summoning something back at the resort.

"I sent you into the wilderness to live a life, to become your own person. There are thousands of you out there, old man. You are all my clones seeking your own way through life... mechanics and butchers, schoolteachers and homeless. So many paths, so many lives. But in the end, you all come home to know the truth. You all do. But you, old man, you rose above the rest."

The man shook his finger.

"You have always been my favorite. Your journey has been quite exceptional."

Several figures moved around them, a semicircle formed. The men were dressed as servants, a variety of formal butlery and disheveled janitorial attire. Some of them were balding, others slightly hunched.

All of them Marcus.

"It has been such a pleasure watching you grow. And it makes my heart heavy to bring you home. But you needed to be healed. Do you know what I'm talking about? Do you know who infected you?"

Marcus looked from face to face, all of them him. Exactly him. They were his brothers, his clones. And in that realization, the earth stood still. There was just the ocean breathing. Just the night sounds, the cool caress of a dewy breeze.

And Marcus began to laugh.

A guffaw burped from his cracked and tired lips and erupted into a madman's hysteria, crumbling between fits of wet coughing. Dream or not, this was how his life would end.

The truth is not what you expect, Marcus. It is often quite inconvenient.

Mother told him that. She knew this was what he would find. And she abandoned him to fall into this absurd truth, to drown in the irony. Helpless, afraid, and alone.

So he laughed until tears fell.

The others did, too.

The man took half a step back and joined the hilarity, his laughter rising above the rest. "No one has ever found the beauty of this moment."

There was no beauty for Marcus. He laughed at the divine justice. *Do you want to know the truth?* Raine had asked.

In that moment, his life was emptied of meaning. All he could do was laugh.

I deserve this. Of course I do.

The man snapped his fingers. One of the servants, an elderly Marcus wearing white gloves, delivered a plastic tub of water. He placed it at the foot of the wheelchair.

"You have been an utter disaster, my son. A beautiful utter disaster. You have ruined lives, sought delusion and grandeur, taken the world to heights it never could've reached without you."

The man kneeled before him, took one of his bare feet from the chair's stirrups and placed it in the warm water. The crowd of Marcus clones gathered closer as he washed his feet.

"Your journey has been long. Share your disasters so that I know more, that I may be more. Now that you know the truth, give yourself to me."

The soapy water was warm.

The man took his other foot, the bad knee biting the nerves, Marcus's eyes filling with tears. His life, once filled with purpose, drained into the sea.

He didn't want this. Didn't want any of this.

I am a clone. An insignificant clone. A copy of this man.

Did that make him nobody? Or was he more than that? Was there no separation between them? Was he a god that wanted to know himself, to be lost and now found?

The man looked up. He would take the salt of Marcus's life, absorb him like the ocean. Own him like the ones around him.

Yes. It is a fitting end.

More clones joined them. Marcus saw them just outside the semicircle. They were three deep; they were waiting for it to happen. *Is that what they all did, too? Did they go into the world and return to be emptied? To serve?*

The man stood.

The grains of discomfort trickled out of Marcus. A numbness took hold, filling him with apathy. He no longer cared about truths or lies. He would give himself. Give it all.

There was no choice.

The smile that appeared bright across the man's face suddenly collapsed. For a moment, he appeared troubled. A ripple of discomfort shot amongst the clones, a fidgeting itch that caused them to dance.

Arms darted from behind the man and latched across his chest, a stiff hug, a locking embrace.

And then he was gone.

A blank space was left in the semicircle, the grass matted where the man's bare feet had stood.

There was time for the clones to look around before they collapsed. Marcus felt a smile grow. In the moments before the world would fade around him forever, a sense of divine justice filled the empty numbness.

Marcus was indeed the son to be, but who was the one to lead? The one to dream and bleed? They had all bled. Now they all see. They would all lead. Maybe he wasn't the son to be.

Regardless of the prophecy's meaning, he realized in that final moment that he served the world after all. He found the truth. He served God.

Divine justice, he thought. *Indeed.*

CHAPTER THIRTY-FOUR_

*W*HAT…

That was as far as the archetype's thoughts went before the sharp edge of the horizon flipped into the curved line of desert sand. Somehow he had crossed into another reality, one of endless sand.

Steel bars locked across his chest. A warm breath on his ear.

The archetype had not experienced surprise in recent memory. He knew all. He saw everything.

But this he did not see.

A small worm of excitement turned in his stomach. This was something new, something he could discover. The palatial resort had vanished. The lawn, the servants, the old man… they had all dissolved. The archetype was the eater of dreams, the consumer of dreamlands. But crossing into these dreamlands, to actually exist in them rather than absorb the essence of their reality, that would be something entirely new. The possibilities would be endless.

The worm continued to dance.

The desert gave way to misty plains of the prairie laid out in golden waves. The archetype reached up to feel the clasped hands of the steel bars that embraced him from behind, the grip of a man determined never to release. *Is he carrying me?*

The prairie transformed into the rainy streets of a city. The goliath skyscrapers shrank into rows and rows of farmland across land as flat as the ocean.

The scenes continued flipping, worlds shuttling past in colors that never existed, realities on the fringes of the familiar. There was no sense of falling, no motion or vertigo. He was a traveler of dreams. The man behind him turning the dial.

There was a moment that stretched out longer than the others, a place on the side of a modest hillside overlooking pastures and fences, barns and horses. It was that moment that perhaps the archetype could have stopped him, could've broken the grip, willed his way back to the sand and surf and island... but he was soaring in the eternal cosmos, seeing the endless realities that interpenetrated all existence.

And he had grown so tired. So bored.

Dreamlands continued.

The cold, craggy white peaks of a snow-dusted mountain range were before him.

The bottom of the sea, red deserts, titan forests, mountains of ice, glassy cityscapes, spiny creatures, cold space, blue suns, white moons, craters.

Faster they flipped. Further he went. Until it all blurred. It all turned gray. Gray that stung his flesh. Gray that ate his bones.

It was the gray between channels, the static that hissed. The gray where nothing existed.

In his last moments of sentience, before the archetype dissolved like an ink drop spit into a mad, churning sea, he recognized this nothingness. He remembered this place called nowhere, a corner of the universe where nothing existed. A reality, he thought, where they had sent the souls of boys.

And then he returned to the primordial soup of the universe.

CHAPTER THIRTY-FIVE_

It wasn't clear if the archetype could feel Paul behind him, but there was no reaction. So absorbed with the old man, he didn't hear Paul approach, didn't feel him throw his arms out. It was only when he locked his hands did he know something was amiss.

Something new.

The archetype shuddered with pleasure instead of fear. Paul expected more of a fight, perhaps for the man to even disappear wizard-like. He wasn't sure any of this would work. If it didn't, he was sure to be tortured again. But this was why Mother had fabricated him.

Did she see this far into the future? Did she know I would sacrifice everything?

Maybe she'd tried this before with others, stood by passively as the archetype sent illusions of fiery ants over their bones, watched them collapse in a heap of agony that only death could absolve. Paul wasn't fool enough to believe he was the only one in the universe to save... *to save what? All of existence?*

Maybe she had fabricated him many times already, sent his clones out into the world like Marcus. He just didn't remember.

With the archetype in his arms, he spun the dial and began to bridge through countless realities, searching for the one place that was inescapable, the one place where nothing existed. The place where the wealthy men sent the identities of children. A place the archetype would know. One he deserved. A nowhere.

And Paul would deliver him.

Real sacrifice is a lonely endeavor.

All those years he thought he had been hallucinating, was he really bridging into another reality? Those times the monitors couldn't find him, those times he saw Cali in the trees, saw her on the farm... had he really been somewhere else?

Paul and the archetype flipped past mountains and deserts, sea and sand. As realities fell like cards, there was a long pause on a hill-side that overlooked a farm where horses were in a pasture and a woman in tall rubber boots was hauling buckets. The hesitation stretched out; doubt quivered in Paul's resolve. A moment longer, he might have let go and run down the long gravel road, hopped the split-rail fence.

He plunged forward.

Realities blurred together like smeared pastels, blazing in a long stream of endless existence until they were enveloped in a never-ending cloud of swirling gray, of endless despair. A place created by the forefathers of foreverland, the precursor to biomites and dream-lands, where the souls of children were disposed to empty their bodies. This was the place of nothingness, of absolute inertia.

Nowhere.

Paul and the archetype dissolved into the roiling static, their memories diluted, the particles of their existence pulled further apart until the fray consumed them. Unknowing. Unbeing.

Inescapable.

The last memory of their existence was of a barn and a pasture.

CHAPTER THIRTY-SIX_

JAMIE JERKED AWAKED.

The sudden movement bit her leg with an odd sensation, the slide of her bones that wasn't quite right. Grimacing, she glimpsed the cell door through welling tears. She slid onto her elbows and shivered, afraid to wipe her eyes and find out she was dreaming, that the iron bars were still in place. She had lost track of the nights, sleeping through most of them, waking long enough to chase painkillers with long swallows of water.

But the pill bottle was empty, the water nearly gone. She was shivering with fever, infection setting in. She didn't want to die alone.

He promised.

The morning she woke to find Paul's makeshift bed empty, there was a bottle of water and a few items of food. She woke later that night to find more water and food.

How many days ago was that?

All her memories were washed in a drugged haze. She had come in the cell for... something. The door slammed on her leg and Paul swore he'd get her out. *Where is he?*

She rubbed her eyes to find the cell door was open. And she was awake.

"Paul?" she called. "Paul?"

Blood pounded her temples when she shouted. She squeezed her head with both hands and then with methodical effort, used the bars to pull herself up. Gravity flooded her legs; blood slammed into open nerves and ignited raw pain. She clung to the cage, eyes closed.

She managed to drag herself into the aisle, periodically stopping to breathe. A blanket had been neatly folded and placed in the doorway. Next to that was an aluminum crutch.

"Paul?"

She stood in the doorway, shivering. The morning sun was warm and welcome. The dewy grass was silver, a long pair of footsteps dragging through it.

The path through the trees was webby and dripping. Several times she stopped but found that restarting the trek was too difficult. She crossed the grassy field in one long stretch, tracing the trail of dewy footsteps past the sundial. The dorm was locked. The window Paul had punched out was too high for her to reach.

The footsteps led around the building.

Jamie found herself in the thick jungle behind the dorm, the path narrow. She came to the foot of the tower, condensation steaming off the walls, sunlight flashing off the reflective panels. The footsteps ended where a glass wall had been shattered. The furniture was trashed, the monitors dark. The elevator doors were open. She hobbled to look inside, cautiously keeping her distance.

A wheelchair.

Jamie wedged the crutch between the doors and lowered onto the wheelchair. The sudden relief was tear-worthy. Once her leg was in the support, she considered rolling out of the building but wouldn't get far, certainly not down a path. For now, she needed to sit.

She would need food and water if she wanted to survive. That meant getting back to the dorm. She would also need medicine. Assuming she could get all the above, she might survive long enough to die a long, slow death.

When the doors began quaking, she rolled to the back wall of the elevator. It stopped. The second light was glowing. The elevator was being called up. That was where they woke up.

She leaned over to grab the crutch. If the old man was still up there, the crutch might be a good enough weapon to keep him off her. He couldn't be much of a threat. Last time she saw him, he could barely move.

The doors opened on the second floor. The smell was foreboding —a rich, clayey funk of death seeped from the hallway like an infection. Someone was talking. She sat and listened, recognizing the dialog as a newsfeed.

"Paul?" she called. It was hopeful but not loud enough.

She cruised down the corridor, the smell coming from the left. That was the room where they woke up. She peeked inside and saw the beds and computers. Monitors were flashing. The floor was littered with syringes and plastic tubing, vials, boxes, and debris.

The newsfeeds poured over her.

Tragedy had struck the mainland. Over half of the human population had been wiped out, some estimates as high as sixty percent. The apparent cause was the sudden collapse of biomites.

All of them.

Every single biomite in existence, preliminary reports suggested, had been deactivated. Only people with a minimal amount of biomites survived. Or those who were clay.

Biomite technology faced a terminal fate.

Where's the old man?

He was up to something, but what? Again, her memories were sun-bleached objects, faint glimmers that warned her to be careful.

The monitors that weren't spewing dire newsfeeds were projecting views of the resort on the other side of the island. Paul had mentioned that building, said it was massive. He was right.

As she rolled closer to the nearest monitor, she saw the bodies on the back lawn. There was a group of them near the dock, dumped into randomly splayed positions of death. They were dressed in uniforms, some of them wearing white gloves. They seemed to be surrounding a wheelchair that contained an equally limp body that was bald and helpless.

The old man.

Furthermore, the servants resembled him with bald scalps and fringes of white hair. Remembering the voice activation, she began calling for the views to enhance. There was a quick zoom of the bodies.

A ship eased onto one of the monitors.

She wheeled back and watched it pull into an empty slip. It was more of a yacht with slow-spinning antennae. Someone was arriving to find an island full of dead bodies. They'd find Jamie, too. *And I'm fabricated.*

She wasn't going to the Settlement.

She would fight with her very last breath before surrendering to that life. Years ago, Paul thought it was wise if they went peacefully, that they would be treated fairly. But there was no justice on the Settlement. If he had to do it all again, he would hide.

That was exactly what she would do.

The crew leaped into action and secured the yacht. There was no movement behind the tinted windows that ringed the ship's bridge.

Jamie was feeling faint and found water in a small refrigerator in another room. When she returned, two more ships had appeared, these less luxurious than the first. They looked more like cargo ships and entered the two remaining slips.

The crew disembarked from all three of them.

There were quite a few men and women on the second two ships, all dressed in plain clothing. They appeared to walk with purpose, just short of marching, and dispersed toward the resort. In small teams, they entered various doors.

A small group exited the yacht.

A woman led four others. She listened as the crew appeared to be giving updates as they entered the back of the resort. There was a lot of activity, boxes carried into the resort, items carried out to the back lawn. Some things were loaded onto the ships.

And then there were more bodies.

The first one was carried out of the resort between two men, the arms dangling, head nodding. Jamie called to the monitor, asking it for a close-up. The dead man was wearing a servant-type uniform like the other bodies on the lawn (most of which had been already loaded). The servant looked a lot like the old man. She assumed Marcus was in the wheelchair, but that was him being carried off the portico.

But there was a second body hauled out, and then a third. Both of them looked like the old man, taken to one of the ships, each of them limp and lifeless. All of them bald.

All of them Marcus.

"What the hell?" she whispered.

The crew cycled in and out of the resort, bringing out boxes and other items, but mostly bodies, some lugged in the open while others were in brown vinyl bags. Movement caught her eye on one of the other monitors.

Someone was approaching the tower.

It was the small crew led by the woman with short hair. They were followed by other men and women and marched around the tower. Some continued toward the dormitory like orders had been given. The yacht crew, however, paused outside the tower.

Jamie spun the wheelchair and pushed into the hall.

The crutch was still in the elevator. She jammed it between the doors, gasping with effort. When she got back to the lab, the crew was walking around the first floor. They had spread out and sifted through the wreckage, occasionally lifting a finger to their ear like they were listening to a call. Jamie cringed.

Are they clay?

The elevator doors tried to close.

They rattled against the crutch. The woman's face filled one of the monitors, looking down, perhaps waiting for the elevator. When it didn't arrive, she looked directly at Jamie.

The elevator stopped making noise.

"Jamie? Are you all right?"

Jamie wheeled back. Her image must be projecting to the first floor.

"Arrangements have been made to take you to safety, Jamie. You have nothing to fear. I know about your leg and I know it must be very painful. I'm here to help. This island is finished and we want to take you back. Can you hear me?"

Jamie looked around. She needed space, needed time to think. *How do they know I'm here?*

"Do you know why your leg isn't healing, Jamie?" The woman offered a sympathetic smile, a slight head tilt. "Do you know why you can't sense any thoughts or control your nervous system? It's because you're clay, Jamie. Your body contains no biomites."

"Who are you?"

"I'm a friend. You can trust me."

"You're lying."

"You're not going to the Settlement, Jamie. I promise you."

She shuddered. "How... how do you know that?"

"I made arrangements for this day. I know all about this island, Jamie. All about you. Your body is a clay incubation, not a biomite fabrication. The person responsible for bringing you here is no longer. All of them."

All of them? "I want to see Paul."

"He's not here."

"Where is he?"

The woman was distracted, listening to an urgent message with her finger to her ear, nodding as she did. She gave curt orders then returned to the monitor.

"Jamie, can I come up?"

"Not until I see Paul."

"You're safe. Do you understand that? You're safe now. Be here and let me help you."

Those were things Paul would say, things he had said to her in the past. But there was no Paul, only a stranger on a strange island. And if Paul wasn't there, no way was she opening a door.

She began wheeling away from the monitor. They couldn't get to her without the elevator. She would stay until Paul arrived.

"Jamie." The woman sighed. "The sooner we get up there, the sooner we can help you. Your leg is broken; you're dehydrated and malnourished. Infection has set in. If you want to wait, I can't help you. But we will be clearing the island and I want to bring you with us."

"Where are you taking me?"

"Back to the world."

She wanted to believe that, wanted to think they would just drop her off at a port and wish her luck. But these people had lied before. As soon as they had her, she'd find out that she was biomites and not clay.

And the Settlement was the only stop.

"You're not going to the Settlement."

"How are you—"

"You have an apartment waiting for you back in New York City," the woman said. "In addition to a sizeable inheritance."

"Inheritance? What are you saying? Are you saying Paul is dead?"

"I'm saying that arrangements for this day were made long ago, Jamie. I can explain more if you just let me up."

"Who?" She wheeled closer. "Who made arrangements?"

"There's nothing I can say that will convince you, Jamie. You will have to trust me. The island is not sustainable and there's nowhere else to go. Paul wants you to come with us. His footsteps led you here, did they not?"

"How do you know that?"

The woman was interrupted by one of the crewmen. She turned her back and mumbled. Jamie called for more volume but couldn't make out what they were saying. The crew was now returning from across the grassy field, each of them stopping briefly for a word. One by one, they took the path toward the resort.

There were footsteps that led her to the tower, but that didn't mean it was Paul. *But she's saying everything Paul would say, everything Paul would want.*

Jamie checked the other monitors. The lawn had been cleared. One of the cargo ships was easing out of the slip, but the other two were firmly docked. There was nothing to trust on the island. She would stay in the tower, starve if necessary. Self-medicate to control the pain.

I can't control the pain because I'm... because I'm clay.

Yes, that made sense; it would explain why she couldn't control the agony, why she couldn't accelerate healing.

This is a dream. A mad, mad dream that won't let me wake. And I'm damned if she's getting anywhere near me. Someone killed Raine, killed the old man. And Paul is missing.

I'm not going anywhere.

For a moment, the woman was gone. It was just a second, but then she was back, like the monitor experienced a hiccup or an empty splice. The woman was alone, hand held above her head. An offering was intertwined in between her fingers, dangled in clunky measure. Jamie wiped her eyes, leaning closer because it looked like...

The elevator rang.

Her heart thudded in her throat. Her hands shook on the rubber wheels as she steered toward the doorway, almost driving her broken leg into the wall. She edged into the hall, facing the elevator in time to see the doors ease together.

The crutch was gone.

It was there. It was keeping the doors from closing and now it was just gone. She had no time to search for it. There would be no use in finding out where it went or how it could've moved from between the doors. All she could do was watch the lights above the door switch from the second floor to the first.

She backed down the hall until the wheels bumped into the glass wall that overlooked the island. Another bell rang and the doors opened again.

It was her.

The woman observed her down the long corridor before stepping out, her pace even and careful. Jamie wanted to shout, wanted to protect herself. But her leg was broken and the glass was at her back. Alone, she watched the woman slow, something clattering in her right hand.

Jamie had the sudden urge to ask for her name. *Had she seen her before?*

The woman cupped the object in both hands as she approached, an offering once again.

"It's nice to finally meet you, Jamie," she said.

"Do I know you?"

The woman knelt in the glass enclave, coming eye level with her. She took Jamie's hand and poured a necklace into her palm. The shiny rocks clattered quietly.

Rocks smoothed by a river.

Rocks drilled and strung together so many years ago.

Rocks to never forget.

A necklace long lost and buried was now pooled in her hand.

"Who are you?" she whispered.

"An old friend."

"What does this mean?"

"Paul never left you, Jamie."

The colors of the stones bled together. Her eyes misted. She tried to say something, but sobs filled her throat.

"Where... where is he?" she finally asked.

The tears played tricks with her eyes. When she looked up, the woman looked older, her hair closer to white than gray. She was holding her finger to her lips, a pose that suggested deep thought.

"You'll see him," she said, "the next time you dream."

MOTHER'S KNOWLEDGE_

It was a frigid morning.

She lay beneath thin covers, thinking it was about time to pull the heavy comforter out. Her breath streamed in wispy clouds. The furnace would need to be serviced before winter stepped any closer. She enjoyed these moments, the still crisp air that slipped past window frames and invaded the house with winter's kiss.

Downstairs, the coffee machine belched. When it was quiet again, she quickly dressed and descended to the first floor, the worn steps protesting each step. The kitchen silence was broken by the second hand of an old clock.

The first sip of coffee was the best part of the day.

She stood at the sink, gazing out of a dusty window, caffeine flooding her senses. The sun had yet to rise above the low-lying hills, casting a shadowless gray pall over the fields. It would be mid-morning before sharp shadows fell on the frosted turf, melting the icy crystals that painted the earth a white haze.

The horses were usually at the fence, waiting for their buckets. Perhaps they were at the round bale. She would eat breakfast first, let them wait. The coffee wasn't strong enough to snap her fully awake.

She was feeling a little weak, a bit shaky. Sometimes her blood sugar was out of balance. Eating would help.

She had grown weary lately, feeling the drag of the musty walls and chipped paint, the old bones of the house draped around her like a frayed sweater. Living alone all these years had healed her soul, but there were mornings she felt as tired as the house.

With half a cup of coffee in her, she turned on the radio. Jazzy sounds filled the house. The iron pan was heating on the stove when a haze of static crackled through the soothing music. It was overcast. Sometimes reception wasn't good.

Pulling open the refrigerator, she pinched two eggs between her nervous fingers and watched them slip out. They cracked open on the floor in a one-two punch. A tiny curse slipped between her teeth. The static cleared from the radio and music played as she cleaned the mess and washed her hands.

Someone was in the pasture.

His figure was still and gray, the details diluted in the pale morning. She continued drying her hands with a towel. This sort of thing happened from time to time. She would often feel him out there first. Sometimes she would see him by the driveway or on the hillside. He was always at a distance, always watching her.

The fantasies of a lonely woman.

She assigned her delusions to her guilty past, a wish to undo her regrets. A wish to be somewhere other than here.

This morning he didn't disappear.

She would sometimes stand in the pasture with buckets and stare at the apparition until it went back to the ethers of her past. It was her way of confronting her agitated mind, a way of not backing down. She no longer assigned guilt for the things she had done.

So she watched this time until the kitchen filled with smoke, butter crackling on the heated pan. And then he began walking.

He climbed over the fence.

He walked around her truck.

He crossed the driveway, his gait as confident and slow as she remembered. And then she lost sight of him as he rounded the house. Standing in her kitchen, hands clenching the towel, she figured that was his disappearing act. A little different than all the other times.

But she waited.

She watched.

The railing wobbled outside. The slats on the porch creaked.

When the door opened, she dropped the towel. A small sound escaped her lips. Her heart swelled. He stopped inside the mudroom, his features obscured in the smoky air, the pan spattering hot butter against the splash guard.

But she could feel him, smell him.

She swallowed down a ball of hope that refused to go quietly.

He moved closer, his boots loud and final. His whiskers were salty, his eyes worn leather. When he reached for her, when he cupped her cheek with his callused hand, the smell of perspiration musky and familiar, she closed her eyes.

Afraid to open them, afraid she would wake alone in the kitchen with only his lingering scent, she spoke in the darkness of hope.

"Am I dreaming?" Cali whispered.

He put his arms around her, pressing his beating chest to hers. His lips to her ears, he whispered.

"We all are."

WHAT TO READ NEXT?_

They woke on an island, in the wilderness, and in prison. Only one thing in common. No memories.

FOREVERLAND

---

bertauski.com/foreverland

REVIEW HALFSKIN!_

If you enjoyed this ride, please drop a review on your favorite vendor. It doesn't have to be long and complicated. Throw some stars on it and write *Loved it!* or *It was really, really okay!* or *Meh.*

Reviews make the difference.

bertauski.com/halfskin

BERTAUSKI STARTER LIBRARY_

ABOUT THE AUTHOR_

My grandpa never graduated high school. He retired from a steel mill in the mid-70s. He was uneducated, but a voracious reader. As a kid, I'd go through his bookshelves of musty paperback novels, pulling Piers Anthony and Isaac Asimov off the shelf and promising to bring them back. I was fascinated by robots that could think and act like people. What happened when they died?

Writing is sort of a thought experiment to explore human nature and possibilities. What makes us human? What is true nature?

I'm also a big fan of plot twists.

---

bertauski.com

See more about the author and forthcoming books at http://www.bertauski.com

www.ingramcontent.com/pod-product-compliance
Lightning Source LLC
Chambersburg PA
CBHW051008180726
48291CB00006B/2021
* 9 7 8 1 9 5 1 4 3 2 2 2 5 *